MW01046012

# A Cover Too Deep

*Elaine M. Litster*

To Brian + June
Enjoy!
Love
Elaine

PublishAmerica
Baltimore

ISBN: 1-4241-3593-1
PUBLISHED BY PUBLISHAMERICA, LLLP
www.publishamerica.com
Baltimore

Printed in the United States of America

*A Cover Too Deep* is dedicated to Bill, my husband, for all his hours of editing and his unfaltering belief in my ability to write.

# I

When Nathanial Bowman walked to the podium in a classroom at Camp Peary, he expected the chatter in the room to stop, and it invariably did. The men and women in the room enjoyed socialising as much as the next public employee, but even at this early stage in their careers they took their jobs very seriously. They had come from all walks of life, and had been carefully selected from a large pool of candidates. They had been trained in firearms, unarmed combat, languages and far more intriguing topics that came under the umbrella of intelligence gathering.

"Good evening," Nathanial started. "Well, tell me…how do you like it so far?" It was his standard opening, and the smiles and comments it generated helped to relax his audience. His speech today to the new group of Central Intelligence Agency trainees included his usual combination of advice, warnings and good-natured bantering with the audience. In the next two hours he would give them examples of the type of fieldwork they would be doing in the coming year, their relationship with their teams and senior officers, the temptations and traps inherent to their job, the lifestyle they would be living, and a variety of other "do, don't and be careful" scenarios. Most of this they had heard from various sources during their training year, but because Nathanial still did active field work the trainees always listened with rapt attention.

Nathanial Bowman, his first name shortened to "Nat" only by friends and senior officers, had a dual role with the Company. It was his own choosing. After seventeen years of faithful and appreciated service, he could have been a full-time trainer or competed for a variety of other positions. He liked training and working with new enthusiastic officers, but Nat also had a love of field work. He was good at it—always had been. From the beginning he had discovered a natural sense for it. At forty-three years of age he felt that he was not ready to take an administrative role. He kept himself sharp and he fought any tendency to take life too easily. The young people kept him on his toes. So he had carved out a role for himself which gave him the best of both worlds: part time in the field by himself; part time training green officers in the field; and part time lecturing and training new officers in the classroom. It was a good mix.

"The better you become in this game, the more valuable you are to the Company. Yet the more valuable you are to us, the harder our opponents will try to reach you and sway you to their side." It was the "morals" part of his speech. "Remember where your loyalties are and do not forget that bad habits can be used against you.

How many in today's audience would still be here five years from now, Nat wondered. In the front row he saw one of Tony's new acquisitions. Sheila Day-Jones had a varied background at twenty-eight years of age, that included years of volunteer work at a rape crisis centre. Her formal background was in political science, and she had published a few works that the Company had liked. Sheila was supposedly a cool number, with no real attachments except for a sister in Vermont. Tony rarely picked women for his team, so Nat knew Sheila must have some real smarts underneath that cool exterior. As if reading his mind, Sheila looked up from her notebook and gave him a level stare. She was a good-looking woman with short dark hair, a very direct gaze and an excellent taste in clothing.

"You will need someone to trust," he continued, "someone to turn to in this job. There may be times you will lose track of your mission and perhaps your own values." These people were really too new to appreciate what Nat was trying to tell them. They were so idealistic now, but someday it would hit them—that "what am I doing and why?" feeling. It could be the end or the turning point in an officer's career. "You will find that you need to open your gut to someone. Make sure it's not that old college buddy who just happened to major in journalism." The audience chuckled, believing that they would never be that foolish. "The men and women who lead the teams you will be joining have been exhaustively trained and hand picked to be leaders. There's nothing you can think of that they have not experienced, thought about or been tempted by." He paused for effect. "Talk to them—anytime, anyplace, if you are having doubts. Lack of communication can be a great enemy. If you screw up, you'll find they have expected it. Just make sure you do not repeat the same mistakes again. Mistakes grow in costliness as your involvement grows."

As he continued to speak, Nat thought about his current assignment. With the support of their former Deputy Director for Operations, their unit of the Covert Action staff had secured a finding that had allowed him to infiltrate a group of rebels in Cuba. The rebel group was in a building stage. They called themselves the Sierra Maestra Liberators, and their stated goal was to liberate the mountains and the rest of the country from the Communist Government, replacing the current historical places on the Cuban map with a few lugares históricos of their own. They knew Nat as Sam Turnbull, an executive with Westcor, and also as a bored financier looking for adventure. They believed that he was at home in the financial institutions of North America, but was a man who spent as much energy robbing those financial institutions as he did investing their money.

"Never stop training. A rusty Operations officer can become a danger to himself and everyone he connects with. You've seen the facilities we have here—use them whenever you are home." It was one of his pet peeves. Nat hated sloppy and out of condition co-workers. If you were working someplace where you had to depend on your fellow officers to stay alert, you wanted them to be in peak condition. That went for mental training, too.

Next week he would be entering Cuba with Aaron. All the preparation and the cover stories were ready. They would be landing by boat at night on the south side of the island, west of the village of Pilon and south of Alegría de Pío. From there they would travel by horseback up into the Sierra Maestra range of mountains. Horseback, of all things. It was going to be a long, sore ride, and Nat did not even like horses. Oh well, no one expected a businessman from the United States to be familiar with horses, so he didn't have to pretend to have any expertise or fondness for the beasts.

For an unknown period of time, the rebels had been contacting American companies who used to have financial holdings in Cuba. The sales pitch had been inviting. "Send us money and we can change the government and then open the country up to you again and do business." It was enough to make some executives drool. What actually happened is that once the business (or a private individual) started to send money, they had to keep it up, or a threatening letter was received. Then the blackmail would start, and the threats had two punches to them. The Cuban authorities would be informed for the purpose of political embarrassment, and the American government would also be informed so it could take its own action against the business or individual. The CIA had no idea yet how many American businesses or individuals were involved, but with the help of the FBI they were doing their best to find out.

One of their own young officers had come to them with the story. Scott Andrews, another member of Tony's team, came from a family of well-heeled businesspeople. One night his father had called him into the study after a business associate had stayed for dinner. The business associate had become involved with the rebels and then started having doubts. After receiving the first letter "reminding" him of an overdue payment, the man had panicked. He had used the business investments to generate the income, and had absolutely no intention of getting himself involved any deeper. He was looking for a way out, and knew his friend's son had started working for the CIA.

Scott had met with him, made no promises but said he would do what he could. A well-trained man with hopes of a long career ahead of him, Scott had gone directly to Tony with the story. After much debate and scheming, Nat had "become" the businessman, Sam Turnbull, and the payments had continued, although different finances were used. While Nat played with the rebels, pretending a great interest in their cause, James Thompson, an experienced Operations officer, was sent into Cuba to make contact.

To that point, everything had been going well. James met Alfredo Pérez, who became an agent for them. Through James, the CIA learned that the rebels were actually quite large and active. They were also very deeply involved in selling drugs and weapons to buyers in the United States. Soon after that, James had disappeared. Nat was still corresponding with a rebel called Osvaldo Rodríguez, who was Sam's contact. The communication continued, but James was not heard from again. "Sam" expressed interest in seeing the Cuban operation for himself. Osvaldo was receptive and arrangements were made. Sam was to meet a drug dealer named Taz, and come with him by boat.

Taz had been a real person. It was he who first approached the real Sam Turnbull. Drugs were never mentioned to Sam—only American business interests in Cuba. Osvaldo had been in direct contact with Taz, but had never seen him. Taz was an American, and had been introduced to the rebel leader, Jose Luis Sánchez, through a chain of American contacts. There was another piece of luck—Taz had been arrested by the FBI on American soil and questioned exhaustively. Once the CIA had enough information for a cover, Aaron St. Pierre was chosen to be "Taz".

Aaron did not like his cover. Posing as a drug dealer was no problem for him, but it was the other habits Taz had developed that turned everyone's stomach. During their investigation of Taz and his activities in the United States, the FBI had solved a few other mysteries of their own. Taz turned out to be the individual responsible for a variety of serious crimes throughout the eastern states. Most of his record was for crimes that netted him financial gain, but he had one perverse hobby. Taz was wanted for rape in five different states. Some of his victims had lived, others had not. The women who had lived reported terrifying experiences of being confined, sometimes for days, toyed with and tortured until Taz had simply disappeared and they were found or escaped. He was a man of many disguises, but he was always very tall and strong with blue eyes and dark brown hair. In addition, he liked to scream a lot in Spanish. At six feet, two inches, powerfully built and with dark hair and blue eyes, Aaron fit the description. Also, he had become proficient in Spanish over the last few years.

While Aaron knew he was going into an all-male camp and even if one of the rebels had a girlfriend he certainly would *not* be expected to go near her, much less assault her, he hated even being associated with that part of the cover. It gave him the creeps. Tony had told him that he was fussing over nothing, but Tony didn't have to look into his girlfriend's eyes and wonder what she would think if she knew he was going to work disguised as a rapist. Nat was more understanding and knew that the cover wasn't sitting well with Aaron, but he assured Aaron that he had nothing to worry about. They would only be there for a couple of weeks. Just go in, find out exactly what was going on, then get out. Those were their orders from a nervous administration who hated making mistakes in Cuba. Besides, if you were pretending to be someone, you had to be the whole reputation, desirable or not.

"Let's talk about your love lives." This always got these young folks' attention. "Depending on where you will be working in this company, maintaining a marriage may be easy or it may be extremely difficult. If you are on a computer in an office five days a week, it's your own fault if you are a lousy lover. However, if there's a chance you may be spending months in the field on an assignment far away from home, you'd better have married someone who can live with that. If they are jealous or possessive, the times when you are home will be hell. Or you may come home and find that your family has moved somewhere else without you. Hell, I was divorced fifteen years ago and it was five years before I even found out." The resulting laughter was nervous, because they sensed that there was some truth to what he was saying. In fact, the divorce had been by mutual consent. Nat sensed early on that he was captivated by this job, and it did not seem fair to ask a good woman to take permanent second place. He had also learned very early that there was no shortage of eager women wherever he went, and he personally found it very difficult to turn them down. A good-looking, fit, six-foot sandy-haired man with an easy smile and an apparently free lifestyle, he chose carefully from the selection available to him and left no bad feelings behind. You never knew when you might need a friend to help you out in a tight spot.

Aaron had learned that from him. Aaron was the rising young star of the Covert Action section, and Tony's pride and joy. During his almost five years on the job, Aaron had exhibited negotiation and acting skills that were making him very useful as a clandestine officer. Add to that an analytical brain, steady nerves, an aptitude for firearms and unarmed combat plus a thirst for the job that had no sign of being quenched, and you had a twenty-eight-year-old with a great career ahead of him. Under Tony's watchful eye and Nat's guiding hand, Aaron had successfully completed every assignment thrown his way to date. It was time to see how this young man could handle himself on a riskier assignment.

Reaching the final stages of his speech, Nat felt his usual eagerness to get back to his assignment. He wanted to see if Aaron handled himself as well as Nat expected him to. They worked well together, which would come in handy on this assignment. A year ago, the difference in their years and experience had suddenly seemed to disappear one night in Peru after they had got themselves out of a bit of a scrap. Due to no fault of their own, they had almost got caught in a building where they had no reason to be. They had escaped detection by seconds and had been sitting in the car after, laughing in relief, trying to pretend they hadn't been scared. Neither one of them was fooling the other, but the teacher/student relationship had faded into the background.

Tony worked hard with his officers, and he put a high value on integrity and loyalty. Nat was also on Tony's team, and he knew the calibre of his teammates. By the time the new ones were sent out with Nat for seasoning, they were still green, but they were absolutely committed. Tony would never stick his senior Operations officer with a young person who had not proven he or she was absolutely trustworthy. At first, Aaron had extended his sense of loyalty to Nat just out of respect for the senior officer and Aaron's belief that any friend of Tony's had to be worthy of the same respect that Tony had earned from him. That night in Peru, Nat had instinctively known that he and Aaron had become friends, and that Aaron had just mentally included him in a small circle of people to whom he gave his personal loyalty.

"Remember," Nat concluded, "that if today, tomorrow, next year…you wake up and realise that you do not like this job any more, or you are no longer committed to it, or you think the hours suck…get out of it. Do not drag on year after year because of the perks or the prestige, or because of some fear you have that to quit is to fail. I never want to find myself in a crucial situation where my backup is someone who would really rather be an accountant. That is not my idea of security." A pause for emphasis. "Good luck, enjoy yourselves, and give it everything you've got."

# II

Surveying the three prisoners and five dead bodies, Gavin knew his men had been lucky. Hammond and Finch had been expert, as usual. They had been outnumbered, which they had already known, but their opponents had been in possession of a couple extra weapons that Gavin had not noticed yesterday. The three officers of the Special Operations section of the CIA had used the element of surprise almost to perfection. Almost. Gavin knew he could have done better. He was responsible for these men, and he could have done better.

Finch worked at securing the last prisoner. Only then could they relax. Hammond wandered over to Gavin, who was staring at one of the bodies. "What's up, Gavin? You expecting him to come back to life?"

Gavin let out a long breath. His adrenalin was subsiding, and his muscles ached from being cramped in hiding and then exploding into combat. "I wish he could. This one didn't need to die."

Hammond laughed, relaxing with the release of tension. He was younger than Gavin, but his muscles ached as well. "Didn't need to die? He was grabbing a machine gun, for Christ's sake!"

"I was close enough," Gavin stated bluntly. "I could have taken him. I didn't need to shoot him, and I should have known about that machine gun. By not knowing, I put you two in a position of unacceptable risk."

"No, Gavin, you're talking crazy." This came from Finch, who was finished with his prisoner and had wandered over, taking a long stretch. "You don't always have to live up to your legend, you know."

Gavin saw red, and whirled around to face Finch. He did not like that sound of sarcasm. Gavin had *never* encouraged that "legend" nonsense. Throughout his career he had done a job to the absolute best of his ability. Period. Finch's jealousy was not appreciated. Especially not now, when Gavin felt like he had made an error.

"Hey, hey, easy, Gav." Alarmed, Hammond had grabbed his arm.

Finch faced him, but had jumped nervously at the look on Gavin's face. "Sorry, man. Hell, I didn't mean anything by it. I just meant that you expect too much from yourself."

Gavin took a deep breath. *What is the matter with me this week?* he wondered. *I'm losing my temper over nothing.* "Naw, it's me that should be sorry," he admitted. "I must be getting too old for all this." He felt Hammond release the grasp on his arm, and he forced a grin. "Time for a vacation, huh?"

The tension disappeared as fast as it had arisen. The assignment had been gruelling, and Gavin realised he actually *was* tired. He knew he had not needed to kill that last man, but he had misjudged and hesitated too long. He had made a mistake, and mistakes were dangerous things to make on these assignments. No one would have expected him to do better, but Gavin liked to demand the maximum from himself. Pushing yourself to the limit; that's what gave him the rush about this job. It's what kept him in the field. But he was forty-three years of age now, and perhaps it was time to take Moseley's advice and have an occasional vacation between assignments. Not that he had anything else to do. This job was his life, and he was basically a loner. The officers he looked after were the only family ties he had. Perhaps, though, it was time for a change of scenery. Maybe he should go home, use the gym, drag Moseley out of the office, play some pool and see if there was anything interesting going on in town.

"Home", to Gavin, was Langley. Gavin had no other place he called home. Moseley was the head of the Office of Special Operations, and had been a very good friend since they had been Career Trainees together. Moseley, however, had been promoted to his present position five years ago. He was good at it, but Gavin missed him. Moseley was his boss now, but that had not changed much, except that they did not see as much of each other as they would have liked, and Gavin always remembered to call him "sir" in front of most people.

"I will contact Moseley and report in," Gavin offered. "Could you two start the cleanup? I think I'm actually going to ask for some time off."

# III

Aaron St. Pierre and Scott Andrews were jogging around the small track that circled the gym in the basement of one of the buildings at Langley. For the first twenty minutes they usually kept pace with each other, chatting away amicably. At twenty-eight years of age, Aaron was very pleased with the direction his life was taking. He had been an officer with the CIA for almost five years now, and he knew that his superiors were very pleased with his performance. That made him happy, so he gave the job all the energy he could. After his training period had ended, he had been assigned to Covert Operations and placed with Anthony Dune. It was a good match. Tony was renown for his redheaded temper, but what people did not take time to understand was that Tony only got upset about things he really cared about; like his officers. He would go up one side of you and down the other if you messed up, but it was because he wanted you to excel. Aaron had no fear of Tony's temper. The man had a heart of gold hidden behind that gruffness. Once you found it, and he knew you had, you had an ally for life.

Tony had recently accepted a promotion, an acting promotion actually. He had been asked to head up the Covert Action section after the man who was in that position had been asked to resign. There were a million rumors about it, but the truth was not being distributed to front line staff. Tony had accepted the post conditionally, because he was not sure he wanted the administrative work. An arrangement was agreed upon where Tony could try it for six months and a final decision would be made at that time. Aaron and Scott had been afraid that they would be reassigned, but because Tony, Aaron and Nat were assigned to the Cuban operation, most of the team was allowed to stay under Tony. That included the new trainee, Sheila, who had just finished her first year and was on the team for a field placement. It also included Dan, who was an experienced officer. James was missing in action, and Kevin Whalen had just asked for, and received, a transfer to the Office of Technical Services. Kevin had started with Scott, which gave him one year field experience following the two-year training program. Two other experienced men had transferred to other station chiefs in Central America.

Nathanial Bowman was another good friend. In fact, during this last year Nat had become somewhat of a mentor to Aaron. In addition to Aaron's regular job as an Operations officer, he had been placed on two short covert operations with Nat. Nat had figuratively held his hand through them, and ensured that a successful conclusion was reached. Of course Nat, being a generous type of man, had given a lot of the credit to Aaron's participation. It had earned him Aaron's unfailing devotion. Now Nat was taking Aaron on a much riskier operation in Cuba. There would not be the safety of diplomatic immunity on this assignment. They would be in a hostile country without any paperwork to protect them. Their only method of rescue was to signal the base at Guantanamo Bay, and that would depend on their ability to send a signal in time.

While Aaron was lost in his daydreaming, Scott turned on the turbo jets. Aaron tried to catch his friend, but it was a wasted effort. With legs that churned effortlessly, Scott seemed to fly around the track. He was incredibly fast, and Aaron always came in a poor second. During his school days, Scott had accumulated a variety of ribbons and trophies for speed and sports that required quick reflexes. He was murder on a racquetball court. Now Aaron's goal was to prevent Scott from lapping him.

By giving it every ounce of speed that he possessed, Aaron managed to keep Scott from gaining a lap on him…barely. Slowing to a jog, Aaron fought to regain his breathing while Scott moved easily beside him.

"You're slowing down, Mr. St. Pierre," Scott teased. "Were we asleep on the switch?"

Aaron gave up and walked. "I guess you could say that," he gasped.

With his usual grin, Scott turned and jogged slowly backwards at Aaron's side. "Well, I'm glad there is something I can beat you at. Were you thinking about Cuba?"

"Yeh. Cuba, Nat, Tony, you name it." He could breathe regularly again.

"I hear Tony, Nat and Moseley are going golfing on the weekend," Scott stated. "Did Tony invite you?"

"Me?" Aaron laughed. "Hardly! I don't play very well." Pulling the T-shirt out at his waist, Aaron used it as a towel to mop his brow. "Besides, it would cramp their style. They talk work on the golf course. They could hardly talk policy stuff in front of me, could they?"

Scott looked puzzled. He had slowed to a walk beside Aaron. "Nat golfs with them, and he's technically the same level we are."

"Oh, yeh, but look at the history between those guys," Aaron replied. "They've known each other since they started working here. Nat knows when he's not supposed to have heard something. Tony and Frank know he can keep their secrets. Besides, Nat says if anything really sensitive comes up they just give him a 'sorry can't talk in front of you, old chap' look and change the subject. He says once in a while they forget he's there, and really put their foot in it. Then they look embarrassed and tell him that he didn't hear what they said."

"Golf courses sound like a great place to pick up gossip," Scott observed, leading the way to the change rooms. "Maybe we should go and hide in a sand trap." He winked at Aaron. "Then I'd really know what Tony thinks of me."

Aaron laughed. "Quit worrying. Tony thinks you're doing just fine, I'm sure. Believe me, you'd know if he didn't."

"So why'd he give me a feminist for a partner?" Scott asked. "He's trying to torture me. I think he's making a big comment on my lifestyle."

"Sheila will be good for you," Aaron teased. "She'll teach you how to work with a woman."

"Shit, now you sound like Tony," Scott protested. "She's supposed to settle me down, whatever that means, and I'm supposed to make her loosen up." He shook his head. "Hell, Tony's either yelling at me or hugging me. I don't know which is worse."

"That's just the way he is Scott. You should know that by now. He's a bit emotional."

"A bit?" Scott snorted.

Aaron slapped his friend on the shoulder. "You don't really mind. Trust me, if he didn't bother yelling at you in your first year on his team, that would mean he didn't figure you were worth it. Look, he didn't yell at Kevin much, did he?"

"No," Scott admitted. "Tony didn't like Kevin for some reason."

"Right, and now Kevin has transferred out. That's my point," Aaron insisted. "If Tony yells at you, he's planning to keep you and wants you up to his expectations. And," Aaron added, "he's such a softy inside that he feels guilty for yelling at you but he can't seem to apologise, so that's why you get hugged every once in a while. Once he decides that you know what you're doing, the yelling will stop and he'll back off. I told you he wasn't easy to learn to work for, but trust me, it'll be worth it in the end."

Scott looked at Aaron. "Actually, I do know that. I can see him with you guys. He really backs you up. I'm just looking forward to the day he decides I can be trusted on my own."

"It won't be long, Scott," Aaron assured him.

Aaron had met Scott at the end of Aaron's training program. He had been sent on a winter wilderness expedition in the Salmon River Mountains in Idaho. His assignment was to take a new trainee into the mountains with a survival kit, stay for two nights and bring him home safely. The whole exercise would take three days: one day up the mountain, one day on the mountain, and one day to get back to base. Food for four days would be carried on their backs in case they were delayed. If anyone had not returned by the morning of the fifth day, the search would be on. Searches were embarrassing for trainees, but occasionally necessary. For the graduating trainee, it was a chance to use the survival skills learned previously. For the new trainee, it was the opportunity to learn those same skills from their partner. The exercise was taken very seriously by all parties, and Aaron had done a lot of studying and practicing prior to the assignment.

Actually, Aaron had always enjoyed winter camping and ice fishing. He experienced only one misgiving. The trainee with whom he was paired turned out to be Scott Andrews. At twenty-three years of age, Scott was bright and well educated. However, he was also rich and had a very cocky air about him. Blond, five feet, eleven inches tall and very attractive, Scott already had a reputation as a womaniser. People said he was superficial, spoiled and undependable—a real playboy. Apparently he rarely socialised with other trainees, and never invited anyone to his family's home. Since Aaron had not been given a choice of partners, he had to make the most of it.

On first impression, Scott struck Aaron as being too casual and laid back about this assignment, acting as if he were going on a picnic. Once they got out on their own, however, Scott started concentrating on what they were doing. Whenever Aaron stopped to teach him anything, Scott listened and watched with rapt attention. It was only during their rest periods that Scott reverted to his carefree, flippant nature. By the first nightfall, Aaron had decided that people were misjudging the "spoiled rich kid". Scott had character hidden under that facade, and could be worth knowing.

Born in Waterville, Maine, Aaron spent many holidays during his youth at his uncle's home in Grand Falls, New Brunswick. When Aaron tried to teach Scott the ice fishing skills he had learned from his uncle, city-bred Scott had been horrified. Fish was something he was served at dinner with tasty sauces. The sight and smell of the real thing being cleaned and gutted was revolting to him. However, Scott had managed to watch bravely and learn even that disgusting trick.

Disaster struck on the return trip during the last day. Somehow, Scott fell through some snow into a hidden crevice. He landed feet first, but the rock on each side of him was smooth and slippery. His head was three feet below the ground. It was pure luck that the snow had not fallen in on top of him and hidden him from view. Scott was stuck. The survival kit included a rope, which Aaron passed down so Scott could secure it around his waist. Unfortunately, no tree was close enough to secure the other end, so Aaron had to wrap it around his waist and brace himself against rocks made wet by snow while Scott pulled himself up.

Slipping and sliding on the rocks, it took all of Aaron's strength to hold on. A very sober Scott finally emerged from the crevice, and Aaron collapsed. He had been soaked in sweat and soon became very cold. Scott set up their little tent, wrapped Aaron in a blanket and lit the small heater. By nightfall Aaron was sick. He had visited a friend the day before leaving on this expedition, and that friend had the flu. Normally Aaron's body had a good resistance to germs, but getting cold and tired must have let the flu bug get a start. He spent the night and most of the next day throwing up.

The next day was the fourth day, and Aaron had no wish for a search party to be sent out. He told Scott to leave him and return to the base. Scott could assure the trainers that Aaron would return to the base the following day when he had enough strength to scramble down the mountain. Scott, however, had refused to leave him, insisting that he would not leave Aaron alone and defenceless where some cougar or man-eating fish could get him. Trying to assure Scott that there were no man-eating fish in the cool mountain streams was a waste of time. Scott refused to leave. Aaron had actually been relieved. He felt horrid and rather helpless in this weakened state.

Scott had played nursemaid, keeping a steady supply of boiled water available so Aaron would not become dehydrated. Knowing that Aaron would need to eat for energy as soon as his stomach settled down, Scott saved the travelling rations for the following day and actually went fishing for his own supper. Sick as Aaron was, the sight of Scott catching a fish through an opening in the ice, and curling his nose in disgust as he prepared it for cooking, made him laugh in amusement.

The next morning they were able to continue, and waved away the helicopter that spotted them at noon. By the time they got back to the base, they were good friends, and in a quiet way of expressing that friendship, Scott had invited Aaron home to meet the family that Scott guarded so carefully. That's where Aaron had met Susan.

Following his training, Aaron had been assigned to Tony's team, and Tony had noticed the friendship between Aaron and Scott. Tony had checked into Scott's training and talked to Aaron about him. Among trainees, Tony had a reputation for being a difficult man to work for because of his temper and the fact that he wanted to spend a lot of time with his officers. Some people saw this as being intrusive. People who were placed on Tony's team either gave up in frustration or became devoted. In Aaron's eyes, Tony was the best man to work for, so he told Scott the pros and cons. Scott was a bit wary, but was impressed with Aaron's strong feelings for his boss. When Tony met Scott one day to ask him if he had chosen all his placements for the coming year, Scott expressed interest in working for him. Partly due to Aaron's recommendation, Tony took Scott on. It wasn't a perfect match, because Scott still had a flippant side to his nature that did not suit Tony's style. Fortunately, Tony was able to see past the flippancy and find the same character and sharp mind that Aaron had talked about. Tony had decided to invest his time and develop Scott. Aaron worked with Scott to teach him, among other things, how to put some of the flippancy away, especially around Tony. It worked, and Scott had been a permanent team member for a year, as well as becoming Aaron's best friend.

# IV

The office of Congressman Richard Harvey reeked of luxury. An image of power and competence was being portrayed, so the dark wine-coloured leather furniture and even the paintings on the wall had a standard to maintain. There was no dust and no clutter. Books were neatly arranged in the oak bookcase with the glass doors. Lamp covers were clean and co-ordinated to the furniture. A Tiffany lamp hung over the desk. Richard Harvey had not been born to poverty, and had no intention of ever experiencing it. He was a pragmatic, opportunistic man who did not plan to err.

Right now, though, he was worried. A couple of years ago he had made connections with the Cuban government. Absolutely against policy, of course, but Richard Harvey followed policy only when it assisted his career. Policy was for other people. He knew best what was good for Richard Harvey. Interacting with Castro's government had proved lucrative. Resources can always be directed towards friendly hands, no matter how poor the country, and the Congressman had received his share. All he had to do was send them some business connections…unofficially and very quietly, of course. He had a couple of connections in the CIA who had been willing to help. Having connections in key institutions was always helpful. The compensation he had obtained had to be hidden, of course, but any financial advisor worth his paycheque could help with that, and Richard Harvey could afford very good and discreet financial advisors.

Everything had gone well until he was contacted by a man named Taz. No last name—just Taz. Clearly an out and out criminal, but he represented a group who called themselves the Sierra Maestra Liberators. Taz had given him a pitch about supporting the group and helping them overthrow Castro. When he had not expressed any interest in the proposal, Taz had referred to his involvement with the Cuban government. There had been no overt threat of blackmail, but Richard Harvey was not fooled. The threats would come later.

However, he was not without resources. Richard Harvey had sent for his own people, people he did not publicly acknowledge, to assess his position.

They had reported back quickly. Taz did represent this group, and had good information, which he was using to blackmail American businessmen and officials alike. The rebel group was obsessed with overthrowing Castro and being in power itself.

He had pretended to go along with Taz and had sent a large donation to buy himself time to think. An idea slowly began to take shape. His sources in the CIA said that the rebel group was growing, and, given time and money, could possibly meet their goal. Castro was old, and his followers were very busy juggling for positions that would ensure their own leadership once he was gone. None of these people were acceptable to the American government because of their communist commitment. The rebels were not communists. Their leader was more apt to become a dictator, but that had not been a problem for Washington previously. If Richard Harvey could help the rebels take power, they would be very grateful. The rewards would be lucrative. And the American people would see this coup as a direct result of Congressman Harvey's own actions. He would be seen as a leader. Who could imagine how far that would take him? The press would be good—very good.

There was one hitch. Last week he had told Taz to inform the rebel leader, Jose Luis, of his support and his hopes for their success. Now Jose Luis was testing him. Any fool could see that. Taz had suggested he come to Cuba to meet Jose Luis and demonstrate his good intentions. To Cuba, of all places. It was politically very dangerous for him, especially since the passing of the Helmes-Burton law. But the results would be well worth it in the end. Richard Harvey had learned long ago that you got nowhere unless you took risks. This was a very big risk, but the reward would be sweet. Visions of a future election were constantly on his mind. He could make it to the top if he played it right.

He would go to Cuba. It would be difficult. A private flight, followed by a long boat trip. The landing would be at night; very secretive. Then he would be taken to the camp in the mountains by horseback. Very clandestine, but somehow exciting too. He told himself not to worry. With a little detailed planning, everything would run like clockwork.

# V

"Why can't those people wave us through? You would think that people would take the time to learn the rules of golf before they went to a course like this!" It was the ever impatient Tony sounding off. Anthony Dune, Frank Moseley and Nathanial Bowman were waiting to tee off on one of their favourite golf courses. The morning weather was perfect—a little on the crisp side with a pure blue sky. It was a lovely, well-maintained course, with a few too many trees for Tony's temperament, but his favourite course nonetheless. The sand traps were made with silica, the fairways well cut, and the greens were manicured regularly.

"I thought we were here to relax," Frank remarked drily. "What's the hurry? It's a beautiful day and we are out of the office."

"Here they go," Nat announced. "Why don't you go ahead, Tony?"

Tony stepped up and addressed his ball. It *was* a beautiful day. He wished he had Frank's temperament. Nothing upset Frank except an overcooked steak. Striking the ball, Tony groaned. "I hooked it. Damn!" It was the waiting around that bugged him, but it was inevitable that the course would be crowded on a day like this. "Go ahead, Frank. Show us how it's done."

Nat and Tony watched Frank address his ball. Frank had a beautiful swing—slow and easy, but with a surprising touch of power. The ball usually went where he wanted it to go, and it obeyed today.

"Beauty, Frank," Nat said. "A short iron will take you to the green." Now it was Nat's turn. He was a little more erratic than Frank, but had just as long a drive. Unfortunately, when he sliced he was often well off the fairway. This time he was lucky, and his ball ended up slightly to the right of Frank's. "I'll take that one," he stated proudly.

They always walked the course because it gave them time to talk and settle down for the next shot if they had blown the drive. The three men had all started working for the CIA seventeen years ago. Gavin Weeks had started with them as well. All four men were good friends, although Gavin and Frank did not get to spend as much time together as Nat and Tony. Since Gavin worked for Frank in the Special Operations section, he went wherever Frank had to send him. Nat worked for Tony, but they usually worked in the same place. None of them had known each other before being hired, but like employees the world over, they had eventually found common interests and gravitated together. The bonds of friendship had formed slowly and cautiously, as they each had brought a well-developed scepticism to their jobs, but now they were as comfortable and intertwined as old men on a porch step watching the setting sun. Communication was often a look or a gesture, rather than words. They were not, however, old or bored. All four were deeply involved in their jobs.

Frank Moseley was in charge of some very specialised teams, like the paramilitary unit Gavin led. All his teams received specialised training to suit their function. Usually their activities were denied or hidden from public view. His teams had to be ready to be sent to any part of the globe at a moment's notice. Like his friends, Frank was married to his job and his teams were his pride and joy. He was in complete control of them, yet was very conscious of the dangers of miscommunication, or the damage that his teams could do with even the slightest error of judgement on their side or on his. He expected, and received, the best from his people, but never relaxed until an assignment was successfully completed, reported in detail, and any "damage" cleaned up.

Damage could include civilians caught in crossfire, reimbursing an official whose car got blown up by accident, or a variety of other situations. Moseley had the pragmatism necessary for his position. Once he made a decision he felt was right, he did not stay up nights worrying about it. If he was proven wrong, he accepted the blame, which was why his men liked working for him. Frank viewed life in the same way he viewed his superiors…unpredictable. One day they wanted a civil war started in an unfriendly country, so he obliged. The next day he had to repair the damage because the country was now friendly. It was all an elaborate game and a huge adrenalin rush.

Frank considered his two golfing friends to be "softer", but he didn't respect them any less for it. They were each as much a perfectionist as he was, in their own positions. Tony and Nat could never handle his job, but they were experts in their own. Frank's men were highly specialised and trained for action. They were not expected to expend a lot of energy wondering if what they were doing was morally correct. Good and bad were fickle concepts in the political arena anyway. It was Frank's job to decide if they were being used appropriately, and if not, then hash it out with his Deputy Director. Tony's field was different. His men convinced people in other countries to supply information, which was then accumulated and sent up the ladder. They were also occasionally involved in operations like this Cuba assignment, and if they got into trouble, Moseley's teams were available to help them out. Tony needed people who could think a situation through and change directions in mid-stride if need be. Frank would have found the elasticity of Tony's assignments too frustrating because he liked clear parameters. Tony saw parameters as guidelines.

Frank differed in physical appearance from his two friends as well. He had short, straight dark hair and a thin build. He was forty-five years of age and stood five feet, ten inches. Like Tony and Nat, however, Frank spent a lot of his spare time at the gym. He rarely took holidays, because the people he wanted to be with were the ones he worked with. His two attempts at marriage had not lasted long. He really couldn't be bothered with the emotional demands his wives had made. Like Nat, Frank spent his leisure time with a few *very* discreet women. He had to be even more careful than Nat, because Moseley knew too much about the Company's less publicised activities to be careless. Like Tony and Nat, his seventeen years of good conduct had earned him the trust of his superiors, but Moseley knew that his superiors were political animals, and he trod a very careful political line himself to avoid getting caught up in their personal games. As a result, he was seen as a loner, devoted to his teams and the Company in general. Only when he was with Tony, Nat or Gavin did he truly relax.

They had reached their balls. Tony was furthest from the hole, but landed a well-hit five iron on the edge of the green. "Now that's what makes a day beautiful," he laughed

Nat used a seven and dropped his ball about five feet from the pin. Obviously pleased, he stood still to watch Frank.

A seven was Frank's selection as well, but he hit it too fat, and it left him with a ten-foot putt. "Ugh!" was all he said.

Nat never ceased to be amazed that Tony and Frank were friends. Their temperaments were so opposite. Frank was so calm, and Tony was such a firecracker. Perhaps that was the answer, though. Before the day was out, Tony was bound to throw a club, and Frank would just laugh at him. Nat was somewhere between the two in temperament. He watched Tony prepare to putt. Tony was the same height as Frank, but was a thicker, more powerful build. His hair used to be red, but had darkened to an auburn shade and was curly. At forty-two, he was the youngest of the four friends. Tony had the kind of morals that caused him to stick with a loveless marriage for sixteen years before his wife committed suicide. Even before the suicide, Tony had always buried himself in his work, perhaps in an effort to avoid the marriage. That was how he developed the habit of virtually living with his new officers until he knew he could trust them with his, or anyone else's life. However, Tony still had the needs of the average mature male, so Nat had introduced him to a couple of women who knew a good thing when they saw it, keeping their mouths shut and their bodies available. Nat also knew that Tony hated the fact that he couldn't just work and forget his sexual urges. The bad marriage, the wasted commitment and the suicide had destroyed in Tony any desire to remarry, yet everyone but Tony knew that Tony *needed* to be married. He was the devoted, marrying kind, and it was just plain sad that his first choice had been such a cold disaster. Now he was so afraid to risk losing another sixteen years that he was throwing his future away. The Company had worried about Tony when his wife died, but three years had passed now, and Tony was as solid and dependable as ever. His wife, Carolyn, had been no long-term loss for him.

Once they had sunk their putts, it was on to the next hole, and another wait on the tee-off. "Did I tell you guys that Gavin's on his way home?" Frank asked.

Both men were glad to hear it. "End of an assignment, or is he coming home for his annual dose of socialising?" Nat asked. Gavin usually scorned taking time off. He liked to visit his friends briefly between assignments, but tended to avoid being around other people for any length of time. About once a year something inside Gavin reminded him that he was a human being and human beings needed company. At that point Gavin would become temporarily homesick.

"That usually lasts about five days," Tony added.

"You're right," Frank grinned. "Then he starts begging me to find him another assignment." The foursome ahead of them were now out of range, so Frank indicated to Nat that he had the honours. He was quiet while Nat lined up and sent a ball straighter this time, but caught a fairway bunker. "Tough luck, but your line is good," he told him. "No, this time it's partly a need for company—at least he has threatened to drag me out of the office to do the town with him—but he's a bit tired too. He actually asked for a vacation."

"Gavin asked for time off? Real time off?" Tony addressed his ball, considering the concept of Gavin the loner wanting a real vacation. This time he tried to relax his swing and keep his left arm straight. It paid off, and the ball went true, landing a five iron from the green. "Better." He picked up his tee. "What on earth for? Gavin doesn't have any outside interests that we know about. The only places he spends time when he isn't with us is the gym and the gun range." Gavin was Nat's age and the same height, but he was a lanky, sinewy man without an ounce of fat. Living a life of action far from the public eye had given Gavin a severe, cautious look. His eyes were a steely shade of blue/grey, and his face had a hard look to it. If he had wanted to, he could have risen through the ranks in the Company, but he had absolutely no desire to do so. However, he was their friend and shared the same unwavering commitment to the Company. In fact, he was viewed as the Company watchdog and would fight any attack ruthlessly. Gavin would have been lost in the politics of the office, but in the field he was a formidable foe to their opponents.

"I don't suppose the impossible has happened and Gavin has fallen in love?" Nat asked, the twinkle in his eye showing he was not serious.

Frank laughed and stepped back from the tee. That had ruined his concentration. "That'll be the day. I'm not sure if Gavin even bothers with sex—it would take too much time, and he'd consider it too untidy. He'd have to remove about six weapons from his body just to get undressed, and then he'd really feel naked. Can't see it happening." Stepping up to the tee again, Frank managed a hook into the trees lining the left of the fairway. "That'll teach me to concentrate," he muttered.

This conversation was getting unkind, thought Tony, as they walked up the fairway. "Give the guy a break, fellows. He's not a machine. There is a real human being behind those steely blue eyes."

"Relax, Tony," Frank responded. "You know how much I think of Gavin. There's no one I'd rather have watch my back. But you must admit he tends to give trainees the creeps, and the stories that circulate among the rest of the staff make him sound like the bionic man. Why would he want to spend time around here when he can't walk down a hall without people staring at him?"

"Speaking of trainees," Nat interrupted, "I saw your newest placement in class today, Tony. Nice-looking woman."

"A woman?" Frank had started to look for his ball among the trees. "How's that going to fit your team building strategy? She might not be too receptive to you spending all your time with her. I mean, it's one thing to watch TV with Scott or Aaron until one a.m. and then sleep on their couch. You'd better not try that with a woman."

Tony chuckled, helping Frank look for his ball. "Wouldn't even try it," he assured. "She's already given me the 'not now, not ever, not while I report to you' look. Believe me, that woman would not bother with harassment complaints—she'd tell you straight to your face and damn the consequences. However," he continued, "she actually approached me. Seems like she'd done her homework first and decided she liked the way my team worked together. Here's your ball, in this grass."

While he managed to hit it onto the fairway, the hook had already cost Frank a stroke. "Well, you probably won't have as much time on your hands now anyway." He chose a three iron, slowed his swing down, and was pleased with the result.

Nat led the way to the bunker. "You'll have to adjust your style, Tony, but it's time you got a life anyway." He grinned to take the punch out of the words.

"Look who's talking," Tony commented. "Actually I think it will work out. I've decided to pair her with Scott for the first few months, presuming she'll stay past her placement." Expecting a reaction, he paused.

"With Scott?" Nat reacted first. "Why?"

Frank was less personally familiar with Tony's team but Nat's response supported his suspicion. "Scott is your rich kid, isn't he? He's only been in the field a year, Tony. He's surely not ready to be paired with a trainee! You've still got Dan, Aaron and Nat here. Why choose Scott?"

Tony waited until Nat escaped the bunker with a well-hit four iron. He was enjoying the reaction. It was fun to be able to throw a curve at his friends. Nat looked pleased with himself, but then he turned to Tony. "Okay...explain. With Scott's reputation, which is worse than mine even, it can't be that he's the only one you would trust with a woman."

"Hardly," Tony protested, as they walked on. "Scott's almost ready to fly," he began. When Tony used the word 'fly', he meant that Scott was ready to do some real work on his own. The amount of support provided by the team to a new officer depended upon the person's abilities and the complexity of the assignment. He felt that Scott was ready to start his job as an Operations officer on his own. So far, he had done well with team support. "The man is bright," Tony told his friends, "he's got a big heart, he's eager and he's taken his training seriously."

"But?" prompted Nat, hearing a condition in Tony's voice.

"But I need him to settle down a bit more," admitted Tony. "Remember, he's a playboy—good looking, rich, and very busy living up to his reputation as a ladies' man. I need to see a little more maturity. I'm afraid he could make an error in judgement if he doesn't take life just a bit more seriously. I like the kid," Tony assured, "don't get me wrong. There's integrity under that playfulness, or I wouldn't put up with it at all."

"I still don't get the link with Sheila," Nat admitted. "She's hardly his type."

Tony nodded agreement. "Exactly. She's a woman who is quite different from his reputed conquests. That's why I'm doing this. Sheila is serious. Too serious if anything. If it works out the way I'm hoping, she will settle him down and force him to view women in a different light. He, on the other hand, will lighten her up a bit."

Frank was shaking his head. "Tony, even if that works, where's the leadership? Scott's barely got his feet wet, and Sheila hasn't even started."

"Frank is right, Tony. I think you are asking for trouble. Who is teaching who what, here?"

"Take it easy, fellows," Tony grinned. "You've forgotten about me. It solves my problem with Sheila and the time I need to spend with her. I'll be spending it with both of them. I have already warned her about that. She and Scott will be seeing a lot of each other and a lot of me. I need to spend a couple more months with Scott anyway. Then I'll know if he can put aside the rich kid image. In the meantime Sheila has a chaperon and can get comfortable with my constant presence. After a couple of months it will be no big deal for her. After all," he concluded, "she's no shrinking violet. I think she's more than capable of looking after herself." Tony addressed his ball. A bit of a breeze had sprung up. He chose the five iron, but it lost momentum in the breeze and landed short of the green. Frustrated with the wrong choice, he jammed the iron back into his bag.

On the next hole there was a line-up and the three men had stood slightly to one side so they could continue chatting. Nat had asked Tony how he liked his new job.

"Too early to tell," Tony responded, "although I have to admit it is really interesting to see the larger picture. When you are involved in one area of the globe, you tend to get out of touch with what everyone else is doing. Now it's my job to know exactly what everyone is doing. My head is spinning, but Frank's been a great help."

"It'll come together," Frank assured him. "You get so you can deal with a lot of pieces at one time. By the way," he asked, "how do you like Walsh?"

Carl Walsh was their new Deputy Director for Operations. Two weeks after Tony's predecessor had been removed from his office, the Deputy Director had a fatal heart attack. It took everyone by surprise, since there had been no suspicion of heart disease. When the doctors opened him up, they found four solidly blocked arteries. The man had been a walking corpse and didn't know it.

Losing the head of the Covert section plus the Deputy Director within two weeks of each other had put the CIA into a near panic. Tony did not know his job yet, and had suddenly lost his boss. Frank had brought in his reassuring voice and started doing double duty. While upper management scrambled to find a replacement for the Deputy Director, the section heads managed to work together without incident. Only when Carl Walsh was put in place did some people start to protest.

The foursome ahead of them had just teed off. It would be several minutes before they were out of striking range. Tony had given some thought to Frank's last question. "He's a bit reserved, and seems to be feeling his way, although I can already tell I would hate to be on his bad side."

"That's for sure," Frank agreed. "He's had each of us in for private meetings so he can get to know us." Frank grinned. "Translated, that means he has researched everything we've been doing and he's making sure he has no bad apples in his barrel."

"That is his job," Tony stated.

"Yeh, but it's a hell of an interview, I can tell you."

"Sure seems to be a lot of upset people over that selection," Nat added. "He's not one of us, is he?"

"Nope," Frank said, moving up to tee off. "He's army Intelligence, or at least he was. There are a lot of people walking around with their noses out of joint about that."

"Well, you can have the politics, Frank," Nat stated. He waited until Frank hit, then walked up. "I hear he's quite the dandy."

"Wears a three-piece suit and his shoes shine like glass," Frank agreed, "but I wouldn't use the word 'dandy'. That doesn't quite fit. Whatever you do, though, never drop into his office when you're off duty unless you have your suit on. Yesterday I could hear him giving someone hell for coming in on his day off with a golf shirt on."

Nat hit, followed by Tony. Tony's ball made a direct flight into the creek, resulting in a series of obscenities. "Tony, I can't believe you don't have high blood pressure," Frank finally remarked.

"I don't keep things bottled up," Tony explained shortly.

"That's one way of putting it," Nat muttered. "By the way, I'm glad the team was kept together, at least some of it. Aaron was walking around looking like he had lost his best friend when you took that promotion."

Tony tried not to look pleased. "Aaron likes stability in his personal life. He'll go anywhere and try anything as far as the job is concerned, but he's the type that needs his personal life to stay on track."

"Puppy dog," Frank supplied.

That pissed Tony off. "Don't call him that, Frank. He hates it. And he's a professional. Just because he likes to have a heart-to-heart conversation with me if something goes wrong in the field doesn't make him any less effective."

"Sorry, sorry." Frank threw up his hands in surrender as they walked down the fairway. "You know I don't mean anything by it. I'm just jealous because he wouldn't work for me."

"No, he couldn't handle that," Tony admitted, "but he's no pushover."

Nat laughed. "I will *never* forget that scene in the cafeteria two years ago!"

"I wish I could," Tony said. "I felt like an incompetent boob and I've never been able to use that trick since."

"What was that?" Frank asked, having gotten a few feet away from them.

"Remember when Tony was calling Aaron every couple of weeks during his first few months on the team? Tony would disguise his voice and kept offering him bribes to see how he would react."

Frank laughed. "I remember. You had told him before that to report any such attempts at once to you. He did at first, didn't he?"

"Oh yeh," Tony agreed, "he sure did. But then he stopped. That brain of his kicked in. He wasn't even as far along as Scott is now, but I guess one day he sat down and really thought about it."

"How did it go?" asked Nat. "He figured that he wasn't worth bribing yet, so what the hell was going on?"

"Yep. He knew that he didn't have access to anything of importance yet, and because he was still new I was watching him like a hawk." Tony shook his head. "Man, did he ever throw me for a loop when he stopped reporting my calls. Then on one call he started fishing to see what I wanted. That really made my skin crawl, because I had started to respect the kid, and I didn't want to know that I'd made a big mistake."

"You didn't have a clue that he suspected you." It was a statement. Frank had witnessed the end result and would never forget it.

Tony stopped near where his ball had entered the creek. He dropped another ball and selected a three iron. "Hell, he was new. I was supposed to be smarter than him. It was a very humbling experience, I'll tell you. Especially to find that he had broken into my home and put a bug on my phone. Who on earth would expect a new officer to do that?" For a minute he concentrated on his ball. The three iron hit true and he rolled onto the green.

Nat was chuckling at the memory of the scene in the cafeteria late in the evening. "Remember how mad Aaron was? He stormed into that cafeteria, slammed the transcripts of the calls down on the table in front of you, actually pulled you off the chair by grabbing your jacket lapel, and demanded to know what game you were playing."

Frank had sent his ball into some bushes to the right of the green. "Shit! Yeh, Nat and I were ready to grab him. He was a big, strong, angry young man, and you really pissed him off. I thought he was going to hit you."

"I was glad you were there, too," agreed Tony. "Since you were, I decided that I'd already gone so far that I'd go all the way and test his control, too. So I taunted him. I needed to see if he could keep his cool, or if he'd strike me. If he lost control while he was that junior, I'd have had some hard decisions to make. It was one thing to be angry at me, but you don't walk into a cafeteria and punch out your boss."

"He didn't," Frank remembered. "In fact, he stepped away from you with a stunned look on his face. He was disappointed in you."

"He said, 'If you can't trust me by now, cut me loose, but do it right now because I won't waste any more time playing games.'" Tony smiled. "The kid was shaking. His future was on the line and he knew it. And I knew I had exactly what I wanted on my team."

"You had some repair work to do," Nat added. "His feelings were hurt."

"Yeh," Tony admitted. "So I told him that I had needed to make sure I could trust him completely, and he had just shown me that I could. I promised there would be no more games, and I told him he was ready. And he was."

Nat hit his ball with an easy stroke onto the green. "We took him to a bar and spent the rest of the night trying to get him drunk," he remembered. "He needed to relax. That was a pretty traumatic scene for a new guy. Especially admitting that he'd broken into your house. But by the end of the evening he was feeling pretty good, though."

"He's got the best potential I've seen yet," Tony stated simply. "I can't wait to see how he does with you in Cuba. Oh, Frank, if Gavin's around, are you going to use him on Nat and Aaron's backup team?"

"Sure, Gavin would be more than happy to help you guys. It's your putt, Tony."

Tony putted badly, watching his ball roll past the hole by six feet. He wasn't concentrating on this game. He tried not to swear this time.

"Aaron sure hates his cover," Nat advised, having sunk his putt.

"I think it's a terrible choice for him," Frank added, looking at Tony. "Sorry, Tony, but I do."

"Why, Frank?" Tony asked. "That is exactly what the real Taz is. Remember that Aaron's hobbies at university were acting and drawing. He can pretend to be almost anything." It wasn't like Frank to concern himself with Tony's operations. It made Tony uneasy.

Frank looked briefly at Nat, then stared into Tony's eyes without blinking. "You know why. You don't like me saying it. It's that puppy dog part of him."

Tony slammed his club bag down in frustration. "Come on, Frank. Just because he's not one of your machines doesn't make him any less a professional. He's years ahead of any of the guys he started with. So it upset him once that he had to gut a fanatic with a knife when the guy was trying to blow everyone's head off with a shotgun. That doesn't make him soft."

"There you go again, jumping all over me," Frank protested. "And my men are not machines. All I'm trying to say is that if anything goes wrong in Cuba, his only protection is a cover that is violent. Aaron is not a violent man."

Realising that some of his frustration was caused by that same fear, Tony looked to Nat for help. "You're confident that there is no risk of him having to actually prove that aspect of his cover." It was a statement.

"I would never have suggested it otherwise," Nat insisted. He counted his arguments off on his fingers. "One—Osvaldo has informed me that Jose Luis allows no women in the camp. Two—the camp is in the mountains and is isolated. Three—he assures me that security is tight and no one will wander in or out. Taz would not be allowed to go into town even if there were a town close by, which there isn't. Four—we'll both be watched closely because we are strangers. And five—I'll be there to get him out if things start to unravel," Nat concluded.

The final hole was not much fun for Tony. Hearing Frank's worries had bothered him, and it did terrible things to his golf game. He shanked his drive, sending it into the trees, then launched his second shot into the creek. By the time he landed his nine iron shot in the sand trap, his temper blew.

"Here we go," warned Nat. Sure enough, Tony's nine iron became a lopsided boomerang, and went sailing off after the ball. Tony never threw anything *at* anyone—he had enough control to keep from doing that—but he left Nat and Frank shaking their heads. "It's a mind game, Tony," Nat called back as he and Frank walked towards the green.

"Nat, you won't be armed in Cuba, will you?" Frank asked.

"Nope," Nat replied. "Wish I could be. Makes me feel rather naked, but Sam Turnbell is a businessman. They will expect me to be unarmed. At least Aaron will be expected to carry a knife."

"A knife. Some help."

"Oh, you should see Aaron in action with a knife. However," Nat sighed, "it is going to feel a little strange sitting among all those weapons and having nothing on me. But," he smiled at Frank, "not to worry. We're just to go in, size it up and bring back as much information as we can glean."

"You remember the signals?" Technical Services had provided a signalling device that Nat and Aaron would use when they were ready to leave, or if they needed to be rescued.

Nat rested his hand on his friend's shoulder. "Frank, please, a little faith. Okay, one signal to tell you we are on our way out so you can meet us in the sugar cane field by the sea in behind the old fishing dock. Three signals with a day and time means we need you to send in the troops on a certain day at a certain time. Five signals with one repetition means we need immediate rescue." He smiled at his worried friend. "Feel better?"

"I don't like that country," Frank said by way of explanation. "You are in there with no protection: no diplomatic immunity, no papers to pretend you are Canadian, no way of pretending you are Cuban, nothing. Anything goes wrong and you have nowhere to turn. Hell, I don't know which would be worse, being caught by the rebels or being caught by the Cubans."

"Cheering him up, Frank?" Tony asked pointedly, having caught up with them.

"Sorry." Frank gave himself a mental slap. This was no way to send someone to an assignment. "That country gives me the creeps." He put on a grin and turned to Nat. "You two will do your usual excellent job, and you can laugh at me when you get back."

Knowing he couldn't push it further without sounding like he was questioning Tony's judgement, Frank gave up. Sounding worried in front of Nat had been stupid. Tony's operations, especially the ones involving Nat, were always good. Frank would just have to live with it and look forward to getting the two men home safely.

# VI

Mary told herself to drop the pace a bit. She could get carried away by the music, but as an instructor she had to remember to stick with the pace of the class. If people couldn't keep up, they would lose confidence. The cardio section was almost finished. She would try out her new abdominal exercises on them, then go into the cooldown.

Since she had been off work on sick leave, she had been teaching aerobic classes four times a week. The classes were helping her more than her doctor had. His diagnosis was that she wasn't dealing well with the stress in her life. She could have told him that.

Mary had the class do a heartbeat check, then slowed the pace gradually. Most of them knew her routine, so followed her easily. During the cooldown, she thought about the last two years of her life: her twelve-year-old son, Steven, being hit and killed by a car while crossing the road to school; the way she had shut herself off from her passionless husband, Vincent; Vincent's eventual affair; the inevitable separation; and her decision to re-enter the workforce with rusty skills. It had been too much change, too fast. One day she hadn't been able to get out of bed. She simply could not face the day. Fortunately her friend Lori had called her during the day, and then had come over and practically dragged her out of bed and to the doctor. Now she was on sick leave. She didn't feel sick, but there was definitely an emptiness inside her.

The last stretching exercise was finished, and the class was over. Now for a warm shower and a shampoo. It was a nice way to end the evening. There were mirrors everywhere in the change room, and Mary looked into her own face to search for life. It was improving. Her light brown eyes had no sparkle yet, but they did look livelier than they had for weeks. For the millionth time she wished she wasn't so ordinary looking. At five feet, two inches, she had a slight, petite build, and although her figure was well proportioned and her muscles toned, people did not notice small women with medium-length medium-brown hair, brown eyes and a pleasant complexion. She was invisible. She knew she had absolutely nothing to be ashamed of; everything was just fine looking—but she was so damned invisible. Sometimes she got the feeling that people didn't even know she existed. Why couldn't she have been tall, or blond, or a redhead, or anything at all? No, she was perfectly fine, perfectly ordinary, and perfectly invisible.

*Shake it off,* she told herself suddenly, *and give yourself a break. This feeling sorry for yourself is what you are* not *supposed to do. Vincent was not the right husband for you. He never made you feel wanted or desirable. You are wearing his disinterest like a suit of armour. Maybe if you had been kinder after Steven's death Vincent would still be your husband, but would you be any better off? I think not. Steven's in heaven, but you have a life to live, so get on with it.*

Putting the thoughts aside, Mary got dressed and then walked to the front counter to talk to Lori. Lori worked at the club full time, and taught aerobics as well. She had a kind heart, but she was everything Mary wasn't. Lori was outgoing, tall, thin, blond and very confident. At twenty-seven years of age she had learned how to put on a good "dumb blonde" act to suck the guys in, then sweep the rug out from under their feet when they were in the middle of their macho act. Life was one long laugh to Lori. Any guy who was good looking and didn't insult her with the macho act was almost guaranteed access to her bed. Protected access of course. Lori was a modern woman who took no chances with health or safety. She lectured Mary constantly on this. While Mary did not approve of Lori's hobby of recreational sex, Mary couldn't criticise. Lori was emotionally healthy and in love with life. Of that, Mary was jealous.

"How was class, Mary?" As usual, Lori's counter was surrounded by young men who were clearly loitering in the hopes of securing Lori's favours.

"Good. Tried my new tape. The class seemed to like it." Mary noticed that as usual, the young men gave her the quick once-over with their eyes, a polite smile, then turned back to Lori. Although it was expected, it did not help to cheer Mary's spirits.

Lori noticed it too, and in defense of her friend decided to dump the lot of them. "Bye, guys. My working hours are over." To show them what they had missed, she let her hips sway as she walked out towards the door with Mary, blew them a kiss, waved at the girl who would be closing up, then grabbed her coat and escorted Mary out.

"Where did you learn to walk like that?" Mary asked, wrapping her scarf around her neck to keep out the cold January wind. "I wish it was contagious."

Lori gave her a quick hug. "You just gotta let yourself go, hon. You have a terrible image of yourself, and you wear it like a chastity belt. Why don't you let me recommend a couple of the nicer guys from the club to you? They're decent, and trust me, they'll make your night worthwhile."

"You know I can't do that."

"Why not?" countered Lori. They had to wait to cross the road at a streetlight, and the wind was whipping at their coats, tunnelling through the highrise buildings around them. "You are 'footloose and fancy-free', as they say. When are you going to start living again?" As soon as she said it, Lori was apologising. "That was thoughtless, Mary. I'm sorry."

It should have hurt, but it felt so true that Mary couldn't even deny it. In her own defence, she made an instant decision on something that had been playing around her mind. "I'm going to have to start from scratch, Lori. Start all over again. But I will. First I think I should go to Cuba for a couple of weeks, lie in the sun and redesign my life. I haven't been there in years, but I used to love it. It would give me some uninterrupted time to think."

Lori was ecstatic. "Cuba! Sun, sand, *warmth*! Yes!" This time Lori gave her a bear hug and whooped in her ear. "That's my Mary. You can do it, you know. You can put everything behind you and start again however you want."

The excitement was catching. Maybe a holiday would be a good idea. Maybe she could start again. Maybe. "Lori, I'm thirty-six years old," Mary despaired. "I have one failed marriage and I've lost my only child. I'm on sick leave from a job I took on the rebound when my marriage was failing. I think I'm a screwed-up mess. I want children in my life but by the time I find a husband it's going to be too late."

"Honey, you don't need to be married to have kids," Lori stated. "You can raise a child by yourself."

"I know," Mary sighed, "but I'd like a real family. And the way guys look right through me, I think I'll be single for the rest of my life."

"Oh, piss on that," Lori snorted. "You are a kind, loving, intelligent woman who does not look thirty-six, and who fails to appreciate that she has a great figure, lovely skin and beautiful eyes. Go forth and learn to value yourself a little more. Go to Cuba—I'm as jealous as hell." Lori pulled her coat tighter. "I will stay here in the frigid bowels of Ontario and dream of you lying on the beautiful sand, soaking in the warm rays of the sun, drinking rum and cokes, and contemplating life." They had reach their cars. "You sure you don't have any room for me in your suitcase?"

Mary unlocked the car and slid into the driver's seat. "Come with me," she offered.

"Can't." Lori responded. "I'm using my vacation time to go skiing in two weeks. I'll be here when you get back."

"Who are you taking this time?" Mary asked, making sure her voice was teasing and not preaching. "Ted, John, Lawrence, or someone I haven't met yet?"

"Oh well, I'm not sure yet." Lori bent down to Mary's car door to close it. "I guess it depends on who's the hungriest." She winked.

"Incorrigible," Mary yelled, and drove away.

# VII

Up in the hills of the Sierra Maestra mountain range, accessible only by horseback, there was a waterfall. It was a beautiful place, the falls about sixty feet high, the rocks covered with green shades of moss, dampened by the cool, clear mountain stream that bathed the grey rocks. At the base of the falls lay a crystal-clear pool, reflecting the shades of green, grey and brown back up at the sky, creating the illusion that the colours continued down into the pool. All around were rugged hills of rock, wearing sparse caps of shrubs, small, hardy trees and grass made brown by the dry season. It was a sight to raise the spirit, and make a Cuban breast swell with pride. This was beauty—unspoiled and clean.

Hugging one side of the mountain, a hundred feet from the pool, hid an old wooden cabin. Long ago deserted, it was an ideal hiding place, being hidden from the view of planes by the mountain and bushes nestled above it. There was only one large room in the cabin, but it was large enough for twenty men to lie on the floor with blankets and sleep. Another small room would be useful for storage. The roof had been thatched years ago with the foliage of the two royal palms between the cabin and the pool. Now the thatch was a bleached-grey colour that blended in perfectly with the mountainside.

Alfredo Pérez and Osvaldo Rodríguez surveyed the scene with approval. It was ready to accommodate the twenty men who formed the Sierra Maestra Liberators. Their leader, Jose Luis Sánchez, was considered to be brilliant by both Alfredo and Osvaldo. Who else but Jose Luis could have convinced corrupt Cuban officials that the rebels were strong enough to overthrow the government? Jose Luis had become tired of selling drugs and weapons for cash. He had wanted more money and more excitement. He would drop a choice tidbit of information, wait for an official to sniff at the bait, then string him in. By the time the Cuban knew what was happening, he was being blackmailed for his association with an insurgent group. Then the official was used to draw in more victims. Being exposed for plotting against the government was a threat that made most of them quake in their shoes. Some actually changed to the insurgents' side willingly, and Jose Luis used them more carefully. If the others tried to get out of Jose's clutches, one of his group was sent to kill the man.

Jose Luis had not stopped at that, either. The money "donated" by the Cuban officials was used to set up a contact in the United States. This caused great amusement among the Liberators. The contact, code name "Taz", was a smooth-talking negotiator. He managed to convince some American companies that the Liberators were preparing a coup, and, if successful, would reward their backers by returning property previously owned by the companies in Cuba. The speed at which some of the companies responded, and the amounts they donated, was mind-boggling. Other companies wanted no part of it, but that did not matter. The number of donators was growing steadily.

Then came the joke of jokes—the Congressman! Taz had outdone himself there. Congressman Richard Harvey had been a businessman himself, and his business had lost a great deal in Cuba. Jose Luis had done his research carefully, and the results had delighted them. The Congressman had been supporting Castro's government financially for the last two years. An opportunity like this for squeezing money out of a rich political figure did not present itself every day. It was risky. Congressman Harvey was known to be a man who stayed to the right of centre, politically and personally. He was a supporter of institutions such as the armed forces, the CIA, the FBI, etc., etc., but Jose Luis had examined his personal history thoroughly. Richard Harvey was basically a power-hungry man who would go to any lengths to protect his political future. Taz had been given the go-ahead to approach him with care and dangle the bait in front of him. Both Taz and Jose Luis had been aware that there was a chance the Congressman would report the contact, but somehow Jose Luis doubted that would happen. Jose Luis was right as usual.

Congressman Harvey had sent a generous donation. His motives were crystal clear to the Liberators, of course. If the Liberators took over the government and returned American interests, the Congressman would be a hero, his political future guaranteed. What a fool!

Now, however, the game was changing. Both the Congressman and one businessman, Sam Turnbull, wanted to see the operation. They were both welcomed by Jose Luis, and were coming next week. Sam Turnbull would be here on Monday, and Taz would be with him. No one had seen this Taz before, but he had worked well for them, so they waited eagerly to meet him. Alfredo particularly wanted to meet Taz, because Jose's research had found that Taz had the same appetite for women that Alfredo did. The thrill of domination and control was not something that many men wanted to discuss. While Alfredo was sure that other men must feel the same, many were too scared to admit it. This Taz had a record for forcing women to give him what he wanted. Alfredo felt that a kindred spirit was coming to visit.

Congressman Harvey and Sam Turnbull were going to be sorry they asked to come here. Of course, once they saw the size of the group and knew who its members were, they became a danger. Before they died, however, they were worth a high ransom. And the Americans could hardly turn to the Cuban government for help, could they? Oh, it was going to be a most amusing week. The Congressman was coming on the Sunday after Sam Turnbull arrived, so that would be the day of action.

As if that wasn't enough entertainment, the Liberators were looking forward to the furore over the ransom demands. Surely the CIA would want their Congressman back, but the Liberators had some news to ruin the CIA's day. The infiltrator whom the CIA had sent down had been fed false information. Even the CIA thought the Liberators were a force to contend with. It had been a stroke of luck that the infiltrator had asked him, Alfredo Pérez, to spy on Jose Luis. Of course Alfredo had said yes, and he and Jose Luis had a good laugh about it, too. Alfredo had told the spy, who had looked Cuban and called himself Dennys, all kinds of nonsense to report back. Then Osvaldo, who was also a good negotiator, had convinced the spy to work on their side. Dennys had never known he had been discovered, but he was a greedy man and had agreed to work for them. It had come in handy, because Dennys knew even more businessmen and individuals whom Taz could contact. Jose Luis could never bring himself to trust the spy, however, so Osvaldo killed him. Alfredo had planned to turn him over to the Cubans as one more American spy for their jails, but Jose Luis said the spy knew too much about the Liberators, and he could not rest until Dennys was dead.

While Taz was down here, he would be negotiating purchases of drugs and weapons on behalf of other American contacts. Sam Turnbull had been told to bring names of potential supporters and their backgrounds for discussion purposes. Sam was not to be alarmed until Sunday, when the Congressman arrived and they could be taken together.

Surveying the camp, Alfredo was pleased. It was basic, but the Americans could rough it for a few days. The rebels were used to rough living. A scowl crossed Alfredo's brow when he remembered what Jose Luis had said about girls. Absolutely not in camp, under no condition. Jose Luis did not approve of Alfredo's appetites, but he said nothing in reproach because Alfredo was loyal. The reason he gave for saying no girls were allowed in camp was because they were a distraction and made men careless. Oh well, Jose Luis was a leader and a good one, so Alfredo would have to go without. He consoled himself with the knowledge that he would have to go with Jose Luis and Osvaldo into the village during the week to meet with a Cuban official they were setting up. If all went well, Jose Luis might permit him to use that time to look for an available woman. A thought cheered Alfredo. Perhaps Taz would come to the village with him and find out what a Cuban woman felt like. He whistled to Osvaldo. Everything was ready here and they could go home. Next week was a week to look forward to.

# VIII

Susan Andrews gave the lounge crowd a smile and a little bow of appreciation. It had been a good set, and it was apparent that she was pleased with the band's performance. The band was called Transitions, and Susan maintained that they had chosen the name because they were trying out a variety of musical styles in search of the one that would take them to fame. She sometimes got discouraged when she thought about how far they had to go, but the lounge owners kept encouraging her. And well they should, Aaron thought. Transitions had done wonders for business.

There was only one table reserved on a permanent basis during Susan's performances. Scott, Aaron and Sheila occupied it regularly, with a variety of other friends. Aaron noticed that Scott was beaming with pride at his twin sister. Scott was only a couple of minutes older than Susan, but he carried the responsibility for both of them. Aaron knew how devoted they were to each other, yet their personalities were very different. Susan was as quiet as Scott was boisterous. Scott was a playboy, but Susan had been intimate with very few men. They were born into a family that had been making money in the mining industry since the turn of the century. Fortunately for Mr. Andrews, there was an older son, who had already followed their father into the family business. Susan was still debating whether to join her father or give her music career a serious chance. That was the real reason for naming the band Transitions. She was trying to make up her mind. Scott was a lost cause, as far as Mr. Andrews was concerned. While he had no head for business, Scott did have brains, and he had shocked his father by applying for the CIA. Mr. Andrews had not fought the choice, mainly because he never expected Scott to survive the discipline of basic training. Even now he occasionally looked at his younger son in amazement, but he had finally accepted the career choice. Secretly he probably hoped Scott would tire of his choice eventually, and join him in the business. Aaron knew that would never happen. Scott was hooked on the job, and his father would ultimately be disappointed.

As Susan left the stage to change, Aaron caught her eye and received the smile he always looked for. While Scott had introduced him to Susan after that winter wilderness experience, it had been close to a year and a half before she had agreed to go out with him. Six months ago he had finally gotten up the nerve to ask her out, and they had been dating regularly ever since. Well, whenever he was home. This job did not make love affairs easy. Fortunately for him, Susan was very independent. She didn't sit around waiting for him to come home. Also fortunately for him, Susan was constant, unlike Scott.

Scott was a charmer. He and Aaron had always told each other about their conquests. In fact, Scott used to turn their sexual escapades into scoring matches. Aaron never knew which one of them was winning, because you could never prove who had slept with whom. Besides, neither of them would ever admit defeat. Young men in the prime of their years, neither Scott nor Aaron had any interest in settling down. But Aaron had thought about Susan a lot. He knew she was the kind of woman who was faithful. He knew it without proof, just as he knew the sun would rise in the morning. That was one of the reasons he had waited one and a half years to ask her out. You didn't trifle with a woman like Susan. He had known that he was not ready to make that commitment, and he would not be unfair like that. The other reason was because she was Scott's sister. You had to be careful with a friend's sister, especially if your life might rest in that friend's hands someday. And this was a twin sister, which made them even closer. When Aaron was finally ready, and he and Susan had started dating, Scott had not approved. He had said nothing, but it was his silence on the subject that told Aaron that he did not approve.

There was no spoken commitment yet between Aaron and Susan, but he loved her absolutely. He also knew that she loved him, but that she had doubts. He could sense it.

The fact that she had gone to bed with him in the first place and kept welcoming him back surprised him. He knew she still believed that he, like Scott, had women stashed all over the globe. After the second month he had guessed this, and had told her there had been no others since they had been together. He had wanted her to know that, and he was also tired of practising safe sex when they didn't need to. She had stopped insisting on it, since she was on the pill by then anyway, but he sensed she didn't totally believe him. With a brother like Scott, it was probably hard for her not to have doubts. Susan had become a passionate lover, but she didn't give herself lightly, and Aaron knew he somehow had to quell those doubts of hers, or someday she would pull away and look for more security elsewhere. First, though, he had to convince Scott, or the fight would be lost before it began.

Aaron took a deep breath. He had already made his decision, but it was a big step. Scott was seated next to him, and they could talk privately in the noise of this lounge for a few minutes before Susan joined them. "Scott, I need to talk to you."

His fair-haired friend gave him a sober look and leaned closer. He had hazel eyes that winked readily at friends, but which could turn quickly serious when the situation warranted. The playboy act was fast becoming more of an act and less of a lifestyle. Scott was learning life's lessons quickly. "What's up?"

*How do you say this?* Aaron wondered. All the speeches he had practised the last few weeks sounded ludicrous. *Oh well,* he decided, *just say it.* "I want to marry Susan."

"What!" Astonishment. And Scott did not look thrilled. It was not the response Aaron would have liked, but it was expected.

Quietly, Aaron started what he knew would be a hard sell. "I want you to be my brother-in-law."

Well, he had Scott's attention, and it was one of the rare times he had seen Scott look actually angry. "Whoa! Just a minute here. This is me you're talking to, remember? I wasn't very thrilled when you decided to start balling my sister, but I will really object to you conning her into a marriage that you know is a little one-sided."

That was too much, and Aaron was shocked. "Hang on there! I am not just 'balling' her, Scott. I happen to love Susan."

"Maybe you think you do," Scott relented a little, "but it wouldn't be fair to her. You'll never be home on a regular basis, and she will expect fidelity. You know she will. You can't promise that." His hazel eyes were challenging and the conversation was being conducted in fierce whispers.

"You're wrong, Scott," Aaron replied evenly. "I can and I am. Faithful, that is."

"Bullshit!" Now Scott pushed himself back from the table, but remained seated. "You're not even being truthful with me now. How can you say that?" But mixed with the anger was the hint of a plea.

*Keep calm and don't get riled,* Aaron told himself. *Scott wants this as much as you do, but he has to believe in it first. He's the family guard dog, and he'll fight to protect them.* "Tell me the last time you saw me with another woman," Aaron demanded.

"Hell, we went whoring with Randy and Alex two weeks ago," Scott retorted. "Don't you remember the Three Bells Pub?"

"Yes, I do," Aaron replied. "Now, tell me who I was with all evening. What woman?" he insisted.

There was a pause. "I don't know. All I remember was you talking to Malcolm at the bar. Oh yeh, Sheila was there too." Scott looked a little perplexed.

"Right. Now, when else?" Aaron prompted.

Stealing a look across the table to ensure that Sheila and her friend weren't listening, Scott leaned closer again. "A month ago, in Boston."

It took an effort for Aaron not to smile. "I remember your brunette model, but who was I with?"

Scott concentrated. He'd been very drunk that night. "Oh yeh, Tony was there, and you got into an argument with him." It looked like Scott was starting to take this seriously. "Okay, two months ago. Rex's stag. They brought in that escort service."

"Again—who was I with?"

"Hell, Aaron, I can hardly remember who I was with that night." He thought hard, then gave up. "I don't remember you with anyone."

"That's because I left," Aaron reminded him. "Those weren't the kind of people we should be hanging around."

"Shit, yeh!" Now Scott remembered. "You gave me that damn lecture and threatened to drag me out of there. I really did hear you, but I was too pissed off at your attitude to want to be around you. You were right though," he conceded. "I had a good case of the shivers in the morning when I remember some of the people who had been there. I was just lucky that night. It taught me a lesson."

"Next?"

But Scott was shaking his head. He was staring hard at Aaron. "Are you serious? Don't play with me, not about this. But come on, Aaron, it's too easy, too tempting. What about this score chart we've been keeping?"

"When did we stop counting?" Aaron asked.

Scott looked surprised. "Well, it's been…a few months?"

Aaron smiled at him. "We stopped keeping that four months ago. Before that I was lying." It was true. Aaron had continued playing the game for a few months to save face until he was sure of himself with Susan, then grown tired of it.

By this time Scott was looking at him in astonishment. "This is real? You've only been with Sue?"

Aaron looked him square in the hopeful hazel eyes. "I haven't wanted anyone else since Susan. There is no comparison. I fell in love with her when you first introduced her, but we were having too much fun. Six months ago I knew I couldn't live without her. She wasn't going to wait forever."

A delighted grin lit Scott's face, and he gripped Aaron's wrist. "My god, it's true. You're serious." For a minute he looked like a child on Christmas morning. Then he got serious again. "Aaron, you've got some work on your hands. First, she doesn't like our job. She has this thing about me going into other countries and breaking their laws." His voice trailed off. Susan had walked through the archways. As she did, a man approached her, took her arm and seemed to gaze into her eyes.

A strange sensation started in the pit of Aaron's stomach. "Scott, who is that?"

"That, Aaron, is your competition," Scott responded in a dull voice. "While we've been away he's been trying to make tracks. His name is Stein," Scott continued. "He's a friend of the family. Loaded...old money...best schools...all that the family likes. He's a banker," Scott concluded.

"A banker?" Aaron stared at the man. He started to recognise the feeling in his gut. It was unfamiliar. It was jealousy. "What do you mean competition?" The man was pleasant looking, well dressed, with the appearance of a man accustomed to working in an office. Probably as polite and dependable as hell. "I hate him," Aaron muttered.

"Fine, hate him," Scott encouraged. "But get a move on with Susan. It's not serious yet." He saw the questioning look in Aaron's eyes. "It's not—yet. You know she wouldn't do anything without letting you know first. But, Aaron, women have these biological clocks built in. I think hers has started. You need to be aware of these things."

Watching Susan, Aaron could tell that Scott was probably right, that he still had a chance. She was being attentive and polite to this guy—you could see that from a distance—but that was all she was being. Susan did not have the look on her face that she wore when Aaron was with her. He sat back in the chair, relieved. "Okay, Scott, I get the picture. No more time to waste."

But Scott turned his chair to face Aaron, his back to the table. "Listen to me," he insisted, dropping his voice. He had to make Aaron understand. "Stein has an advantage. Understand what I'm saying."

"Then what are you saying?" Aaron asked, confused. "Spit it out, for God's sake."

"Bankers," Scott started, "work a basic nine to five, five days a week. Sue's thinking about that. What's more important," he pressed on, "is that bankers are not apt to shoot people. And if a banker wants information from someone, he can buy it. If the person doesn't want to give the information, the banker goes elsewhere. The banker is never in a position of having to force information out of someone who doesn't want to give it." Now Scott had Aaron's attention, as Aaron's eyes left Susan and focused with alarm on Scott's face. "That's what is on her mind, Aaron. I'm sure it is. That's your real competition."

"Fuck," was all Aaron could manage. "What the hell have you been telling her?"

"Nothing," Scott insisted, "but it's in her head. You've got some real convincing to do." Scott straightened up a bit, but he wasn't done. "Oh, one more thing…as a friend…"

Reaching for his drink, Aaron managed a smile. "Okay, sport, let me have it."

Scott reached for Aaron's closest bicep and put a hand against it so his thumb touched the top and his fingers touched underneath. He squeezed it, just so Aaron couldn't mistake his meaning. The muscle underneath did not give. "Stein, as I said, is a close family friend. His parents and mine have known each other for a long time. I don't want Stein to be my brother-in-law, believe me, Aaron. But I don't want him to come in some day with a black eye or worse. I wouldn't want to have to explain that to my father. If, heaven forbid, you lose Sue, you might get upset. Don't take it out on Stein. You'd only hurt Susan more."

"I was never a school yard bully," Aaron replied, "and I'm not going to start with that pansy. Nor will I do anything that would hurt Susan," he promised. "And, Scott, I have no interest in doing anything that would come between you and me. So the banker pansy is perfectly safe. But I still hate him."

Taking his hand off Aaron's arm, Scott drew a slow breath. "Work on her, man. Please. I want to be your brother, I really do."

To his relief, Aaron saw Susan remove her arm from Stein's grasp and make her way to their table. It was a circuitous route due to the proximity of the tables. Just the way she moved excited Aaron, and when she reached his side and smiled as she sat down, he had to fight the urge to pull her onto his lap and run his hands over her body. Neither of them were comfortable with overt public displays of affection, but the desire was always there. It was when they were alone that the fireworks took over. But he had better get his mind off that now, because he had a lot of talking to do tonight.

Gazing at him with those hazel-coloured eyes that she shared with Scott, Sue seemed to read his mind. She put her hand into his and squeezed. Was she just making up for being with Stein? No, Aaron decided, she was pumped up from a good performance. He could see the desire in her eyes. They wouldn't be staying here long.

While the others conversed with the band members, Aaron glanced at Sheila Day-Jones and caught Scott's eye. "How are you two getting along?"

Someone had lit a cigar at the table behind them, so Aaron wasn't sure if Scott coughed to cover a laugh or because of the smoke. "Okay now," he answered. "We are kinda different, but I think we're getting pretty comfortable with each other. By the way," he added, "I don't think those butch rumours are true."

Aaron couldn't suppress a smile. "No, they're not."

Scott stared. "Damn you, you said—"

"Shhh! She'll hear you! You're making assumptions, anyway," Aaron reassured. "It was just a look. I was talking to her in the pub and we just happened to think the same thing at the same time. You know how you can tell. The difference from before is that I was thinking she looks pretty good, and she was giving me the look back, when both of us seemed to realise, *Uh-oh, no way,* at the same time. She blushed, and I'm damned sure I did too. So I bought her a drink and we started over again. She's a good sport."

"What are you guys up to?" It was Sue's voice in his ear, and Aaron just had time to see Scott wink at him before Aaron turned around to her. Sue had rested her cheek against his shoulder, and the wavy shoulder-length blond hair lay on his jacket. She was beautiful, and she was driving him nuts. "Ready to go?" she asked, her eyes shining at him.

"Ages ago." He would take her back to his apartment, and he would talk to her tonight. He had to make her understand that they should spend their lives together. He would tell her what he could, and he would make whatever promises he could to her. He would keep any promises he made, and he would try his best to lay her fears to rest. Then just maybe, when he lay in her arms tonight, it would be with the knowledge that she would always be his. He wanted that. He would work hard for that. It was worth it.

When they reached Aaron's one-bedroom apartment, it took all of his resolve not to sweep her into his arms first and procrastinate on the discussion. Susan dropped her sweater and purse on a chair in the living room and turned to him. Then she sensed his hesitant attitude, and took a step towards him.

"What's on your mind tonight?" Susan looked up into the face of the man Scott had brought home to dinner two years ago and introduced as his friend.

The family had known two things about Aaron from the start. He worked with Scott, and to be introduced as a friend meant he was a basically decent person. Scott was very selective with whom he brought into the family fold. He was strangely protective that way. Susan had known two additional things about Aaron. Scott had told her one—Aaron had a way with women. That meant that he was attractive to women, nice to them, and slept around a lot. It was Scott's way of warning her. The second additional thing had been known only by Susan and Aaron. It had been love at first sight. Just like in the fairy tales. Their eyes had met and something had clicked between them.

At twenty-three years of age, having grown up in a very protective family with a twin brother who had decided that he was her personal bodyguard, Susan's experience with men was somewhat limited, but she had known that Aaron wanted her. She also knew that she could not settle for being one of an unknown number of girlfriends. So she gave him no encouragement, yet could not get him out of her mind. Occasionally she would date someone, but no one else compared. No one else could look at her and cause those sparks to fly.

The next year and a half had been painful for her. Aaron was at the house frequently with Scott, and always looked for her. She was included in the conversations and was often invited along in visits to local pubs or theatres. If Scott guessed her feelings toward his friend, he said nothing. Aaron always treated her with kindness. It seemed as if he knew she would want what he wasn't ready to give. He made no approach to her, yet appeared to crave her company. She settled for that, and hated herself for being so weak.

A year and a half passed, during which time they learned much about each other. Only their desires were never mentioned. It was almost a relief when Aaron was working out of the country, because having him close was a bittersweet experience. Then one day he had come to the house alone and asked her out to dinner and a show. Susan had accepted, although she had always told herself she wouldn't. Getting dressed to go out, she had been in a near panic, determined to stay out of his bed, but knowing inside that if he asked she would not be able to say no. It had been a strange night. Over the year and a half they had learned to talk comfortably together, but that night conversation had been awkward. They had made it through dinner, but in the car on the way to the show he had pulled suddenly to the curb and blurted out how much he loved her and wanted her, and, well, they hadn't gone to the show after all. Her resolve had been pathetically weak anyway.

So she had gone trembling to his bed, sure she would be compared to all his other conquests and found lacking. It didn't turn out that way at all. It had been a wonderful night for her, and Aaron seemed to feel the same way. When Scott found out about her date, he had sat her down, held her hand and told her that she shouldn't expect Aaron to keep himself for her. He told her about their lifestyle since they had met. Scott wasn't trying to be cruel, he just wanted her to walk into this with her eyes open. Susan had already known about their lifestyle, and assured her brother that no promises had been made between them. She promised Scott that if it became too difficult for her, she would walk away from it.

Two months later, Aaron had told her that he was not seeing anyone else. Since then she had been trying to believe him, but from Scott she had learned how easy it was for them. So she tried not to think about it, took gratefully what Aaron offered her, and despaired at wanting him so badly. He did love her, she could tell that, and she loved him deeply. However, she knew that one day she would have to be sure about him or move on with her life without him. She had no set time line for that—it was too unbearable to think about. Now she was standing in front of him, seeing him hesitate. He reached for her hand and led her to the sofa.

Aaron pulled Sue down beside him, forgetting all the words he had planned to say. It came out simply and without fanfare. "Will you marry me?" In her face he saw a progression of emotions: surprise and happiness, but then confusion and doubt. His heart had lifted at first, but dropped when he saw the doubt.

"I…I…want to," she stumbled, "but…oh, I don't know!" It came out as a plea.

*Steady,* Aaron told himself. *You've got to feel your way through this. Find out what the problem is, then look for the solution.* It was his way of calming himself. "Tell me why you wouldn't." She remained silent, but was clearly stressed. "Talk to me, Sue, please. Is it because you still think I'm sleeping around?" When she looked at him, he knew he had been right. He had found one of the reasons. "I'm not, I swear it. I haven't been since before we went out. I told you that; it was true. I don't want anyone else." *How do you undo a reputation?* he wondered. "Look, talk to your brother tomorrow, okay? You know he wouldn't lie to you, and it's very important to me that you believe that what I used to do with him is finished—in the past."

"But, Aaron, even if you aren't now, you could be away for months at a time. And did you ever notice that the men you work with all seem to have had poor marriages or are divorced?" At least her voice was working again, she thought. If only she could stop shaking and say this so he would understand.

"You know how it is when we're together. When we make love you make me glad to be alive. I can't bear the thought of you sharing that with someone else. I really can't."

Without realising it, Aaron found that he had taken her into his arms. "Sue, when we're together, that's not just me, that's *us*." He kissed the top of her forehead, and rested his head against hers. "If I promise, would you believe me? I can do this, Sue, I really can. I won't risk losing you."

She nodded, but she was playing with his shirt collar. There was something else…he knew it. They had to talk about everything. She had to be sure. "There's something else," he prompted.

"Your job," she blurted, as if she was forcing herself to say it. "I don't know what you do. Scott never talks about it. I mean, I know sort of what you do, and of course who you work for, but it's the things I don't know that frighten me."

For the next half hour he told her what he did in his job, in general terms, realising that he should have had this conversation with her months ago. Scott had never expected them to marry, so had never bothered to talk about anything that would be important to a wife. She hadn't even known that she could be with Aaron most of the time. By the time he was finished, Susan seemed more content. He smiled at her. "Anything else?"

"Yes." At first she looked away, then took a breath and looked him in the eye. "I need to believe in you. I need to know that when you are out doing your job you are doing what you're supposed to do. I know that some people change sides, that people get killed and some people hurt other people. So I have to be able to believe that you wouldn't do any of that."

"Wow." Aaron leaned back and pulled her against him. "Sue, I think you are just going to have to trust in my character for that one. I can't possibly predict everything that's going to happen in the future." He lifted her chin with his hand so he could see her eyes. "Do you really think I would intentionally hurt someone, or kill someone just for the hell of it?"

"No," she admitted. "But what if you got into a situation you couldn't walk away from? What if you didn't have a choice?"

"I can't imagine that happening," he replied. "I think you're worrying too much, I really do." He smiled at her again, sensing that the conversation would soon be over. "So, do you think I'm a sadist?"

She shook her head. "No, of course not."

"I don't think I'm going to change now, then." He liked the way her eyes were starting to shine again. This was actually going to work out. First, though, he needed to tell her one more thing. "Sue, it does happen in this business that people occasionally get killed. I don't like it, and I probably won't want to talk to you about it."

A wrinkle crossed her brow. "How will I know then?"

"Why would you want to?" he countered.

"Because you'll be my husband. I don't want to be thinking that you are upset, and insisting that you talk if you need to be left alone. How will I know the difference between you being grouchy and truly needing some space?"

The word "husband" had distracted Aaron so much that he almost forgot to answer. "Huh? Oh." He pulled himself together. "You'll know."

"How?"

"Remember in June when I came back from Peru?"

"Yes." Suddenly Susan looked contrite. "Are you going to tell me that argument we had because you wouldn't meet me and my friends at the zoo like you promised was because of that? Oh, see! That's exactly what I mean! The zoo wasn't important. I would never have given you a hard time about it if I had known!"

"Don't worry, it's not important." *It sure isn't now,* Aaron thought. *Damn, I want to marry her. I want her to have my children. I want it all.* "Look, Sue, what do I have to do to convince you? I love you, and I want you to be my wife."

A smile played on her face, and Aaron felt his heart racing. "Three bedtime promises," she whispered, as she moved against him and kissed his lips.

"Tell me," he demanded. *And please, God, let them be promises I can make.*

"One—no women except me." There was a pause while she started to unbutton his shirt. "Two—thou shalt not kill…unless there's no other way." She searched his face, saw him swallow and nod, then finished unbuttoning the shirt. "Three—never, ever hurt anyone unnecessarily."

"Promise."

When he tried to kiss her, she spoke again. "Oh, and four…"

"Four?"

"Four—always bring yourself home to me safely." Susan shuddered. "Four is very important."

Four didn't need a promise. It was understood. Just as it was understood that talking time was over, and tonight was going to be the best it had even been between them.

# IX

"I want you two to know that I appreciate you coming to see us off," Nat said sincerely. "I know you both have a pile of work you could be doing." Tony and Frank had driven him to the airport, where Aaron was to join them. Nat and Aaron were flying to Montego Bay, Jamaica, to meet Alfredo Pérez. From there they would take a night boat trip to their Cuban destination. On the southern Cuban shore they would be met by another member of the rebel group, who would have the horses waiting. The ride through the mountains would take approximately two hours.

"Speaking of 'us,'" Frank commented, "where the hell is Aaron?"

"Not like him to be late," Tony responded, frowning. Then a familiar figure could be seen dashing into the airport. "Here he comes."

Aaron hurried up to them, looking abashed. "Sorry, fellows. Sue dropped by to say goodbye."

Nat grinned. "Then I guess we should thank you for getting out of bed in time to catch the flight." For that he received a playful punch on the arm.

"You should be congratulating me," Aaron announced, looking very pleased with himself. "I'm getting married."

"Excellent!" Tony cried, shaking Aaron's hand.

"We were wondering how long it would take you to get around to asking her," Frank added, smiling and also shaking his hand.

Nat followed suit, then gave him a quick embrace. "You've got taste, my boy. She's a good woman and she's got class."

"I didn't think you approved of the institution of marriage, Nat," Aaron teased.

"Not for me, I don't," Nat admitted. He gave Aaron a knowing look. "But for you, it makes sense. You two will have a good life together."

"You guys weren't exactly a lot of help," Aaron informed them, looking for his plane ticket. He found it tucked into his bag. "Sue was worried about the fact that the people I work with aren't married. I had to do a real sales job to convince her that people can do this job and have good marriages."

The three now unmarried men looked at each other. "I guess we aren't the best role models in that field, are we?" Frank asked the other two.

"Come on, you two," Tony cut in. "You've got to get on that plane."

"Good luck," Frank said to both of them. "And, Nat...don't you be shy about calling me in, okay? I'd rather do too much than too little." He looked at Aaron. "Don't let Nat be a cowboy. The first, *the first*, sign of danger, you make sure he signals me, or you do it yourself. Got it?"

"We'll be fine, Frank," Nat insisted, smiling at his friend and shaking hands. "See you in Cuba." Then he shook Tony's hand.

"Good luck," Tony said seriously. "I'll be waiting here for you."

Then Aaron shook hands with the two men they were leaving behind, and accompanied Nat to the plane. Once on board, Aaron did a final check to make sure he had everything. He was carrying Taz's passport, because the two men were similar enough for Aaron to pass as Taz. Nat had, with special permission, been given a passport made up by Technical Services, making him into Sam Turnbell. The passports were to get them into Jamaica without questions, because Alfredo believed both men to be American citizens. After that point, the passports were worse than useless, because the officers could not risk encountering any Cuban authorities while illegally in Cuba. Their passports would have been a one-way ticket to a Cuban jail.

"All set?" Nat asked, having watched Aaron checking everything.

"Yep." Aaron got up and put his bag in the compartment over their heads, then sat down and leaned back in his seat. "I brought a dozen granola bars with me in case the food sucks."

Nat laughed. "Well, that should keep you for about a day. I've seen you eat." He got more serious and lowered his voice. The other people on the plane were making a considerable amount of noise jostling for their seats and luggage compartments. "Remember now, from here on in you are Taz. As soon as Alfredo lays eyes on us you must *be* Taz, and I am Sam. He must not be in doubt even for a split second. Our cover is our only protection, so why don't you use the trip to change your mind-set and become that lovely character. I'll be doing the same thing."

Aaron had planned to think about Susan and their afternoon together. If he closed his eyes he could still feel her touch, and the smell of her hung deliciously in his senses. As soon as he got back home they were going to plan the wedding. He would take her home to visit his folks again. They had liked her. Giving his head a shake, he forced his mind to switch to his job. Nat was right as usual. It was crucial that Aaron be able to act his part to perfection.

Lovely thoughts of Susan would have to wait for the return flight. He was Taz, and Taz was not a nice person. Impossible to think of Susan and Taz on the same flight without being sickened. He locked Susan away in his heart and turned his attention to his job.

The meet in Jamaica went well. Taz was a drug dealer, and Sam was a convincing businessman. Immigration looked at them closely and seemed puzzled by their travelling together. They made a strange pair. Aaron had let his hair grow scraggily and had failed to wash it well. This morning he had not shaved. Other than that, he had worn casual clothes, but no disguise. Taz had not been seen by the rebels, although they would have a description of him. Looking like the character you were pretending to be had a definite advantage. Nat had darkened his hair and his eyebrows in case Taz had given the rebels a rough description of him. While Nat did not look like Sam Turnbell, there were no striking features that made him look particularly unlike Sam. They were a similar height, although Sam was slightly heavier. Alfredo looked at their passports and then accepted them for who they said they were.

They landed without incident on the coast of Cuba. Both Aaron and Nat were glad to get out of the boat. Alfredo looked like he lived on the fringe of civilisation. His clothes were worn and grubby, and Nat noticed that personal hygiene was not of crucial importance to him. Aaron tried to do nothing to indicate that he noticed the odour, although he exchanged a brief knowing look with Nat. In fact, true to his Taz act, Aaron stood close to Alfredo and sized him up with a challenging type of look while they waited for the horses.

Alfredo returned the look. "I've looked into you," Alfredo said in Spanish. "You've been a bad boy in your country."

Spanish was no problem for Taz, although Aaron remembered to speak it just poorly enough for a Caucasian who had learned it as a second language. Taz had learned the language as a child, but his first language was English. "So?" he replied. "Is this a problem for you? If you don't want me working for you, just say so. I have other businesses I can be taking care of that are just as profitable."

"You misunderstand me," Alfredo reassured. "I meant only that we might have some interests in common."

Taz looked bored. "Money? We all have that interest. Or maybe you mean the power that goes with it. That is of more interest."

"No," Alfredo pressed. "I was thinking about the female population…"

The horse's arrival was signalled by the sound of hooves. Aaron left Alfredo hanging for a few minutes while they mounted. Fortunately the horses were small and thin, because Nat looked awfully uncomfortable in the saddle. It was late in the evening, but the full moon gave lots of light reflecting off the sea. In fact, there was too much light for safety, so they moved out quickly for the cover of the hills.

Alfredo cantered up beside Aaron. He seemed determined to pursue the conversation, and Aaron had an uncomfortable feeling he knew where this conversation was heading.

"It makes me glad to hear of your reputation, since we will be spending several days together," Alfredo continued.

Aaron decided to play dense. "I don't know what you're talking about."

"Aye! But I forget—how can you understand me?" In the moonlight Alfredo grinned lewdly. "I am sorry to cause you confusion. You do not know of my own fantasies with the female world. We have similar tastes, shall I say?"

*Good grief,* thought Aaron. *Is this smelly idiot telling me he knows I rape women and he likes to do the same?* It took a real effort on Aaron's part to remain in character. If that was true, this was going to be a rather sickening assignment, especially if Alfredo had this desire to talk about his "tastes". Aaron looked pointedly in Sam's direction. "Perhaps that is something we can discuss at another time. Not everyone shares the same fantasies."

Alfredo followed his gaze and grinned. "Of course. Everyone goes his own path. We may be able to do little more than talk in any case. Jose Luis is a strict man."

"A pity," Aaron replied, disappointment sounding in his voice, "but clearly necessary and admirable when results are important."

The conversation lapsed as the long ride into the mountains continued. Aaron felt as if he had passed the first small test. He was glad that they rode in single file, because conversation would have to be carried out in a loud voice, and that was too dangerous. Therefore there was little conversation. A Cuban called Lino Viltrez led the way, followed by Nat, then Aaron, with Alfredo bringing up the rear. The ride seemed to go on forever. Fortunately the horses knew the way, and picked their way over rocks and streams in a steady upward climb. Once in the cover of the mountains, the moon was often hidden from view, but as they climbed higher it could be seen once again between the sparser trees.

When they arrived at the camp, Aaron was surprised to see the waterfall. In the moonlight it was lovely. The horses were taken by Lino to a location undetected by Aaron. Nat was rubbing the inside of his thighs, and moving very stiffly. To avoid laughing, Aaron looked away, suspecting that he too would have sore leg muscles in the morning. Alfredo led them to the cabin, which was a small, basic affair filled with men. There were no washroom facilities, but an area a little distance from the cabin had a pit dug in the ground for that purpose. Aaron was glad Nat had told him to bring toilet paper, Kleenex, soap and a towel. Water would obviously be no problem.

The air temperature was warm and the air had a clean feel to it. This part of the island was mainly agricultural and lacking in air pollution. Nat had disappeared, supposedly using the latrine, but Aaron suspected he was also secreting the signalling device. Nat suspected that their possessions would be searched as soon as their back was turned, if not actually searched in front of them. That signalling device was their only contact with the outside world, and must not be discovered. It had a global positioning device that would pinpoint their location for rescue, if needed. Aaron had been leaning against the doorway. The cabin contained about twenty men, as far as he could tell, and they were all sitting around with various weapons, drinking rum and smoking. The air was thick with smoke, and Aaron, who was a non-smoker, was reluctant to enter.

Alfredo looked back at him. "Where's Sam?" he demanded, walking over to Aaron.

"Out back, I think," Aaron replied carelessly, pointing a thumb in the direction of the latrine.

"Uh." Alfredo pointed toward the east wall of the cabin. "You two can find a spot over there to sleep."

"Yeh, sure." *Should smell wonderful,* Aaron thought, keeping his expression neutral. "Which one is your boss, Jose Luis? You haven't introduced me yet."

Alfredo told him that Jose Luis would be arriving in the morning. He was meeting with some important people today, Alfredo added.

To Aaron's relief, Nat came back in, and Alfredo went over the plans for the next few days. Osvaldo Rodríguez, who was in town tonight with Jose Luis, would be discussing the names and backgrounds of the business connections Sam would be providing. Taz would be busy negotiating the purchase of drugs and weapons on behalf of his own contacts.

Then Alfredo said something which made the Americans realise that it wasn't just the American businessmen who were being blackmailed. "Taz, some of these people you represent, well, they are in debt to us...for past services, let us say. They have given to you, for sure, a price. But maybe they have told you not to turn down what we see is a fair offer." Alfredo was being polite on the surface, but his eyes and his manner were very serious.

Aaron put a grin on his face. Blackmailing drug dealers? Boy, these guys liked to live on the edge. "You, of course, are not asking me to reveal my bargaining positions before we even start." He said it as if it were an inside joke that Alfredo would understand.

It made Alfredo laugh. "It was just my puny attempt to make you show your hand. We are much happier when you are working directly for us. Please, take no offence." Alfredo was now deciding to be a good host. "Let me get us some rum," he insisted. "It will help pass the time."

After Alfredo left to get the rum, Nat judged the noise level in the cabin and the distance to the nearest Cuban. He then spoke quietly to Aaron. "I brought a black ball hat. If we need to talk, I'll put it on. I have a dreadful feeling that Alfredo is going to start talking to you about his sexual exploits once he gets drinking. You will have to join in and build your cover. I will pretend to find you both nauseating, which won't be difficult considering what you will probably be discussing. We will have little to do with each other after that." Alfredo was on his way back, so Nat finished quickly. "You know what your job is. Tomorrow I'll show you where I hid the transmitter."

Aaron and Nat sipped at the rum Alfredo brought over. It had been a long day, and Aaron would have preferred to sleep rather than drink rum. Alfredo guzzled, and it occurred to Aaron that the most difficult part of this job might be pretending to get along with Alfredo. It was hard to imagine that James, the missing CIA officer, had actually stomached using this man as his agent. He was obnoxious.

It was such a beautiful night that they sat outside the cabin under the stars, listening to the waterfall as they talked. Sleeping out here, Aaron considered, would be vastly preferable to sleeping with all those men in that small cabin, breathing in the smoke from their Cuban cigarettes and cigars. If they planned to keep that up, Aaron planned to spend most of his time outside. He hoped it would not rain while he was here, and was glad that his cover did not require him to smoke.

Once Alfredo got on the subject of girls, Aaron knew what Nat meant. This guy was sick, and didn't care what anyone thought of him. He talked about the thrill he got when a woman tried to fight him off, and how he knew that deep down they were actually repressed and really wanted someone to take the decision out of their hands. Nat was fortunate. He did not have to hide his disgust. Alfredo seemed to actually enjoy Nat's discomfort. It was taking real work for Aaron to control his emotions and actually join in on the conversation. Sure, he had acted in school, but in a play everyone was pretending. Alfredo wasn't pretending. His eyes were bright and his skin was flushed. This man was a pervert, and right now he was testing Taz. He would know by Taz's reaction to his stories whether Taz was genuine or not. It was absolutely crucial to Aaron and Nat that Taz make no mistake tonight.

*You must be the character you portray,* Aaron kept reminding himself. *You are Taz. Think like Taz. How would a rapist respond to this conversation? What would he say? At first he'd be cautious,* Aaron decided, *while he felt out the audience. You wouldn't brag about stuff like this until you were sure you weren't being set up. Then, after you got comfortable, you would start showing bravado. After all, it's a power and control trip, isn't it?* That's what Sheila had told him in one of their conversations.

When "Taz" had reached the "comfortable" stage, and was matching Alfredo story for story, Nat had heard more than enough. Jumping to his feet, he stated he couldn't take any more of this, and stalked away to look at the waterfall under the moonlight. *Lucky Nat to be able to walk away from this,* thought Aaron. *He's probably sick to his stomach by now.*

The testing lasted through two bottles of rum. Aaron was amazed, since he had drunk very little. Fortunately rapists were not necessarily alcoholics, and the real Taz had shown no signs of alcoholism. Alfredo's capacity for the liquor was incredible. When he finally announced that it was time to turn in, Aaron followed him into the cabin and gagged. It stunk, and the smoke was making his eyes water. A coughing fit came naturally.

"Can't take the smoke," he gasped. "I'll sleep outside."

Alfredo did not protest. The running eyes and sniffing nose were too real to be faked. "Take the blanket," he offered. "Even in our beautiful country the night air can be cool."

Nat was staying inside the cabin. It was too risky to be seen together very much. Finding a comfortable spot on some soft ground, Aaron surveyed the skies. The full moon hid some of the stars, but Aaron was amazed at the number that he could see. In the city he scarcely ever bothered looking at the night sky because the stars were hidden by lights and pollution. Whenever he got away from the city, though, he found a peace in himself when he looked into the stars. Thank goodness for the stars and the weather here, because other than that it looked like it was going to be a thoroughly unpleasant assignment.

Next morning, after breakfast, Taz started bartering for drugs. While Alfredo mentioned nothing other than quantity, quality and price, the prices were unpredictable and at times made little sense. Aaron managed to buy the same quantity and type for three different contacts for the same price. Then he would try to buy it for a fourth contact and find that the price had quadrupled. It only made sense if you assumed that the fourth contact was in debt to the rebels or was being blackmailed. For other contacts, Aaron found Alfredo negotiable, but not on the high-priced ones. Taz carried a clipboard and kept extensive notes, since there was no electricity in the cabin even if he had been able to bring a laptop computer. Aaron had already discovered that his belongings had been searched while he was out of the cabin for a few minutes, so he knew he could not risk leaving any private notes in his possession. Only transactions and contact codes would be left on the clipboard. It would be expected that he could not keep all the transactions in his memory.

Once he got back to the United States, he would be asked to translate the codes and share the names with the FBI for internal investigation. The names were real, because the real Taz had kept records. Quite a few people were going to be facing some tough questions when Aaron got this information back to Langley.

Occasionally, Aaron and Nat would "bump into" each other when emerging from the cabin for a break, or on the way to the latrine. During their brief meetings they compared their findings, and Nat was able to show Aaron where the transmitter was hidden while he pretended to examine a palmita bush. Aaron was able to report that Alfredo appeared to have assured himself that Taz was the genuine article.

"Nat, he's making me ill," Aaron had complained.

"Don't call me that even when we are alone," Nat reprimanded. "It's too easy to make a slip—and much too costly. And watch yourself around Osvaldo. I don't think he trusts us."

"Right." *Sam, Sam, Sam…don't screw up whatever you do,* Aaron chided himself. *Stay in your role.* Being Taz wasn't a problem, except around Alfredo. Then it became morally reprehensible. But it was working. Nat, no, Sam, had been right about the choice of cover. Aaron would just have to put up with Alfredo and be careful not to make any slips.

Osvaldo had returned with the leader of the Liberators, Jose Luis Sánchez. Both were serious men, and Aaron noticed that Alfredo showed deference to Jose Luis. From the behaviour of the other Cuban rebels, it was clear that Jose Luis was their undisputed leader. There was far more discipline in the camp when he was present.

After one break, Aaron sat in his usual chair (their were only two in the cabin) and waited for Alfredo. To his surprise, Jose Luis sat across from him, his brown eyes guarded. "I think you are probably wondering about price differences among our suppliers," he stated in a carefully controlled tone.

*How should I respond?* The price differences had nothing to do with suppliers. Aaron thought quickly. Jose Luis had a purpose here, and Taz would approach this carefully. "Perhaps I was wondering why some customers pay one price so easily, yet others pay so much more," Aaron responded, holding the leader's gaze. "Perhaps I have noticed that the difference is not with the suppliers. Is this something you would want to explain to me?"

"Not yet," Jose Luis replied bluntly, "but your work for me in the United States has been very impressive. I was watching you this morning, and Alfredo speaks highly of your negotiating skills." He took out a package of Cuban cigarettes and offered it. Aaron declined with a shake of his head. Jose Luis lit up, then continued. "I am very grateful for the work you did with Mr. Turnbell and Congressman Harvey."

Aaron almost choked. Congressman Harvey? Mr. CIA supporter himself? Good God, what was this about and how on earth should he respond? Carefully, very carefully. "I'm glad to know my work has pleased you, and I hope it brings benefits to us both."

"He will arrive at noon on Sunday, instead of during the night. I contacted him from town yesterday, which did not please him. He is used to dealing with you." Jose Luis smiled. "I hope his phone is bugged. I called only to put some pressure on him to ensure that he does not back out. The man is a fool, but a rich one. That will come in handy." Alfredo was approaching, and Jose Luis apparently felt that he had talked enough, surrendering his seat to Alfredo.

This time Aaron found it harder to concentrate on the negotiations. Richard Harvey was actually *travelling* to Cuba to meet the Sierra Maestra Liberators? Why? It sounded like he was walking into a trap. Aaron needed to talk to Nat about this, and pump information from Alfredo without letting Alfredo sense that "Taz" didn't already know about it. Aaron cursed the FBI investigators. Why hadn't they found out about this? If the real Taz had any indication what might be going on, he was probably laughing himself to sleep every night in his jail cell.

On the second day, Aaron was finally able to talk to Nat about this development. Nat received this information with the same astonishment that

Aaron had felt. "He's coming here? Why on earth would he take a risk like that?" Nat thought for a minute. "He must be supporting them. Hell, he knows enough of our people, he probably got hold of our information that reported on the inflated size of this group. Harvey probably thinks the Liberators can overthrow the government here and he'll be a hero for backing them. I wonder how long he's been doing it."

"I don't know," Aaron replied, "but I'm going to try to get Alfredo drunk again and bring up the topic. I'm supposed to take James Thompson's place anyway, and convince Alfredo to work for us."

"Whatever you do," Nat warned, "don't get drunk yourself. And check Alfredo out carefully before you make your approach. I don't think that man is as stupid as he appears to be." He contemplated their options. "I think I'll send Moseley a signal and ask him to come in here about two o'clock on Sunday. It will be risky enough here without having a Congressman with us, even if he does finally realise he's walked into a trap. On our own we can elude pursuit if need be, but Harvey's built like a miniature elephant. I don't feel like risking my life for someone who doesn't have the sense to know when he's being set up."

Later, Nat had given Aaron a sign to say that the signal had been sent. Aaron was glad. Today was Wednesday, which meant that Moseley would send his people in to rescue them in four days. It would be good to get away from this camp and Alfredo. The rescue would have to be done at top speed and would be very risky. Cuba was a small island and the American helicopters would be reported by anyone who spotted them. Only the isolation of the camp would work in their favour.

In the evening, he convinced Alfredo to sit outside and drink rum with him. It was harder this time, because Alfredo was conscious of Jose Luis' presence in the camp, but after a few drinks Alfredo loosened up. As he listened to Alfredo talk, Aaron found himself holding back. It should be easy to convince Alfredo to supply him information, since he had already worked for James, but Aaron felt the hair on the back of his neck twitching when he thought about letting this man know who he worked for. He was safe as Taz, but he felt no safety with Alfredo otherwise. Something was telling him that this was all wrong. First, the man was an absolute scuz. *Is this the best James could do?* Aaron would have tried Lino, if he had tried anyone. More importantly, Alfredo had a loose mouth. He talked too much. Aaron believed that a person who was so willing to blabber to a stranger like himself was apt to spill information both ways without thinking about what he was saying.

Tony would not have encouraged Aaron to approach a man such as this. Or was Alfredo really what he pretended to be? An uneasy thought stirred in the back of Aaron's mind. He decided this needed further consideration, and a few minutes later almost fainted in relief that he had waited.

Alfredo had been talking about his close relationship with Jose Luis. "I saved Jose's skin last year," Alfredo announced proudly. "We had an American in camp, but I didn't trust him. We decided to feed him bad information for a few months while Jose Luis used his Yankee contacts to check the results." Alfredo lit another of his cigars. "The Yank was a spy all right. Osvaldo wanted to kill him, but Jose Luis said to use him for a while longer." This time Alfredo laughed loudly. "He called himself Dennys, and he actually asked me to spy for him. We had so much fun over that one."

"What did you do?" Aaron asked, remembering not to hold his breath, and preparing himself for the worst. They had believed that information, although they now knew it was false.

"Paid him to turn," Alfredo answered. "You Americans love money too much. It was easy. We dropped a few hints and then offered him a cut. He told us who he worked for. He was CIA. What a laugh those guys are." There was nothing restrained in Alfredo's laughter.

"So he kept sending bad information to the States," Aaron guessed.

"Oh yeh! Told them how large and powerful we were getting. Do we look large and powerful? No," he answered himself, "but it worked. People started contacting us. People who will be here on Sunday from the Cuban government and your Congressman. These people will be like money in the bank for us. The CIA is like a sieve," he concluded. "All you have to do is tell them what you want, someone leaks it out, and someone else with money and power hears about it and tries to cash in."

"Where is this spy now?" With some effort Aaron kept his voice casual.

"Dead," Alfredo answered. "A few months ago. He had served his purpose and Jose Luis never really trusted him. I wanted to give him to the Cuban government as a present, but Osvaldo killed him instead."

*Why, James, would you trust a man like Alfredo?* Aaron wondered. *What was it about this motley crew that would make you want to sell them information? What possible advantage could they offer you?* Tony would be very hurt by this news, Aaron realised. James had been a trusted member of the family. It hurt to know he was dead, and was hard to accept that he had sold out. These thoughts flashed through Aaron's mind as he concentrated on his facial expressions. Thank goodness for his second thoughts about using Alfredo! It would have meant death.

"Hey, Taz, I meant to ask you something."

*Uh-oh.* Aaron looked at Alfredo's face, but saw nothing alarming in it.

"Just an idea," Alfredo continued. "Osvaldo and I are taking Jose Luis to the village tomorrow. He has business to do. We'll be there until Sunday morning, when we return with our guests. There'll be nothing to do here while we are gone. You could come along," he offered.

Now what was all this about, Aaron wondered. Three days in a small village with Alfredo? There would have to be a big advantage to make it worth Aaron's consideration. "What's in the village?" he asked.

Alfredo grinned. "For Jose Luis, it's work, but for Osvaldo and me, it's a chance to go to this certain house—you know—where there are a couple of girls who will make us happy."

*Oh shit, and I can spend the plane ride home practising my explanation to Sue of how I managed to get a dose of the clap...or worse.* Aaron's thoughts raced frantically. The excuse would have to be good. *Use your cover when in trouble,* Nat always said. But how...? He thought of something. "Now Alfredo, you know what I've been saying to you the last two days. I don't go for those kind of girls unless I'm desperate—and I'm not usually desperate. I like to pick my own. Watching them, man; following them. It's the middle class married ones who aren't looking for it that give me a hard-on. The ones with the hubby and kids. They're usually clean...they don't fool around much. I like watching the fear in their eyes when I come up to them. They've made a mistake and let me catch them unguarded. The moment they know they are in trouble—wow, that's the moment for me. Playing with them is fun. They get so scared that they sweat, and that gets me really horny. It's best when I can hide them away someplace. I don't like to share. I like them all to myself. Then I can take a few days to train them to do and say anything I want. After that I get bored with them, so I take them someplace and kill them."

Aaron noticed that Alfredo's eyes were shining, and he had actually licked his lips. *God, I've never wanted to go home so much in my life,* he realised. He forced himself to continue. "So don't think I don't appreciate your offer, I really do. But it doesn't do it for me, man. No, I'll stay here and enjoy your beautiful weather, if you don't mind. It'll be my vacation." *My vacation from your disgusting presence,* Aaron added silently.

"You are a bad boy, man," Alfredo laughed. "Many people are not so honest with themselves as you and me. I know your meaning. Enjoy your vacation."

64

It had worked, and Alfredo walked away looking pleased. Instantly Aaron decided that the first thing he would do when he got back to the good ole U.S. of A., would be to run, not walk, to Susan, take her in his arms, and hold her until his sanity returned.

# X

As the sun rose the next morning, Aaron heard Alfredo, Osvaldo and Jose Luis leave the cabin and walk to where the horses were tethered. Once they had left, the atmosphere around the camp relaxed, and the men found places outside to lounge in small groups and talk. The remainder of the Cubans were just your common criminal type, who liked to goof off when the boss was away. Aaron felt much more relaxed with Alfredo gone. He and Nat would probably pass the next three days chatting to the others, who would not notice or care if Sam and Taz occasionally liked to speak English to each other.

When Aaron noticed that Nat was wearing his ball hat, he wandered over to sit beside him. Aaron told him what he had learned from Alfredo about James. Nat was saddened, but not terribly surprised. "I knew it had to be something like that," he stated. "James had too much experience to just get lost and disappear. I wonder why he did it though. What fucking advantage would there be? Money, I guess," Nat answered himself out loud. "It's such a fine line we walk, between right and wrong. Some people lose their way."

Nat seemed preoccupied and was silent for a minute. "I don't think I can stay until Sunday," he said unexpectedly, looking over at Aaron. "My cover has been compromised."

Aaron felt a tension start in his jaw. "What do you mean?"

"It's Osvaldo," Nat admitted, glancing casually at the Cubans to ensure they could not overhear. "I've seen him before. I can't place him—perhaps he looked different. He's watching me. He may be trying to place me, too." With an encouraging smile at Aaron, Nat continued. "We should be okay though, since they'll be gone until Sunday. Then our friends will be here to help us."

"Why risk it?" Aaron asked. "Let's change the signal and go. Nothing is going to happen here over the next three days. Moseley can come back in to scoop the Congressman on Sunday."

At first Nat didn't answer. When he did his words were chilling. "There's another problem. The damn transmitter is broken."

"What!" The word was emphatic, but Aaron had remembered to whisper.

"Don't worry," Nat reassured. "The signal for Sunday went out okay, but when I checked it this morning there was no life to it. Frank will have taken a reading on our position as soon as we activated it. We just have to stay put."

"We're stuck here," Aaron stated. "I don't like this, especially if Osvaldo is suspicious."

Nat shook his head regretfully. "Trust me, I don't like it either, but we have no choice. There will be no boat waiting for us at the shore, and it's at least 250 kilometres to Guantánamo Bay across the mountains. There's a road along the shore, but we only have American identification. We can't pretend to be lost Canadians without someone checking us out very thoroughly, and we sure can't pass as Cubans."

Trying to lighten up a bit, Aaron offered an alternative. "We could go into hiding until Sunday and live off granola bars."

Nat almost smiled. "Yes, I actually thought of that. If things go wrong, watch for my signal and we will do just that." He looked around at the waterfall. "It's a beautiful place, isn't it?" Then he looked at Aaron. "We'll be okay," he assured. "Don't worry. But just to be safe, slip this into that waterproof lining in your jacket, okay?" He handed Aaron a piece of paper. "It's the names of the companies and individuals Osvaldo is planning to hit up next."

As Aaron slid the paper into his jacket, he saw Nat looking at him intently. "If for whatever reason I can't get out of here, I want you to remember something."

"You're getting out," Aaron interrupted tersely. Anything happening to Nat was unthinkable. He wouldn't allow it to happen.

"Remember to trust Tony," Nat continued quietly. "Trust him absolutely and with everything. All damage. Don't hold back. He'll stand behind you to the end. He'll tell Mr. Walsh what needs to be told. Walsh relies on him for that. But Tony backs us. Totally. Mr. Walsh is good too, I believe, but he's new to us, and he's agency first. That's his responsibility. Don't hold out on Tony. And keep to your cover. It will be your only protection until help arrives."

"You're getting out with me," Aaron insisted. "Period. I won't let anything happen to you."

"Of course I am," Nat smiled. "No problem."

# XI

Mary wiggled her toes in the sand and watched tourists strolling by. So far it had been a lovely vacation. She had gone snorkling, horseback riding, walked along the beach, and joined the other Canadians drinking rum punches around the pool. This was restful. No decisions and no hassles to face, and no snow. The other tourists were happy and friendly, and the Cubans always returned her smiles and were eager to talk. Mary had studied Spanish in university and was glad that she had taken the occasional conversational Spanish class since then. You could get much more out of a vacation when you could communicate with the people.

It would have been nice to share this with Lori, but maybe they could plan to come here together next year. Mary was wearing one of her two-piece bathing suits. It was modest compared to the suits that Lori wore on a beach. Women were not supposed to go topless on a Cuban beach, but some did. Tourists were informed that it was not illegal, but was considered in bad taste. Mary would never have considered it in any event. Somewhere in this country was a strict government, but Canadian tourists meant money to the Cuban economy, so the government kept itself relatively invisible to tourist eyes. You could find it if you looked, but most tourists did not care to look. Like Mary, they wanted sunshine, warmth, clean air and relaxation.

The rules were simple for tourists. No taking pictures of military people or establishments, and no black market activity. Other than that, you could wander almost anywhere. A Cuban who injured a tourist would be in very serious trouble, so the resorts in Cuba were very popular with senior citizens who liked feeling safe.

The morning was wearing on, and the sun became stronger. Feeling well cooked already, Mary pulled on her track pants and top. Her room key was in the secret pant pocket, but all her other valuables were in a personal safe located in the lobby of the resort. It made life easier, because you never had to worry about leaving your purse some place. Nothing in her room was irreplaceable, and there were no reports of theft anyway.

On her way back to her room to change into shorts, Mary spotted a large iguana past the hotel, on the drive out toward the road. It had wandered out of a clump of trees and was resting on the edge of the pavement, only a couple of hundred feet from the front of the hotel. Mary decided to approach it cautiously, to see how close she could get before it scurried away.

When she was about forty feet away, Mary noticed a late-model white Mitsubishi L300 van approaching. It would probably scare the iguana. The van slowed as if to watch the iguana, and Mary prepared to give up as the iguana moved nervously. As the van kept coming, the iguana moved into the grass. When the van passed her, Mary saw two Cubans in the front of the van. *Thanks a lot for ruining my fun,* she grumbled to herself. Since it was a lovely morning, Mary decided to keep walking anyway, at least to the road and back. After that she would have a swim to cool off. Happiness seemed to be returning to her, and Mary was very pleased that she had taken the first step into her new life.

Up on the road, Mary turned around to head back. The drive twisted and turned, so you could not see the resort even though it was very close. Around one bend, Mary met the white van again, and moved over to give it room to pass easily. Without warning, it swerved into her path. Startled, she tripped on the curb as she heard the doors of the van open. Two men jumped out and before she could gather her senses together one man clamped a tape over her mouth and held her arm tightly, dragging her to the back of the van. She fought as hard as she could to prevent herself from being placed in the van, but the two men picked her up easily and threw her onto the floor, jarring her shoulder.

*No!* Mary tried to scream, but the tape stifled her yell. One man had jumped in the back and hit her across the face. She fell back from the pain in her jaw. He tied her feet, then yanked her arms together and bound the wrists tightly. The van had already started moving fast. There was another woman tied up in the van near Mary's feet, but she seemed to be unconscious. Mary's captor pulled out a pack of cigarettes and leered at her. He spoke to her in Spanish.

"Taz will like you. You're perfect for him. He will like my present to him." The man broke into a laugh. "Yes, this will be a good three days. It will give me pleasure to watch Taz in action." His eyes studied her body slowly. "Yes, Taz will now truly enjoy his vacation."

Mary did not bother to acknowledge that she understood. His words were horrifying, and for some reason she felt safer pretending not to understand his language. She remained silent.

The white Mitsubishi van travelled for about an hour. It stopped on a dirt road that was more of a path than a road, outside a small village. The house at which it stopped appeared to have several men inside. Mary peered out the front of the van. There was a Jeep in front of the house. For half an hour the two Cubans who had kidnapped her argued with one of the men inside the house. Finally her captors appeared to win. They came back to the van, removed her and the Cuban girl, who was starting to wake up, and forced them into the back of a green Jeep. Securely tied, Mary was helpless.

The trip continued on an old, apparently abandoned path up into the mountains. It was a very rough ride, especially when your movement was restricted. On the way to wherever they were going, Mary caught glimpses of mango trees, sugar cane and banana trees. Occasionally they passed a small cabin with chickens, goats and pigs milling around. Twice, small children stood near the road edge, but the adults were all occupied, and the Jeep did not slow down enough to let anyone have a look inside anyway.

It seemed that this part of the trip went on for hours, but Mary had not bothered with her watch this morning, so had no real idea of time. The Cuban girl was awake and holding her head. Mary was very scared, and the fact that their captors had not bothered to blindfold them was the most terrifying part. *If they do not care that I can see where we're going,* she reasoned, *it seems as if they do not expect me to escape.* That thought was only causing her to panic more, so Mary made an effort not to think about anything except the scenery. Such a lovely, peaceful-looking day. Being a hostage seemed too unreal on such an otherwise perfect day.

Finally, the Jeep pulled into an overgrown drive. It led to some sort of ranch. Most of the buildings were dilapidated, but the barbed wire fences were intact. Horses stood in the paddock, huddled together in the shade. Like other Cuban horses, these were small, thin and bony, but they seemed in better condition than the ones ridden by tourists at the resort.

The driver drove the Jeep into the building that looked most like a tiny drive shed. A thatched roof was still in existence, but was missing the north quarter. They parked in a spot covered by the roof. The driver and his partner got out, leaving the women tied in the Jeep. Mary and the Cuban woman struggled against their bonds, but finally had to give up. They exchanged looks, and Mary could see deep fear in the Hispanic eyes.

A neighing sound and the appearance of horses was the next surprise. Horseback? Surely not. Where on earth were these men taking them? But horseback it was to be, and in due time the women were dragged out of the

Jeep one at a time, the ropes binding their legs were cut, and they were hoisted to the backs of two horses. Mary found herself tied securely to the saddle with knots that would take a day to undo. Finally everything was apparently ready, and the strange trail ride began.

One Cuban led, and the other followed behind. These were no slow trail horses, and they started out covering ground quite quickly. It had been years since Mary had ridden, but she had no fear of falling off unless the horse went into a bucking fit. Since the horses were attached to a rope held by the lead Cuban, she was quite sure bucking would not be a problem.

It had to be a two-hour ride, winding forever up the mountain. Thank goodness for her track pants, because she soon got sore, but at least her legs were protected from the rough saddle. The Cuban girl wore shorts. *She's going to be rubbed raw,* Mary knew. They went places a Canadian horse would not venture. A rocky riverbed was crossed at least three times. Each time, the horses picked their way among large rocks and slippery stones. Where the ground was smoother, they loped, and Mary held on to the saddle horn. They passed more mango trees and grape trees. Cactus grew tall in the open areas. The much-disliked marabu bush grew too close to the path in places, and caught at her pant legs.

As they climbed, the scenery was breathtaking. The little horses were quite surefooted, even on steep slopes. There were no more farms or houses in this area. In fact, it seemed deserted of human life, the silence disturbed only by the calls of the Toti and other birds Mary could recognise but not identify. The sun was getting very hot and starting to dip towards the west. It must be around two o'clock, Mary guessed. The trip had not taken as long as it had seemed. She was very thirsty. The horses were allowed to drink in the streams, but no such consideration was given to their female riders. Her body felt dehydrated, and she was getting hungry.

Eventually they arrived at their destination. It was a beautiful waterfall with a pond at the base. The hills on three sides rose far higher than the waterfall, the hill faces steep with only the hardiest vegetation surviving amid their rock surfaces. A small meadow was nestled between the hills. Vegetation was sparse at this time of the year, but there were trees scattered about. A shack of a cabin had been built years ago, nestled tightly against the eastern hill face, and was well obscured by overhanging palm trees. Two royal palms rose majestically from the meadow floor about fifty feet from the cabin. In front of the cabin stood a group of men watching their progress across the meadow.

# XII

By three o'clock, the afternoon sun had reached its full Cuban intensity for a clear January day. Like the Cubans, Aaron and Nat were sitting under trees, drinking beer on the east side of the compound. They sat with separate groups, maintaining the perception that Sam wanted nothing to do with Taz. It was a good opportunity to gather information and practise Spanish to keep themselves sharp. With Alfredo gone, Aaron did not have to work as hard at his cover. Other, more general subjects could be discussed, although the talk was usually political. Aaron already knew who was who in Cuban officialdom, but he feigned ignorance.

Unexpectedly, four horses appeared at the start of the trail, disturbing the lazy afternoon and signifying the start of the worst nightmare of Aaron's life. Alfredo was on the lead horse, waving and grinning widely. Behind him were two women on horseback, followed by Osvaldo. Aaron was careful not to show his alarm or look at Nat, but his heart was suddenly racing, and his palms were damp. He was very conscious of the close proximity of the Cubans sitting around them to their weapons. *Control,* he said to himself, taking a large swig of beer. He would distract them and give Nat a chance to disappear and get a head start. It was a crisis, but there was no sense presuming the worst. *Nat's been in this game for seventeen years,* Aaron remembered. *He'll know what to do.*

Alfredo was clearly pleased with himself. "Hey, Taz—got you a present!"

Getting to his feet, Aaron kept the beer in his hand and sauntered over. What the hell was this about? *Keep relaxed and be ready for anything,* he told himself.

But nothing could have prepared him for what came next. As he started to approach the horses, Aaron saw Alfredo drag the women off the horses one at a time. With horror starting in his gut, Aaron realised that the women were tied to the saddles. He couldn't prevent his jaw from falling open. *No, please, God, tell me this isn't what I think it is!* Alfredo was waiting expectantly for Taz to say something, and Aaron struggled to get his thoughts together. Say something…react…trouble. Use your cover.

Taz responded with a whoop. "Alfredo, what ya doin' with the bitches?"

"Got you some company for your vacation." Alfredo laughed and pointed at the smaller of the two women. "This one's for you." Then he indicated the Cuban woman. "This one is for me and the boys."

"But where did you get them?" *Stall for time; time to think, time for Nat to think, time to plan.*

"This one we got from that house I told you about," Alfredo replied, looking at the Cuban woman. She looked to be in her early twenties. By her dress and the obscenities she was voicing at her captors, Aaron learned that she had been offered money for sex. Obviously she had not expected to be kidnapped. "She's feisty, with hot blood in her," Alfredo stated. Then he turned to the smaller woman. "This one was very risky to take. We stole her from the resort."

A tourist. Alfredo had kidnapped a tourist. She was petite, a little over five feet tall, and was watching him with terror in her eyes. Aaron felt sick. This was his fault. He had told Alfredo that he liked middle-aged, middle-class women. Now this innocent little woman with brown hair and scared eyes had been dragged from her secure world, kidnapped and presented to Taz as a gift. Alfredo expected Taz to rape her—there was no doubt of that. It couldn't happen. The agency had limits, and even if they hadn't, Aaron could not rape. But they had made Taz his cover. Christ, he was dead.

*React, talk, buy time...where are you Nat? I need help here.* "She's a pretty bitch, man," "Taz" observed, tossing his beer away. Aaron had reached the place where the horses stood, and noticed that he was being followed by Nat and the Cubans. He walked around the woman, seeing her brown eyes following his movements. "A tourist, huh? What's your name, little bitch?"

"Mar...Mar...Mary," she stuttered.

"Taz" broke out laughing while Aaron ran accents through his memory. "Mar...Mar...Mary," Taz hooted. "That's some name. You ain't a Yank, are you, Mary?"

"No," she responded.

"Canadian, eh?" Taz laughed again, looking at the crowd for amusement value. Nat was there, watching him intently.

"You like her, Taz?" It was Osvaldo, who had been quiet up until now, neither smiling nor amused.

Suddenly Aaron knew exactly what was going on. It was the ultimate test. Osvaldo was suspicious. Taz was doubted. Taz was to be tested. How? No decent man would rape. The CIA did not hire rapists. If Taz was actually an

American spy instead of a drug trafficking rapist, Taz would not rape. Aaron was in big trouble. The Cubans were finding the show amusing, not realising what it was really about, so to buy more time, Aaron kept it up.

"She's really for me?" Taz asked. "Exclusive-like? You know I don't like to share, Alfredo."

"She's all yours," Osvaldo stated, watching him.

"I did a good thing, yes?" Alfredo had an evil grin. "You can have the Cuban girl if you want, but the tourist looked more your style."

"She's perfect." Taz paused. "But what about Jose Luis? He said no girls. He might not like this."

"Jose Luis is most willing to please you, Taz." It was Osvaldo again.

*I'll just bet he is,* thought Aaron. *You told him why you are doing this, didn't you, you bastard.* Turning his back, Aaron wandered over in Nat's direction. "I'll bet you're jealous," Taz taunted Sam. "I got me a Canadian tourist woman. She's all for me. Bet you'd like a piece of that." Taz indicated Mary. "Nice bit of tail. She looks about your age, too. Hey little bitch," he called over. "How old are you?"

"Thirty-six." Her scared voice was a dagger in Aaron's gut. *Help me, Nat,* he prayed.

"You disgust me," Sam said. "Leave the poor things alone. In case you didn't know, the Cuban government does not look favourably on rape, abduction and forceable confinement. Or maybe you want to spend your pathetic life in one of their lovely jails. Believe me, they make American prisons look like the Holiday Inn."

*Thank you, Nat.* Taz paused, as if considering the wisdom of upsetting Castro and his friends. Unfortunately, things suddenly took a turn for the worse.

"He doesn't have to worry about that." Motioning one of the Cubans to hold the horses, Osvaldo followed Taz over to where Nat was standing. "You see, we got company coming Sunday. The girls can't be around to see the company. So," he continued, staring into Aaron's eyes, "you've got until Sunday to play with them, then we have to kill them."

Forceable confinement, rape and murder. It took a supreme effort for Aaron to keep his face from showing his horror. *This cannot be happening to me,* his mind pleaded. Taz turned to Sam and gave another hoot. "Hey man, it's a snuff film! You really gotta love this place!"

"Snuff film?" Alfredo had not understood the English slang Aaron had thrown in.

Just then Osvaldo stood in front of Nat. Aaron hadn't noticed that he had pulled a gun out of his pocket. "Unfortunately, Taz, 'Sam' won't be able to partake in your fun. Will you, Mr. Bowman? Or have you forgotten a man called Greco in Peru?" Osvaldo looked at a speechless Taz. "Mr. Nathanial Bowman is an officer of the American Central Intelligence Agency."

"NO!" Aaron had screamed it out loud, to his own horror. Nat looked at him with a flash of real fear in his eyes. Aaron reached deep into his soul for control. *Don't blow it, you fool. Nat's life is going to depend on you now. Get a grip—fast.* Taz actually scuttled back ten feet and turned a panic-stricken face to Alfredo. "They hate me, man. It can't be true. He would have killed me by now." Think faster. "There was this bitch, see? I didn't know she was a wife of one of those guys. They all know my face now, that's why I always gotta be so careful. He would've killed me on sight if he was CIA. It don't make sense." Pause and calm down. "No, he can't be, Osvaldo. You gotta be wrong in this. Besides, look at him." Disdain filled Taz's voice. "Does that look like a spy to you? He's a wimp who doesn't even like getting his hands dirty. Hell, he looks more like a queer than an Intelligence fuckin' officer."

A quick survey of his audience told him that Alfredo was having doubts. Unfortunately, Osvaldo wasn't.

"There's no question, Taz. I was a bit slow putting it together, 'cause he looked different in Peru. But this is Nathanial Bowman."

It became clear that Nat knew Osvaldo now, as a look of resignation shadowed his face. Aaron's heart sunk. Nat wouldn't give up this easily unless he knew that Osvaldo actually did recognise him. Then Nat did something surprising.

"You're a fucking pervert," he snarled, looking directly at Aaron. "I should have killed you as soon as we got here. Instead I forced myself to wait and listen to your sick talk. That woman was a wife of a friend of mine. Oh, I'll do you," he promised, "don't worry. I owe it to someone."

*What the hell are you doing, Nat? You just admitted it!* But Aaron knew in his heart that the game was up for Nat anyway. At least for now. There were too many Cuban rebels and too many guns for Aaron to even dream about starting a fight. He was good at close combat, but there were limits. No, he'd have to come to Nat's aid later. Nat had just tried to put distance between them. Aaron would be useless if he were discovered as well. *Use your cover. Oh God!*

"Go ahead, pervert." Nat actually spat at him. "That poor little woman is doomed anyway. You want her for yourself? You want to show everyone what a big man you are? I hope you rot in hell!"

*Oh Nat, you're killing me. It's about staying alive, isn't it? Staying alive and getting the hell out of here. Hopefully getting the women out of here too. If I die, you and the women also die, and all for nothing. And what damage will be done before we are all allowed to die? If I stay alive, just maybe I can save all of us and nail these bastards to the wall. But at what cost, Nat? At what cost to her and me? For me to stay alive, she has to suffer. Yet if I walk, or I'm caught, you and the women will suffer anyway. Can I live knowing I let you die for nothing? This is no choice, Nat.*

But choice it had to be. Stalling for time was over. Aaron had to stay alive. Had to try. Couldn't give up.

"Well, Mr. Bowman," Taz drawled. "Watch and see what I did to your friend's wife." Spinning around, Taz strode over to Mary, took out his knife and cut the rope that was still binding her to the saddle. *What do I do, he wondered? How am I supposed to do this?* A snippet of conversation floated into his mind. Sheila had been talking about rape one day. *"Rape is not about sex, not really. It's about control, domination and a hatred of women. Sex is just the manifestation; the method of dominating."* What else had she said? *"Rapists use fear and intimidation to control their victims, as well as force."* Fear and intimidation. Okay. He was six feet, two inches. Mary had to be a foot shorter. Time to show her the real Taz.

Mary was trying to back away from him. Taz grabbed her by the hair. "Come here, bitch." Then he literally picked her up and threw her over his shoulder. There was a piece of softer ground to the south side of the building where he had been sleeping. Aaron noticed everyone following him. Great— an audience. Life didn't get much worse. At least they were not bringing Nat with them.

Now what? Physically overpowering this little woman who was crying and pleading with him to leave her alone would be easy, but he had two problems. First, how could he force her to have sex without breaking any bones? He was much, much stronger than she, and if she struggled, she was apt to be hurt. Yet the Cubans were expecting Taz to put on a show. It had to look realistic, but he didn't want to hurt this woman. She was going to hurt, he was sickeningly aware, but if at all possible he wanted to keep the harm minimal. *Fear and intimidation.* Okay, he'd put on an act that would frighten the devil.

Second problem. Big problem. Sex was not going to be possible unless he had an erection. Being violent with this woman was not going to do it for him. His body was already telling him that. So what to do?

Taz had to start his act. The ground was mainly sand with a sparse layer of grass. There were no rocks in sight. Mary's hands were tied in front of her. He swung her off his shoulder, turned her face forward so she could see the ground, then threw her about eight feet in front of him. Her feet hit first, as he expected, then her hands took the rest of the fall. She lay there, crying. As he approached her, she looked up and begged him not to touch her.

*I'm sorry, I'm sorry, I'm sorry,* he apologised silently. *But I have to do this. Believe me, if I could think of another way...* but for her it was either him or them. He would try his best not to hurt her too much. He wished she could understand that it was either one of him or all of them. Not that the thought made this any easier for him. This was going to be his step into hell, and it would be at this innocent woman's painful expense.

Alfredo and a couple of the rebels had started with the other girl. They were only a few feet away. It was too close. Taz grabbed Mary's hair, waited a second for her to reach up and grab his wrists in an instinctive protective gesture, then dragged her another dozen feet away. Her feet were scrambling, and he knew that her weight was being supported through her hands and arms. She was surprisingly agile, he thought.

*Okay, now what? Fear and intimidation.* He had to become Taz long enough to get past his scruples. Taz would have an erection because he would make Mary give him one if need be. *Okay, you are Taz. Think like Taz. Feel like Taz. Lives depend on this.*

Taz took out the razor-sharp switchblade he always carried. "Okay, little bitch, let's see what you look like." Grabbing her sweatshirt, he sliced it from neck to waist. There was a bathing suit underneath. The knife had terrified her, and she had screamed. "Get those clothes off NOW!" Taz hollered at her. "Or I'll cut them off you!"

In a panic, Mary managed to pull off the track pants, shoes and bathing suit, crying and shaking through it all.

"Now kneel!" Taz ordered, then laughed hysterically. He was speaking in English to her, but then repeated his words in Spanish for the sake of his audience. This was about survival and maintaining his cover, so the rebels needed to be convinced of his intentions. He stood in front of Mary, towering over the slight form, then knelt. The knife in his hand was close to her body. "See this?" he asked unnecessarily. "It's very sharp. It can cut very easily." Slowly, he placed it near her face. "Don't flinch. I'd hate to slip and cut off that cute nose." Then he let the knife travel down her body to her breasts. "Oh, they're pretty, little bitch. You didn't tell me how pretty you were."

Amazingly, Mary spoke. "You don't need….need the knife. I'll do what you want."

It almost ruined Taz's act. Taz could not feel sympathy. "But I like the knife, little bitch. It makes sure you'll behave. If you don't, I cut off one of these cute little nipples. You wouldn't want that, would you?"

"No, please!" She was shaking and crying again.

"Then you're going to help me, aren't you?" Taz stood up and unzipped his pants. He held the knife at the side of her neck and moved into position. "Now you behave. If you do anything bad, you get cut."

Well, it worked—just. At least the dampness of her mouth on him would make his entry a little easier for her. When he was ready, Taz whooped it up, put the knife away, grabbed Mary by the hair and pushed her onto her back. Mary tried to struggle, but Taz was easily strong enough to restrain her. Yet she still tried to avoid him, and Taz was going to have to subdue her. She was making it worse for herself, although it was quite a show for the others. With an open hand, Taz slapped her once across the face, then was in position. "Lie still," he commanded. Strangely enough, she stopped moving and he pushed into her. She gasped and whimpered.

Finally it was over. "Over," he heard himself whisper before he caught himself. Taz wouldn't say that. *Taz can go to hell,* Aaron decided, as he pulled out of her. *That was the worst sexual experience of my life.* Catching his breath, Aaron noticed that his victim wasn't looking at him any more. *Right…humiliation.* That was the other part of rape. Fear, intimidation and humiliation. Three days of this? He had found hell.

The others were still at the Cuban girl. She was getting punched and beaten in the process. Aaron tore his eyes away and looked for Nat. No sign of him. Alfredo was grinning at him, as if satisfied with his performance. Now Mary had to be tied up, but Aaron did not trust the others yet. He would stay with her a few more minutes. Putting on a subdued Taz act, Aaron knelt beside her.

"Okay, sit up."

She did, but still wouldn't look at him. The rope that bound her wrists was dangling on the ground, but around the wrists it was tied much too tightly. He struggled to untie it, but then gave up and cut it. Her wrists were already swollen, so he rubbed them and then retied the rope more humanely. A second piece of rope cut from the first long piece, and tied to the rope that bound her wrists, would serve to fasten her to the tree.

"There's some rules you need to follow." Taz could not be seen being kind to the prisoner, so he decided to taunt her, switching back and forth from

English to Spanish. "First—no other guys. Since we're going steady now, I don't want you fucking around." He pointed to the Cubans. "Those guys…you don't know where they've been. I don't want to get a case of the clap from you. So if they ask, you say no."

Mary was staring at him in astonishment. *She thinks I'm crazy,* he realised. *Good.*

"Second—you never say no to me. See that girl?" Pointing at the Cuban girl, he didn't look. She was screaming profanities at the departing Cubans and getting abused and kicked for her troubles. "She keeps saying no. You do what I want, and I don't have to hurt you too bad." The rebels were entering the cabin after tying their victim to a tree. Aaron finished with the ropes and led Mary to the same tree.

"That's all for now," Taz decided. "Let's tie you to this tree. I'll be back later." In his pocket, Aaron had some Kleenex. He tossed this at Mary, gathered her clothes and tossed them as well. Then he went inside for a very large glass of rum and to try to find Nat.

An hour later, Mary was still leaning in shock against the tree Taz had tied her to. She was all cried out for the moment. The girl beside her had said her name was Juany Martínez. Juany was in a great deal of pain. Compared to what she had endured, Mary had gotten off lucky. Some luck. That had hurt a lot, and she'd never been so scared in her life. She had been sure that Taz was going to cut her with that knife. That was her worst fear. Physically she was not badly injured, except for a sprained wrist and a small amount of blood from her vagina. Some torn skin, probably. Nothing that wouldn't heal if left alone…if left alone. The trembling started again, so Mary practised breathing exercises to try to calm herself. *At this moment in time you are safe,* she told herself. *Hang on to that thought.*

Taz was a stark raving lunatic, Mary realised. She hated him. His only redeeming feature was that he didn't seem to want the others to touch her. He was insane, she decided. Going steady? Don't fuck around? Was this guy for real? He was probably schizophrenic too, although she didn't know much about that. She knew he had two voices, and seemed to have two personalities. Just before he had penetrated her, he had barked a command in a low, authoritative voice. *"Lie still,"* he had said. She had. It was a voice you obeyed. Then he had undone those ropes that had hurt so much and rubbed her wrists. First he violates her, then he worries about ropes. Definitely schizophrenic.

By the time the sun was starting to set, Mary's stomach was growling for food, and she was extremely thirsty. The royal palm she was tied to beside Juany gave shade from the sun, but Mary had been offered no food or water during the day. Only a few hundred feet away was a beautiful waterfall and a large pool of clean-looking water. There was probably little pollution up here, Mary decided. No sign of civilised life, anyway. This crew of outlaws had picked a great place to hide out. Actually, the mountainous scenery was beautiful. It would be a lovely spot under different conditions.

When the cabin door opened and the Cubans spilled out, Mary felt the panic again. Taz was with them, and they all made their way over toward the women.

Aaron had spent the last couple of hours wondering where Nat was. He was nowhere to be seen, and Alfredo had changed the subject when Aaron had asked. It would not be wise to press the subject, so Aaron had been forced to act like nothing was bothering him while his mind was in turmoil.

Taz grabbed Mary's hair again. Quickly she grasped his wrists to protect her scalp. With little effort she was pulled to her feet. In Spanish, Taz told everyone that he was going to do what Alfredo had requested. Alfredo had wanted to see how to train a bitch. Removing the ropes that had tied Mary's hands to the tree, Taz gave her a violent shove away from the cabin. Somehow she managed not to fall this time.

"On your knees, bitch!" Taz screamed in English. Then he laughed hysterically. Suddenly the laughter stopped, and he glared at her. "Why are your clothes still on?" With a quick movement, he pulled out his switchblade, but Mary hadn't waited. Anything to avoid the knife. She scrambled out of her clothes.

Aaron forced an evil grin onto his face and surveyed the audience. He pulled one of his supply of granola bars from his pocket. In Spanish he announced, "Let's see how hungry the bitch is. Maybe she'll beg for food." He had hoped to leave Mary alone tonight, but the others had wanted a show. He had declined as long as possible, but it was dangerous to keep refusing, and one of the others had suggested that he share her. That had made up his mind. While he was stalling he had figured out a way to at least get some food into her body. They were definitely not planning to do anything to keep these women alive. Female yelling told him that Juany was being abused again. *Okay, do it, Taz. She'll hate this, but at least it won't hurt her.*

Aaron had to harden his resolve when he saw Mary kneeling naked, quivering at the sight of the knife. "Hungry, bitch?" He cut off a small piece of granola bar and held it out towards her in his fingers. "You have to beg. Be a good little dog. Bark." He repeated it in Spanish for the Cubans. Mary's look was pathetic, but she had to obey him. His knife made a menacing gesture. She barked like a sick dog. Degradation and humiliation. He felt sick. "Good doggie." He made her sit, beg and roll over for pieces of food. In his pocket he had another bar which he had hoped not to use, but the Cubans wanted to see sex. He opened the second bar as the rebels crowded around.

"You'll like this one," he announced. Being Taz and not showing any weakness in the role was extremely difficult. He had to focus intently on his role, pretending that it was all make-believe and they were all part of a bizarre theatre production. Tonight was an X-rated show called oral sex. *Taz, Taz, you're Taz,* he kept repeating to himself, *and this is your audience.* Mary cried through the entire play, and Taz let her cry. It was more convincing for his perverted audience, and she deserved to be able to cry.

When Taz was done, Mary picked up the piece of Kleenex he had thrown at her. Then he let her put her clothes back on. Mary didn't look at anybody, but just followed him meekly back to the tree. *The bastard...the horrible, cruel bastard.* Doing that—taunting her and completely stripping her of any dignity. *May he rot in hell,* Mary cursed to herself. She sat in silence as he tied her up again without a word. *You're an animal,* she fumed silently at his back as he followed the Cubans back to the cabin.

About an hour later, Mary saw Taz come out the door by himself. He did not look happy. She started to tremble and could hear her own breathing coming in gasps. Taz walked over to her, but this time he didn't yell and scream.

"You need to go to the bathroom, little bitch?"

Actually she did. She noticed that his voice had changed to that authoritative voice she had heard earlier. Cautiously she nodded her head. Was this a trick? Juany had fallen asleep. Taz knelt down and untied the tree rope. He seemed cold and distant, but at least he didn't drag her around. She was led by the arm to a dirty latrine area. *Don't look,* she determined. She hadn't bothered to put the bathing suit back on. It seemed safer to leave it lying by the tree. Taz was a little too reckless with that knife. She was relieved to see that he wasn't watching her urinate. It stung her torn skin and she gasped.

"Problem, bitch?"

"It stings," she replied tersely. *As if you care.*

"Take your time," he replied.

Back at the tree, tied up again, Mary watched Taz walk away. He'd even pulled a roll of toilet paper out of his jacket and left it with her. Definitely schizophrenic. Taz during the day had been a cruel lunatic. This Taz she called Taz II. An impersonal issuer of orders, he thankfully seemed uninterested in hurting her. She would try to figure him out.

Juany woke up as Taz II left. She had been thrilled to learn that Mary spoke Spanish, but had promised not to tell. Somehow Mary felt safer with the men not knowing that. Juany was in a great deal of pain again. She was bruised and bleeding, as she had been roughed up by a couple of the men.

"You are lucky to have only one animal at you," Juany stated forlornly. "I will kill all of them if I have a chance." She talked for a while longer, then fell asleep again.

Mary tried to reassure herself by analysing what had happened. It was impossible to think while Taz was attacking her, because fear blots out reason. Now she could think with a clearer head. Juany had been right. For some reason Osvaldo had given her to Taz. Taz had wanted her for himself so he wouldn't catch any sexual diseases. That seemed peculiar, but Taz was obviously a North American male, and perhaps he was worried about AIDS. Mary was, too, but she had no choice in the matter. Whatever his reason, Mary was glad she only had "one animal" to deal with. It had been a terrifying day, but now that she thought about it, she had not been badly hurt. Sore, terrified and humiliated, yes, but she was alive and relatively unharmed. Now she had to figure out how to stay like that.

*First of all, don't piss him off,* Mary decided. *You do not want Taz to give you to the others. How on earth does Juany bear it?* Mary decided she would try to figure out what Taz wanted, and just do it. Rules of decency and sanitation did not exist here, and why should she care if all those criminals watched? Pain avoidance was important. Perhaps if she followed all of his rules, Taz would stop terrorising her. Maybe he would even put the knife away.

Aaron was inside the cabin, fighting down panic. Where was Nat? Alfredo had finally mentioned that Osvaldo had taken him somewhere for questioning. Tomorrow, Alfredo said, they would find out what he knew and if he had managed to send out any information about the camp. It was crucial that they know this.

"Did you know, Taz, that Osvaldo suspected you, too?" Alfredo raised a hand. "I told him he was crazy. Now he knows. As if a CIA officer could do what you did today." Alfredo laughed. "It's crazy."

*Yeh, crazy.* Aaron felt overwhelmed by something he suspected was depression. This was the worst day of his life. Alfredo would not tell him where Osvaldo had taken Nat, and Nat was nowhere near the camp. Hellish.

"I'm turning in," he announced. They were used to him sleeping outside, so suspected nothing as he left. He couldn't help Nat right now, but as long as he didn't give himself away he could protect Mary.

Juany was asleep. When Mary saw him coming, she jumped nervously. Her hands pulled the cut sweatsuit tight, and she was shaking. Aaron removed his jacket. She was probably cold from the cool night and the shock of the day.

"Put this on, little bitch." He pulled out a small flashlight and some cream he had taken from his medicine kit. Also, he pulled out a whisky flask from his shirt. He had dumped out the whiskey and filled it with water. Holding the flask out to Mary, he saw her draw back. She had to be thirsty, but thought that it was alcohol and knew it would make her thirst worse. Aaron wanted anyone seeing it to think it was alcohol. He couldn't be seen being nice to the victim.

"Drink," he ordered.

The tears started again, but she reached out for the flask and took a sip. Then she glanced up at him curiously and continued to sip.

He turned the flashlight on to put cream on his finger. "Pants down," he ordered. She whimpered again, but was afraid to say no to him. With one hand she pulled them down to her knees. He took a tissue and placed it between her legs. Taking it away, he saw traces of blood, but no flow. Minor damage, he decided, trying to keep his emotions out of his head. She cringed when he touched her to apply the cream, but relaxed as soon as he was finished. "Okay." He needed to give an explanation to explain away his actions. "I don't want you catching anything down there. I got enough problems without getting any diseases from you."

Again the look of astonishment. *Well, that confused her,* he decided. *It's better if I don't make sense. She can go on thinking I'm crazy.*

As he walked out of her reach and lay on the ground, Mary shook her head in disbelief. *Make that a paranoid schizophrenic,* she decided. Oh well, at least Taz II was human.

"Hey, little bitch," he called over. "You married?"

When she glanced over, she noticed that he seemed to be writing—-no, drawing. The stroke of the pencil looked like drawing. "Divorced," she responded, reaching into the pockets of the jacket out of curiosity. There was a granola bar in the right pocket and the antiseptic cream was in the left pocket.

"What do you do for a living?"

*Must be question and answer period,* Mary thought. *Oh well, can't hurt.* "I teach aerobics part time."

"What about the rest of the time?"

"I work as a clerk with a company that makes parts for that space arm. But I've been on sick leave." *Why did I tell him that? Damn it!*

"What for?"

*It's too late to take it back now,* Mary knew, *and I'm too tired to make up lies.* "Stress."

There was no response for a moment, then Taz II spoke again. "The divorce?"

*Sure, spill your guts to a lunatic. What difference does it make?* "Partly. My son was killed and I lost interest in life. By the time I stopped blaming my husband for my son's death, my husband had found someone else."

Taz II had folded his drawings and put them in his shirt pocket. He turned on his side as if to sleep. Mary heard him mutter what sounded like "a fucking Canadian tourist, middle class aerobics instructor, off for stress because her kid died." She didn't know whether that meant he did not believe her, but she couldn't have cared less. He obviously was not planning to rape her again tonight, and that was all she needed to know.

"By the way," he added, "you can have anything I leave in those jacket pockets. It's a reward for good behaviour."

Mary thought a few choice obscenities, ate the granola bar and fell to sleep.

Aaron turned onto his back and stared up at the stars. Tomorrow he would take the jacket back and hide the drawing in the inner lining. Lacking a camera, he planned to draw all the rebels for identification purposes later. Drawing also helped him relax. He had given Mary the jacket to keep her warm during the night, but there was another benefit to doing that. If Osvaldo had any remaining doubts, he would never expect Aaron to let any evidence out of his possession. Osvaldo had searched Aaron's possessions carefully, but had missed the jacket lining. Once he noticed Aaron letting Mary wear the jacket, he would not suspect it to contain anything important.

*I cannot keep talking to Mary,* Aaron knew, wishing he could sleep, but knowing he wouldn't. Sleep seemed an impossibility after today. Getting to know Mary as a person would only make his job much harder, and it was too hard already. Unbidden, thoughts of Susan crept into his conscious. He had been trying to keep them at bay, but now her vision floated into his mind, and his conscience cringed. *Susan, how will I ever be able to touch you again without remembering this? How will I even be able to tell you about it?* Aaron knew if he survived until Sunday that he had to tell Tony all about this. It would affect his credibility, and the rebels had seen him do it. Incredible as it seemed now, Aaron suspected that his actions would one day be public knowledge and Susan would know if he hadn't told her first. His life, as he knew it, was over. Today he had crossed a terrible line, one that he had never wanted to cross.

To punish him, his mind went further, taking him to a small house in Maine, where two good people, who were his parents, waited for his letters. He could imagine his letters now. *Dear Dad…I know you always told me that women were gentle creatures that I should love and cherish, but instead I decided to assault and humiliate one.* Aaron groaned. Why was it that when you needed the people you loved the most, they were the ones you couldn't bear to talk to? How would he ever look his parents in the eyes again?

And Nat. Where was Nat? Nat was depending on him, but Aaron didn't know where to find him. Was he hurt tonight? Was he scared? Was he waiting for Aaron to find him and set him free? Aaron rolled over and laid his head on his arms. *They took you while I was putting on their show, Nat. How can I help you when I don't know where they've hidden you? They don't trust me that much yet. I've searched all around this area. You're gone. Please don't die on me. Give me a chance to help.*

Eventually he must have fallen asleep, because when Aaron awoke it was morning and the start of another hell day.

# XIII

Anthony Dune sat in Carl Walsh's office, bringing his boss up to date on the various covert actions that needed Walsh's approval, or were significant enough that Walsh needed up-to-date briefing. Cuba was but one of the many operations that staff were currently undertaking, and Cuba was by no means one of the biggest. However, Tony was directly responsible for the Cuba assignment and Cuba was a thorn in the Company's side, so Walsh had taken a personal interest in it.

While they were talking, a knock on the door interrupted them, and Mr. Walsh called the person in. It was Scott, which surprised Tony. It was very unusual for a junior officer to disrupt a briefing session, but Tony noticed that Scott entered confidently, as if he knew he should be interrupting. Accustomed since birth to being around powerful business people, it took a lot to make that young man feel uncomfortable.

"Yes, Scott?"

"Sorry to interrupt sir," Scott addressed both men, "but we have some information we think you may wish to know."

Tony had directed Scott to coordinate with the FBI and try to discover all the individuals and companies involved with the Sierra Maestra Liberators. "What is it?"

At Mr. Walsh's indication, Scott came over and took a chair at the desk. "About Cuba, sir. A signal was received requesting Mr. Moseley's intervention for Sunday afternoon at 2:00 p.m. Then the signal died. It appears that the transmitter is down."

That caught the attention of the two men. "Broken?" Mr. Walsh asked, casting a concerned glance in Tony's direction.

"Yes, sir," Scott answered. "Mr. Moseley is preparing his team now. But there's more," Scott continued. "Mr. Dune asked me to trace the contacts and intermediaries involved with the rebel group in Cuba. One of the FBI men stumbled upon a contact with direct links to Congressman Harvey."

"I beg your pardon?" Mr. Walsh was clearly shocked.

"*Richard* Harvey?" Tony demanded, aghast. Harvey was a powerful player in Washington. He was also a vocal supporter of the CIA.

Mr. Walsh did not want to believe this. "Mr. Andrews, are we SURE about this?"

Scott continued to deliver his message in a matter-of-fact tone. "Sir, the FBI have uncovered information that suggests Mr. Harvey is actually arranging a secret trip to Cuba on Sunday."

"Sunday." It was Tony's comment. Two events of that magnitude happening on the same day could not be coincidence.

There was no sound in the room for almost a minute. Knowing his seniors were running the implications through their minds, Scott waited quietly.

Finally Mr. Walsh spoke. "I need absolute verification on this one, Tony. We cannot walk up to Richard Harvey with this kind of accusation unless the proof is rock solid."

"Yes, sir," Tony responded.

"A Congressman going to Cuba on the sly," Mr. Walsh mused. "Incredible. Why the hell would he take a risk like that? What is he up to, or perhaps I should ask what has he gotten himself into?"

Walsh and Tony stared at each other. Tony said it first. "I know, sir. We've got something important going on down there, and we underestimated. We have only two officers on site, one of whom is relatively new to Covert Operations, and we have a one-way transmitter that is now broken."

"And it's an unfriendly country for us," Walsh added. "We can't ask that government for help, and we cannot walk in openly, say, 'Excuse us,' and go to our officers' aid. It is already a huge risk sneaking Moseley's team in and out, and it has everyone very nervous." For a minute he stared at the ceiling. "Suggestions, Tony?"

*Why didn't I arrange better backup?* Tony asked himself. *Why didn't I listen to Frank? It was supposed to be a routine investigation, except for the country involved. They were supposed to find out exactly who was involved by completing the deals, try to find out what had happened to James, then return with the information. Just a little investigation into a group trying to blackmail US businesses. Frank never trusted anything in that country. I should have listened to Frank. Too late now.*

"Leave it as it stands, sir," he responded to Walsh. "If Harvey really is planning to go there, why ruin his fun? We can catch him at the scene. It sounds like our people know he is coming there. If we go in too early, we'll ruin that. If our people were in trouble, the signal would not have specified Sunday, it would have been immediate. Our danger, of course, is that Nathanial and Aaron now have no way of altering the signal to us if they get in trouble. They'll be on their own, but they are both resourceful. Nathanial was instructed to leave at the first sign of trouble. They are both capable of living in hiding for a few days."

Mr. Walsh was nodding. "All right, let's go with what they requested and hit hard and fast on Sunday. But, Tony, make sure Moseley is briefed on what we know and remind him how crucial this entry and exit is. I want our men out of there safely, and I'd hate to miss catching Richard Harvey in the act."

# XIV

Friday morning started quietly enough for Mary. Taz woke up as Taz II and took her to the latrine without comment. Then he demanded his jacket back and went into the cabin. Things were quiet for about an hour. The sun was warm in the morning, there were birds singing and the air was fresh. Inevitably the cabin door was thrown open to ruin the peace of the day, and Alfredo came out, laughing and heading in the direction of the women.

Alfredo was yelling in Spanish to Juany, saying obscene things, and Juany was yelling back. It was a horrible conversation to listen to. Then Alfredo hit Juany hard in the jaw. Since they were only about three feet away from her, Mary was forced to listen to the following slaps and punches. She moved away as far as the ropes would allow, but it only gave her another foot. Mary prayed that Alfredo would stop hitting, but then to her horror Mary saw him take out a knife. When he deliberately cut a two-inch gash in Juany's face, Mary screamed in terror. In an instant she realised her mistake.

"You want the knife too, bitch?" Alfredo threatened her in Spanish, turning and waving the knife.

Panic welled up in Mary as he approached, his eyes cold and expressionless. There was a sickening grin on his face. The knife was inches from her face.

"Such a pretty face. Such a shame to ruin it."

"No, please!" Instinctively, Mary put up her hands to try to protect herself, but help came from a surprising source.

"Alfredo, my friend—what'cha doin'?" Taz was there, a hand on Alfredo's wrist. "Don't do that, man. I hate an ugly bitch." He stood close to Alfredo with a leer on his face. "Man, when I have a bitch do a blow job for me and I look down, I like to see a pretty face. Nothin' worse than looking down at something ugly, man."

Alfredo snorted. "Didn't mean to touch your property, my friend, but I was pissed off and she got in my way."

Taz looked menacingly at Mary. "Well, if she pisses you off, my friend, you make sure you tell me. That means she needs more training. I'll take care of her for you."

"Yeh," Alfredo laughed, looking a Juany. "This one needs to be taught a lesson too. I think it's time for some fun, right?"

"Yeh, time for fun," Taz responded. The usual audience had joined them. Not all the rebels raped, Aaron noticed. There seemed to be seven regulars. The others stayed away, and Aaron was matching names to faces for future reference. If not all the rebels could be removed to the United States for trial, he wanted to be sure which ones should come, and which could be left behind. With an effort he turned his mind back to the task at hand.

In his hand, Aaron was still holding a greasy piece of bread that was supposed to be breakfast. It was lathered in a tasteless butter, and his stomach had rebelled at it. It was barely edible, but it gave him an idea.

"Okay, bitch," Taz yelled, "let's party." He brought out his knife and sliced the rope that fastened her to the tree. Then he grabbed her hair, paused to put the knife away and let her grab his wrists, then pulled her about twenty feet away. "Kneel," he commanded.

Making no effort not to cry, Mary obeyed. What now? At least he had saved her from the knife, but what torment would she have to endure for it this time? He was laughing and talking like a lunatic again. This was Taz I, and he was terrifying. It was going to be awful.

"Had breakfast yet, bitch?" Taz unzipped his pants, pulled out his penis and wrapped a piece of bread around it. "Want a sandwich?"

Mary leaned away. What the hell was he doing? What did he want from her? For Pete's sake, couldn't the guy just have sex and be done with it?

"Not hungry, bitch?" Taz slapped Mary across the face. It almost knocked her off balance. "Get those clothes off—NOW!"

Face stinging, tears flowing and her breath coming in gasps, Mary somehow removed her clothes.

She was sitting on the ground. Taz grabbed her hair again, forcing her to lean back. Then he rubbed her crotch with the bread. It was greasy. His wild face was only inches from hers. "Or maybe you prefer girl smell," he snarled at her. When Mary didn't respond, but only stared at him, Taz wrapped his hands around her throat. "Not talking? All choked up?"

Taz moved his hands to her armpits, and with surprising ease Mary found herself lifted from a sitting position right up until her feet were about three feet off the ground. She shrieked, expecting to be thrown again. Instead, Taz walked over to a large tree and shoved her against the trunk. He leaned against her torso, then put his hands around her throat again. All the time he was cackling and whooping. Mary's back was scraped against the bark, but she dared not move. If Taz moved back, all her weight would be borne by her throat.

"This is fun, isn't it, bitch? Now you're not short any more. If I drop you, you know where you'll land, don't you?" Taz positioned himself beneath her, and let her settle onto him. "There, that's what you've been waiting for, isn't it?"

Mary's back was taking the brunt of this. As he let her down so he could penetrate her, she heard one of Taz II's terse commands. "Wrap your legs around me." She obeyed. Taz II expected to be obeyed. Now he was supporting her weight, although her back still rubbed the tree. She groaned with each thrust, but with all the grease that had been smeared on them, it wasn't the thrusts that were hurting. It was her back. *It'll be over soon,* she told herself, as she gritted her teeth. *At least I only have to do this once. It'll be over in a couple of minutes.*

It was done. "Over," Taz II whispered. His hands were on her waist. Mary felt him pull her forward against his shoulders. She leaned there in relief. Over for a while. The back was scrapped, but otherwise she had survived. They were both breathing heavily for different reasons. Alfredo and his friends were clearly amused at the show. *Sadistic animals,* she thought. She refused to look at Juany, afraid of what she would see. *They are going to kill her,* Mary knew. *She's not a human being to them.*

Taz drew a deep breath and let her down. He then took her to a royal palm further from Juany then before, and tied her to the new tree. When Mary looked at her previous place, Taz II grunted. "You don't need to watch that." Then Taz brought over her clothes and the roll of toilet paper. The others were wandering away, realising that the show was over. Taz handed Mary the whiskey flask, and commanded her to drink. She sipped it gratefully, returned the flask to him and was left in peace.

Inside the cabin, Aaron put his head in his hands. He kept an ear tuned for Mary in case anyone outside tried to touch her. They had to get through this afternoon and tomorrow. Help came on Sunday. How many more times would he have to put on a show? Hurting her was eating him alive inside. He reached for a bottle of rum, but changed his mind. *No alcohol. You're not going to start drinking right now.* It was important to try to stay alert for Mary's sake, for his own sake, and for Nat's sake, if he were still alive. The lack of sleep last night was probably going to be repeated tonight. Most of the food stuck in his throat. He had lost his appetite. He knew he was very close to giving up in despair. If he did, Nat and Mary would be left to the hounds, and nothing would be accomplished for it. He had to remember that. And he had to put on these theatrics with Mary or Alfredo might want her for himself. He shuddered. He had seen the Cuban girl. She wouldn't live to see Sunday.

By not letting anyone know she spoke Spanish, Mary occasionally picked up bits and pieces of conversations as the Cubans came outside to swim or drink in the shade. Alfredo had a loud voice that matched his personality, and he talked more than the others. That afternoon, Taz was swimming at the base of the waterfall. Alfredo came out to sit beside the Cuban they called Lino, who was playing a guitar and humming a Cuban folk song. Lino had brought his guitar out yesterday evening as well, and chose a spot halfway between the women and the cabin. Since she had not seen him anywhere near Juany during the assaults, Mary realised that this man was not a personal threat to her, so she had relaxed and listened to his music.

Now, Alfredo seemed to be goading Lino. Mary had a feeling that Lino did not approve of Alfredo and Alfredo sensed this.

"What do you think of the present I gave Taz?" he asked Lino, pointing at Mary. "He was surprised, wasn't he? It was a good surprise."

At first, it appeared that Lino was not going to answer, but then he did. "A surprise, yes," he said without emotion.

"Taz did well for us by convincing Congressman Harvey to come here on Sunday," Alfredo said proudly. "Did you know," he continued, slapping Lino's shoulder, "that this Congressman is believed to be a big law and order man in the United States? He is known to support the CIA. What a laugh—if they only knew!" It was too ironic to Alfredo, and he started to laugh, which caused him to choke on his cerveza. "For many years the Congressman has been working with the Cuban government, using some contacts he has in the CIA. Boy, you can't trust anybody in that outfit. They do not know what each other is doing. Mr. Harvey knows how to stay rich."

"What do you want him here for?" Lino asked.

"Can you be so stupid?" Alfredo demanded incredulously. "We have told him we can remove Castro, and he believes us. He will give us lots of money."

"Not once he sees how small we are," Lino protested.

"Ahhh, fool," Alfredo stated rudely. "He will give us money because we will not let him return unless his government pays a big price for him. In the meantime, we will find out all he knows about our own government that we can use, and he will tell us the people in the CIA that will work for us." Alfredo waved away a raven-like toti that had landed near him. "Oh yes," he concluded, "the Congressman will be a great help to us."

Now Alfredo got up to leave. "Jose Luis is impressed with Taz. He will be most happy when he learns on Sunday that Osvaldo was wrong in his suspicions." With that, Alfredo left Lino to his songs.

Mary did not know the names of any US Congressmen, but the conversation had been chilling. During the day she had heard various Cubans mention drugs and guns, but this sounded much more sinister. Who were these people, and what on earth would a Congressman be doing here? It was her first clue that Taz was new to this group. Alfredo had made him sound like an outsider, and if he was involved in talking a Congressman into coming here, Taz was very probably American.

Judging by the sun, it was only slightly past noon when Mary noticed two Cubans laughing and walking towards her. Lino was nowhere in sight, and Taz had strolled off about half an hour ago. At first, Mary suspected that Juany was in for more abuse, but when they were closer, Mary heard them referring to her.

*No, oh no! They aren't supposed to touch me.* Mary drew back from them. "Leave me alone," she cried in Spanish. "Stop it!"

They had no intention of listening, and started grabbing at her, one trying to pin her down while the other struggled with her clothes. For some reason she didn't stop to analyze, she screamed at the top of her lungs. "TAZ!"

It startled the Cubans for only a few seconds, then they recovered and renewed their attack. Mary tried to fight, but didn't have a chance, and was losing badly when Taz hollered from the pathway and dashed over.

"Hey, hey, hey—none of that," he said as he pulled one Cuban off her with surprising ease. "She's mine, boys. Alfredo's present."

They must have sensed the warning in his voice, because they backed off, almost apologetically, muttering, "Sorry," and giving excuses. Alfredo's orders were not to be trifled with, and the American was no weakling.

Then Taz turned to Mary. She knew he was angry and he had people watching him. This would not be good. It did not surprise her to be slapped and grabbed by the hair. Taz dragged her about thirty feet from the tree and ordered her to "sit." Mary sat and waited, her face stinging, her heart racing again. *It will end,* she told herself. *It always ends eventually.*

"What did I tell you about two-timing me?" Taz demanded in a rage. "You're nothing but a slut!" Then he leaned down towards her. "Or maybe you want these guys, is that it? Is it?"

"No," Mary pleaded.

"Take the clothes off!"

Off with the clothes again. Again the racing heart, the panic and the sweating palms. *Is it possible to die of fright?* Mary wondered? Taz grabbed her clothes and threw them towards the tree.

"Don't look at me!"

It was a Taz II order. Mary obeyed instantly and turned her head as far around as she could, looking at the mountains. Shivering, she waited.

"You think those guys want you? Well, let's see how desirable they find you now."

He was not even finished speaking when she felt it. Warm, wet and disgusting. Oh God, he was urinating on her! This was really too much to bear. She kept her head turned and began to cry. It was making her feel subhuman. This wasn't something you did to a person. She had no dignity left. When he finished, the Cubans laughed and walked off. The fun was over for them. Mary wouldn't look at Taz. It would be too degrading to see him laughing over this.

"Back to the tree," he ordered. His voice held no expression.

Mary walked back. She had never felt so dirty in her life. Taz said nothing further, but tied her to the tree without letting her put her clothes on. She didn't want them on her body now. Her body was too dirty. After he walked away, Mary sat in the heat of the Cuban afternoon in abject misery. Why couldn't he just kill her? She would welcome that now. She smelled terribly, and her skin was hot and sticky. Why had he done that?

After about an hour, Taz returned with a towel and a bar of soap. She no longer cared what he did to her. He said nothing as he untied her, and she wouldn't look at him. Defiant, she decided not to move. He would have to force her.

"Come on, little bitch. You smell. Let's have a bath." It was Taz II.

Mary felt herself start to cry again. *This man is tormenting me.* "Why did you do that?" she whispered. *Go ahead; hit me for questioning you. I don't care any more.*

Taz didn't answer her, but grasped her arm and dragged her up gently this time. "Let's go," he said as he led her towards the water. At the edge of the water, he released her arm. Mary stood still and waited. "In you go," Taz directed.

Knowing it would feel cool and delightful, Mary waded in. Blissfully, she jumped into deeper water, held her breath and dove down to get totally wet. She kept a wary eye on Taz, waiting for orders, but he was sitting on a log staring into the waterfall. Only when voices could be heard around the cabin did he stir.

94

"Come out now," was the next command.

Mary obeyed instantly. *I feel like a well-trained dog,* she thought angrily.

"Sit," was next. So she sat. He had a bar of soap, which he rubbed into a lather and then rubbed on her wet skin. *He wasn't kidding,* Mary realised with astonishment. *I'm actually getting a bath.* Like any good little dog, she sat as he scrubbed her down. While he did, Mary looked around in pleasure at the blue sky and steep, jagged cliffs with auras, the turkey vultures, flying overhead. The waterfall had created a clear, sparkling pond beneath it, and the mosses growing on the rocks underneath and around the falls created an iridescent green and blue effect. *Beautiful,* Mary thought. *Too beautiful for so much horror.*

Taz had rubbed soap in her hair. As he finished, Mary heard Alfredo's voice.

"What the 'ell you doing, man?"

"She stinks," Taz responded.

"Yeh, so I heard."

"She's getting a bath," Taz continued. "We've got a date tonight."

Alfredo walked over. "You know, Taz, you are really weird."

Taz stared up at him. "I get bored," he stated. "And you know how I can't be in a small room with those damned cigarettes."

"No offence," protested Alfredo. "She's a good-looking bitch," he added, running his eyes over Mary's soapy body.

*Burn in hell,* Mary wished. *You brutal, subhuman piece of slime.*

Alfredo saw her look. "Ooh, she's a wild one," he taunted.

"She's under control," Taz responded. "She's getting well trained."

This amused Alfredo, who slapped Taz on the back and strolled to the cabin. Taz continued to rub soap into Mary's hair in silence. It was badly tangled, and his fingers kept getting caught.

"Rinse," he ordered.

*So much for the purity of the environment,* Mary reflected, as she went into the water. It took a couple of submersions to rid her hair of soap. When she came out she felt alive again.

"Sit."

*Roll over,* she thought. But she sat without a word, the passive, well-trained victim hoping to avoid brutality. When he pulled out his knife, she started to shake. Taz II had never pulled out his knife with her.

"Relax, little bitch," he said. "You need a haircut."

*A haircut? This oughta be good,* Mary thought. *Now he's a hairdresser with a switchblade. Oh well, hair always grows back...if you're alive.* She would sit still for the haircut.

It was going to be a bad haircut, Mary knew, as Taz hacked away at the tangles that wouldn't seem to come out in his fingers. This man was no barber. She contented herself with trying to name the plants that were growing around the water.

Suddenly the quiet day was interrupted by a man's scream from the cabin. Mary jumped, bumping Taz's arm, which had stopped its cutting movements at the sound of the scream. Laughter followed from the cabin, but above her head Mary heard Taz curse. She looked up at him and panicked. An inch-long knife gash had appeared below his left eye, and she had caused it by jumping. She had cut him with his own knife and nearly put his eye out. Now he would retaliate, she knew. He would cut her face with the knife just like Alfredo had cut Juany.

"I'm sorry," she pleaded. "I didn't mean to do it. It was an accident. I'm sorry, I'm sorry." It was getting hard to breathe, she was so scared. He was wiping at his face, smearing the blood, but *he had put the knife away. Thank You, God,* Mary prayed. Taz's jacket was beside her, and Mary quickly found a Kleenex and the antiseptic cream. She tentatively touched the wound with the Kleenex. Would he let her help? Yes, he did. Taz glared at her, but let her press the edges of the wound together to stop the bleeding. Her hands were shaking so badly that she could hardly keep them in place.

"It was an accident, little bitch," he said simply.

The knife had been sharp, and the cut was thin. It finally stopped bleeding and Mary applied the cream. Taz seemed to have no desire to do any more hairdressing. Mary's hair had been shoulder length, but it was shorter now. She had no wish to look in a mirror. The sun was now low in the horizon. It had been an emotionally tiring day. Taz led her back to the tree and let her put her clothes on. He seemed almost human when he helped her put his jacket on. Then he tied her up. Taz had said very little during the afternoon, but Mary had the strangest sensation that he was feeling guilty. It didn't make sense, and she was probably imagining it. Or maybe it went with the schizophrenic personality. Didn't much matter, Mary decided. Taz II was much preferable to Taz I.

After he walked away, Mary searched the pockets. Two granola bars this time. *Definitely guilty. Strange man.*

# XV

A few minutes after Aaron had settled down under a tree near the cabin with a beer, the sound of horses caught his attention. At the end of the path, Osvaldo came into view on horseback, leading another horse that carried a man who looked unwell. It was Nat. Aaron forced himself not to jump up and run to him. Slowly he got to his feet and stretched.

One of the rebels helped Osvaldo remove Nat from the horse. It appeared to Aaron that Nat was alive, but he fell to the ground and had to be dragged. Nat was unable to walk, and Osvaldo was trying to decide where to put him.

"Tie him with the bitch," Taz offered. "That way we can keep an eye on everyone at once."

It must have made sense to Osvaldo, because to Aaron's relief Osvaldo and the rebel half carried, half dragged Nat to the tree beside Mary. The fact that Nat was still alive and Osvaldo was paying little attention to Aaron reassured Aaron that his cover was still intact, but the next few minutes could be critical. If he was safe, he would get Nat and Mary out of here tonight.

They secured Nat to the tree beside Mary. She was watching with a look of horror on her face. No wonder. Nat had been beaten. His feet had no shoes and they were swollen and blue. It took all of Aaron's self-control not to take his knife and slice Osvaldo's throat from ear to ear. It would not help. Not now. There were too many rebels watching. *Later,* he promised himself. *I'll kill him for you later, Nat. Promise.*

Osvaldo looked at the women, then looked at Aaron. A quiver of fear travelled down Aaron's back, but Osvaldo's words were unexpected. "I'd rather deal with him than work with you," he stated venomously, pointing at Nat. "At least he's got guts. You are scum." He turned and led the others away.

Aaron nearly lost it. *I'm scum? After what you did to him?* He took a step after Osvaldo, ready to tear him to pieces, but a groan from Nat stopped him in his tracks. Aaron turned to his friend, but again had to control himself. It would be suicide to appear to be too concerned about Nat. Nat was watching him, breathing shallowly and leaning back against the tree. Mary was sitting quietly, a sad look on her face as she studied Nat. *I cannot stay here right now,* Aaron knew, exchanging a look with Nat. *I'll be back, Nat, promise.* He spoke to Mary, but held Nat's pained gaze. "I'll be back a bit later, little bitch. Better watch this guy, he looks dangerous." That earned him another of those incredulous looks of hers before he turned away.

Once Taz had left, Mary examined the man tied to the tree immediately beside her. The royal palms in this area were developing quite a history of hostage-holding. It did not seem fitting for such a magnificent tree to be so badly used. This poor man beside her had been hurt a lot. His breathing was laboured, his feet were a mess, and the rest of his visible body was badly bruised. He was looking at her, though, so he was still alive.

Mary moved as close to him as she could. *He must be terribly scared,* she decided. *Maybe he'd like someone to talk to.* "Hi. My name is Mary."

"Nathanial," he breathed.

"Are you hurt inside, too?" she asked.

"Probably," was the answer. He managed to straighten himself up a bit against the palm tree. "Are you badly hurt, dear?"

*Why are you worrying about me?* she wondered. *You can see there is no comparison between our injuries.* "No," she answered. "Nothing like you. I only have to put up with one of them, and at least he doesn't beat me." She glanced toward where Juany lay and shuddered. "Not like they do to that poor girl."

That seemed to relieve Nathanial. "I'm glad. Does he frighten you?"

To her chagrin, Mary felt tears well up. Really, he needn't waste energy concerning himself with her. But she heard herself reply anyway. "Yes, he terrifies me. I don't know what he wants. He's like a crazy person, and I can't figure him out. I try to do what he wants, but it's different every time. He's raped me twice and made me do other stuff."

"I'm so sorry, my dear." Nathanial reached over and touched her hand. "Well, at least I've been spared the agony of watching that," he stated in a lifeless voice.

Carefully, trying not to hurt the bruised hand, Mary closed her own hand around it. He was so nice. "It's not so bad," she said bravely, feeling badly for complaining to him. "I can bear it. If only he wouldn't use the knife. It scares me so!"

"Has he used it yet?"

"No," she admitted, "but it's always around my face and…other areas. If I don't do what he wants, he might use it. But I don't know what he wants!" She swallowed and sniffed.

Nathanial smiled at her. "He may just be trying to intimidate you, my dear." He was quiet for a moment, then spoke again. "Do you think he could be putting on a show for these guys? You know, trying to look tough to them?"

"Maybe." It was possible. "But he's like a madman. You never know what he's going to do, and I can't think of anything when that knife is near me."

"Well, my dear," Nathanial continued, "I want you to do something for me."

"What?"

"I think that if Taz has not used the knife yet, then he has no intention of doing so. I think it's all part of some tough guy act." Nathanial managed a smile. "The next time he has his knife out, I want you to think of me. Think of me, and remember that I don't believe he'll use it. Can you do that?"

"I'll try," Mary promised.

They talked for almost an hour. Actually, Nathanial seemed too tired to talk much, so Mary held his hand and did most of the talking, telling him the names of the lizards with curly tails, the bayoyas, the toti birds and the various trees and bushes around them. It was wonderful to have company.

So engrossed was she in talking with her pleasant visitor, that Mary did not notice Taz approach until he was a short distance away. Mary panicked and snatched her hand away from Nathanial.

"What's the matter, dear?" Her action had surprised Nathanial.

"It's Taz. He's going to be mad. I shouldn't have been touching you. It was one of his rules." She could hear the panic in her own voice.

"My dear, I don't think he'll care," Nathanial assured her. "I'm no threat to him."

*Poor man,* thought Mary. *Don't upset him. He's put up with too much already.* "Look," she whispered, "don't mind about it, please. He doesn't hurt me too badly. Just don't look."

Aaron had reached them. Seeing Mary holding Nat's hand had given him a perfect excuse to come over. He put on a subdued Taz act. "Little bitch, you're holding on to a corpse, you know. He's a dead man."

When she heard his voice, Mary stopped cringing. It was Taz II. Perhaps she wasn't going to be punished.

Taz was looking at Nathanial's feet. "Well, Bowman, it looks like someone did not like you."

"Osvaldo," Nathanial breathed. "He's not finished yet, either. Thinks I have more things to talk about. Tomorrow he wants to have another chat."

"Mm." Taz was quiet for a minute. "Can you walk?" he asked suddenly. Nathanial sighed. "Not a prayer."

This news seemed to agitate Taz, Mary noticed. He turned his back to her and stood with his hands clenched. Nathanial continued to speak to his back. "I really have only two hopes left in this world," Nathanial said slowly, as if daydreaming. "To die in my sleep, and to be buried in my hometown in Kentucky."

Taz seemed to be stuffed up, because Mary heard him sniff. He was staring intently off into the hills. Then there was a movement beside the cabin, as a couple of Cubans got up and stretched. Taz coughed and spun around. "Bathroom, bitch," he ordered hoarsely, untying her. This time he half dragged her to the location, avoiding her gaze. *He's upset about something,* Mary knew, *but thank goodness it has nothing to do with me.*

Before retying her, Taz ordered Mary to stand still beside the tree. He quickly grabbed an extra length of rope from her previous tree. Now when he tied her, she had another two feet of leeway. It seemed peculiar, but she sure wasn't going to argue. She sat down in the same place she had been, but Taz glared at her.

"Hey, bitch, I thought you wanted to hold hands. This man is your guest. The least you can do is be nice to him. What kind of hostess are you?" Taz pointed towards Nathanial. "Get over there and hold the corpse's hand."

Mary scooted over. This Taz was nuts. *Hostess? Guest? Sure, Taz, whatever you say. It's an easy order to follow.* She was close to Nathanial now, and, remembering to take his hand carefully so as not to hurt it, she rested it on her leg with her own hand covering his. *Happy now, Taz?*

Nathanial sighed again and gave her a little pat. "Thanks," he whispered, but his eyes were closed, so Mary didn't know if he was thanking her or Taz.

"I sleep out here, Bowman. To make sure the little bitch doesn't get away," Taz informed. "She's usually asleep before 10:00 p.m."

"See you later, then," Nathanial responded in a weak voice.

Taz turned and strode away.

"He's weird," Mary told Nathanial. "I think he's schizophrenic. He's like two different people."

Nathanial opened an eye. "Well, my dear, it looks like you'd better keep playing along with him. It seems he's the only thing keeping you alive out here." His voice trailed off. He needed to sleep, but first he wanted to say one more thing. "Mary, if you get out of this place, will you do me a favour?"

"Of course," Mary promised.

"If you meet...a man who knows me named Tony...give him my love. Tell him it wasn't his fault. And should you... meet a man named Frank...tell him he was right...but not to feel bad about it. Will you do that, Mary?"

"Promise," Mary responded. "Now go to sleep. You need rest."

About an hour later, Mary saw Lino approaching. He had been playing his Cuban folk songs with a few Cuban-style North American songs thrown in. Since Lino always kept his distance from her, Mary did not worry about him. This was the first time he had walked over to her, so Mary watched him warily. He pulled an orange out of his pocket and peeled it slowly, speaking at Nathanial as he did so.

"This is not a good place for you to be, Mr. Bowman," he stated quietly in Spanish.

Nathanial had been dozing, but currently was awake. He looked curiously at the Cuban. "No," he replied cautiously.

Lino pulled the orange into sections, and handed Mary a piece. Surprised, she took it gratefully. As Lino had reached down towards her, Mary had noticed a gun tucked into his belt. It seemed that Nathanial's eyes spotted it too. Then Lino spoke again.

"It doesn't have to be like this. There are people you could be helpful. ..." He broke off abruptly, hearing the cabin door open. Casually, he broke off another piece of orange and once again gave it to Mary.

Taz had come outside, seen Lino's back, and started on a direct line towards them. As Lino turned slowly and glared at him, Taz stopped. Lino then proceeded to give Mary the rest of the orange and returned to his normal sitting place. Taz also seemed to change his plans, and walked towards the latrine. Mary looked at Nathanial, who seemed as puzzled as Mary had felt. She wondered what Lino had been going to say. Oh well, the orange had been a nice snack.

Late that night, Mary heard Taz approach. She was having trouble getting to sleep, thinking about Nathanial and Juany and her own position here. Nathanial seemed to be sleeping, and Mary lay on her side facing him. She was keeping very quiet so he wouldn't waken. The moon was just a slice tonight, and she was lying in the shadow of the royal palm. Nathanial was lying in the moonlight, partially propped against the base of the his tree.

Taz did not go to his usual spot. Instead he knelt on the far side of Nathanial. Mary was surprised to see him touch the older man's shoulder and wake him up. Mary decided to lie very still and pretend to sleep until she figured out what was going on.

"I'm getting you out of here," Aaron whispered in Nat's ear.

"Impossible," was Nat's response.

Aaron felt his heart sink. "I'll carry you. I can hide you somewhere and go for help or hide with you."

"Give it up, Aaron." Nat looked kindly into his young friend's face. "It's 250 kilometres to the base. You can't stop anywhere without paperwork to protect you. Besides, if we're both missing you know perfectly well the operation has been wasted and Jose Luis won't rest until he finds us. I can't travel, and if you move me Moseley's team won't find me. You can't reach the base in time to inform them of the new situation." He grimaced. "And how long do you think we could hide from them even if you did stay with me? I can't move around to get away from them, and we would absolutely have to be close by if we hoped to be rescued."

Aaron was silent. *My God, to have Nat back and now I can't even help him. How can I have let this happen? There must have been an answer I missed.* He felt Nat's eyes on him. It was hard to meet them.

"However did you not talk?" Clearly, Nat had suffered greatly today. Carefully Aaron took his hands to examine them. Anger surged through him.

"Oh, I talked," Nat admitted. "Believe me, I talked all day." He stared at his feet. "Osvaldo is brutal, but fortunately he is not sophisticated enough to ask the right questions. He was too focused on what we knew about them. Nothing I said today did any real damage to us." Pulling his hands back, he took a couple of breaths and coughed.

"I can't take another day of their torture. You know that, Aaron. I think I only survived today because I knew you were depending on me." He waited until Aaron looked directly at him. "Don't let me die by their hand, Aaron. Please."

Aaron knew what Nat was asking—had known it since this afternoon. It was inconceivable, but he knew. "I...can't..." he choked.

"Yes, you can", Nat insisted quietly. Always calm, always the teacher, Nat spoke as if to a child. "You know how. You only have to find the courage to do it."

"Not...you. Don't ask...don't..." Yet Aaron knew it was the only sure way out for Nat. He knew he had to.

Somehow Nat continued to smile as if he was making the most natural request in the world. He continued to speak softly and calmly. "It's okay, Aaron, it really is. I know that you love me enough to do this."

With a groan and a breaking heart, Aaron accepted his duty to his friend. He shifted his position so that Nat was resting back against the left side of

Aaron's chest. Aaron kept up a steady murmur of encouragement into Nat's hair as his hands guided Nat's neck into the best position to expose one of the carotid arteries. "I'm right here with you, Nat. Don't worry, I'll be with you until the end. It won't hurt, I'm right here." He never stopped murmuring. Nat had relaxed completely in his arms, and had placed a hand on Aaron's left wrist as if to comfort him. Aaron kept his left arm around Nat's shoulders and leaned his head against Nat as if protecting him from the cool night air. It was impossible to do, but somehow Aaron made his fingers find their mark. He closed his eyes and held his friend close as he pressed.

It took only seconds, but it touched Aaron's life as permanently as it ended Nat's. Nat was alive in his arms; then he was dead.

Mary lay totally still in shock. What was this? These two men had been friends! Why? And who was Aaron? Aaron had just killed his friend and had hated doing it, and Nathanial had asked him to. Something to do with not wanting to tell things to Osvaldo, who was torturing him. Nathanial had told Mary not to be afraid of the knife because Taz was just putting on a show, and Nathanial knew what he was talking about because he knew that Taz was not Taz. Taz was Aaron. Or Aaron was Taz. But who was Aaron? Who had Nathanial been? And who was coming to rescue them on Sunday?

She heard Aaron stifle a sob. For heaven's sake, this man was not what he was pretending to be at all. He was human. Why had he pretended to be Taz? Why had he raped her? Now the schizophrenia made sense. There was no Taz I or Taz II. It was all Aaron Someone pretending to be somebody else. Putting on an act.

As Aaron finally walked away, Mary watched him. If she could find Aaron under the surface of Taz, perhaps there was hope. It explained so much to her—the lack of sexual arousal, the consideration for her when no one was around to watch the act, the lack of outright brutality. Now she could sleep. Where there was kindness there was hope. She mourned for the loss of Nathanial. Then she mourned for Aaron's pain at killing his friend.

In the morning, Mary woke to find a drawn-looking Taz—no, Aaron— standing close by. The sun was up; she had slept longer than usual. Nathanial's body was still tied to the royal palm. Perhaps Aaron planned to bury him. Nathanial had wanted his body taken home to Kentucky, but how could Aaron do that?

And who were they anyway? All the questions from last night came flooding back. This morning felt like a new beginning—a time of discovery.

Perhaps it would be safest for her to continue to view Aaron somebody as Taz, because otherwise she might ruin his act, and for some reason it seemed important for him to be Taz to the Cubans. Believing now that Aaron was only acting made Mary feel far more confident, although still very confused. However, she knew she might only be engaging in desperate wishful thinking, but the Aaron of last night surely could not be the mean creature that was Taz.

Taz "discovered" Nathanial's death and got a couple of the Cubans to help him remove Nathanial's body a decent distance away behind a clump of struggling orange and mango trees. Then came the usual morning routine of being led to the latrine and giving him back his jacket. Juany was not moving around much. Although not a very religious person, Mary found herself believing that Juany had more than paid for any sins she may have committed on earth that would have kept her from heaven.

What horrors would today bring? They seemed inevitable, but Mary felt she could face them today. She would look into Taz's face to find Aaron. Tomorrow they planned to kill her, but perhaps Aaron would help her.

Tied to her tree, Mary stared up at the leaves of the royal palm, that throughout their history had been used as thatch for roofs. An aura soared in the blue sky, looking for small prey below. After a while, her little friend the bayoya lizard came out of its hiding place and stared at her. It looked like a four-inch dinosaur with a curly tail, and was good company in this lonely place.

Today the morning was half gone before the perverts emerged from the cabin. Only Taz looked different. He seemed tired and lacking his usual nasty spirit. There had probably been little sleep in Aaron's night. Alfredo was in top form, grinning wickedly and addressing the general population. For the first time, Mary wished she did not understand Spanish. He was being crude, and he was goading Taz. Alfredo thought it was a lovely morning for anal sex.

Oh no! Mary's resolve not to be scared evaporated. That would be too horrible. As Taz reached her, she started shaking her head. She hadn't pleaded with him since the first day, but she was pleading now.

"No, please…don't do that," she begged, as he dragged her away.

"Shut up," Taz commanded, and slapped her. "Don't ever say no to me."

The slap had no force to it this time, but Mary hardly noticed. She had been wrong. This hard-looking man was no gentleman. Aaron must have been some third personality.

When they were behind some low bushes, Taz pushed her onto all fours. The Cubans were close, but the bushes gave her some concealment. She waited, trembling, for the pain, trying to block out Juany's feeble cries. Taz was in position and had yanked her track pants down to her knees, but then something surprising happened. He pushed close, but did not enter her. He did not even try. At the same time she realised this, he reached forward and twisted her breast. She screamed in pain and he released it immediately. Why did he do that? Now she was gasping in fright and confusion. What was she supposed to do? Then it dawned on her. *He's faking it, for heaven's sake, and I'm supposed to be in pain.* As his hand reached for her breast again, Mary simply screamed 'no', hoping it would go away. It did. Now her cries were tears of relief. She had found Aaron. *Follow his cues and do whatever he says.*

When the act was over, Aaron knelt beside Mary, holding her in his arms. He was shaking from exhaustion, relief that she had caught on, and fright that he was taking a huge risk with his cover. *This is dangerous,* he knew, *but I simply cannot hurt this woman any more. I've taken as much as I can bear in this hell. I need to be kind to her as much as she needs it from me.*

For the sake of appearances, Aaron pulled out his knife. Alfredo chose to look over at that moment. "Did she like it?" he asked Taz.

*Animal.* "Of course," Aaron answered. "I'm going to stay here and play with her for a while." He wiggled his knife to show his intentions. Again for appearances he ran the knife over Mary's body, closing it as he ran it between her legs. Alfredo walked away without further comment. Mary shivered in his arms, her right fist gripping the front of his shirt as the weight of her upper torso was supported by his right arm. Her head lay against his bicep. Suddenly she turned moist brown eyes on his face and murmured, "Thank you." It almost killed him. The things in life he had taken for granted! Of course any woman he held in his arms would feel safe, wouldn't she? Now he was being thanked by a woman for not hurting her. Inside he felt sick to death and lonely...horribly lonely in this hell.

"Shhh," he whispered. "That's okay...it wasn't my favourite kind of sex either." For a moment he was afraid she would question him, but she seemed content to lie quietly in his arms. As the rebels left, Aaron stroked her back with his left hand. Mary sighed and her brown eyes closed. *I know how you feel,* he thought. He was exhausted and his soul was weary. If only he could pick her up and carry her home. Any more sex was out of the question. He had no arousal left.

*I found him,* Mary knew. *This is Aaron Somebody. Aaron who has been pretending to be someone he isn't, and at the same time was protecting me from the others. Aaron, who was going through great theatrics but not hurting me very much.* Lying against him with his hand rubbing her back was such a comfort after two days of fear. *Be careful,* she told herself. *Don't give him away. You don't want this kindness to end.*

Her eyes had asked him who he was, but she wouldn't put it into words. It was his secret, for whatever reason. She pondered the possibilities: a rival gang, a mercenary, or a spy for the Cuban government since this group was working against the authorities? Something more fantastic tickled her brain. Aaron was not Cuban. Nathanial had been American, and Aaron was his friend. Americans were not supposed to be down here, but Nathanial had information he had not wanted Osvaldo to know. Americans might have spies down here. She glanced at Aaron again. What did a spy look like? No idea. Not that it mattered. As long as he was Aaron and not Taz. She smiled up at him, but that seemed to disconcert him, so she turned her head away.

This time, when Aaron tied her to the royal palm, Mary watched with regret as he walked away.

# XVI

Sitting at his desk, with the telephone receiver pressed against his ear, Frank Moseley concentrated on Gavin's report on the training exercise. Everything seemed to be going well, and Frank could picture each manoeuvre as Gavin described it. Out at Harvey Point in North Carolina, Gavin was moulding a small group combined of selected officers from their own paramilitary unit and some men on loan from the army into a cohesive rescue team prepared for any eventuality in Cuba. This wasn't turning into much of a holiday for Gavin, but hearing that Nat and Aaron could be in trouble had motivated Gavin to request the command of the rescue group. Frank hadn't hesitated in acquiescing. It was reassuring to know that the rescue team's leader was a man who had years of experience with delicate operations. By the time Sunday rolled around, the rescue team would appear to have worked together for years.

While Frank was talking with Gavin, Tony had knocked on the office door and entered with a young man Frank recognised as being on Tony's team. This was Scott, the man Tony wanted to "settle down". After hanging up, Frank greeted them and indicated that they should sit.

Tony came right to the point. He and Frank were both busy men. "Scott has asked to be part of your rescue team in Cuba." He said no more.

At this, Frank glanced at Scott, and then returned his gaze to Tony. For Tony to bring Scott in here and make that request for him informed Frank that Tony was in favour of this request. Otherwise Tony would have told Scott no himself. The fact that Tony did no more than make the request also signified that Tony knew Scott would need some fast, serious training that Frank might not wish to provide. After all, the rescue team was working together around the clock under a very tight time restriction. Sunday was coming very quickly, and only Frank would know it if was possible for Scott to fit into the schedule.

Frank hesitated. This was a serious operation; one in which mistakes could not be made. He looked at Scott again and saw a physically fit, confident young man waiting for his decision. It was a risk putting an untested man who had little more than basic training in with seasoned fighters. Tony encouraged his men to ask *why*. During the rescue there would be no time for *why*.

"You would have to obey orders *without question*," Frank stated, staring at Scott.

"Yes, sir, I know." Aaron and Nat were down there, and Scott wanted to help. He could follow orders to the letter when he had to.

"And do you have any idea what could happen if you screw up and put my men at risk?" Frank continued.

Scott swallowed. "Big trouble," he answered. "I could get people killed." That's why he knew he would have to do exactly as directed.

Frank looked at Tony, who left the decision entirely up to Frank. "Okay," Frank decided. "I'll give you a chance. You'll join Gavin Weeks immediately and train under his direction. The final decision will be his, based on your performance during training, and you will respect that decision. Is that clear?" Frank watched for the reaction.

Scott remained serious. This was no lark or adventure; it was serious work with consequences he could only imagine as yet. "Of course," he replied. "Thank you, sir."

Scott and Tony stood to leave, but Tony remained behind. "Thanks, Frank."

Getting out of his chair, Frank walked around his desk, leaning against the front of it. He grinned at Tony. "Did you want to go down there too?"

A knowing smile crossed Tony's features. "You can always read my mind." But he shook his head. "I wasn't even going to suggest it. I'm not in that kind of condition any more, and in any case I can't drop all my work to train for it. Besides," he added, "Walsh would never agree. There's no reason for me to be there, except personal."

"That's all true," Frank observed, "and I'm out of condition for that kind of intensity, too. Plus, there is no reason for me to go either, but I am."

At Tony's surprised look, Frank nodded. "I want to be there to oversee it, since we may have to scoop Richard Harvey. Of course, the fact that Nat and Aaron could be in trouble also gives me personal incentive to be on the scene," Frank admitted. "I thought you might feel the same, so I've talked to Walsh and he has agreed on two conditions."

"Which are?" Tony could hear the eagerness in his own voice.

Holding up two fingers, Frank counted them off. "One—we are in and out—no hanging around and risking our people a second longer than necessary. Two—you and I are to be sufficiently armed, but are to stay out of the line of fire. He insists we keep back until the way is clear. Walsh does not want to lose either of us, and particularly not both at once. Not," Frank laughed, "that it's a personal thing for him. He's thinking of the fact that he would have to replace us."

Tony shrugged. "Can't blame him for that. What else would you expect? We don't even know the man personally."

Once again, Frank got serious. "One thing we absolutely cannot afford, Tony, is any confusion in command responsibilities if we go. Gavin is in charge from the moment we step into the choppers. We are just along for the ride and to assess or prevent political damage. I have no problem switching roles, as it were, with Gavin. How about you?"

"I wouldn't dream of getting in his way," Tony promised. "This is out of my field, so I'll feel much safer doing what he says."

"Okay, then it's settled. I'll let Gavin and Walsh know. On Sunday we'll go down and get this thing over with and done. Hopefully," Frank prayed, "we'll all be back here in this office Monday morning, when Nat and Aaron can tell us all about their escapades."

# XVII

Drawing the people around him helped Aaron pass the time and gave him a purpose. When they got these bastards in court, he would have no problem remembering what each of them looked like. As he finished each drawing, Aaron would slip it into his pocket until night, when he transferred it to the waterproof section of the jacket lining. No one paid any attention to Taz scribbling in his clipboard, because Alfredo had told them that Taz was doing some bookkeeping for a variety of deals, and Aaron made sure that any drawing he was working on was beneath several pages of figures and bogus transactions until it was ready to be transferred to the jacket. That was just in case someone caught a glimpse of the clipboard close up. Drawing also gave him an excuse to sit in the shade for periods of time and guard Mary. This afternoon he had chosen the tree right beside her, where Nat had been tied. After this morning Mary must know he was a fake, but Aaron could only hope she would have no desire to tell anyone in this place about the fact that he was drawing. Currently he was reworking a picture of Alfredo, and he had pulled it to the top of the clipboard. Fatigue was making the work difficult, so he rested the clipboard on the ground and closed his heavy eyes.

"Taz." One of the rebels had walked out of the cabin and was approaching the place where Aaron was sitting. There was no time to hide the picture without being seen doing it, so Aaron jumped up to meet the Cuban at a safe distance away. He found out that the Cuban had just returned from a trip to the closest village and had brought back some sweets. Aaron declined politely and turned back towards the tree as the Cuban walked away. Then Aaron froze. Alfredo must have returned from the area of the horses. He stood now beside Mary, *with Aaron's clipboard in his hands*, leafing through it. Only one picture was attached to the clipboard, but it was Alfredo's, and it was on top. Fighting panic and preparing a story, Aaron strolled over.

Alfredo looked up at Aaron's approach. "Too complicated for me," he stated briefly, handing back the clipboard. The picture was missing. Aaron told Afredo about the arrival of the sweets and Alfredo dashed away. Perplexed and breathing heavily, Aaron stared at the clipboard and the ground around it. Had Alfredo taken the picture? Was the axe now ready to fall on Aaron's head?

"I hid it." Pulling a piece of paper out from the front of her track pants, Mary handed it up to Aaron. "I took it out to look at it," she confessed, "then I saw him coming. I didn't think he knew about you drawing things, so I hid it."

*Wow.* Aaron knelt down beside her, fighting a desire to wrap his arms around her. "Thank you." It seemed like an insignificant way to reward her, but it had given him a scare and he had better join the others for a while. Glancing to make sure no one was watching, Aaron slipped the picture into his pocket. He looked at Mary again before getting up. "Thank you," he repeated, backing away.

Mary peered around the tree to look over at Juany, then wished she hadn't. Juany's body was a pattern of purplish bruises and there were knife marks on some of the areas that Mary could see. Juany was lying on her stomach, for which Mary was grateful. The bloody smears on the side of her thigh were enough to tell the story of what lay underneath. It was hard to tell if she was still alive, but Mary thought her back was rising faintly, as if the body still had enough strength to draw air. There had to be massive internal bleeding, after the abuse she had endured. *The poor thing,* thought Mary. Her life may not have been easy, but her death was a horror.

During the afternoon, the cabin door opened and Alfredo came out on the run, followed by Aaron, who shut the door carefully and quietly behind him. *Oh no,* thought Mary, *not again.* She mentally prepared herself as Aaron ran to her side. Alfredo pulled out a knife as he ran over to Juany.

"Shut up and don't watch." It was the voice of Taz II, but the voice was whispering.

*Oh God, poor Juany,* Mary thought, as she saw Alfredo's arm rise and fall out of her peripheral vision. Aaron lifted Mary to the far side of the tree. He placed her on her knees, and positioned himself behind her, one arm around her body and his right hand on her throat. This was different, and Mary felt her fear rise again. Was it time to die? It was supposed to happen tomorrow, not now. She wasn't ready now. Aaron had her pressed tightly against his body, his face resting against her head so his mouth was near her ear.

"You must be very quiet," he warned. "There is a little group of tourists coming, and if they see us they will be slaughtered."

Tourists. Real people. Riding up here in the hills so far from anywhere? Mary could feel tears start to gather. She remembered riding in the hills with other tourists. Before…when she was free.

Aaron kept whispering. "No, no crying, Mary. You don't want them to hear, do you? They look like your countrymen; innocent little tourists with families and friends and jobs, on those funny little horses they rent down here. You don't want to kill all the tourists, do you, Mary?"

No, of course she didn't. Mary shook her head, then lay back against Aaron's shoulder. To be so close to the real world and rescue, but to be unable to reach it was almost more than she could bear. But they were not to be her rescue, were they? If they spotted her, they were to be executed by this group of animals. If they didn't, she would be the only victim. It was not a choice. Her life was almost over. She prayed that they would keep riding those little horses right past the cabin without dismounting. Right past, and then back to wherever on earth they had come from.

It was a long, quiet fifteen minutes. The group did pause to watch the waterfall and gaze at the hills surrounding it, but they did not dismount. When the Cuban guide had led his pale companions around a bend in the trail, Aaron spoke quietly again. "Good girl, Mary. That was a brave thing to do."

Alfredo got up from his hiding place, and started to walk back to the cabin, but then he changed direction and approached Aaron and Mary. "You've trained her real good, Taz. Now that our bitch is dead, how about you share with the men?"

"Tomorrow," Aaron replied. "We've got a date tonight, but you can have her tomorrow." As Alfredo walked away, Aaron knew tonight was decision night. Mary's eyes, large and terrified, stared up at him. She must have seen the look Alfredo had given her. "They are going to kill you tomorrow, Mary." He took a breath. "You know that means they won't care what they do to you first."

"You could let me go," she replied hopefully. "I wouldn't tell anybody. I could go back to the resort and make up a story. They'd let me go home."

"That's not an option," Aaron stated in a dull voice. If she lived, as soon as the rebels discovered Aaron's role down here, they would find her. Mary would be brought as a witness against the CIA. An independent witness who had been raped and abused by the very officer who was producing the evidence. No jury in the country would find him credible when they heard what he had done to her. To make things worse, his employers had sent him down here with that damned cover. He had used it for protection against a Canadian tourist, for God's sake. The international community would crucify the CIA for this one. They already had their feathers ruffled by the Helmes-Burton Act, and the CIA had made too many mistakes on this damned island in the past. They would not be forgiven for abusing this small woman, and the rebels would go free. It was his obligation to protect his employers from this disaster, but it meant killing Mary. He couldn't let her go free, but he would not let her suffer.

Mary knew somehow that it would do no good to protest. Why she had to die, she had no idea. What was it that was so important that she couldn't be allowed to live? She remained still, feeling sad. His arms around her and the palm rubbing her throat continued absentmindedly for a few minutes. It felt sensual, as did his cheek against her head. Strange how the slightest of touches seemed so wonderful after the days of rough, uncaring treatment. And he had finally called her by her name this time. Aaron the friend of Nathanial was not a cruel man.

Mary made a decision. "Please don't let them touch me, Aaron. Don't leave me to them." A breath that sounded suspiciously like a sob sounded in her ear.

"I won't leave you to them," Aaron promised in a whisper. "I can do it tonight if you want." He turned her face towards him with his hand. "It won't hurt…I promise. I'm not going to hurt you or scare you any more." For a moment he held her close. "Time to go," he said regretfully. "I'll be back tonight when it's dark. Give me your decision then."

*He doesn't want to kill me,* Mary knew, as she watched him leave. *It has upset him so much that he did not even hear me use his real name. Aaron will end my life tonight, but he'll do it gently like he did with Nathanial. Tonight I will join my son—it won't be so bad. I was not meant to have a real life. At least someone will be here to hold my hand while I die.*

Shortly before midnight, Aaron joined Mary at the royal palm. He noticed that she was awake and sitting up, so he handed over a sandwich he had made earlier in the evening for her.

*My last supper,* Mary realised. After a couple of bites she could eat no more, and handed it back. Her throat was constricted and she gulped back tears. Aaron was staring at the partially eaten sandwich, and seemed to be waiting for her to say something. Somehow she managed the words she knew he expected. "Will you do it, please?" Aaron answered by pulling her close and nodding. It was too much. Why should her life end in this remote place so far from her home? What had she done to deserve this? Unable to check her tears, Mary stuffed her knuckles in her mouth to silence her sobs.

"Okay, it's okay," Aaron whispered, having a hard time trusting his voice. He kissed her forehead, then pulled her hand from her mouth. She looked up at him and he lightly kissed her mouth. "Don't be scared…I'm here with you," he murmured.

*That was nice,* Mary thought. *The kiss was warm and nice and I deserve another one. I deserve to be held for a while before he takes everything from me.* His voice and his eyes were gentle, and Mary reached up with her hand and caressed his face. There were bristles growing for tomorrow's shave. Aaron, at least, would have a tomorrow. He didn't pull away from her caress, and his lips were close, so she pressed hers against them.

To her delight, he responded. Well, why not? She would not see him or anyone else in the morning. This was completely out of character for her, but what reason was there any more to follow rules of decorum? Being shy was a waste of time. *In fact,* Mary decided, *Aaron owes me a lot. I've put up with his abuse, now he can love me just a little.* Hardly believing she had the nerve to do this, Mary continued to stroke Aaron's face and neck with her hand, looking directly into his now questioning eyes.

This time when Aaron kissed her, it was longer, and he put a lot more feeling into it. Then he pulled back and could hear his own breathing. He wanted to make sure he was reading Mary's signals right, because they were unexpected. Her hand on his face had felt like a balm to his troubled soul. It cooled the hot guilt he was carrying, and told him she knew he was not Taz, but a real human being. Aaron had wanted so badly to show her that he wasn't the animal he had pretended to be. Now she seemed to be offering him the chance. "Is this what you want, Mary?" he whispered against her cheek.

Mary nodded and smiled at him. Aaron took out his knife and cut her ropes. This time Mary showed no fear of the knife. He placed her gently against the ground and let his hands and lips do the rest of the talking. She responded to his touch and he moved slowly and with as much gentleness as he could. Her body was willing, and a pleasure to touch. Aaron felt both a great peacefulness and an urgency to please her.

The night unravelled slowly, and Mary gratefully let Aaron lead her from one ecstasy to another. *This man has been well taught,* she realised. Throughout her marriage to Vincent, sex had been polite and civilised. She had experienced neither complaint nor passion. Her marriage paled sadly when compared to the passion she felt this night. But something was still missing. Aaron clearly expected tonight to be a one-sided affair—hers. He remained fully dressed, probably assuming that the last thing she wanted was more intercourse. As Taz, Aaron had never seemed terribly aroused, but tonight his breathing was giving him away. Now he pushed himself away, as he had a couple times previously. *No cheating, fella,* Mary decided. *If this is my vacation, I want an all-inclusive.* Reaching over, she unbuckled his belt.

"You don't have to do that, Mary," Aaron breathed. He made no real effort to stop her, though.

Reading that correctly as permission to continue, Mary smiled, said, "I want to," and sneaked her hand into his pants. It was immediately apparent that Aaron did not share Taz's problem. He groaned at her touch, and she didn't have to ask twice. *Yep, an all-inclusive,* she thought happily in his arms again as he slid gently into her. She wriggled contentedly against him as he placed kisses on her face. They were as close as they could be now, under the stars in the clear Cuban night.

Everything comes to an end eventually, and finally Aaron lay beside Mary and held her hand. Wow. After the hell of the last few days, making love had felt fantastic. She had gone a long way toward making him feel like a real man again instead of that shameful thing he had portrayed. If they could only run away together now, and he could forget about the importance of tomorrow. But running away wasn't possible. He took a deep breath and squeezed Mary's hand. "Go to sleep, dear. I'll take care of things later."

She looked at him with absolute trust in her eyes. "Don't forget," she begged.

How could he? "No." As she turned to her side, he curled up against her back. "Goodnight," he whispered, "and thank you. Thank you more than you can imagine."

Aaron continued to lie deep in thought, close against Mary's back. Happiness was being able to show someone that you weren't an animal. He stroked Mary's arm, and was rewarded when she snuggled closer into his chest. Happiness also was a woman who felt safe in your arms. After the nightmare of the last three days, Aaron felt an incredible relief now. He had needed desperately to be kind to this woman. Her healing touch had soothed his tormented soul. It had been a joy to make love to her and give her pleasure.

Now he was supposed to kill her. This place had made him an angel of death, and he was supposed to take the life of yet another person who deserved to live. Aaron rested his chin on the top of Mary's head. After two nights of little sleep and the emotional strain of the days, he was so tired. Could he just let Mary go? Moseley's men would be arriving tomorrow afternoon. If Mary managed to make it out of the hills tonight, how long would it take Cuban officials to organise and come up to investigate? He suspected it would take awhile, but could he take that kind of risk? Aaron listened to Mary's breathing. He really did not want to kill her. Surely there was another way. But even if she didn't tell anyone about the rebels' camp, the rebels would suspect she was alive as soon as they found out that Aaron wasn't who he had pretended to be. Once it was known that a member of the CIA had spent three days raping a Canadian tourist, every newspaper and radio station in the world would carry the story. The political fallout would be unbearable, and the rebels would walk. The people who had tortured Nat would get off scot-free. Aaron couldn't bear the thought of that.

Damn. He couldn't even think of how to get around this. He was so tired. So damned weary.

Sleep was impossible, although Mary wanted to go to sleep. Well, she did and she didn't. To be alive in this place tomorrow was too horrible a concept to think of. On the other hand, she felt very much alive right now. If, by some freak chance, she lived to be back home again, she knew one thing for certain. She would appreciate being given the gift of life. Life was very precious. Life in a country like Canada was a blessing she had taken for granted. Her future, if there was one, would be different. Her future...

*No ropes...there were no ropes tying her.* Taz, no, Aaron Somebody had not tied her. Mary smiled to herself. Of course he hadn't. Aaron did not tie women to trees. Taz did. Taz was gone. Aaron was beside her, snoring on his back. While he was asleep, she could pick up her clothing quietly and escape. But what if he caught her? He had said he could not let her go. Why, she did not understand. Something was terribly important about Sunday. But so what if he did catch her? Aaron would not hurt her. He could no longer pretend to be Taz with her. Aaron had revealed his true nature. Perhaps he could still kill her. Perhaps he had to. But he would never hurt her again. She knew that with certainty. Besides, she considered, if the final end was to be death, why give up without trying? It was impossible not to try when the chance offered itself and she felt so alive.

Quietly, ever so quietly, Mary stood up and gathered her clothes. She also took Aaron's jacket. The moon was bright and half full, which was an additional blessing. She would be able to see where she was going. All she had to do to find the road by the coast was to keep going downhill and follow Orion's belt, keeping the Big Dipper well back over her left shoulder. Then she probably had to head east, depending upon where she came out. It didn't matter, because soon Russian-built tractors and trucks would be travelling the roads, taking their loads of workers to their jobs. She would stop the first vehicle that was carrying Cubans to work and ask for her resort by name. The general Cuban population was very helpful, and they would make sure she arrived safely. Tourists were welcome to hitch a ride, although a tourist at this time of the morning so far from a resort would be a cause for talk and concern. That didn't matter either, as long as Mary got back to the resort. Today was Sunday. Her plane was leaving Monday morning at 10:45 a.m. She planned to be on it.

The hardest part of her escape was the first part. Mary did not try to put on her clothes until she was hidden behind a clump of the weed-like marabu bushes. There she dressed. Without an ounce of guilt, she put on Aaron's jacket. He probably wouldn't have minded anyway, she told herself. Her sweatshirt was cut down the front, and would cause concern among any Cubans she met. She wanted to get home without any fuss. Now she was dressed in her bathing suit, dirty trackpants, a cut sweatshirt, Aaron's jacket and running shoes. The jacket was huge on her, but Mary knew it helped hide the dirt of the track pants and the cut sweatshirt. In the pockets, she could feel one of his drawings and the remainder of the sandwich. Aaron had left the drawing in his pocket probably expecting that she would not need the jacket tonight. Oh well, she would keep it as a souvenir. Mary had no expectation or desire to see Aaron again. Surely he belonged in some very different world. It was a world she had no desire to know about.

Mary had to move quietly, which meant going very slowly and carefully. The waterfall's roar offered protection once she crossed the meadow. Now she could move more freely, but it was crucial not to turn an ankle or break a limb on the descent; a descent designed more for mountain goats than people.

The trip to the resort took a long time. Going down a mountain on a little-used trail travelled only by horses was treacherous. Mary tripped and fell several times, making a great deal of noise. She startled a couple of the Trogun birds from their sleep, and had more than one fight with the hated thorny marabu bushes. These bushes were her friend and her enemy. She could grab them to avoid a fall, but at the cost of sending spikes into her skin. At times the path seemed to disappear, and twice she had to backtrack to find it again. The stars were her encouragement, but also told her that time was passing. She had to be on a travelled road by morning, in case she was pursued.

As she descended, Mary noticed the vegetation changing, and welcomed the sight of Mango and orange trees. Sugar cane plots told her she was approaching civilisation, but she pressed on in her effort to reach the road by daybreak.

Near the start of her descent, Mary had thought she heard the sound of someone pursuing her, but the sound had stopped. Either she was hearing an animal knocking stones down the path, or it was Aaron. Would Aaron pursue her? When would he waken? Would he trust her not to talk to the Cuban officials? All she wanted to do was to get home. Get back to her safe little home in the cold January snow and forget about the last three days. How could she report a man for rape when she had asked him to make love to her? And who was he? A friend of Nathanial's, who had been a kindly person. A man who, yes, had raped her, but had kept her alive and protected from torture for three days. There was so much she didn't understand, but she knew that while she would have reported Taz gladly, she would not report Aaron. Aaron could have his Sunday to meet the Congressman. Why a Congressman would come to that place was beyond Mary's comprehension. *That's Aaron's business,* she decided. *I want nothing to do with him ever again.*

If it was Aaron Mary had heard behind her, he was no longer in pursuit. Thirsty and half starved, but not willing to give up, Mary forced herself to continue. When she eventually reached the road, she cried from exhaustion. Her track pants were torn from the marabu thorns, and she was bruised and filthy from her falls.

When a truck full of workers finally came into sight, Mary could not even climb into the back when it stopped for her. Several Cuban men jumped down and with the encouragement of Spanish chatter from the women, they collectively hoisted Mary into the truck. There was concern. The tourist looked worn, tired, and dirty. It was most unusual. Tourists usually looked rested, well-fed and carefree. What was she doing out so early in the morning? Had she been hurt? No one in the truck spoke English, but they quickly discovered that she spoke Spanish. They offered to take her to the doctor, or get the police if she wished. No, no, she emphasised. She wanted to go to the resort. She insisted that she had been foolish and gotten lost. Someone had given her a ride, but she had given the wrong directions and ended up in the wrong village. Then she had tried to take a shortcut over some hills and become totally lost. No one had hurt her. She had fallen several times, ripped her clothes and gotten dirty. Nothing had happened to her. There was no need for police or a doctor. All she wanted was to go back to the resort, get cleaned up and have some breakfast because she was very hungry. The Cubans gave up, clearly with misgivings. The resort management would know what to do, and would take care of her, they knew.

Aaron awoke with a start. He had fallen asleep, for God's sake. At least it was still dark. The heaviness in his mind was because he had to kill Mary. He remembered this with extreme regret. Then he rolled over and knew panic. Where was she? Silently he jumped to his feet and searched the immediate area. She was gone, and so were her clothes. He had not thought to tie her up. More panic—she had taken his jacket! The jacket held the lists he and Nat had compiled. They were in the waterproof lining with his drawings. He had to get them back.

Even as he pursued her down the trail, tripping, falling and jabbing himself in those prickly bushes, part of Aaron was happy. Mary deserved to be free and live. Personally, however, it was a disaster. If she went to the Cubans with her story and they acted quickly, the operation could be finished before Moseley arrived, and Aaron was in big trouble if caught. He would have to stay extremely alert and be ready to run for it at the first sign of Cuban officialdom. That would leave Moseley's team in danger of being detected, or, worse still, being caught on the ground. And it would mean leaving Nat's body behind…never returning him to the States for a decent burial. Aaron felt depression creeping in.

Yet Mary had promised not to tell anyone, and Mary now knew he was not Taz. They had shared a night of intimacy, and just maybe she would go straight home. Aaron had no doubt that she would get back to the resort now. Once she made it to the road it would be light, and all she had to do was go up to a Cuban, say, "Canadian," and ask for her resort by name. The Cubans and the Canadians seemed to have this understanding between them, that riled Aaron's administration to no end. Mary would be safe.

Suddenly Aaron stopped. He had reached a crevice in the rocks. Ahead, he could hear signs of Mary's progress, as stones occasionally clattered down a riverbed. He had just made a decision. He would pretend to have killed her. There would be no awkward explanations required. He had simply gotten carried away. She had run. It was a snuff act, right? Okay, that's better. Keep working at the story.

Pretending to have killed someone took a little thought. What did you do with the body? How did you kill her? Survey the terrain, make sure you are too far from the camp for anyone to bother checking. Get some blood on your knife. She fought and you killed her. The blood on the knife is hers. They can't prove otherwise. Finally the details were figured out. He returned to the camp and sat down under the tree to wait for morning. *Run, Mary,* he prayed.

*Get out of Cuba somehow. Go home. I'll find the jacket later. Please just don't make a scene when you get home. I didn't want to kill you, but you could destroy me so easily.*

Morning came. Aaron was trusted, his explanation about killing Mary was not questioned. Alfredo was disappointed, but was too excited about the day's activities to be very upset. The guests started arriving at 11:00 a.m. With amazing pride, Alfredo introduced Taz to several of them. Aaron kept a close watch on the arriving horses. Finally he saw the large American Congressman. So it was true. Incredible, but true. And just in time, because it was almost 1:00 already. Aaron kept hidden from the Congressman. Richard Harvey had never met Aaron St. Pierre, but Aaron did not know if Richard Harvey had ever met Taz, and Aaron had no intention of finding out. One more hour and it would be over. One more hour to hold together, then he and Nat could go home.

# XVIII

The sun was cooking down on Moseley's team. Scott was sweating. Although the trees offered some shade, they had to move from one tree to another, quickly and very quietly. Everyone had made it out of the helicopters without incident. Gavin had been worried about Tony and Frank, since the two men had very little recent experience with this type of demanding physical activity. They were not expected to do anything but stay with the group and keep as invisible as possible. Keeping hidden from any view from the air was crucially important.

Scott was gaining an appreciation of why they were wearing these khaki and green outfits, in spite of the fact that they made you feel like you were in an oven. In addition to the protective colouring, long pants and long sleeves were protecting his body from all these prickly bushes.

At least he was carrying less weight than some of the men. Gavin had discovered that he was very fast, and had decided to leave Scott relatively unencumbered so he could chase people. Hopefully, he could run fast enough in this heat to do the job for Gavin.

Ten more minutes passed, and the camp came into view. Several horses had been tethered a few hundred feet back, but Gavin had removed their bridles. The thankful horses never made a sound. From where the team was hiding now, Scott could see a number of Cubans, but neither Aaron or Nat were in view. There was a waterfall and an open meadow between where they crouched and the cabin at the opposite side. Gavin signalled that they would have to make an indirect approach to stay amid the shrubs. As leader, Gavin was giving the signals, and the team had practised well. All Scott had to do was watch, listen and obey instantly. He wondered if Gavin still got nervous. Scott's adrenalin was building fast.

They crept forward, circling the meadow. In a thick clump of palm-like bushes, Gavin gave Tony and Frank the signal to stay and hide. Both men had been equipped with personal sidearms for defence, but were to stay out of any danger. The rest of the team continued their approach. Finally they were close enough. "Now!" A whispered command in the tiny earphone, and the unit exploded into action. The Cubans standing around had no time to sound an alarm. The inside men grabbed for their guns as their door and windows were invaded, but were so shocked at the assault that they failed to move fast enough. It was over in minutes, with only three Cubans dead. Scott hadn't even had to chase anyone.

Where was Aaron? Scott checked outside, and found him sitting at the back of the building with a terrified Richard Harvey beside him. First Scott put handcuffs on the Congressman and led him over to where the prisoners were being gathered, then Scott returned to Aaron. Aaron was still sitting against the cabin. Just sitting. Scott hardly recognised his friend in this ill-kempt, silent, haggard-looking man. "Aaron, you okay?"

"Is Tony here?" Aaron whispered. "I have to report damage to Tony."

Scott did not like Aaron's voice. It was monotone and lifeless. "Yeh, he's here. He's out front. Come with me. I'll take you to him." Aaron stood up and started to follow passively, but then spotted two of the team leading a Cuban out of the cabin door. Aaron muttered something about "kill Osvaldo," and before Scott realised what he meant, Aaron had his knife in his hand and was running towards the Cuban.

Scott had not been expecting to chase Aaron, and Aaron already had a head start. The two officers striding ahead with the Cuban had put several more yards between them and Aaron, but it still didn't give Scott time to think twice. It was high gear and out of the shade of the building into the sun. Scott estimated it to be about a hundred-foot dash from himself to this Osvaldo. Very little distance when the other person had a head start. *"Give it everything you've got,"* Moseley had said about the operation. Scott did. He tackled Aaron about four feet away from Osvaldo, hoping he was doing the right thing. It was a stroke of luck that no one was slashed by Aaron's knife.

"No, Aaron, not like that," Scott gasped, pinning his friend's wrists to the ground.

But Aaron didn't try to struggle. His breathing sounded erratic, and he simply screamed, "Tony! TONY!"

Scott listened in shock. *What the hell...?*

"I'm here, son." It was Tony. He knelt down and helped Aaron into a sitting position. "Deep breaths," he ordered. "Calm down now, it's all over. Calm down, I'm here."

It worked a little. Aaron's breathing changed from gasps to a steadier rhythm. He had the front of Tony's shirt clenched in his fists. "Damage," he said between breaths.

Tony motioned to Moseley, who was assisting with the securing of prisoners, and directing the removal of the three dead Cubans. Moseley trotted over to Tony's side.

"Aaron, where's Nat?" he asked urgently.

Aaron stared up at Tony. Nat had said to report all damage, but Nat had not known he would die by Aaron's hand. Nat, Tony and Frank were close friends. You couldn't tell your boss you had killed his best friend. You couldn't tell anyone. Murdering your fellow officer would surely not be tolerated. It was a dark secret that would haunt you for the rest of your life. "He's dead," Aaron answered. "Osvaldo tortured him, and he died."

Anger crept over the two men's faces. A terrible anger caused by sorrow and loss. "Where is he?" Moseley choked out.

Aaron pointed at the gully where Nat's body had been dumped by the rebels. He died Friday night," Aaron warned. The rebels had not buried him. Nat and Juany had been tossed in the gully together. Moseley took a deep breath and wandered over. It was no place to say goodbye to a friend.

Catching his breath, Aaron looked at Tony again. "There's more." He saw Tony fight to keep himself under control and put a neutral expression on his face.

"Tell me only what we need to know now," he instructed Aaron. "We don't have much time. Details can wait until we get you home."

"There was a witness," Aaron began. "A Canadian tourist."

"A tourist?"

Aaron closed his eyes. "A woman." He opened them up again and saw Tony looking at him nervously.

"A woman…"

"They brought her here to test me." Now he couldn't look at Tony, so stared at the ground, the vision of Mary in his head. "After Nat's cover failed. Osvaldo and Nat had met before, but it took them a couple of days to recognise each other. I had to stay alive, to try to help Nat…" It sounded feeble to Aaron's ears. He forced himself to look at Tony again. "I raped her, Tony. I raped a fucking innocent Canadian tourist aerobics instructor." His breathing was becoming irregular again, and his body started to shake.

"Is she dead?" It was Tony's voice, but it sounded strangled. "If she's dead, we deny, Aaron. No matter what the Cubans say, we deny."

"No," Aaron replied dully. "She got away last night." No one will know about last night, Aaron decided. Mary wouldn't like that. It was private and no one had witnessed it. It mattered to no one but them.

Tony was looking grave. "Where is she, Aaron? Where did she come from?"

"A resort somewhere nearby," Aaron answered. "She lives in Toronto. She's probably on her way back there now." He saw Moseley returning. Moseley looked ill.

"Do the rebels know she's alive?" Tony asked.

"They think I killed her last night," Aaron said, "although they've probably started doubting that by now."

At Moseley's approach, Tony turned. "Frank, there's a witness to this."

"Good. These bastards are going to pay for what they've done," Frank promised, his fists clenched.

"No, not good," Tony responded, helping Aaron to his feet. "Not good at all. Aaron had to rape the witness."

Moseley looked at Aaron, stricken. "Good God. There's a woman's body with Nat," he stated, disbelieving. "Tell me you didn't have a hand in that."

"No," Aaron responded instantly. "Hell, no. That's Juany. I never touched her, Frank, I swear. They did that to her in front of us."

Relief flooded across Moseley's face. "You poor bastard," he stated unexpectedly.

For Moseley to show sympathy surprised Aaron. He hadn't expected Moseley to understand.

"What shape is this Mary in?" Moseley asked, still addressing Aaron.

"Bruised, scraped, and I slapped her around a few times." He remembered Mary's fear only too vividly. "Christ, Tony, I raped the woman. Scared the life out of her, humiliated her. She probably suffered more from that than anything I did physically to her." Then he remembered his jacket. "She's got my damned jacket, too. She's carrying the evidence that Nat and I collected in the lining. Plus a bunch of drawings I did of these characters. We have to find her and get the jacket back."

Scott had been kneeling beside Aaron in shock. He was having a hard time believing his ears. Now he stood up. Here was something he could do. "I'll find her, sir. After we get back I'll trace her and find the jacket. Sheila could come with me; she's worked for years with victims of rape, sir," he explained to Moseley. "She'll know what to do and say."

Tony and Frank exchanged a look Scott didn't understand. As a single unit, they turned and walked several feet away, and began talking very quietly.

Frank spoke first. "We cannot survive a witness. Not a raped Canadian tourist. It'll bring us down."

"The fallout from the international community would be devastating," Tony agreed. "The Canadians are already in hysterics over Helmes-Burton. Can you imagine them finding out we were involved in the kidnap and rape of one of their citizens? And don't imagine for a minute that the Congressman won't try to make this look like something we did out of negligence, or perhaps even intent. He'll do anything to extricate himself from this mess."

"Our credibility will crumble," Frank agreed. "Options, Tony," he requested.

*Oh boy,* Tony sighed. This was dangerous. These were not front line decisions. "We could take no prisoners. Forget about court and deny everything the woman says."

"Execute them all?" Frank bit his lip. "I wouldn't ask the men to be a party to that."

"We'd have to do it ourselves," Tony realised, hardly believing he was having this conversation. "But we've got a US Congressman here as a witness."

Frank raised an eyebrow. "Are you prepared to execute a Congressman?"

"Hell, Frank, you asked for options," Tony protested. "I'm just thinking out loud. I'm not prepared to do this at all."

"Where does that leave us, then?" Frank asked. "I can't get past the obvious."

"Damn it, Frank, neither can I." Tony ran his fingers through his hair. He was getting a headache. "Would Gavin do it?"

"If we explained the danger." Frank stared at Tony seriously. "You know that we'd be on our own on this one. You have to understand that Walsh cannot approve this."

Tony nodded. "He'd send it up the ladder."

"And what fool would give special approval to kill a citizen of a friendly country and accept responsibility for it?" It was not really a question. Frank knew full well no one would approve it.

"Not a chance of it being approved." Tony was following Frank's thoughts. "But they won't know what to do either. It'll create a panic. It's a lose-lose situation. We're doomed."

"Which brings it back to us," Frank agreed. "What would Walsh want?"

Tony looked directly at Frank. "To not force him to ask for a decision. He doesn't want to know about this. The consequences of knowing when you cannot take action to fix it are disastrous. Everyone is ruined."

"It's a risk. I don't like it," Frank stated.

"Neither do I. We have absolutely no authority to do it, but we have to protect the Company." Tony sighed. "It's more important than one tourist." Well, at least they agreed, Tony thought. "And there can be absolutely no trail back to the CIA."

"It has to be Gavin," Frank insisted. "I won't trust it to anyone else."

"He won't like it." Gavin, Tony knew, would do almost anything to protect the Company, but he would personally see this as overstepping their mandate in a big way. "But he'll do it because he'll understand there is no other way."

Frank nodded, and the two men returned to Scott and Aaron. Scott repeated his offer, but Tony shook his head. "Thanks, son," he said, "but this isn't a job I'd ask you to do." Tony turned to face Aaron, who was standing now, and put his hands on Aaron's shoulders. "I'm going to take care of this for you. I'll take you home, let you recover and then we'll prepare to send these bastards away for good. You have nothing to worry about. I'll fix it."

Aaron relaxed. Nat had been right. Tony would back him.

Scott looked puzzled. *How do you "fix" rape?*

Aaron's sense of relief was short lived. Moseley turned to Scott. "Go and get Gavin," he ordered. "Tell him we have a job for him."

"NO!" The yell was from Aaron, as the truth dawned on him. "No, not Gavin. Don't send Gavin. She doesn't deserve this, Tony. Don't do this."

Scott stopped in his tracks when he realised what was being proposed. The rape victim was being seen as a security risk. Gavin was known to take care of security risks.

Tony and Frank had seized Aaron's arms and started pushing him into the cabin. Moseley looked over his shoulder at Scott. "That was an order, Mr. Andrews. Get Gavin and get Doc."

Doc was not a real doctor. He was a member of Moseley's team. Doc had some medical training and could help with bullet wounds, gashes and broken limbs. He also carried a variety of drugs and sedatives. As Scott left to find him, Gavin passed him and entered the cabin.

Inside the cabin, Frank turned to Gavin and filled him in. Gave him his orders. Gavin glanced at Aaron and then turned his attention back to Frank.

"We are talking about a Canadian national, sir. I need to be perfectly clear on this order. You are deeming her to be a threat to the agency and you wish the threat eliminated."

"That is correct," Frank responded.

Suddenly, Aaron felt he was arguing for his life. Mary's life actually, but he knew if he allowed them to kill Mary now, something inside him would die with her. She had escaped and he had been happy. For the sake of his own soul he needed to apologise to that woman, and help her put her life back on track. Aaron started doing something he hadn't done since he was ten. He started to stutter.

"D...on't do th...is, Tony. Don't...don't fuckin' d...o this," he repeated. "She was he...held hos...hostage and r...r...raped by me for th...thr...ee days. She does...doesn't deserve to be k...killed by us, t...t...too!"

"Aaron, she is a threat to us." It was Tony; a hard, businesslike Tony, who would protect the CIA at all costs. "Has it not occurred to you that this woman would be called as a witness by the defence? What do you think is going to happen when the jury hears how you treated her? What will they think when they hear that you stood by while the Cuban girl and Nat were tortured, and you spent your time tormenting a Canadian tourist? She'll be a wonderful witness for the Congressman."

Aaron was furious. "Do you think I 'stood by' from choice, sir? Is that what you think? That I was having *fun* here?" They were face to face, and Aaron refused to back down. His anger had displaced the stutter, but he hardly noticed. Moseley and Gavin stood close by. Doc followed Scott through the door into the cabin.

"Of course I don't," Tony responded, "but they will. Your credibility will be shit, Mr. St. Pierre, and the jury will let those animals walk. Not because we don't have enough evidence. Because the key player in this—you—will not be trusted. You will fall, and the entire Company will fall with you. They'll say we couldn't control one of our own. We put innocent people at risk and we were responsible for crimes against a citizen of one of our closest neighbours. We sent you into a situation over which we lost control. The validity of the evidence depends on your credibility, and it will be in serious doubt, Mr. St. Pierre. I will not risk your career, this operation and the reputation of the agency for this woman."

Aaron collapsed into a chair, leaned his elbows on the table in front of it and put his face in his hands. Tony had reached his limit of tolerance, or he would never have called Aaron by his last name. He knew that Tony was right, too. Morally wrong, but chillingly right. That's why Aaron had known that it had been his duty to kill Mary. But that was before. She was a person to him now. It wasn't right. Doc came toward him with a needle, but Aaron waved him off.

Gavin walked over to where Aaron was sitting. Aaron glanced up at him and then looked away. He knew what Gavin was probably thinking. Gavin's code name was "panther", a far cry from Aaron's nickname of "puppy dog". *He probably thinks I'm the weakest excuse for a covert officer he's ever seen,* Aaron thought. However, Gavin gave no such indication. He squatted down beside Aaron, his right hand on the back of Aaron's chair, his left hand on the table. "Just so you'll know," he said quietly, "I won't hurt her. She won't be hurt and she won't be scared. She won't even know I'm there."

It was true, Aaron knew. Gavin wasn't cruel. He was very professional. Cool and professional. He was employed to do very specific jobs, and he was very good at it. This was not personal for Gavin. Few jobs were. Aaron looked into the steady, cool grey eyes, and saw Moseley's right arm and main Company protector. No, this wasn't personal. "I know, Gavin," Aaron said finally. "But I still can't live with it. If you do her, you might as well take me too...because I'm dead inside." It wasn't a lie. The darkness that had been threatening to creep into Aaron's soul in the last days felt icy and empty. And it felt very close by.

Gavin said nothing, but stood up. Yet before he moved away, he slid his right hand from the chair and laid it on Aaron's shoulder. Aaron was surprised. Support had come from an unexpected direction. But it was Tony's operation. Tony and Moseley had to agree, and Tony had to be convinced before he would attempt to sway Moseley. As angry as Tony seemed right now, Aaron still had to keep trying. "Do you know what Mary was doing all Friday evening?" he asked, looking up at Tony. "She was holding Nat's hand, for hours, talking to him and keeping him company."

Tony exploded. "Damn you, Aaron, that's not fair!" His face was red, and his hands shook.

Then Aaron knew. Tony did not want to give this order. He would protect the agency at all costs, but with reluctance. There was a chance.

Aaron kept looking into Tony's face. Tony, who, in spite of being very angry, had not left his side. A man who defended his officers; went to the wall for them; almost lived with them. The man Aaron occasionally called "Dad" out of fondness, when no one could hear, of course. Tony wasn't rigid. If Aaron could think of another option, Tony would at least listen. But Aaron was tired and emotionally exhausted. His brain felt stalled.

"I know I can't stop you," Aaron admitted, giving up. "You'll do what you feel you have to. Just don't let one of your considerations be my career. Because I'm finished for you, Tony. You kill Mary now and I have no hope. My life is fucked. There'll be no career, no marriage. I can't carry this kind of guilt around, you know that. I just can't," he ended lamely. "Is there no other way?"

Tony had shut his eyes. *Shutting me out, Tony?* Aaron wondered. *Or are you looking for a way out? Help, however, came from a different source, although it wasn't offered with any enthusiasm.*

"There is another way," Moseley stated, "but neither of you will like it."

Open eyed again, Tony looked suspiciously at his friend. "Do I want to hear this, Frank?"

"What is it?" Aaron looked from one man to the other. They both had so many secrets up their sleeves, learned from years of fieldwork.

Crossing his arms over his chest, Moseley half sat on the table facing Aaron. "*If* we bring Mary in, this operation could fall apart, as Tony has accurately stated. If you want her alive, you'll have to take the fall."

"No."

"No way."

Tony and Gavin had spoken at once, but Aaron was listening. "What does that mean?"

"It means," Moseley continued, "that we say you acted outside of our interests and our direction. We help Mary charge you with rape, forcible confinement, the whole package. We offer her compensation. We throw our protection into the integrity of the evidence. You are on your own. It could mean prison for you, Aaron," Moseley finished.

*Prison. My God, what have I come to? Some choice,* realised Aaron. This was making suicide seem like a preferred option.

Tony was watching him. "No, Aaron, I will not let you do this. I will not."

But then Gavin spoke. "Sir, if I may make a suggestion. We need to agree on this. Can't we meet Aaron halfway?" Gavin had gained everyone's interest. "I'll go up, assess this woman, and judge our vulnerability with this situation. Then we can make the decision." He indicated Aaron. "I'm having a really hard time with this concept of puppy dog as a rapist. It's possible that this woman may not be the enemy we think. Why don't we take a couple of days to sort this out?"

Support from the most unlikely source. Aaron caught his breath and prayed. Gavin's advice held enormous weight with his senior officers, regardless of the fact that they were friends. And the two seniors were looking for a solution. *Shut your mouth and let Gavin carry this,* Aaron told himself.

Moseley looked at Tony. Tony looked at Moseley. Moseley shrugged. "What's the hurry?" he asked. "As long as we reach her first."

Tony whipped his head back to stare into Aaron's face. "*If* we do this…if she comes in because we see no threat, that doesn't mean you're home free.

We still have to protect the Company. If the case starts falling apart because of this witness, we'll have to cut you loose. It will be too late to do anything else, then. I will have to personally lay the charges against you. If we survive, I can withdraw the charges. If we don't…"

"I go to prison," Aaron finished flatly. It was a gamble. He would be betting his life on Mary. Little Mary, who had endured his terror, put up with his abuse and had started to see through him. Who, in the end, had enough faith in him to ask him to take her life. And who had reached out to him in her final hours, somehow knowing that he was not the animal he pretended, but could give her love. He would bet on Mary. "I'll take the risk," he decided.

There was still a worried look on Tony's face. "Aaron, this woman must hate you. Are you sure about this?"

"She was starting to realise that I wasn't what I was pretending to be." Aaron sat up straight. The immediate crisis was over. "It'll be okay, Tony. I'm sure it will."

Tony leaned on the table and spoke quietly. "You know I'll do everything I can to protect you, Aaron."

This was vintage Tony. Aaron could actually smile again. "Thanks, Dad," he whispered.

"Give him the sedative, Doc," Tony ordered, straightening up. "And, Scott, you will go to Toronto on your own after we get home. We don't need Gavin yet. Find this Mary and call me. Do not contact her on your own, understood?"

"Yes, sir," Scott replied. "I'll find her and call you."

"I'll come up with Sheila—that was a good idea you had. I will do the assessing. Sheila is NOT to know what this is about, understood? I will make a decision when I'm ready." Tony looked at Gavin. "Are we all cleaned up and ready to go?"

"We don't have room for everyone," Gavin replied. "I need Aaron to tell us who to take."

Outside again, Aaron pointed out Jose Luis, Alfredo, Osvaldo, and of course the Congressman. There was room for one more. After some thought, Aaron picked Lino. Lino had not liked the violence, and had sung songs to Mary. He might be convinced to make a deal.

Scott watched Aaron point out the prisoners they were taking. When he pointed at a man named Lino, Lino made an unexpected dash away from his captors. Before Gavin could holler, Scott was in motion. Hell, he was going to feel these muscles tomorrow. Two tackles in one day in a hot Cuban sun.

He did catch the Cuban, although the guy was fast, and managed to hold him just enough until Aaron caught up.

"Come on, Lino," Aaron instructed in Spanish. "Don't be so bloody paranoid. You're just a witness. Who knows, if you're a good boy we might even give you back to Castro."

Finally they were ready and the choppers were brought back. *It will be wonderful to leave this place behind,* Aaron knew, *and to go home. Go home to sanity.* Wait a moment, they had forgotten someone. "Nat," he said to Tony. "We have to take Nat."

"Got him," Moseley replied. "We've buried the Cuban girl, and we'll notify the Cuban government indirectly after we've left. Nat's with us. We're taking him home."

# XIX

He was freezing. Scott wrapped his arms around the front of his chest and huddled into his overcoat. Why would anyone live in this icebox? In dismay, Scott stood outside the Iron Will Gym, where Mary Norland worked, staring at the salt and water eating his Dach casuals. Tony had said to bring boots, gloves and a hat, but had Scott listened to him? *No. I was too damn anxious to get up here to help Aaron,* he cursed himself. Now his hands were hurting with cold, and he had only had a short walk from the subway to here. His ears were starting to ache too, as the bitter breeze stung them. How did Canadians stand this? And why on earth had settlers ever come here in the first place?

Not that he had never been to Toronto before. His previous visits had all been personal excursions, but by luck they had never been in the first week of February, or any part of the deep winter. *Well, get on with it,* he told himself. *It's no fun standing out here, and I'll just have to try to rescue the leather shoes later.*

Inside the Iron Will Gym it was warm, so he took a minute to recuperate while he surveyed the lobby. A very attractive blond woman with the kind of body that was itself a great advertisement for the gym was watching him with interest from behind the counter. There were several steroid-type males circling her and preening. He made a quick assessment. This woman looked like his style—an added bonus. Scott was very comfortable with women, and usually had no difficulty getting information from them. Not to mention the fringe benefits. It was easy…a matter of being pleasant and considerate. He couldn't understand why some guys couldn't figure that out. Of course in this lobby he would have to compete with the steroid junkies. They were bigger and had lots of muscle to show off. He would look almost puny beside them, so he would have to trust to his personality. Listening to their conversation, he decided that some of these guys sounded like they had the personality of a Canadian snow bank.

This proved to be the right tactic. When Scott smiled and approached the desk, the blonde smiled back invitingly, as if she were bored with her current companions. *Okay,* he coached himself, *keep it genuine and friendly. She probably puts up with enough macho in a day to make her ill.*

"Where are your mitts?" she scolded with a smile before he could speak. "You look like Frosty the Snowman."

Her name tag said *Lori.* Scott made an obvious point of glancing at it, then grinned at her. "Hi, Lori. Yes, your winters are wicked."

Lori nodded. "A bit of an accent you've got there. Just visiting?"

Scott noticed that the other men had given him a condescending look, but then gave up and wandered back to their weights. *Good, I was getting claustrophobic with them around.* "Yes and no," he responded to Lori's question. "I have a bit of business to attend to, but I decided to stay with some friends while I was here. They recommended your gym, so I thought I'd check it out."

"Are they members?" she asked. "If they are, I can give you a day pass so you can come in with them."

*You could give me a lot of things, honey,* Scott considered, *all of which I'm sure would be perfectly delightful.* The blue eyes watching him had evidence of intelligence, which he considered a plus, and she had nice white teeth. *Yes, a definite possibility.* "No," he replied easily. "They are more the couch potato type. They heard about the gym from some other people."

"Well," she responded with a hint of suggestiveness. "How about a tour today, and if you like what you see I'll give you a pass for tomorrow?"

"Sounds great." Perhaps the best part of the tour was the fact that Lori was walking in front of him, and he had lots of time to observe her form while she was pointing out various pieces of equipment. *I wonder how many men sign up for memberships after one of her tours without even remembering where the weight room was supposed to be? She's the kind of woman that can get you very distracted.*

Too soon they were back at the front counter, but Scott had the information that he came for. En route, he had stopped at a bulletin board, feigning interest in the activities posted. The aerobics schedule had been on that board and he had pointed it out. Thinking he was interested in aerobics, Lori told him that there were several men that took the classes, and gave him more information about the classes than he cared to know. At least he now knew that Mary was teaching a 10:30 a.m. class tomorrow. It gave him the perfect opening.

"This is a real long shot, but I don't suppose there's any chance that the Mary who is teaching tomorrow morning's class would be Mary Norland?" he asked. "I'm supposed to look up a woman by that name. My father's doing one of those family tree things." He grimaced. "It bores me to death, but he's obsessed with it. This Mary is supposed to live in Toronto and work at a health club. I told Dad I would go through the phone book, but I haven't bothered. I also told him that there was no way I was wasting my time going from health club to health club looking for some umpteenth cousin of his. Even if I find her," Scott continued, "she wouldn't know me from Adam, and we'd have nothing to talk about."

"Have you bought any lottery tickets today?" Lori asked, buying the story hook, line and sinker. "You should, 'cause you just got lucky. She *is* Mary Norland."

Scott managed to look sufficiently amazed. "Well, that just made life a lot easier. I can get Dad off my back now. Maybe I can just say hello after her class tomorrow."

"Sure, why not?" Lori replied good-naturedly. "I'll get you that pass and you can use the gym at the same time." Pulling a card from a drawer, Lori started writing on it.

*Okay, work is over,* Scott decided. *Now comes fun.* "What are the chances of talking you into a tour of the city tonight?"

While the look her blue eyes sent him was telling him she was interested, he could read the note of caution in the way she held her head.

"Let's see," she said pensively. "You're from out of town, out of the country, in fact. I don't know you or your friends, and they aren't members here. You look like the boy next door, which used to be a good thing, but not necessarily any more." She shook her head. "This isn't sounding good."

"Is that 'no'?" Scott asked. It sure didn't sound promising.

"Well, help me out here." Lori looked at him thoughtfully. "Who do you work for?"

*Whoops. I can't tell you that,* Scott realised, *because I'm not supposed to be up here working.* Then he had an idea. "How about lunch? We can walk to a place nearby of your choosing, and you can let your buddies here know where we're going." He grinned at her again. "You can even let them follow us if you promise not to let them sit at our table."

When she laughed out loud, Scott knew he was in. He could tell by her pleased expression. "I'll have you back for your afternoon shift so your boss can't complain," he promised, forestalling any objection from that direction. "And tomorrow," he continued, "I'll try to bring my friends when I drop by to meet Mary. You can decide if they suffice for references."

This time Lori's laugh was one of acceptance. "Oh, you're good," she stated knowingly, her eyes saying something that was affecting his blood pressure. "You may just have won yourself a night on the town."

Lunch had been fun and very promising, but too soon it was over, and Scott was back in his hotel room, calling Tony to tell him of the arrangements. He thought Tony would be pleased, but soon discovered otherwise.

"You did what?" Sitting at his desk, Tony had been catching up on his work when Scott phoned. Yesterday they had buried Nat in his home town in Kentucky, and the emotions of the day had taken their toll. Tony's head was pounding. Nat had been well liked and respected, so the turnout was large and there had been few dry eyes. Aaron had been a mess despite the medication Dr. Hummel had ordered, and Tony had found it extremely difficult not to break down himself. Frank and Gavin had stood right beside them, both of those men better at concealing their emotions than he was. Tony knew they were feeling the same pain, particularly Frank, who would be sharing Tony's feeling of responsibility. Frank had swallowed repeatedly, and had not looked at anyone. Tony had derived comfort from their close presence, and had used that comfort to be strong for Aaron.

Aaron blamed himself directly. He still believed he should have been able to prevent Nat's capture, and had talked to Tony for hours the night before about what he should have, could have, might have been able to do. Listening and trying to help, Tony had told him again and again that it was all hindsight. Decisions were made on foreseeable events, but sometimes things just happened. Aaron and Nat had been caught unexpectedly. It had happened, it was terrible, but Aaron had no reason to spend the rest of his life beating himself up about it. While needing to reassure Aaron, Tony had his own anger, guilt and grief to deal with. It had been a very difficult few days.

Now Tony could feel his nerves being strung. He had told Scott *not* to contact Mary, and here was Scott telling Tony they had a lunch date with Mary and a girlfriend tomorrow. Now Mary had a witness who would be able to identify them if she ever saw them again. "Tell me that you at least did not tell them who you work for," Tony demanded, his temper and voice rising.

"Of course not, sir." Scott was always careful to add the "sir" when he suspected he was in trouble. "I told her that you and Sheila live in Toronto."

"You idiot!" Tony exploded. "I don't even know the main streets in Toronto! Great, just great! Now I can spend my spare time on the way up studying road-maps and practising a Canadian accent. Thanks a lot!"

There was a pause on the phone, then Scott spoke again, sounding defensive. "I'm sorry, sir, but I thought you would be glad to have a meeting arranged quickly."

At his desk, Tony rested his forehead in his hand. He had to stop yelling at Scott all the time, especially since the man tried so hard to do things right.

Tony knew he had let himself get out of control again, so he counted to ten to give himself a chance to recover before speaking. Scott had, in fact, done well to get the appointment. "Normally, yes, that would have been perfect. It's just that I won't feel easy about this woman until I've talked to her, and now you have a third party involved." Tony checked his watch. "We'll be up late tonight, so have a room ready. Dan will drop us off, but he's staying with relatives at night. It's a bit of a working holiday for him." Dan was an experienced officer who had married a Canadian and spent many holidays with her family. Tony had agreed to let his wife travel up with them. She would be spending a month with her family, and Dan could visit when he wasn't needed. "Scott," Tony continued, "you've done very well to make contact so quickly. I apologise for the 'idiot' comment. It was totally uncalled for."

"That's okay, sir," Scott responded. "By the way, there is no press here at all about a Canadian woman being raped in Cuba. Not a peep. It seems that she's staying quiet so far."

"Thank goodness for that," Tony replied. "I really hope she cooperates with us."

"So do I, sir. I'll see you tomorrow." Scott rang off.

"Sir", and not "Tony", Tony noticed. Scott was still offended by the insult. It had been a stupid thing to say. Tony picked up the phone again to call Sheila. He would have to make amends to Scott later.

The next morning at 10:30, Scott brought a tired Tony and Sheila to the Iron Will Gym. They had decided that Sheila would use Scott's pass and take Mary's aerobics class to initiate a connection. Scott would introduce Tony to Lori and they would glean as much information from her as possible. At lunch yesterday, Scott had learned that Mary had recently come back from a vacation that had gone sour, but Lori had offered no further information. During the afternoon Scott had kept his ear to the news and scanned all the papers. No stories were appearing in the media. To be sure, he had called a few papers and checked with Mary's travel agency. It took a little know-how to get information without revealing the reason for your questions, but Scott always enjoyed that kind of game. He didn't know why Mary was keeping quiet about her ordeal, but he and Tony were very happy about it.

At the front counter, Tony noticed that Lori was looking at him suspiciously. *Something's wrong here,* he concluded. He had tried to talk very little, and did his best to disguise what she might recognise as an accent.

On the trip up he had studied a map of Toronto, and this morning Scott had told him that he was supposed to live in an older section of Avenue Road. They had found it on the map and studied the surrounding area. Despite his fatigue, Tony had made a determined effort to be pleasant with Scott this morning. He still felt bad about yesterday, because Scott had not deserved the reprimand. Fortunately the kid was very forgiving, and so far had never let Tony's temper dampen his enthusiasm.

Bringing his thoughts back to Lori, Tony smiled at her.

Lori turned to Scott. "I thought you said your friends were couch potatoes," she accused. "These people do not look like couch potatoes. This guy looks extremely fit," she finished, indicating Tony.

*Whoops…mistake,* thought Scott. *That was a dumb thing to have said. Lori knows fitness when she sees it.*

Tony jumped in, relieved that the problem was so minor. He stared at Scott and pretended to be insulted. "You told her I was a couch potato?"

"Sorry," Scott apologised, letting him lead. "You said you didn't belong to a gym."

"Not right now," Tony admitted, "but a couch potato is someone who sits around watching TV all night with a remote control in one hand and a beer in the other."

"So bite my head off because I used the wrong term," Scott protested, looking to Lori as if for help.

Lori was laughing at them now, probably because Scott had put a comically contrite expression on his face and rolled his eyes. Tony knew it was time to drop it. The mini crisis had passed.

The next hour passed amicably. For the most part Tony watched Scott at work. *I was never that smooth with women,* Tony mused regretfully. *Where do people learn to be so confident? By Scott's age, I had already made the biggest mistake of my life and married Carolyn. Scott will never be that foolish.*

Before the hour was up, Scott had convinced Lori that Tony and Sheila had lived common-law for the past two years in Tony's home, which he had owned for fifteen years.

Tony worked for Bell Canada out of an office in Richmond Hill, north of the city. He commuted daily because he didn't want to ever sell his home. It was the house his university-aged son had grown up in. Tony's previous wife had died in a car crash years ago. Lori bought the whole story, and the questions she asked were easy to answer.

It was almost 11:30 now, and Tony felt a thrill of nervous anticipation. In a few minutes he would meet the woman who was causing such turmoil at the agency without realising it. In that camp of horrors in Cuba, his initial order to Gavin had made perfect sense, but now it seemed terribly out of place. They had been welcomed across the border, and were having a relaxed conversation with a perfectly ordinary person in a city that didn't know it was hosting a CIA officer with an ulterior motive for being there. Today he was supposed to make a decision whether an innocent woman was to live or die, and now the realisation that he was here for that purpose seemed a little shocking. He had made some very serious decisions previously in his career, but never one quite like this.

On their return from Cuba, Tony and Frank had met with Carl Walsh. Walsh had been horrified at their report, sending the news about Nat's death and the existence of a witness who had been raped by one of their officers immediately up the line. Walsh had not needed the implications explained to him. Without hesitation he had approved Tony going into Canada to locate Mary, on the understanding that they were to keep such a low profile that no one would know they were in the country. Going through regular channels on a matter this sensitive would be avoided as long as possible. Once Tony had assessed the damage, Walsh would know how to proceed. Of course Walsh was not told of Tony's real purpose for assessing Mary. If Gavin was utilised, Mary would just disappear and there would be no trail back to them. Tony and Frank would protect Gavin's actions absolutely. It was unfortunate that Scott and Aaron were privy to that decision, but both men were mature enough to know that even if they wanted to tell anyone about that decision, it would never be proven. Had Tony felt any doubt of Scott or Aaron's loyalty, the decision would have been hidden from them.

A few minutes later Sheila emerged, cheeks flushed by exercise. She was walking down the hall with a petite woman who had a trim figure and very pleasant features. The woman had short brown hair and a clear, healthy complexion. Sheila was obviously captivated—they were laughing like old friends. When they came close, the woman looked up and saw Tony looking at her. Her eyes were sparkling with laughter and kindly looking…a genuine type of person. Now the eyes were meeting Tony's directly. Something inside Tony turned upside down. *My God, it's the girl next door…the wife…the mother…this is the woman Aaron raped? No wonder he's such a mess. And I'm supposed to decide whether to kill her? Spare me, please.*

Mary stood still, surprised. This attractive middle-aged man with auburn hair and a pleasant expression had just looked right at her. That wasn't surprising, but he was still looking at her, even though he was standing beside Lori. That was definitely surprising. And he looked…well, interesting. Not a bodybuilder, but a good physique. Perhaps a potential customer for the club. Mary rarely did more than glance at the men here and greet them pleasantly as any good employee should. Staring at men was something that confident women like Lori did. Now she realised that she was still looking at this man. She should look away, she really should, but, well… "Hello," she greeted.

Tony smiled his encouragement. "Hello."

*He has a nice smile too,* Mary decided. Drat, she could feel herself blushing, so she forced her attention away. Lori was almost grinning. *Darn you, Lori, stop that. He's probably married, anyway.*

"Mary," Lori began, once she composed herself, "this is Scott, the man I told you about with the family tree father."

Mary held out her hand to the very attractive blond man who appeared to be in his mid-twenties. "Hello, Scott." This time it was Mary's turn to smile. *Sure, you invited him back for a family tree discussion, Lori. Tell me another story.* Scott was what Mary would call a charmer, although never to his face. Young, definitely good looking, with a manner that struck Mary as pleasant…just Lori's type. When Scott shook her hand without squeezing the life out of it, Mary gave him an extra bonus point.

"And these are his friends, Anthony and Sheila," Lori continued. "You've met Sheila, I see. They live in Toronto."

Of course Anthony would be married, or perhaps just living with Sheila, since neither of them were wearing rings. Mary swallowed her disappointment and felt foolish. Really, she was being absolutely silly today. Anthony had only been polite. Mary exchanged a smile with Sheila and then shook hands with Anthony. Despite her good intentions, she felt a tingle. That had definitely been a tingle that had run up her back. "Pleased to meet you, Anthony," she murmured. *Good heavens, I'm still blushing. This is ridiculous.*

Unknown to Mary, Tony was feeling nearly the same. *This is definitely not good,* he knew. *You have some very serious work ahead of you, my man, and you have to stay objective. So get your mind back on your job—now.* "Hello, Mary," he greeted.

Scott and Lori had already decided to return to the same deli to which Lori had taken Scott the day before. Since they only needed a light cover story for this job, Tony had decided they could use their real names. If Mary was to become a witness, she would be told who they were later, and they would apologise for tricking her if that was necessary. Had they been able to go through normal channels, the cover would have been unnecessary. If Tony had to act independently and bring Gavin in secretly, Lori might know their names, but she would have no idea who they were.

Tony already knew that unless he had suddenly lost his ability to judge character, the chances of him bringing Gavin in were slim to none. For some reason Mary was keeping her horror story to herself, and if he handled this well, it would stay that way. Tony relaxed a bit and listened to the conversation about aerobics. Steering the conversation to vacations was Sheila's job. Tony would only intervene if required. If the Cuba incident arose, Scott was to remain quiet and let Sheila probe the emotional side of it so Tony could get a sense of Mary's intentions. He crossed his fingers and hoped.

When Sheila swung the conversation to vacations, Mary suddenly became quiet. Lori was seen glancing nervously at her. At a look from Tony, Sheila let the silence continue in the hope that Mary would feel the need to fill it. She did.

Shaking her head in an attempt to dispel unpleasant thoughts, Mary looked at the people around the table. "I'm…sorry," she stammered. "I had a bad experience on a vacation. Ignore me." *That was poorly handled,* she decided.

Sheila looked at her compassionately. "Where did you go?"

"Cuba," was the reply. "I used to go there a lot."

"Bad food, bad hotel?" Sheila prompted.

*No, I don't want to talk about this,* Mary decided. *I told Aaron Somebody that I wouldn't tell, although I did tell Lori. She promised not to let my secret out. No one would ever believe, or understand it, anyway.* In an effort to change the topic, Mary shook her head to let Sheila know she wasn't prepared to answer, then asked Sheila what she did for a living.

"I'm a counsellor at a rape crisis centre," Sheila said easily. Since she continued to volunteer at one, this wasn't actually a lie.

"Oh." Mary swallowed, but said nothing further.

Sensing that Mary was not prepared to go any further right now, Sheila swung into action. She talked to Mary and Lori about working with women who had been assaulted. While Sheila knew her job was to encourage Mary to discuss her experience in Cuba, she found herself slipping quite naturally into her social worker role. Drawing Mary out was difficult, so Sheila talked about why women sometimes did not want to tell anyone about rape. She talked about the degradation and humiliation some women were forced to endure, about the fear and the shame they experienced, and about how their experiences could return to haunt them if they were kept hidden inside and never dealt with.

During this one-sided discussion, Lori glanced at Mary frequently, and Mary was clearly feeling distressed. Finally Lori spoke up to protect her friend. "Maybe we should change the topic," she suggested. "This is a bit depressing." Sheila pretended to suddenly notice Mary's distress. "I'm so sorry, Mary. Gosh, that was thoughtless. Look, if you'd like we could leave these guys here and go for a walk."

Mary shook her head, afraid to speak. It felt like Sheila had reached right into her and *seen* how much it hurt inside. She wanted more than anything to talk to Sheila, but if she did, Mary knew she would just cry and tell her everything. That couldn't happen. Mary had promised, and Aaron had been so kind in the end. People would want her to tell them who Aaron was. He would be in a lot of trouble. It was better if he remained unknown.

It was Lori who let the cat out of the bag. "You've got to deal with this someday, honey," she said to Mary.

"Lori, you *promised*," Mary complained desperately.

"Did this have something to do with your vacation?" Sheila probed. Undoubtedly there would be days when she wouldn't love her job, Sheila guessed, and today was one of them. It was apparent that Mary needed a genuine compassionate counsellor, and Sheila was feeling like a fraud right now. She promised herself that later she would sit down with Mary and truly help her, or at least link her up with a crisis counsellor here in her hometown.

"Nooo…well, I met some bad people." Mary tried to stop. Sheila was so easy to talk to, but she was a total stranger, for heaven's sake. Lori was different. Lori was her friend, that's why she had taken her hand now. Just as she had when Mary had told her about the rapes and the humiliation, and people being tortured, and, and… Damn it, her eyes were watering. It was all coming back so vividly. "I'm sorry," she sniffed.

"Were you hurt?"

It was Sheila talking in that social work type of voice. She had that manner that made you cry and blurt out things you didn't want to say, like "I was kidnapped." There was silence at the table, and Mary placed her hands on either side of her place setting. She had to get out of here before she confessed everything.

In an automatic gesture that Tony later attributed to fatigue and a momentary emotional weakness, he reached over and covered the hand that

Mary had laid on his side of her place mat. He held the small, shaking hand without realising that he had done so. Nor did he realise that out of concern he had reverted to his natural way of speaking and said, "I'm so sorry, my dear."

The gesture and his words stopped Mary in her tracks. It was surely coincidence that Anthony had taken her hand and reminded her of Nathanial. It also had to be coincidence that he had used the exact same words of comfort that Nathanial had uttered. But Mary realised that it was no coincidence that Anthony had just spoken those words with the exact same accent Nathanial had. And Nathanial had said, *"If you meet a man who knows me named Tony, give him my love...tell him it wasn't his fault."* It had seemed an odd thing to say, but Nathanial had refused to explain. Mary had put it down to the wanderings of a mind dealing with extreme pain.

Mary was suddenly terrified. She had a jacket that belonged to Aaron Somebody, whoever he was. Mary had found the hidden package in the lining when she had washed the jacket. It had pieces of paper listing transactions and names, so Mary had expected a mysterious phone call, or a letter. She had not expected three strangers to show up pretending to be someone else. Who were they? Were they Aaron's people? Were they someone else? Were they dangerous people? She had only one way to test them.

Tony knew he had made a major mistake. He wasn't exactly sure how Mary had done it, but she had seen through his cover. *I'm really blowing this,* he chided himself. *My two officers are doing an excellent job and I'm the one screwing up.* He saw Mary cringing against Lori, looking at him with her brown eyes wide and frightened. *Now I've terrified her somehow,* he realised. In an effort to look like nothing was amiss, he picked up his coffee cup, thinking furiously. That's when he got the shock of his life.

"Nathanial said to give you his love," Mary said quietly. "He said to tell you it wasn't your fault."

The coffee cup fell to the table with a crash, and then to the floor, spilling coffee everywhere. Tony moved back to avoid it, his eyes staring at Mary in astonishment.

Inside, Mary started to shake. She'd been right. *Calm down,* she told herself. *This is a Toronto restaurant full of people, not an isolated camp in Cuba. This man is a friend of Nathanial's, and Nathanial was nice. Maybe these people just want the jacket.*

"You can...can have the jacket," she stammered. "Then just go away and leave me alone. I don't want to know who you are or what you do. I don't know what was going on down there, and I don't want to know. I haven't told anybody anything, but I will if you don't go away."

When the three CIA officers stared speechlessly at her, and then looked at each other, Mary turned to Lori. "Lori, look what you've done!" Despite her best intentions, Mary was getting quite frightened.

It was Tony who found his voice first. Fortunately, Mary had kept hers low and the restaurant was noisy. The crashing coffee cup had turned enough heads. They were supposed to keep a very low profile, but this situation was on the verge of getting out of hand. If Mary got hysterical in public, Tony would have a real problem.

"Take it easy, Mary," he said soothingly. "You are perfectly safe. Relax and just talk to us. We're not going to hurt you. We just came up to talk to you and get the jacket." Good, her breathing was calming down. She wasn't a hysterical woman, but she clearly was frightened. No wonder, after what she had been through. Quickly he made a decision. Their cover was blown, so they might as well come clean with her now. It would have been preferable to do this in private, but it was too late for that. These women would not agree to go anywhere with him right now.

Mentally, he crossed his fingers while he produced his business card. You could never be sure what kind of reaction it would produce. Mary took it with shaking fingers and read it, looked at him quizzically, and read it again. He noticed that she wasn't overly surprised.

*Well,* Mary thought, *it sort of fits.* "I guess I have to trust that this is legitimate," she stated without emotion, indicating the card. "However would a person really know?" Then she looked at Sheila and Scott, who belatedly followed Tony's lead and produced their own cards. *Oh great,* Mary thought without humour. *Just what I always wanted—a collection of spy cards.*

Mary stared at Sheila, who had tricked her, but it was Scott who spoke up. "Sheila has worked at a rape crisis centre for a number of years, and she still volunteers there."

Once again Mary looked at the cards. Now she just needed Nathanial's and Aaron's. Nathanial...poor man. "So Nathanial was just working—doing the nine-to-five thing, except a little different. Some job." She stopped talking. There was a pained look on Tony's face.

"Nathanial Bowman was a very close friend of mine," Tony stated simply.

"He seemed to be a very nice man," Mary responded honestly. She looked at Lori, smiled, then released Lori's hand, which was probably squashed by now. Then she turned back to Tony. "Nathanial tried to keep me from being scared, but he was in much worse shape than I was. He told me to think of him when Taz came at me with the knife." She shuddered, unknowingly wrapping her arms around herself and cringing again at the memory. Staring at her plate, she thought of one more test. Just to be sure of them, in case they were lying. "What was his name?" Mary kept her eyes down.

Tony knew who she was referring to. "Officer St. Pierre. You knew him as Taz."

"No." Mary looked up. "His first name. Tell me his first name."

Scott and Tony looked at each other, puzzled. Wondering, Tony gave her the answer. "Aaron."

Mary smiled and nodded her agreement. *Aaron…I found you. I didn't want to find you, and I don't want to see you again, but at least you are real. Now maybe I can find out why it happened.* She was too embarrassed to ask Tony. Instead, Mary looked across the table at Sheila, and felt a sense of support. "Why did he do it?" Mary finally asked.

For a long second, Sheila seemed to be forming her answer. Before she spoke, she glanced at Tony for direction, but he seemed willing to let her carry this. Giving Mary her full attention, Sheila did her best. "I can't fully answer that, Mary, because I don't really know what all happened there. Tony would have to fill you in on the *why*. But," she continued, "I do know Aaron a bit. With absolute honesty I can tell you that for him to have raped you, the situation had to be critical. You have no reason to believe this, I know, but Aaron St. Pierre is actually a very kind and gentle man. If I'm permitted to say," here she flicked another look at Tony, "he's under a doctor's care now because of what he did to you. He's having a hard time dealing with it, and he's feeling terribly guilty. Mary, we're all in shock that this happened to you. All we know is that Aaron would have avoided it if he had seen any way out."

Tony waited for the reaction. Would Mary yell, laugh, or simply tell them to go to hell? It was unlikely that "I'm sorry our officer raped you, but it was all in the line of duty" would cut much ice with the victim. A number of expressions crossed Mary's face, but when she didn't respond, he handed her the card Aaron had asked him to give her. "Aaron asked me to give this to you," he told her.

Tentatively, Mary took the card and looked at the front of it. Then she turned it over. On the back of the card was written *Mary—call if you need me or you want to talk. Please. Aaron.* Mary stared at the words as thoughts tumbled through her mind. *They say you are a nice man, Aaron. Are they right?* She sighed and looked up at Tony.

"Where are you staying? I'll get his jacket for you."

*This was much too easy,* Tony thought. *Why isn't she angry? She should be threatening to sue us, and send Aaron to prison.* For now he would take it at face value, but there was still a great deal that had to be discussed. "Mary, we need to talk about what happened in Cuba—but not here," he added, indicating the restaurant. "Members of that group in Cuba have been arrested, and the case is going to court as fast as we can get it there. We need you to be a witness."

"Oh," that didn't sound good. "No, I could never face Aaron again," Mary said in a plea to Sheila. Then she remembered something, and turned to Tony again. "Did you get everyone on Sunday? I promised Aaron I wouldn't tell anyone because he was getting rescued on Sunday. Did you bring Nathanial back? He wanted to be buried in Kentucky."

This time there was no noise, because it was a sandwich Tony dropped. She knew about the rescue and had promised not to *tell*? She even knew where Nat had wanted to be buried! Christ, this woman was no end of surprises. Without a shadow of a doubt, Tony knew he would be keeping her alive and very, very safe, even if he had to guard her himself. "How," he demanded, "did you know about the rescue on Sunday?"

*Oops,* she thought. Who had told her that? How much should she be saying here? Aaron had probably not told Tony about killing Nathanial. "I know it was Sunday because that's why Aaron said he had to kill me. So I wouldn't go free and tell anyone."

Tony had nothing more to drop, but Scott did. This time a glass of water hit the floor and shattered, and now heads were definitely turning in their direction.

"We're out of here," Tony ordered, signalling the waitress. His hands were shaking, and his two officers looked like they had just seen a green Martian. "Scott, for heaven's sake, get it together," he ordered in a whisper. Next he turned to Mary. "Please, Mary, we really need to talk to you. Can we go some place private?"

Private? Mary hesitated. Did she really trust these people?

"Come to my place," Lori said suddenly. "As long as I can stay with Mary. I'll call work and tell them I need the afternoon off."

Mary looked at her in relief. What a friend! Although Scott probably had something to do with that decision.

Scott drove, and Lori sat up front with him to show him the way. Tony sat facing Mary. The backseats of the company car had been designed for people to face each other and conduct business. Sitting across from her allowed him to observe Mary more naturally. She was attractive. Not blatantly, like her friend Lori, but in a natural, understated way. There was no trace of guile on that honest-looking face, either. He shuddered when he thought of the order he had given to Gavin in Cuba. Only a few days ago Mary had been abused and threatened with death by someone she now knew to be one of his own people, yet here she sat without a word of condemnation. That she was scared, he could see. Her colour had paled when she entered the car, and her brown eyes were fearful. But she was here. He fought an insane desire to cross over, take her into his arms and tell her she was safe and not to worry.

Sitting beside Sheila, and across from Tony, Mary sat silently, deep in thought. What would Tony want to know? What did she want to know? For most of the trip, Tony was on the telephone, talking to his office. It gave Mary a chance to observe him. She had been scared at the restaurant, and very nervous about getting into a car with these people, but she felt better now. From some of the things he was saying, there was no doubt that Tony was talking to a real office, because he was asking for legal advice, and he kept calling someone "sir". Legal advice meant lawyers, and lawyers meant that there was some legitimacy to all this, so Mary lost her private fear that Aaron's people might just be more criminals and want to get rid of her.

Besides, when Tony had held her hand at the restaurant, he had given himself away, but he had also given away the fact that he was a compassionate person. Very businesslike on the surface, but there was a nice human being under there. Eyes could tell a lot about a person, and Tony's eyes, when he was being unguarded, told Mary the same thing. They were hazel, and went well with his sandy colouring. Good for admiring only, though, Mary decided. Despite the tingles he had caused, Mary knew she had better keep her distance. Tony travelled in such a different world than she, he might as well be from another planet.

Upon their arrival at Lori's, Mary came to two decisions. She would not tell Tony that Aaron killed Nathanial. That was Aaron's problem, not hers. Nor would she tell him about making love with Aaron on Saturday night. That would be much too embarrassing. If Aaron had told him, Tony would already know, and might ask her about it. She wouldn't lie, but if Tony didn't know, she sure wasn't going to volunteer the information.

As it turned out, the question and answer session was a lot easier than Mary had expected. Tony did not ask her about details of what had happened in Cuba. The lawyers had told him that they wanted the information firsthand.

Tony's questions were more general, and Mary found that he asked her a lot of questions about how she *felt* about what had happened to her. Did she hate Aaron? No, he had tried to protect her from the others. Whom did she blame for being kidnapped? Alfredo and Osvaldo—they had kidnapped her. Did she plan to seek damages from the CIA? Money? she asked. No, she wanted nothing to do with the CIA, or Aaron or those horrible criminals. She wanted to be left alone.

"Have you been to your doctor?" was Tony's next question.

"Yes."

"What did you tell him?" Tony asked.

That had been terribly embarrassing. "I told him I lost my mind and went home with some guy I met in a bar, and he got a little too rough with me." Mary blushed. "Dr. Kline has been my doctor for twenty years. He didn't totally believe me, but he had to take my word for it. He gave me a list of rape crisis centres and told me I could talk to him anytime I wanted. He also insisted on giving me a complete physical."

"Would you give consent for Dr. Kline to talk to our staff doctor?"

"Why?" Mary was sitting beside Tony on Lori's couch. He had a clipboard and was making brief notes. For some reason she had found it comforting to see him pull a pair of reading glasses from his pocket and perch them on the end of his nose. It made him seem more human. Now he was looking at her over the top of them.

Tony wished he could ignore those brown eyes that now stared up at him so calmly. Except for the seriousness of the questions, it seemed like a very intimate atmosphere. To give them some privacy, Scott had taken Lori into the kitchen to chat and make coffee. Sheila was being unobtrusive, sitting in a chair on the other side of the living room. Once again Tony yanked his mind away from those eyes to answer the question.

"We would like to know the extent of the damage you suffered," he responded, "and if there are any...complications," he finished.

*For complications, read pregnancy*, Mary realised. A sigh escaped her. No, she seemed doomed never to raise children. Her period had started yesterday. Not that she would have sought to have a child by a man she didn't know, but it would not have been the disaster Tony obviously thought it would be.

"No pregnancy," Mary answered. "And no damage that isn't already healing. Not physical, anyway." Tony had looked at her intently, so Mary went on to explain. "I've been having nightmares," she informed. At that, Tony scribbled another note.

Gnawing at the end of his pen, Tony watched Mary. *There's something I don't understand here,* he decided. *She should be furious.* Why not? "Mary, why aren't you angry?" That brought up the brown eyes again, and gave him another little jolt in the chest.

"I am angry," she replied. *Does he think I enjoyed enduring all that?* "I was forced to have sex with a man I don't know, thrown around, tied up, starved and threatened with death. I'm very angry."

Putting aside the clipboard, Tony turned towards her. "Where's the anger? I can't see it. I don't know where it's directed."

"Well, that's part of my problem, I think," Mary admitted. "I don't know who to be angry at. There's no one to yell at. I can't yell at Aaron, because in the end he was nice to me. I do believe that he was trying to protect me from the others. And I don't think you guys actually planned to have me raped, although it really pisses me off that you would make someone pretend to be a rapist. I'd like to kill Alfredo and Osvaldo, because they didn't care or even pretend that I was a human being. They are evil," Mary concluded, "but I never want to see them again." She thought about it. "Maybe that's why I have the nightmares. It all seems so unfinished."

*Perfect,* thought Tony. "Let us finish it for you. We'll pay for your lawyer and all your expenses if you'll come to court as our witness. You'll be put up in an apartment or house and I'll make sure you are guarded. Hopefully it will all be over in a couple of months." Even before he finished, Tony knew he was losing her. Her body language was saying no.

"No, I couldn't," she began. "I couldn't stand in a witness box and talk about the things Aaron did to me." Instinctively she looked at Sheila.

He was frustrated, but Tony knew enough to back off for the moment. They had no means of forcing Mary out of Canada to be a witness. She would have to come voluntarily. There was no rush to get a decision today, it had just been a chance. One thing he knew for certain was that Mary was no threat to them. Their lawyers would work with her and she would be treated with kid gloves.

"Do you want to charge Aaron with rape?" Tony asked reluctantly. "We can help you do that."

Mary stared at him. "No." *These people are really hard to convince,* Mary decided. *Obviously Aaron hasn't told them the whole story, especially about the last night.* "But," she added, "I need to know…" she stumbled, embarrassed, and glanced again at Sheila.

Sheila caught on quickly, and finished the sentence. "…if Aaron has any communicable diseases?"

"No," Tony replied. "I meant to tell you that. We had him examined and there's nothing for you to worry about." The blush in her cheeks only made her look more attractive, Tony decided, although he was sorry to see her embarrassed again. With a smile, he dared to pat her hand again. "Let's wrap this up," he said. "That's enough excitement for you in one day." Stretching, he felt the tension leave his neck and shoulders. Now he could afford himself a little luxury and look into those enticing brown eyes.

*I think he's pleased,* Mary decided, although she wasn't sure exactly what he was pleased about. Her answers, obviously, but why? At least he was smiling at her. Now that he wasn't being businesslike, she felt very comfortable with him. Scott came out and handed her a cup of coffee, so she curled her legs up underneath her on the couch and leaned back to relax.

Lori and Scott joined them and bantered back and forth with Sheila about nothing of importance for an hour and a half. Occasionally Mary or Tony joined in, but the younger people did most of the talking. Frequently Mary and Tony had their own conversation, which centred mostly around personal hobbies and interests.

"You didn't tell me where you were staying," Mary reminded Tony, "or how long you plan to stay."

"I'm not really sure," he admitted. "Now that I've found you, it will depend on how we decide to proceed with this, and whether I can convince you to come down and visit the beautiful state of Virginia."

"That means how cooperative I'm going to be," Mary guessed correctly.

"Something like that," Tony replied non-committally. He wasn't frustrated any more. A bit tired from the tension and emotions of the last few days, but feeling quite relaxed in this living room sitting beside this little woman who was doing such strange things to his heart strings. He noticed that Mary had finished her second cup of coffee. They should take her home. It had been a stressful day for her, too.

"Let us drive you home," he offered. When she smiled at him, her eyes twinkled as if she knew a secret. "What? Did I say something wrong?"

"No," Mary answered quickly. "It's just that my house is at the end of this block. I can walk quite easily."

Before she knew quite how it was arranged, Mary found herself being walked home by Tony. Scott and Sheila would bring the agency car. The air was a crisp -12 Celsius, with a lovely clear sky. Tony had worn earmuffs and gloves, as well as overshoes. Mary cast a critical eye at his outfit and decided that he was warm enough for the short walk. The sun was low on the horizon, as the afternoon had passed with amazing speed. Knowing that her new acquaintances might be around for a few days pleased Mary now, instead of frightening her.

"This weather is quite pleasant," Tony admitted, "in a cold kind of way." In truth, he would have liked to walk further with her, but their car had already reached her driveway. He slowed his step, and Mary did likewise. She was looking up at him as he paused. Before he chickened out, or came to his senses, he blurted out what was on his mind. "Once this is behind us," he stated, "I would like to take you out to dinner."

Quite a conservative proposition from an obviously conservative type of man. Mary could feel her pulse quicken. This "date" might be far in the future, and it was quite conceivable that he would change his mind or forget, but the thought of it made her happy. "I'd like that," she answered with pleasure. Impulsively she slipped her hand through his arm, and was rewarded when he covered it with his other hand. Like an old couple taking a walk in the park, they strolled towards her house.

# XX

That evening, from his office in Washington, Congressman Richard Harvey started to make a telephone call. Bail had cost him a ruddy fortune, and his lawyers were going to cost even more. At least the news about his arrest had not hit the papers. The CIA were keeping very quiet about this, and for the time being that suited Richard Harvey perfectly. He was close to ruin, but he would go down fighting.

Jose Luis and his buddies could not get bail, as it was obvious that they would disappear at the first opportunity. They needed lawyers too, and although they had money stashed away, they couldn't access it right now. He had to be the bloody go-between for them and their Cuban contacts. All this and a telephone that was probably tapped by now. What a mistake he had made supporting them. He wished he had never seen that island.

Richard Harvey used a firm of lawyers picked for their legal skills, not for any ethical reasons. They would do whatever he said. Right now he needed to pass on some information from Jose Luis. His lawyers were to check into the supposed death of the Canadian woman at the camp. "Taz" had turned out to be a CIA officer and it was just possible that he had not killed the woman. Highly unlikely that he would let her go, the Congressman thought privately. A CIA officer raping a Canadian tourist repeatedly in front of everybody, and apparently with great enjoyment? What were these guys resorting to? St. Pierre would be a fool not to kill her, but if he hadn't, she would have to die.

It was Alfredo who had discovered that the woman spoke Spanish. There was a chance that she had overheard conversations that tied Richard Harvey to both the Liberators and, previously, to the Cuban government. The woman would be an independent witness, and the jury would believe anything a kidnapped tourist told them. His lawyers were planning to tear Mr. St. Pierre's credibility to shreds. It was their only sure defence. By raping the tourist, he had set himself up, and if he had killed her too, well, he would be finished. If she was alive, they had to make sure she was never seen alive again. Unless, of course, she wanted to be a witness for their side. His lawyers' staff, many of whom had nothing to do with legal work, had developed contacts inside the CIA, and Richard Harvey had a few of his own. While they looked for this woman, they would at the same time be tapping their sources for information. Even if the CIA found her first, Harvey's people would silence her anyway. That would leave St. Pierre as the only CIA witness on site. Nowhere near as good as an independent witness.

Having second thoughts about using his own phone, Congressman Harvey let out a series of oaths and went in search of a phone booth.

# XXI

Dialling Aaron's number, Scott couldn't keep the smirk off his face. That smirk had annoyed Tony so much that the older man had invited Sheila for a drink in the bar downstairs and left Scott with the job of reporting in. Man, he couldn't wait to tell Aaron the news. When Aaron came on the line, Scott skipped the pleasantries.

"Hey, Aaron, I think you can relax," he informed. "Things are okay up here."

"You met Mary?" There was a sign of the old Aaron's excitement in his tone. An excitement that had been missing despite some pretty hefty anti-depressants.

"Met her, and she's got the old man's approval."

"Thank God!"

Scott couldn't hold himself back. "Are you sitting down, Aaron?" he asked.

A pause on the line, followed by a groan. "She's pregnant?"

"No, no...nothing like that!" With an effort, Scott toned himself down. "Well, first I'd better let you know that she saw through you. Or at least she must have, because she doesn't want to charge you, or sue us, or anything." There was no immediate response. "She's a nice lady, Aaron."

"I know that." Aaron had almost whispered.

"But what I really gotta tell you—the old man's gone head over heels for her!"

"What?"

"No shit," Scott insisted. "He's falling in love with Mary. You should have seen them today. They were walking arm in arm down the sidewalk like an old married couple. You can forget about any execution order from him."

No response.

"Aaron?"

"I'm still here, Scott. It's just a little surprising. Tony doesn't know all that happened in Cuba. I'm afraid if he falls in love with Mary he's going to be pretty upset with me when he hears the details."

153

"That's a thought," Scott admitted, "but there's not much you can do about it. Anyway, the old man's so damned proper, he probably won't ask her out until the case is over."

"Probably not. Tony's a little different. Well, at least she's alive. Oh, Scott, I'm scared to death to see her again, but at the same time I really need to. Is she coming down?"

"She doesn't want to, but we'll work on that. Sounds like she feels about the same way you do. She doesn't want anything to do with us." Poor Aaron. He had to get his life back on track. Scott pried a little. "Have you called Susan?"

"No. Not yet." There was another pause. "She's got a road tour tomorrow, and she'll be gone for at least three weeks. I'll call her when she gets back."

*Damn you, Aaron.* "Aaron, she's my sister." Scott knew Aaron didn't need any more guilt right now, but he was avoiding Susan.

"I can't yet, Scott. I'm sorry, but I can't. What the hell am I supposed to say to her? 'Sorry about those promises, honey, but they only lasted four weeks?' Or maybe 'How about we spend our honeymoon in this really nice prison I'm going to?' Look, I want to tell her about this, but we're not even married yet. I don't think she's going to understand. You had better be ready for her to drop me flat."

Scott felt deflated. "Promise me that you'll give her a chance when she gets back. Promise."

"Promise." Silence. "Scott...I'm sorry."

"Not to me, Aaron," Scott rallied. "Save your apologies for Susan and Mary. I don't know exactly what went on down in Cuba, or how you brought yourself to do what you did, but I do know one thing; if I believed for a second that you did that out of choice, I would never let you *near* Susan again, much less be begging you to call her."

"Thanks."

"No problem. Now go and get better fast, okay?" With a sigh, Scott hung up. The road to being a brother-in-law looked long indeed.

154

# XXII

The next morning was spent in the hotel while Tony got updated on some of the other operations under his command. At 11:00 a.m. the phone rang. Scott grabbed it, and was surprised to hear Lori's voice on the other end. "Well, hello there," he greeted.

Lori's voice sounded concerned. "Sorry if I'm interrupting anything, but I wanted to ask you if you have any other guys working with you up here."

That got Scott's attention, and he snapped his fingers at Tony to get his. "No, we don't. Why do you ask?" Tony was beside him in an instant, and Sheila was gathering up the papers they had been working on, sensing that the quietness of the morning was ending.

"There were three men here at the club asking for Mary. I know she was out shopping this morning, so they probably didn't find her at home. I didn't like their looks," Lori stated grimly. "You know—cold, big, eyes looking all over the place. Two of them reminded me of a gangster movie."

"What did you tell them?" Scott demanded.

"That I hadn't seen Mary for two weeks. She had gone on vacation and hadn't come back yet. They were easy to lie to. Didn't like them."

*Whew!* That gave them some breathing room. "Okay, well done. Gotta dash, Lori, and find Mary. If you see those guys again, play dumb, will you?"

"Oh, I can be the dumbest blonde they ever met, if I try," Lori laughed.

"Mm. No comment. Talk to you later." As soon as he hung up and told Tony, Tony ordered him to call Dan. They needed some help. Sheila did not have the experience necessary to hold her own if these were hit men. For that matter, Tony probably didn't think Scott had enough experience either. But Scott knew that although he lacked experience, his reflexes were fast, he was very good with weapons, and he craved excitement. Surely that counted for something.

The next phone call was to Mary's house, but there was no answer. As soon as Dan arrived, they were on their way. This was work, and Tony shut his mind to any personal feelings that were clamouring to be heard.

155

Four bags of groceries could weigh a lot. Although she had gone to the store for bread and milk, Mary had impulsively decided that she would invite her new acquaintances for dinner. The last package was nicely crammed into the small fridge when she heard a car door slam. Normally, she would not have paid any attention, but she hoped Tony, Scott and Sheila would drop by. Now the phone was ringing. When Mary picked it up, she heard Lori's voice.

"Mary, has anyone been at your place? There were some gangster types here, and Scott said they weren't CIA. They asked for you, Mary."

"Hang on, Lori." The kitchen window looked onto the road, and Mary peeked out. She saw a black Jaguar. No one she knew could afford a Jaguar, so she looked closely at the three men around it. Something about them made her blood run cold. What was it? *Process what you are seeing, she told herself. Your gut instinct is usually right, but why are you getting warning bells?* Their manner of dress—bulky topcoats, eyes hidden by sunglasses on a cloudy day. The body language—looking up and down the street as if worried about being seen. The car—money in a neighbourhood complaining about property taxes. They did look like gangsters a bit. Mary made a quick decision. "Lori, they're in front of my house. I've got to run." Hanging up the phone, she grabbed her car keys.

In many of the older Toronto homes, like Mary's, the garages were behind the houses, accessible by a back laneway. Mary slipped out the back and ran to her car. It was a well-tuned Toyota Corolla, and started quickly and quietly. She reversed out the back and down the lane. If she wasn't followed, then she would chalk it up to an overactive imagination. If they followed her, she didn't know what she would do.

A few blocks away, Mary pulled over. *This is silly,* she decided. *I'm becoming paranoid. I'll sit here and see if they are following me. It's probably just Lori's imagination and a lot of coincidence.* Mary checked her rearview mirror. The Jaguar was turning the corner towards her. *That cannot be coincidence.* The little car jumped gamely to her touch, and Mary sped around a few streets. *You know the neighbourhood,* she told herself. *Be calm and drive carefully but quickly. Check the mirror.* The Jaguar was definitely following. *Okay, a couple of detours, then stop at the restaurant with the telephone. There will be lots of people there. It's lunchtime. No time to worry about parking tickets.*

Jumping out of the car, Mary ran into Lee's restaurant. The patrons were mainly Oriental. The telephone was inside and to the right. Mary dialled

Tony's hotel number. No answer in the room. She hung up. That hadn't occurred to her. He was supposed to be there. Now the panic that she had been denying rose in her like a balloon ready to burst. What now? Call 911? By the time she convinced anyone she wasn't crazy or on drugs, these men would be here. *Oh, Aaron, what have you done to me?*

Aaron. She had his card, but he was hundreds of miles away. Maybe he would know what she should do, though. He was Tony, Sheila and Scott's friend. Maybe he would help her. With shaking fingers, she grabbed his card. It told her to call. She would. Somehow she dialled his number. There was no answer, but then a switchboard answered. Well, at least it was a live person. For a second she felt foolish, but then she looked up and saw the Jag pull up behind her car. Her voice almost failed.

"Help, please…I need to speak to Aaron. Hurry! Aaron St. Pierre. I'm in trouble. My name's Mary. Mary Norland. He'll know, please…" The doors of the Jag were opening. "They're coming in…please hurry."

"Where are you?" the calm voice on the switchboard asked.

"In Toronto, Canada. Tony…Tony Dune was here to help me, but I've lost him." Although the restaurant was below street level, the street could be seen through the front window if you peered up. Mary saw legs beside the Jag.

"*Where* in Toronto are you?" the voice demanded.

Couldn't she just put Aaron on the phone? Somehow Mary remembered what street she was on, and also gave the name of the restaurant and the closest intersection. Then there was a slight sound on the phone and suddenly she heard an authoritive voice from Cuba.

"Mary, it's me, Aaron. Tony's on his way. Tell me what's happening."

Her knees almost buckled with relief. Aaron to help and Tony on his way. *Answer him, quickly.* "Three men followed me in a black Jaguar. They're coming down the steps now. They've seen me." Her hands were sweaty on the phone.

"Is the restaurant busy?"

"Packed," she responded.

"Okay, Mary, everything's going to be all right. They will want to take you out of there. *Do not go with them,*" he emphasised. "Stay on the phone with me. We'll stall for time. Tony is only a few minutes away."

Now the men were inside the door. Two of them stayed by the door, while the third walked towards her. Up close, he didn't really look like a gangster. He could have been anyone.

"Hello, Mary," the man greeted. The man, who worked under a variety of names and was currently using Harold Pitt, observed the small woman in front of him. She was clutching the phone and staring at him, terrified. Hard to imagine that such an insignificant-looking person could be worth all this trouble. His instructions had been complicated. Normally he was paid to threaten, kill, or simply teach someone a lesson. Many of these assignments could be given to one of his two employees, who were currently guarding the door. Mr. Pitt took responsibility for the more difficult assignments, like this one.

For this assignment he had come along because it required some analysis. If the CIA had not contacted this woman, he was to bring her back as a witness for his employer. If the CIA had already killed her, as his employer had expected, that was considered good news. Mr. Pitt was to find out how she was killed, plant some evidence, and bring attention to the fact that she had been a witness to CIA wrongdoing and had subsequently disappeared. Enough people had seen her in Cuba after she left the scene of the crime, apparently, so the CIA was taking a big risk in killing her. His job was to tip the scales against the CIA. Proof that they killed her was not necessary. Circumstantial evidence on top of the Cuban witnesses would be more than enough to convince a skeptical public that the CIA had murdered an innocent, abused Canadian citisen. His employers actually preferred this option. The third option was not expected. If the CIA had contacted the witness, and for some inexplicable reason she had agreed to cooperate and not been killed by them, Mr. Pitt was to execute her and make it look like a CIA job.

None of the options were beyond his abilities, but Mr. Pitt did not like complicated assignments. They left room for confusion and error. He did not like to make errors. This employer paid him not to make mistakes, and paid well and promptly. Not that he knew who his employer was. The name was "James" and his money was good. Mr. Pitt had no desire to know more.

Aaron had been listening closely, and had heard Mr. Pitt address Mary. "Say hello," he instructed, "and ask him who he is."

"Hello," Mary obeyed. "Who are you?" He gave her the name of Harold Pitt, which she repeated to Aaron.

"Ask him what he wants," was her next instruction. She did, and felt a stab of fear when his eyes checked out the restaurant. *I think he wants to kill me,* she realised. The men by the door were constantly scanning the street, and she suspected that under their coats they probably had guns.

Mr. Pitt decided to make up an answer for her and talk her into leaving the crowded restaurant. "I represent the legal firm of Duncan, Gillespie and Erikson. We'd like to meet with you about a court case coming up." He actually smiled at her. "It has to do with that awful experience you had in Cuba at the hands of the CIA."

While he wasn't doing anything threatening, Mary knew it was very weird that he didn't seem to care when she repeated everything he said to Aaron. *He doesn't care because he's going to kill me, so what does it matter what gets said? There's probably no such legal firm, and no Harold Pitt.*

"We went to your home," Pitt continued, "but we missed you. We would like you to meet with us for a few minutes. You can pick the place."

*I'll bet I can,* thought Mary. *Choose my own graveyard—no thanks.* Aaron was talking again. "Mary, Tony is just arriving. Tell Mr. Pitt that you are a witness for the CIA, who are just about to enter the restaurant to pick you up."

She did so, and saw the men by the door stiffen and look quickly at Mr. Pitt. Pitt made a small motion with his hand that Mary interpreted as a don't-do-anything signal. Oh, this was awful.

Aaron wasn't finished yet. "Mary, when Tony comes in, hang up the phone and do *exactly* what he says, okay?"

"Okay," she replied weakly. *Please don't anyone shoot.* Out of the corner of her eye she saw two things. Tony was walking down the steps with a black man she hadn't seen before, followed by Scott and Sheila. At the same time, a police cruiser pulled up to the curb. "A police car just came," Mary announced into the phone.

The reply surprised her. "Shit."

Later she would understand that response. Right now she saw Scott and Sheila wait outside the door while Tony came in, followed by the man she didn't know. "Tony's here, Aaron."

"Hang up and do what he says."

With reluctance, Mary hung up the phone. It had been like having a safety line attached to her. She noticed that Tony seemed completely composed. He actually said good morning to the two men at the door as he walked between them. The black man walked a few paces past the two men, then turned so his left side was towards them and his right side was towards Mr. Pitt. Everyone was taking up positions, Mary realised. *Please get me out of here, Tony. This looks really dangerous.*

Tony walked up to her, stopping several feet away. "Sorry we're late, Mary. Ready to go?"

He didn't sound like anything at all was going on, but Mary knew by his posture that he was alert for the slightest movement by Mr. Pitt. Surprisingly, his next words were directed at Mr. Pitt.

"She's under our protection. Your firm will receive full disclosure nearer to the commencement of the trial."

Mr. Pitt merely nodded. He and Tony seemed to be in a staring contest. "Go out to the car, Mary," Tony ordered.

Her legs managed to take her past Tony, past the man she didn't know, past the two men at the door, and out the door past Scott and Sheila. Scott and Sheila's attention was totally focused on the two men inside the door, and they didn't seem to even notice Mary pass between them. As she got to the car, Mary started to breathe again, but then a police officer approached her. It was a friend of hers who worked this area.

Mike Chang was a nine-year veteran of the Toronto Police, with sergeant's stripes, a wife and two preschool children. He had turned thirty years old last month, and was very happy with life in general. Right now, Mary wished Mike was anyplace else but here. The street seemed strangely deserted for the middle of the day, and Mary wished there were more people around. Having opened the backdoor of Tony's company car, Mary saw Mike glance behind her. As he did, Mary heard a sudden scuffle of feet, and heard Tony yell "MOVE!" Almost instantaneously, Mary felt herself pushed roughly into the car, landing on the floor. To her astonishment, she saw Scott shove Mike into the car and jump in with him as the car took off.

Somehow, Sheila had gotten in, and since the car was squealing its tires to get away from the curb, Mary could only presume the other man was driving. Tony had pushed her in, and was sitting facing backwards. Mike was also on the floor, struggling to right himself.

Mary knew Mike was going to be upset as soon as he got his bearings. As she tried to sit up herself, Mary saw Scott make a quick movement towards Mike, who was trying to reach for his gun. Scott grabbed his arm and removed the firearm from its holster. Flabbergasted, Mary looked at Tony.

Tony wasn't looking at her. He was busy opening a compartment in the car and pulling out a couple of serious-looking weapons. *Damn,* he thought. *This is turning into an absolute disaster.* For a few minutes he had thought they would get away safely, but Mr. Pitt clearly decided the stakes were too high to allow Mary to be taken away. The dangerous time had occurred when the street had been quiet, just before they got into the car, and that was exactly when Mr. Pitt and his goons had made their move.

Seeing a uniformed police officer had probably startled them just enough to throw off their timing. Scott had pushed the police officer into the car for his own safety. Mr. Pitt would have shot right through him. But now they had a damned cop in the car. Scott had moved quickly to disarm him. It had been too much to expect an armed police officer to lie meekly on the floor while being abducted in a car full of weapons. He was nervous—you could see it in his eyes, but he wasn't ready to give up. He made a movement to get up. If he grabbed for one of their weapons, someone in this car could get hurt.

"Get down," Scott ordered, but Mike just glared at him. With the revolver that he had removed from the police officer, Scott lightly tapped Mike's temple for emphasis. "Down," he repeated quietly. Mike gave up and sat on the floor next to Mary.

"Easy, Scott," Tony warned. The abduction, weapons, and a car chase were going to be enough to try to explain, without adding a charge of police assault for good measure. Tony handed Scott an Uzi. "Okay, son, I'm counting on you." Tony braced a knee on the car seat against the window as Dan manoeuvred the vehicle sharply around corners, vehicles and other obstructions. Tony knew he needed Dan's experience in the back of the car, but he also needed Dan where he was—driving on streets that only he was familiar with. Knowledge of the roads would be their only advantage over the twelve-cylinder Jaguar. Tony would have to put his faith into Scott's training and reflexes today. Sheila had moved the other two as far into one corner as she could. Scott needed room to move if necessary. He was a lot faster and more flexible than Tony.

Tony noticed that the police officer had his eyes trained on him. *You know I'm running this circus, don't you, Sergeant?* "You are in no danger from us, Sergeant. We just don't have time to be polite." He turned to Dan. "Can you outdrive this Jag?"

"Not on a drag strip," Dan responded drily, "but we're staying ahead. I know the streets. They're from out of town." They whipped around a corner and detoured through an alley to squeal around another corner.

"What the hell's going on here?" the sergeant demanded. Realising that there were no guns pointed *at* him had apparently increased his confidence.

It was Mary who answered, since the others were too concerned with the car following them. "They're guarding me, Mike."

"From what?" he asked sarcastically, eying the guns.

"From some men who don't want me to be alive to testify at a trial," Mary responded. Poor Mike. As far as he knew, the only danger to him was from inside the car. She told him who Tony was, and the little bit of what she knew was going on. It was clear that he didn't like it, but he seemed to believe her. Some of the tension left his body, and he turned to watch Tony again.

*As long as Dan keeps free of the Jag,* Tony thought, *we can avoid a street battle and hopefully lose them. At the first safe opportunity we'll drop the cop off. He'll be angry, but no worse for wear. I had better call Walsh and get some political help started. We are really going to ruffle some feathers today.* While the car careened back and forth, Tony reported in to his once again horrified Deputy Director. *I wish I knew Walsh better,* Tony thought briefly after Walsh had rung off. *Things like this could really shorten a career.*

So far they were keeping out of street fighting range. Tony glanced at the sergeant. *Looks barely thirty. Must be doing something right to have the stripes.* Suddenly the sergeant's walkie talkie came to life. He started to reach for it, but stopped suddenly and glanced at Scott. "I've got a rookie with me today. He's probably following us."

Dan spoke from the front of the car. He was monitoring the police radio calls. "Your rookie is hanging right in there with us. He's a hell of a driver for a rookie." Then he addressed Tony. "The rookie has already called in to report, sir. This officer's people are starting to freak. They want the rookie to try to communicate."

Tony swore under his breath. This was getting worse and worse. "Dan, if the police get a roadblock in front of us, we could end up in a three-way shooting match." He didn't need to say more. He knew Dan could envision the results.

"Doing my best to avoid them, sir."

Allowing the sergeant to communicate to his rookie couldn't make the situation any worse, Tony decided. "Go ahead and talk to him."

"I hear you, Derrick," Mike responded to the rookie.

"Are you all right, sir?" was the anxious question.

"That's affirmative."

"Sir, I'm to ask if you are still armed."

*Oh shit,* thought Tony. *Now all hell will break loose.* He looked at the sergeant, who said a surprising thing into the walkie talkie.

"Stand by." Mike was staring at Tony, as if to say, *"Your move."*

Stand by? This man was no fool, Tony realised. Probably third or fourth generation Chinese Canadian, young and a sergeant. His eyes were calm now, and he observed Tony steadily. So the sergeant had understood the implications of a roadblock. "How long have you been on the job?" Tony asked.

"Nine years."

Experienced. Good. "Married?" He wasn't asking for the sake of social pleasantries. A man with commitments was more apt to be cautious.

"Wife and two preschoolers."

Tony made a decision. "You understand that you have neither the firepower nor are you paid enough to take part in this shit." It was a statement.

Mike nodded. "If it means seeing my kids grow up, I can eat a little humble pie and sit on your floor. I won't interfere."

"Scott." It was all Scott needed for a command. The weapon was returned instantly. "If worse comes to worse," Tony said to Mike, "protect yourself and Mary."

Mike spoke to his rookie again. "That's affirmative, Derrick."

"That made them a little happier," Dan advised from the front, "but they are still planning to get both us and the Jag off the road." It wasn't a high-speed chase—the roads were too congested for that—but Dan was forced to do some dangerous manouvers to keep away from his pursuers. Having cruisers closing in would complicate things.

Tony grabbed the phone again. He needed help. If Walsh was trying to go through official channels, help would never come in time. Walsh answered immediately. He had been standing by, and told Tony that he had four different people contacting various Canadian officials.

"We're almost there, Tony," Walsh informed. "I've got the Toronto police chief on the other line. I skipped a few channels. He's just verifying who I am, then I think we'll be okay. For God's sake, try not to get anybody hurt in the next few minutes."

Tony hung up and prayed.

"I can get rid of that Jag for you," Mike offered, still holding the walkie talkie in his hand.

*Get rid of it?* "How?" Tony demanded.

A little smile played around Mike's eyes. "The rookie is a stock car driver in his spare time, and he also has a passion for those demolition derbies."

*Well, finally,* thought Tony. *A little piece of luck.* "That will cost you some major paperwork, I imagine," he mused. Then he got serious. "Make sure that your man knows there is a lot of firepower in that car."

"Derrick...can you take that Jag out of this race?"

The rookie's voice sounded incredulous. "Easy, sir, but with the cruiser?"

"Of course." Mike went on to warn him. "You only get one chance, then get away from them fast. They are heavily armed. Call for backup and watch from a distance. Try to see where they go, but *do not* approach them by yourself, understood?"

"Yes, sir. I'll have to wait for a spot without pedestrians."

The sergeant was nodding to himself. Their own citizens were their first priority.

"I know a perfect spot," Dan announced as he spun the car into a tight left turn. Three more abrupt turns kept the passengers unbalanced. Tony noticed that the rookie had no problem following. They were now on a street that consisted only of office buildings, where people did not work Saturdays. Today was Saturday. "Financial district," Dan announced. "Lots of cement and not too many shop windows."

There was a pause. "Here he goes," Scott yelled.

*Flawless,* Tony observed, watching the cruiser through the back window. The Jag was hit at an angle that caused the right front fender to hit a lamp post. It spun around and buried itself against a set of cement stairs leading from the sidewalk to a higher walkway into the buildings. No pedestrians, and minimal property damage if you discounted the Jag. The cruiser sped half a block ahead, and pulled over to stand guard until help arrived.

Scott whooped, "Fuckin' got them! Good job! Your guy's out of harm's way, too. His backup is arriving, but the goons just left on foot, running."

*They won't hang around,* Tony knew. At least the potentially deadly situation had ended peacefully. He stored the heavy weapons back in their compartment and sat back in his seat, inviting Mary and Mike to get off the floor. Now the rookie appeared directly behind them, the cruiser damaged, but still quite operational. Together with Dan, the police officers arranged a drop-off spot around the next corner to the left. By the time Dan turned the corner, there were at least eight cruisers sitting in the road, waiting. From instinct, he hit the brakes.

"They don't look particularly friendly, do they?" he observed. "Walsh must have got through, though, because they've been told to keep hands off as long as the sergeant here is returned unharmed."

"They missed me," Mike laughed. "It's okay. I'll get out here and you can slip away."

But Tony disagreed. "That doesn't seem polite, somehow. It's sort of like dumping your date at the curb instead of walking her to the door. No, let's be gentlemanly about this, Dan. Drive up to them. I'd like to thank the rookie, anyway."

Upon Dan's approach, several cruiser doors opened, but no officers emerged. *They are not really sure what we'll do, Tony knew, so they are still ready for another chase.* Tony opened his door, and let Mike out first after the sergeant had said goodbye to Mary.

Mary, Scott, Sheila and Dan all watched Tony wave at the gathering of cruisers and walk with Mike back to the rookie's car. Derrick left his car and was introduced. Handshakes all around, and it was over.

With a sense of great relief, Tony returned to his car. Crisis was over, for now, and everyone was safe. Even Sergeant Chang had seemed to bear no grudge. That was a bit of luck. The poor guy probably had hours of report writing ahead of him now. The CIA public relations team would try their best to soothe the ruffled police and political feathers, and Carl Walsh would have people busy back at the office trying to figure out who had hired the hit men. Someone had been after Mary in a big way.

Dan sped away as soon as Tony entered the vehicle and was seated. A pounding had started in Tony's head; the result of his adrenaline rush. He always had to internalise his tension until the current crisis was over, then his body punished him by giving him a violent headache. It would pound until he took some aspirin, or lay down and rested for half an hour or so.

"Where to, Tony?" Dan asked.

"The hotel first. We'll grab our stuff and then go to Mary's." Tony smiled at Mary, trying to ignore his headache. "Can you get a bag packed real fast? We've got to get you to some place safe. We'll drop Dan at the subway so he can continue his vacation, then the rest of us will drive nonstop to Langley."

Mary stared at him. Go where? She wasn't going anywhere. This was her home, and she couldn't just walk away and leave it unattended. "I can't leave Toronto," she stated. "I live here."

Perhaps if his head hadn't been pounding, he would not have felt so frustrated, but damn the woman anyway. Couldn't she see after what had just happened that people were out to kill her? "Yes you can," he stated. "I can't protect you up here. You have to come down and let us put you in a safe place for a couple of months."

"A couple of months!" Was he crazy? And what was "a safe place" anyway? She hardly knew these people. For all she knew, they could lock her up and throw the key away. Not that she really believed they would, but Tony couldn't just order her around like this. She shook her head. "No, that's all right. I'll stay with Lori. No one will find me there."

Anger boiled up inside Tony. He had just risked the lives of three of his officers, plus his own, caused unknown political havoc, abducted a police officer, and Mary was acting as if it was all in a day's pay! Drop her at Lori's? As if those men would not think of trying there? The ungrateful, stupid woman. When he spoke, it was with a low, icy tone that held no warmth for her brown eyes. "You are coming with us. We are not playing games with you any more."

"Sir," Sheila spoke, "perhaps we can discuss this—"

But Mary interrupted. How dare he! So this was what they were really like. She should have guessed. "And I suppose you think you have enough power to get me past your Immigration kicking and screaming and waving my passport?"

"Oh, I'll get you past," he threatened. His control was slipping away, but he was too angry to care.

Sheila tried to speak again. "Sir, I don't think this is doing us any—"

"How?" Mary challenged, an independent streak and natural stubbornness refusing to let her back down now. "Are we driving out of the province and crossing in a wheatfield perhaps? I'll still make one hell of a noise every time you stop."

"Sir, stop this." Sheila's voice got louder. She had never seen one of her boss's temper tantrums yet, but was not of the personality to stand by and let him threaten a defenceless woman in any case.

It was enough to snap Tony's control. Now he was yelling. "YOU ARE COMING WITH US IF I HAVE TO TIE YOU UP, GAG YOU, AND PUT YOU IN THE TRUNK!"

"THAT'S ENOUGH, sir," Sheila yelled back.

At the same time Mary's voice became very quiet. "Well, it wouldn't be the first time. That's just about what I've come to expect from you people."

Tony saw red, but her words had reached him. They had hurt, and he knew he was making a terrible mistake. However, he had gone too far now to back down. His two male officers were not helping. That meant they believed he was in the wrong. And this brand-new female on his team had the unbelievable gall to yell at him in front of the others, telling him to shut up. Sheila became the target of his anger.

"You keep your mouth *shut*! You've just had one of the shortest careers of anyone on my team *ever*!" There, that would teach her. But even as he yelled, the professional part of Tony that had been screaming for control finally got a foothold. His anger having peaked, and the energy spent, he realised what he had just been saying. Guilt started to settle in. Angrily, he stared out the window, struggling to regain control.

No one besides Dan had noticed that they had reached the hotel and were sitting in the parking lot. Scott's mind had been racing. He had experienced Tony's temper before, but never seen it directed at a civilian in their protection. Probably Tony's frustration was augmented by his fondness for Mary, although you wouldn't know it now. Mary and Sheila did not know Tony well enough to realise that if they had reacted differently they could have diffused a lot of that anger. Now it seemed to be an impasse. If Aaron was here, he could have cooled the old man down. Aaron had always known how to handle Tony.

Well, why not? Scott reached for the phone. The mere fact that Tony didn't stop him told Scott that Tony wanted a way out, but was still too angry to try. Aaron would be waiting for the results of today's near disaster anyway. He answered the phone immediately.

"Hello."

"Hey, guy; could use your help."

At the other end, Aaron heard the tension in Scott's voice.

"What's the matter?"

Scott told him in brief what had just transpired. While he talked, he kept an eye on Tony. Tony continued to stare out the window, hands actually clenched.

"Let me talk to Mary first," Aaron requested. Scott handed her the phone.

Mary took the phone. She felt like she had caused a big problem, but still felt that she was right. It made her feel awful. Sheila was in trouble and Tony looked like he'd love to hit her. "Hello, Aaron," she spoke in a weak, tired voice.

"Hi, Mary." Aaron's voice was pleasant and friendly. It was nice to hear. "So I hear the old man has lost his temper again."

"Yes." Mary felt like crying. Damn, why was she always wanting to cry around Aaron? It was his rescuing voice, she decided. "He said he was going to tie me up and put me in the trunk of the car because I wouldn't go across the border."

"He *what*?" A note of exasperation had entered Aaron's voice, but it wasn't directed at her, because his voice returned to being friendly. "Mary, do me a favour, okay?"

"What?" she asked, wiping at her damp eyes.

"Stare at Scott."

Stare at Scott? Mary was confused, but it was an easy order. She looked at Scott and caught his eye.

"Are you staring at him?" Aaron asked.

"Yes." *But why?*

"Keep looking…has he winked yet?"

Winked? No…there it was. Scott's face broke into a little private smile and he winked at her. It lifted Mary's spirits. "Yes, he did," she answered, now noticing a bigger smile and a slight blush on his cheeks.

"Good," Aaron replied. "That means he's on your side. So Sheila's in the old man's bad books, is she?"

It dawned on Mary that Aaron was trying to cheer her up. Her naturally cheerful disposition thrived on the banter. "I think she just got fired."

"Oh, that won't last," Aaron spoke confidently. "What's Tony doing now?"

"Still not looking at us." Yet as she spoke, Mary noticed that Tony's hands were no longer clenched, and he was rubbing his forehead. "I think he has a headache."

Now Aaron's voice became more serious. "Mary, back at that restaurant, Tony had to walk into a very dangerous situation. He had only one experienced officer with him. That was Dan. Those men were hit men. Tony had to be scared, but you see, he's in charge. He can't look scared, so he comes across as confident as anything. Then they were pursuing you, and he has an abducted uniformed police officer in the car. This has been a really bad day for him. So when the tension finally has a chance to escape, it comes out in anger. That's just the way he is." Aaron paused. "Mary, Tony would not have tied you up and put you in the trunk of the car. He was just frustrated because he wants to protect you and we weren't expecting someone to come after you in such a big way. Did you really think he would put you in the trunk?"

"Not really," she admitted. "He was just mad. Besides, I don't think Sheila would have let him."

Aaron actually laughed. "No. That woman's got guts, I must say." Then his voice softened. "Mary, you don't want to come down here, is that it?"

"Well, no, Aaron," she admitted. "I live up here. Why should I have to leave my home and go down there for a couple of months? I haven't done anything wrong."

"No, of course you haven't," Aaron responded. "Mary, I might be able to get Tony and his boss to agree to a compromise. See if Tony will talk to me."

Tentatively, Mary passed the phone. With relief, she saw Tony take it and listen.

Down in Carl Walsh's office, Aaron leaned on a chair and smiled across at Frank Moseley. Mr. Walsh, Tony and Moseley were arranging to send Gavin up to Mary's house. Tony, Scott and Sheila would stay up there with her. One of their lawyers would conduct the initial interview with Mary in her home. Gavin would provide extra protection for the CIA staff. Dan had offered to help out during the nights. Using Gavin for guard work was a bit of overkill, but it fit nicely into Moseley's plans to let him have a chance to be with other staff for a while. Besides, Gavin and Tony were friends, and Gavin would be more than willing to lend a hand.

Aaron felt better than he had for ages. Since Cuba, that is. Mary had actually called him for help today. Truthfully, he had been astounded. Astounded, but absolutely thrilled. And he had been able to help her. That had felt wonderful. After all the hurt he had caused her, to be able to help had felt absolutely wonderful. Then she had talked to him again, and now he was trying to satisfy everyone's worries, yet keep Mary happy too. He was still embarrassed to meet her face to face, but a lot of his depression had lifted today. He decided to stop taking the anti-depressants, because maybe, just maybe, there was a way out of this mess.

Once everything had been settled in the car, it had taken little time for Tony, Sheila and Scott to check out of the hotel. When they were finally settled at Mary's house, Tony had leaned back on the couch to close his eyes and try to persuade his head to stop aching. It had been a terrible day. Mary came over to him and took hold of his wrist, insisting that he follow her. Not wishing to cause her any further distress, he let her lead him into her bedroom and obediently lay on top of the bed. She drew the drapes closed to block out the light and quietly left the room. Although he did not intend to sleep, it was a relief to close his eyes in the quiet solitude.

A couple of minutes later, Sheila entered with a glass of water and a bottle of aspirins. She handed him the glass, and shook two of the pills into his hand without speaking.

"I'm sorry," he offered.

That earned him a perfunctory smile. In a perfectly professional and respectful voice, Sheila said, "Why don't we leave that discussion for later, sir."

Perfectly respectful, and Tony hated it. It meant *"You're a jerk, Tony."* He couldn't imagine working with people who were always polite and respectful. You would never know what they thought. Sheila was being polite because she knew he needed a rest. Tony washed down the pills and closed his eyes after she left. Later he had a lot of apologising to do.

When he awoke an hour later, his head was clear, but he was confused. Where was he? *Oh yeh, Mary's bedroom.* He opened the drapes to let light in.

169

It was a tidy, simple room, and very clean. On the dresser was a picture of a young boy with brown hair and happy brown eyes. Poor Mary, however did you bear that loss? Aaron had told him about Mary losing her son. Tony had wanted children, but his wife had found excuse after excuse. After a couple of years, as the marriage deteriorated, he had given up asking. He no longer had wanted to bring children into that cold home environment.

As he sat on the side of the bed, Tony tried to remember everything he had said while in his rage earlier. What had he said to Sheila? Oh, great—he had fired her. Actually, he hadn't. It was not possible for him to arbitrarily fire anyone, and hopefully Sheila knew that, but what a thing to say to a trainee. At no time had Tony even considered having Sheila's employment terminated. He was quite impressed with her so far, and he was particularly impressed that she had stood up to him today when she knew he was wrong. Okay, time to repair some damage.

In the living room, Scott and Sheila were chatting with Dan, who was watching the street. The television was on low. "Where's Mary?" Tony asked.

"She heard you get up and went to make a pot of coffee for us, and a hot chocolate for herself," Scott responded. "I'm going to help her with supper in about an hour."

*Good, I've got a couple minutes to talk to Sheila.* Tony waved her over to a chair further from the television. Once Sheila was seated, he pulled a second chair over to hers. "I'm sorry," he offered for a second time. "I was totally wrong today, and you had every right to tell me so. In fact," he added, "I consider it your responsibility to tell me when I'm wrong. Unfortunately," he admitted, "I wasn't listening very well today."

Sheila shrugged. "It's okay, sir."

There was that polite respect again. *Damn it.* "No, it's not okay," he insisted. "I threatened to fire you. I couldn't fire you like that even if I wanted to, which I certainly don't."

This time Sheila looked at him more directly, and there was a flash in her eyes. "All right, I found your behaviour unbelievable. You threatened to tie Mary up and throw her in the trunk...in the trunk! She has just recently been kidnapped and raped! What the *hell* were you thinking of?" Sheila's eyes were blazing now. "And this to a woman who has done nothing wrong and has absolutely no obligation to cross that border and help us, and you know it."

Holding up his hands in a sign of capitulation, Tony offered no resistance. "If you're waiting for a defence, I don't have one. It was a totally thoughtless thing to say. I knew as soon as it was out that I had gone way, way too far."

Having made her point, Sheila backed down. "Sir, before I asked to be put on your team, I checked around with everyone about you. They told me about your temper, but I also learned that the people who have survived being on your team do very well in this job, and really enjoy working with you. So if you want to yell at me and fire me every day of the week, I don't care. I can take that," Sheila insisted, "but I'll never stand by quietly and let you bully an innocent person."

"I don't expect you to," Tony replied. "I wouldn't waste my time with you if you did. Yes-men are a dime a dozen. I don't need them on my team. You are doing very well," he told her honestly, "so just keep it up, and I'll try not to fire you too often."

A smile appeared on Sheila's face. "Can I have some severance pay, Tony?"

He laughed and clapped her lightly on the shoulder, knowing he'd made a good choice with her. Now he had to talk to Mary.

In the kitchen, he asked Mary if he could help make the coffee. She ignored his offer.

"Are you firing Sheila?" she demanded.

*Such a direct person,* Tony noticed. *Definitely not the passive little type she appears to be.* "No, of course not," he answered, leaning his right shoulder against the fridge so he could face her. "She was absolutely right." For a moment he watched her stirring the hot chocolate. "I have a temper, Mary. You saw it today. Actually, I think you've just seen it at its worst. I get unreasonable and say things I don't mean. My people just get used to it and put up with me. It surprises me that they do." He had carried his glass out, and reached now to put it behind the sink. That put him close to her, and on impulse he put his hands on her shoulders and turned her to face him. "I would *never* have put you in the trunk of the car. It was an absolutely thoughtless thing for me to have said to you. Please tell me you believe that."

Being this close, with him looking directly into her eyes, was doing fluttering things to Mary's heart. *You are acting like a child in the midst of a school girl crush, for heaven's sake,* she chided herself. *Get a grip. You're just a job to this man.* Deciding to tease, she poked him in the ribs with her spoon. "Sheila would never have let you, anyway." Then she smiled and felt a responding squeeze on her shoulders. "I never thought you would, Tony. At least not after you walked me home yesterday." Then she blushed. *What a thing to have said!* Then she saw him relaxing. "I'm sorry I said what I did," she continued, feeling heat in her face, "about expecting that kind of treatment from you. I didn't like you bossing me around, so I wanted to hit back. It didn't help the situation, and I know I hurt your feelings. You risked your life for me, and I didn't even thank you. I must have seemed awfully unappreciative. Sorry."

That did it. The blush in her cheeks affected him the way her eyes had last night. Without bothering to worry about his actions, Tony gave her forehead a light kiss. He didn't dare do any more. Awkwardly, he stepped back from her and released her shoulders. He couldn't afford to get this interested so fast. They had a lot of work ahead of them, and things could get tense. Mary had not even agreed to help them yet. These out of control emotions had better take a backseat for a while.

"Mary, we've got a lot of talking to do. We need your help. Let's take the coffee into the living room and sit with the others. We've got all evening ahead of us. Scott will help with supper later. He's quite a good cook."

Once they had settled down in the living room, Tony looked around and noticed that they made a cosy little scene. Scott was lounging in an armchair, and Sheila was on Mary's left side on the couch. Tony was sitting to the right of Mary, half turned to face her. Dan was leafing through a magazine in a wooden rocking chair which provided a clear view out both front and back windows. His eyes never stayed on the magazine for long, constantly scanning the outside views.

Now that an attack had been made on Mary, there could be no question of the need to protect her. She had been seen alive in Canada and in their company. It had become imperative to keep her safe and prepare her for the coming trial. They needed her cooperation, and Tony would do his best to get her to agree to being a witness for them. Aaron had not underestimated the impact her testimony as an independent witness would have on the jury and the media. Lawyers retained by the CIA would try to win the case on evidence, but Tony knew that the case would really be about credibility, and the Congressman had nothing to lose and everything to gain by attacking them. A vicious battle was looming, and everybody knew it. Everybody except Mary. They needed her support, so she had to be given the whole picture.

They talked for two hours. It was an invaluable education for Sheila and Scott. Mary seemed to understand, but for her the important issue was to protect Aaron. Why she felt such a protectiveness for Aaron when she seemed afraid to meet him again, Tony could not understand, but he accepted it with gratitude. Mary had little feeling one way or the other for the CIA. She thought the decision to give Aaron that cover had been extremely ill advised at best, but she had no personal vendetta against them. She would cooperate for Aaron's sake. Period. It was enough. The Company did not seek her undying devotion—just her support through a political land mine.

Cooking was one of Scott's favourite hobbies. While he prepared supper, Tony, Mary and Sheila chatted. Dan would join in occasionally, but he took his guard duty seriously. After supper Scott would collect Gavin at the airport, then Dan and Gavin would spell each other off, with backup from the two younger officers. Tomorrow a member of the legal staff would arrive to talk to Mary and compare her story to Aaron's. Tony would return with the lawyer to Langley. He had a lot of other business to attend to, and Mary would be well protected with four of his people watching her.

Privately, Tony did not anticipate any more attempts on Mary. Whoever was after her knew she was being protected now. He had made that clear to "Mr. Pitt". Most likely, Richard Harvey was behind the attack, but it would be hard to prove. The Congressman had money, power, and was too familiar with the workings of the intelligence community to make the mistake of showing his hand. More so than the members of the Liberators, Richard Harvey had the resources needed to arrange the hit that quickly.

Looking at Mary, Tony felt himself amazed that so much energy was being spent on this little woman. She seemed far too insignificant to have created such a panic among such powerful people. Just then she noticed him staring, and smiled up at him. Okay, insignificant was the wrong word, Tony told himself as his emotions started to play with him. Is it just me, or is she feeling this too? They were sitting side by side, and it felt like electric sparks were zapping back and forth between them. Taking a glance around the room, Tony knew he was among friends. The people you worked with on this job became like family. There were few secrets between them. He decided to take a risk and reached for Mary's hand. No resistance. It came easily and closed around his own. He gave her a thankful smile. Until dinner was served by a discretely smirking Scott, Tony and Mary sat together in comfortable conversation.

After supper, Scott went to the airport to pick up Gavin. Sheila took Mary into Mary's bedroom, and managed to have almost an hour of private conversation with her. Tony had given Sheila permission to talk about Mary's ordeal as long as no details were discussed. That put real limits on the conversation, but Sheila used the time to build Mary's trust in her. They could talk more in the days ahead. When Mary asked who Gavin was, Sheila had laughed.

"You probably won't warm to him," she informed Mary. "He'll give you the creeps. Gavin seems cold because he's all work and no play. For entertainment I hear he sits around and cleans his gun." Then she reconsidered. "Scott tells me I'm not fair to Gavin, and it's because I don't know him. Scott could be right. I will say that if I was ever in trouble he's the person I'd like to see the most. His reputation is phenomenal."

When Scott brought Gavin back from the airport, Mary understood what Sheila was saying. Gavin stood about six feet tall, and was thin, with a wiry, powerful build. His hair was dark brown and short, his clothes were a very dark shade of blue, and his eyes were intimidating. They were a light blue/grey. *Probably the same colour as his gun,* Mary thought, *and they look right into you.* He nodded a greeting, then shook hands with Tony, who greeted him warmly. Sheila had said the two men were longtime friends. An unlikely pair, thought Mary, but friends sometimes had very different personalities. Gavin was not friendly, but he wasn't rude either, so Mary just let him be. *He gives me the chills,* she decided, *but if he's as good as Sheila says, he's welcome to look after me.* Later in the evening she noticed with amusement that he was, indeed, sitting around cleaning his gun.

There would be a one-day delay, Tony announced the next morning. The lawyers were busy at the office analyzing the evidence, and couldn't come up today. He noticed that Mary looked pleased, and he didn't mind the delay either. Today he could handle some of his business on the phone, and between calls he could talk to Mary. Tomorrow he absolutely had to get back to the office and take care of his work, but today he could relax a bit.

At one point during the day, Mary and Sheila talked again in the privacy of Mary's room. Once again the same rules applied about not discussing details, so after a while the conversation moved to other topics. Out of curiosity, Mary asked Sheila about her job and the structure of the CIA. Sheila answered Mary's questions when she could, and sidestepped the ones she felt she shouldn't. When she got to the point about describing her job and how the team worked, she also mentioned that there were other sections in their division.

"Tony's friend, Frank Moseley, runs a section that would be interesting to work for," Sheila stated. "They get involved in situations where there's a need to go into a country and protect our interests. Sometimes they may work with a particular group, or against a particular group, and sometimes they have to go in and rescue our people like they did in Cuba. Or they may be used to eliminate threats to us." Suddenly Sheila changed the topic, and Mary smiled to herself.

*I'd love to ask her more,* Mary thought, *but I think she just remembered not to tell me too much. I wonder what it means to eliminate a threat? It sounds ominous.*

Much of the day was spent playing the trivia "games" Tony's team had invented to pass slow evenings. These games were actually mind exercises to keep them sharp. They had to be up to date on the domestic and foreign political scene to participate with any skill. Sheila was learning quickly, and Scott and Dan thrived on it. This was new to Gavin, but he joined in confidently.

Mary was totally lost in the game, but sat contentedly and listened. She learned more about the personalities of her new acquaintances than she remembered about the political scene of any particular country. All in all, the day passed much too quickly.

# XXIII

Richard Harvey stared at the man sitting across the table at a very exclusive and private restaurant. James Cook was a partner in the law firm of Harrison and Cook. It was a very selective law firm, with a small but wealthy clientele. They were used by important people who found themselves in big trouble. Fees were very high, and payment could not be in doubt. Richard Harvey had used them a few years back to get out of a politically dangerous fiasco. He needed them again now.

James Cook had discovered some bad news in his interviews with Jose Luis, Osvaldo and Alfredo. The Canadian witness was supposed to have been killed in Cuba, but of course Cook had questioned this as soon as he found out that "Taz" was actually Officer St. Pierre. While the assaults by Mr. St. Pierre on the woman were a gold mine for the defence, the fact that the witness still lived was problematic. It had been Cook who had arranged the first attack on Mary, hoping they could bring her as a witness for the defence. She should have been more than willing to prosecute Mr. St. Pierre and his employers. Cook had been quite surprised that the CIA had not already executed her, and was now even more surprised to hear that Richard Harvey's sources inside the CIA reported that Mary was actually cooperating with them. Why? It made no sense.

Now the news from the co-accused had been worse. Mary had been overheard speaking in Spanish on two separate occasions in Cuba. Alfredo had not known she spoke Spanish the morning he had talked to Lino about Richard Harvey, not thirty feet from where Mary had been sitting. Cook was privately disgusted and not surprised to see that the Congressman was now scared. What had he expected, getting involved with such a ragtag group of hoodlums?

"We've got to get rid of her," Richard insisted. "We can't risk her as a witness if she knew the extent of my involvement down there."

"No, we can't," Cook agreed, "but this is going to be difficult. I'll get my contacts to try again. This time they will have to make it look like a CIA job,

176

which should be possible since she is now known to be in CIA company. It will guarantee an acquittal for you, I'm sure."

"Your contacts bungled the last attempt," the Congressman stated bitterly, taking a long swallow of whiskey to steady his nerves.

"It was too complicated, and everything went wrong," Cook replied angrily. "It got out of hand. My contacts do not usually fail. They won't fail again."

Richard Harvey glared at his dinner companion. "I pay you not to make mistakes. This will ruin me if we lose. I cannot afford to lose."

"No, you can't," Cook agreed quietly. *So don't even think of threatening me,* his eyes said, watching the Congressman back down. *You know who's in control here. I provide a service you just can't buy everywhere.*

Resigned, but very miserable, Richard Harvey finished his whiskey. Things were not going well, not at all.

# XXIV

The following day at Mary's house was spent waiting for the lawyer to arrive, and then waiting while the interview was conducted. Tony introduced Mary to Paul Hedley, who would be prosecuting their case. For Paul to have been sent up here to interview Mary personally indicated to Tony just how nervous the administration was about this witness.

. Mary was being very quiet today, and Tony sensed that she was nervous about having to talk about what had happened in Cuba. Paul Hedley addressed her concerns at the start, stating that he would allow Sheila to sit in on the interview due to her past training and as a support to Mary. No one besides himself and the required legal staff, Mary and Aaron would know the contents of the interviews at this time. Mr. Walsh would be briefed, but would not be told specifics. It was all likely to come out in court if the defendants decided to attack Aaron's credibility, which was expected, but until then Mr. Walsh had decreed that to save Mary embarrassment no one else needed to know.

That made Mary feel a little better, and she took Mr. Hedley and Sheila into her den and closed the door. To start, Mr. Hedley gave her a list of proper terms for various sexual acts. Mary was surprised, but he explained that she might find it easier to talk if she didn't have to worry about what words to use.

He was right, Mary found. Actually, the interview was quite painless. Mr. Hedley was quite factual and pleasant. Aaron had admitted readily to three rapes and two sexual assaults. One by one, Mr. Hedley checked their details with Mary. In fact, he asked for minimal details and then seemed to check them against his notes. There was a lot more she could have said, but he didn't seem interested at this point in any in-depth discussion. Mary was glad, but a little puzzled. It seemed more like a summary, but perhaps Aaron had provided the details and Mr. Hedley felt it unnecessary to embarrass her. He seemed to be a sensitive man.

Mary was also pleasantly surprised that no mention was made of the last night in camp as far as the sex act was concerned. Aaron had told them of their agreement to end her life, but had not told Mr. Hedley that they had made love. *Thank you, Aaron.* Mary had absolutely dreaded admitting to that. It sounded so wanton, especially since she had been raped by him. How could she ever explain the emotions of that night to anyone?

Aaron had also said nothing about killing Nathanial. *Okay, Aaron, he was your friend, and it's your job. You didn't want to kill him. I will keep my mouth shut and protect your secret,* she promised. *You will never know that I saw you kill your friend.*

Finally the interview ended, and Mr. Hedley smiled. "I'm very pleased," he announced. They went into the living room to confront a tense-looking Tony. Mr. Hedley shook his hand. "The stories match. We'll be ready," he promised Tony.

Tony went with Paul Hedley to the airport. Mary was sad to learn that she wouldn't see Tony again until they had a safe place ready for her. It would only take a couple of days, and Mary was still very reluctant to go down there, but she was getting used to Tony's presence, and she would definitely miss him.

Before he left, Tony had touched her cheek and whispered, "Don't forget our supper date," into her ear. He was carrying Aaron's jacket, although all the contents were safely secured in Mr. Hedley's briefcase. When he noticed Mary looking forlornly at the jacket, he offered it to her. "I'm sure Aaron wouldn't mind if you kept it."

Why she wanted a souvenir of those days, Mary couldn't have said. Perhaps it was because the jacket had meant protection to her. Gratefully she took it with a blush and said goodbye.

Later that afternoon, Scott volunteered to go out for groceries. Tonight there would be five people for supper, and Mary's food supply was dwindling. He was gone a full three hours, and when Scott finally returned, Lori came in with him, carrying groceries. Gavin and Dan gave him a disapproving look, but said nothing. Sheila raised an eyebrow, but kept her comments to herself.

Lori walked into the kitchen with her bag of groceries, and Mary took Scott's bags and followed. Alone with Lori, Mary grinned at her friend. "What have you been up to," she whispered to her friend, "as if I couldn't guess."

Lori gave her a big wink and a hand signal that indicated that it had been a pretty steamy session. "He's a hot one," she whispered, then blew Mary a kiss and left the kitchen. "Gotta go," she called back. "Cab's waiting outside."

Mary was left chuckling to herself. That was when Scott entered the kitchen to help put groceries away. Mary tried her best to behave, but when he caught her eye, Mary started to giggle, and put her hands against her mouth to control it.

"What?" he demanded. Although Scott was feigning innocence, a little smile was playing on his lips.

"Sorry," Mary apologised, "but Lori and I have been friends for ages. She's not very good at keeping secrets from me."

Now his whole face smiled, but he put a finger to his lips. "You won't snitch on me, will you?"

Mary shook her head. "Of course not, but your friends have probably already guessed."

"Your friend is hot," Scott stated confidentially. "Do you mind?"

"Mind? It's none of my business," Mary protested.

"No," he agreed, "but do you object?"

*Strange question,* thought Mary. "Why would you care if I objected?"

Scott turned his friendly eyes on her, and Mary noticed that he actually looked sheepish. "Because I'm in your home as your guest and you're a really nice person. I don't want to upset you."

*What a sweetheart,* Mary decided. It was like having your very own little brother in your house to protect you. "I don't mind, dear. Lori is more than able to look out for herself. Go ahead and have fun. I won't tell a soul."

"You're sweet," Scott offered. Now his eyes were twinkling. "By the way, I hope you know the old man likes you."

Her heart gave a little bounce, but Mary quickly restrained it. Tony was from another world, and this silly infatuation she felt was bound to bring her crashing down eventually. "I am quite sure the 'old man', as you unkindly put it, likes women on a regular basis. But if it makes you feel better," she confided, "I will admit that I enjoy his attention."

"Oh, but he doesn't," Scott argued, pulling a small bottle of rum out from one of the bags. "Got some coke?" After taking the pop from her, Scott poured them each a drink. "Pork chops tonight," he announced, starting his dinner preparations. "Nope, the boss isn't like me at all," he continued. "He's a real serious type." While he got the food ready to bake, Scott told Mary about Tony's marriage and his current availability.

"This sounds like a sales pitch," Mary interjected, sipping her rum at the kitchen table. "Does he give you a commission for this?"

"Ten percent a lay," Scott quipped, then blushed furiously. "Oh, shit, I'm sorry—I'm not supposed to be so flippant. Tony wants me to become more serious, but I'm having a hard time."

Having almost choked on her drink, Mary laughed until tears ran down her eyes. Impulsively, she reached out for Scott's hand. He sat beside her at the table.

"You're a good sport, Mary."

"I could have used a little brother like you," Mary confessed. "You must keep your family in stitches." Mary saw Scott smile as if to himself, and a thought occurred to her. There was a question she wanted to ask, but it was a bit awkward because of the conversation that might follow. However, Scott was the best person to ask because she felt very comfortable with him, and he knew Aaron. "Scott, is Aaron like you?"

The reaction was instantaneous. Scott's attention was suddenly totally focused on her, and Mary saw his eagerness to talk. He turned his chair so that they were face to face.

"Mary, I've wanted to tell you about him, but Tony's so worried about upsetting you that I was afraid to bring it up."

"I'm afraid to see him again," Mary admitted. "I don't know anything about him and I need to know what he's like."

"The person you met in Cuba was not the real Aaron," Scott told her. He took a deep breath. "Aaron is my best friend, Mary. In fact, before he went to Cuba he was planning to marry my sister, Susan."

"Your sister?"

"Yeh. She's my twin."

"But now he isn't?"

Absentmindedly, Scott's fingers were playing with the watch on Mary's wrist. His eyes came up to meet hers again after a pause. "Aaron is a mess," he said bluntly. "Please believe me when I tell you that Aaron is not a rapist. I know he raped you," Scott said quickly. "I'm not denying that, but he got caught in a situation he couldn't get out of. You suffered because of it. Now the guilt is eating him. He needs to see you."

"I'm afraid," Mary said simply. "After all that happened, I'm too embarrassed to see him again."

"No, Mary, he won't embarrass you," Scott promised.

She tried to explain to this kind, young man. "I'm afraid of what he'll be like when I see him. When I walk into the room, will he act like it was all in the line of duty? Will he be arrogant, or not care about it at all? Has he told everyone about the things he did, and how I had to do anything he wanted…wanted me to?" Her voice faltered, and she felt Scott grasp her hand. "Scott, you can't…can't imagine the humiliation…. If I walk into that room and he looks smug, or someone else gives me one of those knowing looks…I'll just die. Then I'll hate him." Mary coughed to clear her throat. "I think he was nice, but it seems to have been worlds away, and maybe I just hoped he was. That's why I'm afraid."

*Oh heavens,* Scott thought. *I think I am finally understanding this reluctance to see Aaron. But she's so wrong. She doesn't know Aaron—how could she? And Aaron is sitting down at the office scared to see her, too, for reasons that are somehow similar yet from an opposite perspective.* He started to talk about Aaron, what he was like, and how Aaron had been affected by the experience. Then he talked about Aaron's promises to Susan, and told her about Aaron's character.

"Please come down with me and meet him, Mary. I know you told Tony you would, but you don't really want to, and Tony's worried that you will change your mind. I'll be there with you, I promise. I'll walk through the door with you and I won't leave your side. Please."

Well, you couldn't refuse someone when you had just decided they would make a neat little brother, could you? He wanted her to promise, and once she promised him, it would be very hard to change her mind. Mary sighed. "I'll come," she said. "I'll come, and I'll do my best." She pulled her hand away. "Now let's rescue supper."

After breakfast the next morning, Mary called Lori to make arrangements for her house. Lori already had a key, and agreed to come over daily to check on the place. Mary told her that she was welcome to stay there if she wished. The neighbour's teenage son shovelled the driveway after any large snowfall to earn extra spending money. That left plants, mail and flyers for Lori to take care of.

Once she had hung up the phone, Mary noticed Scott, Sheila and Gavin in discussion. Dan had left for the day to visit his family. With glee, Sheila announced that they were all taking Mary to the Eaton's Centre, which was only a few blocks from Mary's home. Sheila had insisted that since Mary was feeling a bit uneasy about meeting Aaron and going to court, the least they could do to increase her confidence, was to get her some clothes that suited the occasion. Mary did not protest too much. She had a wardrobe for work, of course, but it was small and dated. There was no knowing how long she would be away from home, or how many days she would have to be in the witness box. If they wanted to buy her clothes, she would not turn down the opportunity.

Gavin was not thrilled. Going out in public like this would normally be vetoed instantly by him. However, he tended to agree with Tony that Mary's attackers had most likely been ordered off. There had been no sign of them since the attack. It would be a risky hit now, and whoever had hired them had surely realised that it was far easier to wait and try to use Mary's evidence to their advantage. With minor misgivings, he agreed to the plan, but he made one demand. They would not all go in one car. He wanted Sheila and Scott to follow them in the company car. Scott would be able to observe from a selected distance to ensure that no one followed. Mary would drive her own car, accompanied by Gavin.

The men had never been in the Eaton's Centre before, so Mary pointed out the three levels, the eating places and the main stores. It was not too crowded today, so Sheila and Mary had no trouble being waited on. Scott and Sheila were good company, if you could overlook the fact that their attention was focused mainly on the other mall occupants. Having a conversation with people who were constantly scanning their surroundings seemed awkward to Mary at first, but she soon adapted. They were not being rude, she knew, just careful. Gavin stayed a little distance away. It was harder for him to blend in, although on second thought Mary decided that he could easily pass for a disinterested husband waiting for his wife and her friends to buy a dress. After an hour, however, he seemed to become ill at ease, and Mary saw Scott saunter over to him.

"Problem?" Scott asked idly.

"Maybe," Gavin responded. "I wish I knew what those guys looked like. Why don't you buy a paper at the kiosk. Have a look in the bookstore across from it, and the shop two doors down."

However, Scott did not get that far. A familiar voice spoke at his side.

"Is it safe to be around you today?"

Scott turned quickly and had a start. The voice belonged to Mary's police sergeant friend. "Mike! What the hell are you doing here?"

"I live in this neighbourhood," Mike responded. "I should be asking you that question. Weren't you people supposed to go home?"

"Uh, Mary wasn't ready to leave, so we had to stay and watch out for her." Man, surely fate could not be this mischievous! But there wasn't time to worry about coincidence. "Actually, in answer to your first question," he responded, "I think we've got a situation developing here. I have to eyeball someone. Walk with me and tell me if you recognise anyone."

Mike's face became very serious, and he accompanied Scott on his stroll past a couple of stores. Both men recognised Mr. Pitt and his cronies.

"Big trouble," Scott observed to his companion, who was not in uniform today. "You armed?"

"No. Off duty. You got any backup?"

Indicating Gavin, Scott murmured, "Just big brother."

Mike ran a professional eye over Gavin. "Yeh. Well, do me a favour and don't tell me what he's packing, but if he has anything extra on him that's legal, perhaps he could lend it."

Scott knew they could use the help, but worried about involving this man again. "This isn't your problem," he stated. "Why don't you just put some distance between us. They won't recognise you."

"Mary *is* my business," Mike stated, "and I don't like these goons in my city. I'm sticking whether you like it or not. Besides," he added, "I don't like the look of your odds."

"Neither do I," Scott admitted. And even if these guys didn't kill him, Tony definitely would when he heard about this.

"Where are you parked?"

"G3."

Mike led them out a back route to their parking lot. Gavin had already given Sheila the sign, so the women had been ready. It was clear that trouble was brewing, so Mary merely nodded at Mike and stayed close to Sheila. Things went well until they were a few feet from the company car. Gavin hollered at them a few seconds before a shot rang out. Sheila cried out and fell to her knees.

Mary couldn't follow what happened next, because a strong hand had slammed her down and against the side of the car. It was noisy with gunshots for a brief moment, then quiet again. Mary did notice that Mike had acquired a handgun. Sheila appeared to have been hit in the upper arm, but had scrambled to the shelter of an adjacent vehicle.

"We have to separate them," Gavin whispered. "We can't sit here in a group like this. Mary will come with me. The rest of you, cover us, and handle whoever remains."

Scott saw the look on Mary's face. "Mary—trust Gavin. Go with him and do *exactly* what he says." He felt horribly responsible for this. It had been his responsibility and he had put them all at risk. At least Mary would be in good hands with Gavin.

Mary nodded. How could she refuse? She was helpless by herself. Swallowing her fear, Mary looked at the cold, efficient man who was to be her bodyguard.

Trusting Gavin meant doing very scary things, like running from car to car to pillar on command, as fast as you could, without regard for life or limb, only hoping that he had some plan in mind. She made a conscious effort to ignore the occasional fire-cracker sounds that followed her. Adrenalin prepared you for fight or flight, Mary knew, and it was coming in handy now.

At one point Gavin was beside her, and they were crouching behind a car. One of their attackers had been downed by Scott or Mike. That left two, and the one after Mary was persistent. Normally, Gavin did not find himself guarding an unarmed person in situations like this. Usually everyone on his side was armed and trained. It had been a relief to find Mary actually capable of moving quickly and following orders precisely. Had she faltered or been physically unable to move fast, the situation could have been critical. Their two remaining attackers were now separated, and it was time to make the final move. Mary would really have to keep her head for this next manoeuvre

This order from Gavin meant running as fast as Mary could, hunched over, three rows back to her car. It meant controlling her shaking fingers long enough to unlock the driver's side, crawling in, starting the car and unlocking the passenger door. Mary took a breath. *"Keep your head down,"* Gavin had said. Now she was to back out fast—*for heaven's sake don't hit anything*—drive to the yellow pillar, and open the passenger door.

In a flash Gavin jumped in, yelled, "Drive," and they were off.

February in Canada meant wet, slippery ramps out of parking lots, and Mary did not normally drive fast. The Corolla skidded around in rebellion when she hit the accelerator to get up the ramp to the street, but at least they were moving. A few hair-raising manoeuvres later, they were safely on the street.

"What about the others?" Mary asked.

"They're behind us," Gavin replied. "I wouldn't have left without them."

*No, I'm sure you wouldn't,* Mary thought. *You may have been told to look after me, but your priorities are crystal clear. I come second, but I can't blame you for that. The others depend on you, and they are your people. You have no personal interest in me.*

It was true. Sheila had told Mary that Gavin would give her the creeps, but he did not have that effect on Mary. Cool, yes. Professional, yes. Disinterested, absolutely. But not creepy, and not at all nasty. Mary was comfortable in his presence in a detached sort of way. He had protected her, so what more could she ask? Mary stole a glance at him, but he was busy on his cell phone now.

Gavin had dialled Scott. "Everyone okay? How's Sheila?"

"Fine," Scott responded. "Just a graze. Mike's going to bandage her up. Then he gets the fun of reporting the dead bodies to his boss. I'm going to report in for us now."

"I can do that," Gavin offered. "Tony's going to be pissed. I can run interference for you."

Scott's sigh came over the phone. "No. Thanks anyway, Gavin, but I'm responsible for this mess. Tony left me in charge, and I blew it. That shopping trip should never have happened." He managed to laugh. "Hell, I'll probably be pushing paper for a few months."

"I doubt it," Gavin stated. "You'll take it on the chin, but he'll forgive you. The PR boys are going to be really scrambling again, though. Did we get all three of those guys?"

"Yep, sure did. They won't be bothering us again. Are we heading back to Mary's?"

Gavin looked at Mary. His people were taking too many risks and drawing too much attention to themselves in this country. He wished he had been able to talk to Tony about his assessment of Mary. It was time to do some serious thinking. "You go back. Get Mary's things and head home. Drop Sheila at the doctor. I'll call Dan and let him know we've gone. Mary and I will drive down from here."

*So we're going to Virginia,* Mary heard. This time she would not protest. She was tired and badly frightened, and now Sheila was hurt. Tony had been right, and now all this mess was her fault for being stubborn. Three dead people left for Mike to explain, and Sheila with a bullet wound. This time it was Mary who was getting a headache. While she drove, she listened to Gavin call Dan, then put his phone away.

The sun was low in the horizon, and the afternoon was ending when they reached Pennsylvania. In New York State, Gavin had taken over the driving. He had been thinking about his orders from Moseley, and the problems this case was causing for the Company. *"Protect our officers and the Company's interests,"* had been Moseley's instructions. "The Company's interests" had been discussed in Cuba. Was this woman a threat to them? Tony had come to Canada to find out, but if he had made a decision, he had not had a chance to tell Gavin. In the meantime, they were continuing to risk the lives of their officers, spend resources and take huge political risks over this woman. Was she worth it? Would she back them in court, or crucify them? It was time to find out.

Gavin had the ability to make a problem like this simply disappear and never be traced back to the CIA. It was not a decision he wanted to make, but he was paid to do things that were not always pleasant, and certainly not known to the public. For him, the Company came first, without question. It was a part of him. He would question this woman, and then take the appropriate action.

He told Mary that he wanted to pull over at the next rest stop and take a break. Deliberately, he chose a place that had other cars in the lot. This was just the interrogation stage, and he had no desire to frighten or upset her. He wanted Mary as relaxed as possible, so she would answer his questions freely.

Mary *was* quite relaxed. Gavin was a quiet man, so she had spent the ride snoozing. He had parked the car in a well-lit spot that had several other cars around, and had leaned back as if to doze. When he started talking, he made no suggestive remarks or did anything to make her feel the slightest bit uneasy. At first the conversation was quite casual, but it began to occur to Mary that he was asking the same type of questions that Tony had asked. Questions about what happened in Cuba, and how she felt about Aaron and what had happened to her.

It began to dawn on Mary that this wasn't just a casual conversation. *There is a reason for these questions,* she realised, *and somehow my answers seem important to him. Why? Scott told me to trust him. Trusting someone means telling the truth, but something is strange here.* Not that it mattered. Mary knew she was a very poor liar. Those eyes of Gavin's would see right through any lie she could make up. Especially since she didn't know the reasons for the questions. A lie might only make it worse. Therefore her answers had to be the truth, and she could only hope he liked them.

How did she feel about Aaron? Confused, nervous, but she believed he had been trying to protect her.

It must have been upsetting to learn that she had been abused because the CIA had made Aaron a rapist for his cover. Yes, she was really pissed off about that. It had been a stupid thing to do, as far as she was concerned.

There was the slightest change in expression in Gavin's eyes. Barely discernible, but it was as if the emotion that made Gavin human had just been hidden behind a cold steel-grey wall. Somehow Mary knew she had answered a question incorrectly. *One wrong,* she thought. *I wonder how important it was.* She wished Tony were here. Tony cared about her, she knew. He would have wanted her to give the right answers, and would have helped her get them right. Gavin didn't care. Only the answers, she sensed, were important to Gavin.

# XXV

Another crisis. Carl Walsh was not happy. Damn it, they weren't even supposed to be up in Canada, and now the Toronto police had three bodies to be explained away. Of course the public relations staff of the CIA were doing their best, but Carl was very relieved to hear that Tony's people were on their way home. Carl had reported this one up the ladder as well, and his boss was most concerned. At least with the witness safely down here everything would revert to some semblance of normality.

Tony Dune and Aaron St. Pierre were in his office with him. After hearing what went on between Aaron and that woman in Cuba, Carl had gone home and hugged his wife. He had been involved in a lot of sticky situations himself during his career, but what Aaron had got caught up in was enough to make your skin crawl. After he had been informed about all the damage, Carl and the CIA Deputy Director, Peter Geraldton, had sat in Carl's office sharing a moment of dread. The case was a political time bomb, and had to be carefully managed. Somehow, however, it kept getting out of control.

His secretary interrupted his thoughts. "Taylor on line one, sir." Taylor was a PR man. With a sinking feeling, Carl picked up the phone. "Yes?"

"Thought you would want to know, Mr. Walsh, that the men killed in the parking lot have no identification of their own," Taylor announced, "but they planned to cause a major problem for us."

"How?"

"One of them had an authentic identification card of ours."

Sweat was starting to dampen his forehead, but Walsh made an effort not to grip the phone too hard. "Authentic? Whose?"

"James Thompson."

"Thank you," Carl croaked. "Everything else going well?"

"As well as expected, sir," Taylor advised. "We've ticked a few people off with this one, but they'll play ball with us."

"Good." Carl hung up and looked at Tony. "Your officer in Cuba, the one who disappeared, Mr. Thompson…his ID just showed up on one of those bodies."

"They wanted Mary badly," Tony observed, "and they wanted it to look like we did it."

"But why?" Walsh asked him. "Why are they bothering? She's more of a problem for us than for them. She escaped Saturday night. She wasn't around to see the Congressman. For heaven's sake, she was even tied up outside, so she could not have seen the weapons, drugs, transactions, or known for sure who had tortured Nathanial. Having her as an eyewitness will be valuable for us, but it won't make the case. So why is Richard Harvey, and it must be him after her, so scared of her?"

*Poor little Mary,* Aaron thought. *People are trying to kill her and their reasons don't even make sense.* She deserved to be safe after what she went through with him and the threat of the others…suddenly the answer hit him like a stray golf ball on the head. "I know why!" His chair had toppled to the floor, he had jumped so quickly. The eyes of his superiors bore into him. "She speaks Spanish—she speaks fuckin' Spanish!"

"Spanish!" both men had responded simultaneously.

It was coming back to Aaron now. "When two of the Cubans threatened her, Mary let off a torrent of Spanish. I was so busy trying to talk them out of touching her, it completely slipped my mind. And another time she understood something Alfredo said. How could I have missed that?"

"What could she have heard?" Walsh demanded.

Think…had anyone talked near her? Yes! "Alfredo," Aaron realised. "One day I was in the water. Lino was playing the guitar near her. Alfredo joined him and talked for a while. Alfredo has a very loud voice, and is totally indiscreet."

Before they could say more, Frank Moseley knocked and entered. To Tony's eye, Frank looked distressed. His tie was loose, as if Frank had been pulling at his collar, and his normally neat hair looked as if he had been running his hands through it. Frank was not a man to lose his cool, so even these slight signs concerned Tony.

"What's happened, Frank?"

Moseley looked at Tony, glanced apprehensively at Aaron, then faced Mr. Walsh, who was watching suspiciously. "I can't reach Gavin. I expected him here by now, but he hasn't reported to the house we prepared for Mary, and his phone is turned off."

"Perhaps they stopped for supper," Mr. Walsh suggested helpfully.

"Maybe."

There was something wrong here. You could hear it in Frank's voice. Frank should not be this worried over Gavin being behind schedule. "What's wrong?" Tony asked his old friend. "You're not worrying just because he's late."

"He's not answering his phone, and there is no other form of communication in Mary's car," Moseley repeated, walking towards the door and back. "Gavin should not have cut off communication."

For Christ's sake, the man was actually pacing! Tony felt real worry building up in him. "Do you think they've been intercepted?"

"No." Moseley stopped walking, and had obviously come to a decision. He faced Tony. "When Gavin is on an assignment; when he is clear about his orders and his strategy; he will turn off or leave behind his phone so it won't ring at the wrong time. Scott says Gavin has his phone with him and used it before he left Toronto."

Mr. Walsh's stomach was starting to develop knots. "Will you please be more specific here, Frank. You are not speaking plainly. What assignment? He was on his way home with her."

What assignment was indeed the question. Why was Frank so damned stressed? Then Tony caught on. Oh no. Cuba. Gavin had been given specific orders in Cuba. Tony stood up and took a step towards Frank. "What orders did you send him to Toronto with, Frank?" Tony could hear the quiver in his own voice. The expression on Frank's face told Tony that his fears were correct.

"To protect our officers and the Company's interests," Frank answered.

Mr. Walsh was obviously relieved. "So what's wrong? Gavin has never had problems understanding the Company's interests, from what I've heard about him."

"Cuba," Tony almost whispered, and Frank nodded. Behind Tony, Aaron let out a groan.

Mr. Walsh had not reached his position by being slow. There was something he had not been told. "Tell me *now*," he ordered. Then he glanced at Aaron. "Should I be asking Mr. St. Pierre to step out?"

"He's been in this all along, sir," Moseley stated.

Tony started, explaining the scene at the Cuban camp. "I believed that having a witness in that situation was too dangerous for us, and too politically disastrous for you to even know about. I made a decision—"

"*We* made a decision," Frank interrupted, staring at Tony.

"Okay Frank," Tony corrected, acknowledging the support, "we made a decision to send Gavin to eliminate the danger. Gavin was instructed to terminate the witness."

"You WHAT!" It had been an icy, very angry Deputy Director of Operations who responded.

"We changed it, sir," Frank stated quickly, "after Aaron pleaded for her. Aaron was the reason she was spared." They had gone so far now that Walsh might as well know it all. They didn't know him well, but they would probably know him a lot better after he assimilated and reacted to this news.

It didn't take Carl long to picture the scene, calculate the potential political damage the two men must have discussed, and understand their rationale for not informing him of their plans. It had been a no-win situation for everyone, and Carl would not have liked being faced with that decision. However, the decision was absolutely out of the authority of men on the front lines. Carl would not even have dared to risk that decision himself. He believed in process—in checks and balances. The decision on how to proceed should have been his to make. He took a breath to steady his voice. "We are going to move on from here, gentlemen, but before we do, I want one thing crystal clear. I do not care how you operated under my predecessor, but you will keep me informed at all times. Under me, you will make no decisions that are above your authority to make, or outside our mandate. None. I am here to take that responsibility. You will not make my decisions for me. Is that clear, gentlemen?"

The "Yes, sir" was in unison. Mr. Walsh nodded and sat down in the chair he had vacated without realising it. "Now continue, Frank. How do you believe Mr. Weeks has interpreted your orders?"

"I believe he may be interrogating Mary to determine her risk to us," Moseley responded. "There has already been two incidents in a friendly country, and one of our officers has been injured. That will not sit well with Gavin. He understands the political risks, and he does not like us getting bad publicity."

"Yes, his reputation for loyalty is quite admirable," Mr. Walsh mused. "If he does decide that she is a risk…I presume he's good enough to ensure her death could not be traced back to us." It was a statement more than a question.

"Oh yes," Frank replied without hesitation. "He is very careful. There will have been some perfectly plausible mishap—perhaps a car accident—even we won't be sure whether it was real or not. Only Gavin will know. We'll be seen as bringing her here for protection, but she will not make it. Very tidy, very respectable. No trace."

*And she won't even know why he's asking the questions,* Tony knew. In her honest little way she will blurt out her answers without thought. Gavin has little use for lawyers or courts. He may not *see that we can guide her answers.* The memory of the guileless brown eyes stabbed him. Tony looked at Mr. Walsh. "We can send a car to intercept, sir. Perhaps it's not too late."

Mr. Walsh thought for a moment, then, to Tony's horror, shook his head. "No. It's probably too late anyway. If it has happened, we're probably no worse off—better perhaps." He saw Tony's look. "My understanding is that you have a great deal of faith in Mr. Weeks."

"Yes," Tony admitted.

"Then if Mr. Weeks determines this witness to be a threat, he is probably correct?"

"Yes." It was a whisper. Gavin would not take his task lightly. If he killed Mary, it would be only to protect all of them. Tony could put no blame on Gavin. He also knew that Mary would be handled gently. Gavin would end her life with reluctance.

Aaron felt himself falling into a dark well. He had felt so good since Mary had called him. Life had seemed worth living again. He would be here to help her, to beg for her forgiveness. Now that was gone. He had little doubt of the outcome. Gavin was efficient, and had no patience for anyone who would speak against his beloved CIA. The agency was his life, and its officers his family. They had all recognised the risk Mary posed, but they had been willing to take the risk and gamble. Gavin did not gamble. Aaron sat with his head in his hands. Mr. Walsh was talking again.

"There will be no blame placed on Mr. Weeks, gentlemen. He is doing what he believes he has been ordered to do. Frank, I would like you to ask him for the truth, privately, and then just confirm it with me. I don't need details, but I do like to know that our officers have enough faith in their superiors not to keep secrets of this magnitude. And, gentlemen, that goes for you, too. No more secrets. You come to me and we work things out. That is how I was told you both work with your officers, and I expect the same respect from you." He hesitated slightly. "I intend to earn that respect, but for now I suppose you'll just have to take it on faith."

The conversation returned to Mary's knowledge of Spanish, and what she might have overheard. Congressman Harvey had connections in the CIA at different levels. Walsh decided he would meet with the Deputy Director to discuss how to plug any leaks of information that could be used for the Congressman's benefit in court. Tony listened, but part of his mind wandered to the woman for whom he had developed an instant and deep fondness. Would Gavin see the same lack of guile and the same honesty in her personality? He had to tear his thoughts away, because the thought of her death was just too painful.

Their conversation was interrupted once again by the phone. "Mr. Weeks is here, sir," the secretary announced.

"Alone?"

"Yes, sir."

Alone and at the office—not at the safe house. Mr. Walsh hung up and sighed. "Well, gentlemen, here we go. You will not question his story. That's for Frank to do. But, Frank, just clarify those orders, will you? I would like to hear what he believed them to be." Mr. Walsh looked at Aaron, who looked crushed, then at Tony. "Should he stay?"

Aaron looked up and met Tony's eyes. "I have to know, sir."

Tony nodded. Aaron probably felt as sick inside as he did, if not worse. "He should stay," Tony replied. They would put a watch on Aaron until they were sure he had survived the worst of the depression.

As soon as Gavin entered the room, it was apparent that he picked up the tension level. Instinctively Gavin's eyes flashed to Moseley for answers.

Moseley cleared his throat. "Gavin, have a seat, will you?"

Shaking his head, Gavin declined. *He's on edge now,* Tony observed. *Frank is standing and looking defensive. Gavin knows something is up.*

When Gavin did not speak, but continued to look at him, Frank framed his question. "Please tell Mr. Walsh exactly what orders I gave you when I sent you up to join Tony in Toronto." That only earned him a look of suspicion, so Frank continued. "Understand that if the orders were not clear, any misinterpretation is my responsibility."

Moseley and Gavin had a long history of working together, plus years of friendship. That Frank would readily assume full responsibility for this error came as no surprise to Tony.

"*Misinterpretation?*" Gavin's voice was incredulous, and held the start of anger, but he visibly checked it and turned to Mr. Walsh. "I was sent to protect our officers and the interests of the CIA." He looked again at Moseley. "Correct?"

"Correct." Moseley glanced at Mr. Walsh. "Would you please give Mr. Walsh your interpretation of the second part of that order?"

"Frank, that's not necessary right now," Mr. Walsh objected.

Realisation was coming to Gavin, and the colour heightened in his face. Gavin was a blunt, forceful man who had no fear of speaking his mind. Moseley permitted it because Gavin was invaluable to him, but it sometimes meant that Moseley had to swallow a bit of pride. Gavin did not know Walsh, but Moseley had offered to take responsibility, and clearly wanted Gavin to enlighten Walsh, so Gavin would do as directed.

"I was to determine if the witness to the Cuban affair was a threat to us," he advised Walsh. "If she was, I was to eliminate the threat. That," he added, speaking directly to Moseley, "is almost verbatim what you stated in Cuba." He stepped closer to Moseley until he was only about two feet away, face to face. In his hand he held an empty pop can, which now was crushing in his hand. "I hope," he said emphatically, "that you are not going to tell me that you changed YOUR MIND!" At the end, he was almost yelling into Moseley's face.

Mr. Walsh threw a concerned look at Tony, but Tony shook his head. Gavin and Frank had to work this out. Gavin had a right to be angry. He had just killed Mary and was being told it was a mistake. Inside, Tony felt a terrible void. It was over, done.

"You are fucking with my head!" Gavin continued to yell at Moseley.

"This isn't your fault," Moseley insisted.

"*Fault?*" In a furious gesture, Gavin threw the pop can against the wall. "I don't give a damn about fault! You and I cannot risk 'misinterpretations'."

Aaron couldn't stand any more. All he could see was Mary on that last night in Cuba, trusting him after three days of horror. "Oh, Gavin," he groaned. That dark well was pulling him down again.

That stopped Gavin in his tracks. He stared at Aaron as if seeing him for the first time. Then he abruptly strode over to him. "Aaron! No Aaron, I didn't hurt her…"

"I know," Aaron interrupted. He didn't want to hear any more. "You didn't hurt her and you didn't scare her." He lifted his head. Gavin had squatted down beside him, just the way he had in that Cuban camp. "I'm not blaming you, Gavin, I'm not. It's just hard to bear, that's all."

But Gavin shook his head and placed a hand on Aaron's shoulder. "No, man, I mean I didn't touch her. She's here, in Tony's office."

"What?" Brakes came on, and Aaron's fall into the dark well stopped. "She's alive?"

"Yes." His anger seemed to evaporate, and Gavin actually smiled at Aaron. "You guys should have asked me that first, if that's what you thought. She's no threat, not really. She's just angry," he continued, "and why shouldn't she be? But she saw right through you, Aaron." He looked over at Mr. Walsh. "Mary absolutely believes that Aaron was trying to protect her.

She isn't keen to see him again, but she has no hard feelings against him. Of course she's not too thrilled with us right now, but she is still willing to cooperate if she's needed."

Alive and in his office. "Why did you bring her here?" Tony asked, once he had found his voice.

"To leave her car here and pick up Scott after he drops Sheila at the doctor." Then Gavin gave Aaron's shoulder a slap and straightened up. "Tony, you and I have to have a little chat."

Tony glanced at Mr. Walsh, then back to Gavin. "Here and now, if it is about this."

Shrugging, Gavin continued. "I stopped the car at a public place to interrogate her. I said I needed a rest, and it was a well-lit place so she wouldn't have any concerns." A quick glance at Aaron, then he spoke again. "After it was over, she looks up at me with those innocent eyes, and asks me whose 'team' I'm on. I told her I report to Moseley. Then…and then she gets this scared look in those eyes, and asks me if she passed the test. If she *passed the test*, Tony. She fuckin' knew what I was up to."

It shocked Tony. "How could she?" he asked. Gavin was a seasoned interrogator. He would never have given Mary a clue to his intentions.

"Sheila had been talking…"

"No!"

"…in general terms, Tony," Gavin insisted. "Nothing specific. I'm not blaming Sheila, but Mary sees through people. You also told her how politically sensitive this case is. Mary fits pieces together. That five-foot-two-inch piece of innocence sitting beside me had figured out that if she failed this 'test', I would kill her."

This time the groan actually came from Mr. Walsh. This case was one disaster after another. Now an innocent woman who they needed to cooperate had figured out that the CIA had planned to kill her if she said the wrong thing. It was becoming one of his worst nightmares.

"Okay, Gavin, what have you done to repair this?" It was Moseley again.

"Promised her my personal protection," Gavin said simply, "and I meant it. We have done this woman no favours. She's been hurt and threatened by us. I don't like it at all. She's a nice lady." He walked over to where the pop can lay on the floor, picked it up and tossed it in the garbage. Then he looked at Moseley. "Frank, I'm going to take that vacation now, and I'm spending it at the safe house. I'm going to take care of Mary."

"What?" Mr. Walsh was still looking a bit pale.

Moseley intervened. "No, Gavin. You are not to be working on your vacation. You've asked to come in for a while, so if you would like to work at the house alongside Tony's people with Mary, I have no objection. When this is all over, then you can take a vacation before I re-assign you." Moseley turned to Mr. Walsh. "Do you have any objection?"

"Heavens, no. If you can spare him from the field, I have no objection," Mr. Walsh said in a tired voice. "Tomorrow I am really looking forward to meeting this woman. From what I hear, she is so average that people have a hard time describing her to me. Yet," he said in an amazed voice, "she has a Congressman hiring hit men to kill her, she's almost been executed twice by us, she has our female trainee screaming disobedience at Tony, she's been raped by one of our officers repeatedly yet forgives him, and now she has a veteran officer willing to do volunteer work to look after her *after* she figures out that he meant to kill her." He stared at each of them in amazement. "Does this sound like an average person to any of you?"

As soon as he could get away, Tony dashed to his office, entered and closed the door behind him. There she was, safe and sound, but looking small and scared. The visitor's tag hung slightly askew on her blouse. *She looks so tired,* he thought. *What a terrible day for her.* When he had entered the room, Mary had stood up and smiled, stepping forward slightly as if she wanted to come to him. Then she had stopped.

"Hola!" he greeted gently.

"Hola!" she responded easily.

"Como está?" he continued softly.

"Yo estoy…" but she couldn't finish. She didn't need to. He could see how she was. Mary's hands had been clasped in front of her, and now she raised them to her mouth and clamped her teeth on a knuckle. The brown eyes were developing a red brim around them, and seemed to be begging him to bring some sense of sanity back into her life.

Tony had intended to cheer Mary up and try to allay her fears by telling her that nothing would have happened to her; that she had no reason to fear Gavin. He had not intended to walk over to her and take her into his arms, but he was unable to stop himself. And he had definitely not intended to seek her lips and kiss them as if he had been afraid he would never see her again, but that was exactly what he was doing. Her lips were soft and moist, and she was yielding to his embrace. The way she pressed against him was causing flames of heat to shoot through his body.

He had to stop this. They were in his office, for Christ's sake, and anyone might knock and enter with little warning. With a last hungry kiss he moved away, but held on to one of her hands. Without words, a promise had passed between them. *Not now, but soon,* the promise had said. He found his breath. "I'm so glad you are here."

"I needed you today, Tony;" she replied simply. "All day I kept trying to be calm." Then she smiled. "I thought about our dinner date," she admitted. "It kept me going."

"Mary." Catching himself, Tony led her to the chair closest to his desk, then arranged his own chair at a ninety-degree angle to her. Conventional looking if anyone walked in, but close enough to touch her hand. "Tell me about what happened between you and Gavin."

Mary shivered, but she told him. Somehow she had passed the test, even though she knew she had answered some of the questions wrong. It had shown in Gavin's eyes. Gavin had done nothing to scare her, and she hadn't been frightened at that point because he had no look of cruelty to him. The questions, however, had been similar to the ones Tony had asked. Mary had known they were important. Afterwards, Gavin had looked relieved, and had prepared to drive off. Being curious, Mary had asked him a question of her own. Whose team was he on?

It was when he answered, "Moseley's," that Mary had an attack of nerves. Sheila had told her that Moseley's team did special projects, things done behind the scenes. Gavin , Sheila had said, was almost a legend. He was used in situations that were very dangerous or delicate. He was reputed to be a total Company man who would protect the agency at all costs, and eliminate threats. People said if you wanted a job done without anyone knowing about it, Gavin was the man they used.

*Protect the Company at all costs and eliminate threats,* Mary had remembered. Tony had told her how important it was for them that she cooperate. It had dawned on her then why Gavin was asking her all those questions. Protecting the Company meant finding out if she was a danger to it. And she had failed the question about blaming the CIA for her experience in Cuba.

When he had told her he was on Moseley's team, Mary had needed to know for sure if she was safe. It had been hard to ask, but impossible not to know. *"Did I pass the test?"* had shocked him. Then he had looked ill. At least he didn't pretend, Mary remembered. That's when she decided that she liked him. He could have lied—told her she was crazy or mistaken, but he hadn't. Gavin had looked her directly in the face and apologised for scaring her. In fact, he had reached over, taken her hand, and told her that it should never have happened and that she was safe now. Mary had believed him because he hadn't lied, but had sat shaking a little in her small car close to this powerful man. He had made no movement except to continue holding her hand and looking at her, telling her once more that she was absolutely safe now, and he would protect her himself from now on. The shaking had stopped. Then he had taken her to dinner and asked all about her life.

"When you people decide not to kill someone, you're really nice to them," Mary ended, with a tired smile.

Tony died a thousand deaths inside. Thank goodness Walsh didn't hear that one. He would have had a coronary. He had a feeling that Mary had been trying to tease him, but was too weary to carry it off. Tony was saying a silent thank-you to Gavin for bringing Mary home safely to him, when Scott knocked and walked in.

At the sight of Scott, Mary jumped up from her chair again. Here he was, her new friend, smiling and winking at her, safe and unhurt. If he had been killed in that parking lot she would never have forgiven herself. Impulsively, she tried to kiss his cheek, but he laughed instead, and picked her right up off the ground in a huge bear hug. She squealed in delight as her tension evaporated.

"I am *so* glad to see you!" he said. When he put her down, Mary noticed that the finger he was pointing at her was shaking. "No more shopping, no more going out in public for a while. That was totally my fault, and I'm not going to risk losing you again."

Normally, Tony would have disapproved of Scott's familiarity, but he was hardly the one to lecture about that in this case. Anyway, Mary was clearly quite comfortable with Scott, and she could use a few friends right now. So without comment he shepherded them out the door to take Mary to her new temporary home.

Gavin was given the job of driving, and after he had passed the same oak tree twice, Mary was quite sure that they were going around in circles, or at least some sort of figure eight. Eventually, though, they came to a small brick bungalow at 51 Elm Street. It looked well kept, yet had nothing to make it stand out from several other bungalows on the street.

Inside, the house was actually quite remarkable. Half the living room was taken up with computer equipment, wires, phones and what looked like small televisions hooked up to electrical equipment. Being only slightly familiar with even basic computers, Mary had no idea what she was looking at.

Tony saw the look of astonishment on Mary's face. "A little different from your normal living room, isn't it?" he teased. Then he began to explain it, trying to not confuse her with too much detail. There were cameras outside that monitored the street and the grounds around the house. Scott and Gavin could see exactly what was outside at any time, and the images were being sent to an office at headquarters, where they were stored, or could be viewed by someone wanting to check on the house. Some of the telephones were attached to the computers, and one was hooked to a secure line into headquarters. One phone was just your regular type of telephone.

Some of the equipment was actually hooked up to Mary's bedroom. There was a timing device, so the listener could hear into her room for a selected number of seconds at a predetermined interval. This was an extra safety precaution, so that at night in the very unlikely chance that someone was able to get onto the grounds and into her room, any sound was automatically recorded at headquarters. The sounds were also transcribed through a monitor in the living room, where Gavin or Scott would keep an eye on it and respond to anything suspicious. Of course anything out of the ordinary on any system was reported in a signed report that one of the officers had to submit at the end of their shift. Oh, and Tony warned her not to snore too loud, since Gavin or Scott would be listening in at all times, and snoring was hard on the ears. Then he laughed at her look of consternation.

"Do you listen to me in the bathroom, too?" she complained.

"No, of course not," Tony assured her. "When you are ready to go to bed, you poke your head out the door and let them know. Then they will turn it on. We trust," Tony continued, "that when you are awake, you are capable of screaming if need be. However," he continued, "it has been ordered by our Security section that this be turned on by 11:00 p.m. at the latest. So if you are planning any parties in your bedroom, prepare yourself to have them monitored."

The remainder of the house was much less complicated. Mary's bedroom had a little en-suite bathroom, a closet, small dresser and a double bed. Above the bed was a green light. "When that light is on," Tony explained, "you'll have heard a faint click. That means the sound monitor is on."

Too bad, thought Mary, eyeing the bed. Tony was standing close behind her, pointing to the light. She could smell his cologne, and felt his presence acutely. She wished like anything he would close the door, lose his head like he had in his office, and take her to bed. It wasn't likely to happen, and now that she knew people would be listening at night, for sure it wouldn't happen.

*Fool,* she told herself. *A man from a life totally different from your own, who will forget you as soon as your reason for being here is over. I'm not like Lori,* she knew. *My feelings will get hurt and I know it, but he makes me so crazy that I'm willing to risk it. Surely, though, living with a little pain in your life is better than not living at all.* Accidently, she let a sigh escape her.

"You're tired," Tony observed, patting her shoulder. "The rest of the tour can wait. Tomorrow is a big day. We will be meeting with my boss, Mr. Walsh, plus Mr. Hedley, a man from public relations, and Aaron."

*Aaron. Meet Aaron tomorrow.* Mary did not feel ready. It would be awful. "What time?"

"Ten thirty." Tony smiled. "Everything will be fine, Mary. Let Scott make you a good breakfast to give you some energy. He makes a great pancake."

As if a pancake could give her courage, Mary thought, closing the bedroom door behind Tony. Tomorrow would come and surely had to end. Then the first step would be over. *Aaron.* She would know what kind of person he was.

In the living room, Tony selected the large stuffed armchair near the front window, and tried to stop thinking of Mary. He had something else to discuss, so he looked at Gavin and Scott in turn. "Okay, you two...let's talk about that fiasco in the mall this morning. Whose responsibility was that?"

Gavin didn't hesitate. "Mine. I should have vetoed it. If I had refused to go, it wouldn't have happened."

It didn't surprise Tony in the slightest that Gavin would volunteer to accept the blame, but it wasn't Gavin he wanted to hear from.

"No, it bloody well isn't!" Scott had been watching Gavin from where he stood near the computers, but now he walked over to stand in front of Tony. "It wasn't Gavin's responsibility, it was mine. You left me in charge of Sheila, and we were supposed to protect Mary. Gavin was only there as our backup in case things got out of hand, which they did." He shrugged. "Sheila asked me about going to the mall and I wasn't keen about the idea, but I went along with it. Gavin wasn't in favour of it at all. I'm the one who should have said no. It was my responsibility."

"Yes, it was," Tony agreed. He was pleased, but he wouldn't let Scott see that. Scott was standing still, clearly waiting for the expected lecture, but Tony decided that he didn't need one. *Scott knows he made a mistake. He doesn't need me to tell him that. Next time he'll think good and hard before he makes a decision.* "Well, I'm going to make some coffee," Tony announced, amused at the surprised look on Scott's face. *Ah, it's good to give the kid a break once in a while,* he decided.

# XXVI

Tony left the house early the next morning. He had slept on a cot in one of the bedrooms after staying up late with Scott and Gavin. It had pleased him to see that the two men had settled down quickly to work together, and seemed to hit it off well. They were very different personalities in some ways, but each had a sense of duty that Tony liked. In fact, Tony found himself more pleased with Scott's performance with every passing week. That careless attitude that Scott had worn like a shield was disappearing. It did not surprise Tony. He had been sure that there was some good, solid stuff under the rich kid performance. That's why he had kept working with him. Scott today was quite different than Scott even two months ago.

Mary had looked pale this morning, and had said that she did not sleep well. That was to be expected. A strange house with a light coming on over your head and an intimidating morning ahead of her would not be conducive to a good rest. On the drive to his office, Tony thought about what was ahead. Mr. Walsh had consulted with several people, who all thought they knew how this meeting between Aaron and the witness should be handled. Mary was to meet Aaron in a formal office setting, so she would feel protected. Aaron had been given strict instructions, aimed to ensure that Mary felt in control. He was to speak quietly and politely, move slowly and, if he had to get up, to let her know exactly what he was doing. He was not to approach her without someone else by his side, and he was not to tower over her. Above all, he was not to touch her, even by accident. He had raped and dominated her, and she was probably terrified of him. If there was any problem, or if she couldn't face him, he was to leave the room.

Tony had his doubts, but he had been outvoted. Aaron would be stifled. Since Mary had called him for help, Aaron had taken himself off the anti-depressants, and was improving, but he was still depressed and very nervous about today. Knowing Aaron as he did, and with what he now knew about Mary's kind nature, Tony felt that the two of them would get through this much easier if people left them alone, perhaps with Sheila or Scott for support. As Sheila had said to him at Mary's house, Aaron and Mary had a lot of healing to do. How could you start a healing process in a room with your employers, a lawyer and a public relations man staring at you? To make it worse, everyone would be dressed in suits and ties, sitting around that large wooden desk in Mr. Walsh's very formal office. In fact, Mary would have to walk at least twenty feet from the door to the desk with five pairs of male eyes watching her. He shook his head. Mary would need a lot of courage to get through today.

It was Scott's job to bring Mary to the meeting this morning. At 10:30 a.m. he was walking her down the hall towards Mr. Walsh's office, with her hand through his arm. He had butterflies himself, and he knew by the drawn look on Mary's face that she was not far from panic mode. Even the process of getting her past the gates and in through the front doors was an intimidating procedure. Trying to distract her, he pointed out paintings and objects that he could tell she had not the slightest interest in.

"Here we are," Scott announced, pausing outside Mr. Walsh's office. Then he felt her freeze.

"I can't...can't go in there." No, it was impossible. Walk through that door and say hello to a bunch of strange people, and see Aaron? Panic welled up. *He'll look at me. He'll see the prisoner who did anything he asked. He's seen me naked and helpless. I cried and I begged. There's no weakness in me that he hasn't seen. And in the end I begged him to kill me but asked him for sex first. I was his play toy, and now they want me to go in there like nothing happened.*

Scott was worried. Mary was terrified. He faced her, and bent down to whisper. People walking by were giving curious looks. "You can do this, Mary. I know it must be awfully hard, but once you do it, it will be over. It's the first meeting that's so hard. I'll be right here beside you. Please."

"I...no...I can't."

"Please, Mary," he begged. "Do it for me. Aaron needs to apologise desperately. That's all that will happen in here. Then you'll be past the worst, and things will be okay. Please...for me?"

Without him, Mary knew she would have run away. She looked up at him and took courage from his kind face. "Don't you leave me, not for a moment. Promise."

"Promise." He opened the door quickly, and they were committed.

With Scott's arm around her shoulders, Mary got about six feet into the room before she froze again. She hardly saw the other people at the desk.

Only Aaron. It was him, although he looked neat and clean. He was pale, too, as if he had not been well. As she had suspected, he was a very attractive man, and young. Perhaps under thirty. Also as she expected, he was looking at her.

Scott was trying to urge her towards the desk, and was introducing her to someone, but Mary couldn't hear or pay attention. She was having flashbacks. Visions of Taz screaming and dragging her around, and visions of that camp. Juany screaming and Nathanial lying beside her in pain. Scott was whispering her name into her ear now, but Mary couldn't take her eyes off Aaron. The worst flashback came—the last night when she had asked this attractive young stranger to make love to her. *God, what must he think?*

Aaron sat in misery. Mary was so scared she couldn't move. Her left fist was clenched around Scott's lapel, and she probably didn't know it. She had clung to Aaron that way once in Cuba when she'd been frightened. *Hold on to her, Scott,* Aaron prayed. *She trusts you, and she needs to cling to you right now. Poor Mary.* Why on earth did Walsh insist on such a formal meeting? Was it possible to find a more intimidating setting? Why hadn't they let him go over to the house to meet her, with Scott and Tony to support her? It would have been much less threatening. Mary was no coward, but how much could one woman take? Damn them! He should have fought them harder.

Then Mr. Walsh spoke to him. "I think you should leave for a bit, Mr. St. Pierre. Perhaps we can bring you in later."

Ordered out. They were wrong, all wrong. Okay, he had no choice, but they could not prevent him from speaking. "Please don't be scared, Mary," he said as he stood up. "I'll go now." Slowly he walked toward her on his way to the door. "Please don't be so scared," he said quietly. A few feet away from her, he paused. "I never wanted any of that. I didn't want to hurt you, and I didn't want to scare you…I swear." He could hear his voice catch. "I'm so sorry…so very sorry." Mary still stood frozen, but her eyes had followed his every move. He tried again. "I was so happy when you called me for help. I'm here to help you, Mary. Any way I can. Please believe that…" Well, he had better go so she could relax. "Maybe we can talk later," he said hopefully. He backed up a step and turned to go out the door.

He was leaving. Mary fought to gain control over her panic. She had just found him and he wanted to help her. She remembered him now. He was exactly what Scott had said. She remembered his voice. He was the Aaron of the last night, who had tried to protect her for three days. Aaron wasn't laughing or bragging. He was sad and kind. Now he was leaving. With a gasp she found her voice.

"No." It was a croak, but it stopped him. *Try again.* "Don't go. Please." She waited and heard Scott let his breath out. "I can't do this alone, Aaron," she pleaded.

Aaron did not need a second invitation. He turned to face her. "You don't have to be alone, Mary. I'm here to help you. I'll stay. Thank you," he added. He indicated to Scott to help Mary to a chair.

Scott had been trying to introduce Mary to the man directly across from her. Mary decided to take the initiative now, although she was still shaky. Before she sat, she reached a hand across to him. "I'm sorry. That was awfully rude of me," she said to him. "My name is Mary."

"Carl Walsh," the man responded, looking pleased. He proceeded to introduce the public relations man as Mr. Wilkes.

Just then Tony picked up the phone, pushed a few numbers and said, "Okay." *To hell with all this formality,* he decided. He had a little surprise in store for Mary. Noticing Mr. Walsh's curious look, he merely smiled slightly and said nothing.

When the door to the office opened, Mary glanced over and her eyes shone with relief. It was Sheila! Her arm was in a sling, and she was wearing, of all things, blue jeans and a T-shirt that said *Just Do It!* Grinning from ear to ear, Sheila walked directly over to Mary. "Hey, Mar, how ya doin'?" As Mary jumped up to hug her, Sheila glanced reproachfully at Mr. Walsh. "Geesh, you think this room is masculine enough for her?" Although the tone was sarcastic, her smile kept it one step short of insubordinate.

Mr. Walsh glared at Tony, who stared right back. *I'll fight you on this one,* Tony said silently. Mr. Walsh decided that it wasn't worth it, and said hello to Sheila.

"Your poor arm!" Mary blurted.

"A scratch," Sheila insisted, waving the issue aside. "Can I sit with you?"

Aaron watched the two women. Another friend for Mary. Good. He looked his approval over at Tony. *Way to go, Dad!* It would not surprise him to learn that Tony had specifically told Sheila to dress like that. Sheila would not have done that on her own. Good old conservative Tony. Once in a while he just had to break the rules.

Mary had moved over one seat to make room for Sheila. That placed her directly opposite Aaron, with the desk between them. They were at the end of the desk, however, and no chairs separated them. Maybe later he could slide his chair around and sit beside her, too. But it was too soon to push Mr. Walsh again. *Pick your time,* he told himself. *Tony will back you.*

Tony noticed that Mary was wearing a skirt and co-coordinating sweater that had a neckline which exposed her throat plus an extra inch or two. Conservative, but very becoming. He knew that Sheila had helped select it during that ill-fated shopping trip. Who else but Sheila would concern herself with retrieving a package of clothing under gunfire? Tony decided that he didn't want to think about that. Regardless of how she had obtained the package, Sheila's taste in clothing was excellent. Mary looked great.

It was time for formalities. Paul Hedley began by making formal apologies, and then announcing that the statements taken from Mary and Aaron had concurred. He further informed Mary that Aaron had freely admitted to the rapes and assaults, and that she, Mary, was expected to charge him with these offences. It was fully expected, and Aaron would stand trial for them after this current trial was finished.

Mary was perplexed to see Aaron sit without emotion or response while Mr. Hedley talked. Charge him with rape? Send him to trial? Whose side were these people on? She looked at Tony for clues, but he avoided her gaze.

"May I ask questions?" Mary inquired of Mr. Walsh.

"Of course."

Turning to Mr. Hedley, she directed her question at him. "You said that the statements concur."

"Yes."

That meant that Aaron had said as little as she had. Brief descriptions of the assaults. "Did Aaron say why he did it?"

"Mr. St. Pierre told us that he was forced to use the cover that had been provided to him. He stated that it was the only way he knew to stay alive. His hope was to remove you and Mr. Bowman from the situation. He also told us that he attempted to injure you as little as possible in the process, but suspects that he caused you a great deal of psychological trauma."

Well, that was one word for it. Mary looked at Aaron. The room was very quiet. "They want me to charge you with rape."

"Yes." The word was said quietly and evenly.

"Why would I do that, Aaron?" *Please stand up for yourself, Aaron. If you don't, I will have to, and I'll be so embarrassed.*

"Because I raped you, Mary."

Shaking her head, Mary felt her breathing quicken. He was taking the blame for all of this. Why? He did not deserve it, and she had to tell them why. "You didn't tell them everything, Aaron."

His eyes flickered, and he looked down at his hands. What was she going to say? Aaron could feel his pulse speed up. "I think I did, Mary," he answered simply.

"No." Her eyes flashed. "You didn't. You forgot to tell them how you gave me your jacket every night with the granola bars in the pockets, and how you put water in the whisky bottle so I could have a drink when they thought you were being cruel." She took a breath. "And you didn't tell them about how Alfredo was going to cut me with the knife, but you stopped him by saying that when a woman was giving you a..." she skipped the word—she couldn't say that "...you didn't want to look down and see a cut up face."

Aaron thought he was going to die. That's right, she spoke Spanish, and he had not realised it at the time. All those horrible, horrible things he had told Alfredo...she had understood. He stared at her.

"You didn't tell them about the tree—how it looked like you were choking me, but really you were supporting me with your body; and how you had smeared that butter...all over...so it wouldn't hurt." Mary was breathing heavily now.

"Mrs. Norland, please don't distress yourself," Mr. Walsh objected. "Mr. St. Pierre is perfectly willing to accept responsibility for this."

"But it's not his fault," Mary blurted. Then she forced herself to look at Tony. That was difficult to do right now, but she needed to know if she should stop talking. Tony was looking a little unnerved, but he met her gaze steadily. Then he smiled at her—a small, somewhat strained smile, but enough to show that he was on her side. He did not ask her to stop. *"Aaron needs you desperately,"* he had said. *Okay, Tony, I'll fight for him.*

"You told them about...about urinating on me," she continued, "but you didn't tell them you did it to keep those bastards away from me. You felt so bad about it that you took me for a bath later."

Aaron could see the men actually cringing at the visual images. Mr. Hedley was writing notes furiously. Here was little Mary, embarrassing the hell out of herself to protect *him*. "Mary, you don't have to do this—"

"But you won't stick up for yourself," she insisted. "You never told them about putting that cream on me at night, pretending it would keep you from 'catching anything'." Somehow she managed to raise her eyes and look him in the face. "And when Alfredo thought it would be fun to have...have..." she was starting to cry, damn it "...and I couldn't stand the thought, I begged you not to. You *faked* it, Aaron, even with them only a few feet away." Somehow she kept talking, in spite of the tears in her eyes. "And the last night, Aaron, when I begged you to kill me, but then I got scared..."

"No!" *Damn their conventions,* Aaron decided. Mary was *not* going to do this on her own. She was trying to save him, and he would not sit here like a coward and let her do this alone. In a second, he had left his chair and knelt beside her, taking her trembling hands in his. "You don't have to say this, Mary. It's enough to know that you believed in me."

That caused her to smile. "I got scared," she continued stubbornly, "and you held me until I stopped crying. You told me to go to sleep and you would take care of everything when I was asleep." She squeezed his hand. "Aaron, I stopped being afraid of you when I caused the knife to slip and it cut your face." Tentatively, she touched the scar that remained beneath his eye. "If you had been Taz," she shuddered, "you would have cut me to ribbons with that knife. But you didn't. It never occurred to you. Yes, you raped me," she acknowledged, "but you kept me alive for three days in that horrible place, and you protected me from much worse."

"Oh, Mary." To the shock of the men watching, Aaron put his arms around Mary and pulled her close, resting his face on her shoulder. He felt her fingers patting him shyly on the back. He was saved. She had looked past the animal and seen the man. For the first time since Cuba, he felt an interest in being alive.

"Do you know why I ran away?" she asked.

"You didn't want to die," he responded, pulling his face back to look at her.

"Well, that too," she admitted, "but I was afraid you wouldn't be able to do it. I couldn't face the alternative. I knew that if you felt you had to come after me, you at least wouldn't hurt me."

With a groan, Aaron buried his head against her shoulder again.

"I will not let them charge you with rape," Mary insisted, glaring at his employers. "You need to tell me how I can help."

"Help?" Aaron pulled back and held her hands. His eyes were moist, but he smiled up at her. "You have opened the gates to my private hell and let me out. You have no idea how much you have helped me."

It was hard to listen to, especially when you cared about both the people involved. Tony knew Aaron well, and had continued to believe in him, but to have that faith justified was sweet indeed. A glance toward Scott sobered him. Scott had been learning too much, too fast, since that day in Cuba. He had developed a fondness for Mary, but had been isolated from all but the most general of details. This was a shock to him. He was sitting on the edge of his chair, with his hands clenched, staring at Aaron. Tony caught his eye with a firm look, and Scott turned his head abruptly to stare into the middle of the room at nothing.

A thought struck Tony that he had picked a team of chivalrous men. *They are all dragon-fighters,* he realised. Fight for your country, your company and the women you care about. There was a danger, though, that this situation could cause them to fight each other. Aaron was engaged to Scott's sister, and that had to be on Scott's mind right now. *I've got work to do with these two men tonight,* Tony decided. *Scott and Aaron have to be helped to do a bit of healing themselves.*

Sheila decided that her friends should have some privacy. It was long overdue. "Can we give them a few minutes alone, sir?" she asked Mr. Walsh.

"It will make my job a lot easier," Mr. Hedley agreed quickly.

Mr. Walsh seemed more than willing to break the tension now. "Sure. Why don't we get some coffee in here? Tony, open the meeting room door and let them sit in there. The room is completely private, Mary," he informed her. "Take a few minutes, and we will call you when the coffee arrives."

Once Aaron and Mary had gone into the adjoining room, Walsh turned to his colleagues. "How did we miss this? I know he said he tried not to hurt her, but is Aaron that transparent?"

"He fooled all the others," Tony answered, yet he was just as perplexed. Sure, they called Aaron "puppy dog", but damn it, he had raped her. How had Mary known it was all an act? By all accounts it had been a horrifying spectacle. How had she seen through it?

Inside the private room, Aaron and Mary sat side by side. While he was glad to be away from the limelight, and could feel himself unwinding, Aaron realised that the relaxation was bringing fatigue. Beside him, Mary also seemed to be calming down. It was quiet and peaceful in here, and neither spoke for a few minutes. Aaron reached over to cover Mary's left hand with his right. It earned him a timid smile, and her shoulders seemed to relax. Now that they were finally alone, he found that he didn't know what to say. It was nice just to sit here beside her. The colour in her cheeks was fading, and she had stopped shaking. This secure, quiet room seemed worlds away from what they had endured in Cuba.

"I am so glad that you are here and safe," he ventured finally. "I've wanted to meet you and tell you how sorry I am, but I was afraid that you wouldn't come down here."

"I was afraid to come," Mary admitted, her hand turning under his to hold it. "I was too embarrassed, but you have very loyal friends. They kept telling me that you were a decent man, and I had nothing to worry about." Her eyes studied his face. "Finally I had to come. I'm glad I did. I think it would have remained unfinished for me if I hadn't."

*I feel as if I'm sitting beside a long-lost friend,* Aaron realised. Scott had been right about her being so nice. "I don't know you," Aaron mused, "but I feel as if I know you very well." Then he stopped, abruptly, seeing a look on her face. "I'm sorry, that was not a very appropriate thing to say."

Mary recovered quickly. "You know, I think we are going to feel a bit awkward for a while. Maybe we should try not to worry about what's appropriate or not, and just take things a day at a time."

"Fine by me."

Mary stared at his hand for a minute. "You didn't tell them about…"

"That last night?" he guessed. When she nodded, he explained. "I thought it was kinda personal, and maybe you wouldn't want anyone to know. There were no witnesses, and I can't see why it would matter." He could tell by the way she refused to look at him that he'd been right not to tell. She was embarrassed. There was no reason to be, but he suspected that she would never have done anything like that if she had thought she would have to face him again. Part of him wanted to talk about that too, but not yet. It was too early to have a conversation about that intimacy. "I'll leave it up to you," he said. "If you want to tell, we'll tell. If not, it will be our little secret."

She raised slightly pinkish cheeks to him. "Secret, please."

"Okay." For the next few minutes, he told her that Mr. Hedley would be interviewing them again this afternoon, and this time he needed details. When Mary shuddered, Aaron explained that Mr. Hedley expected the trial to deteriorate into a credibility fight, because the defence had no other way to explain away the evidence and the fact that Congressman Harvey had been caught at the scene. Mr. Hedley needed to know everything the defence knew. "Hedley says we're going to feel like we are the ones on trial—me anyway. It's going to be awful."

"Will he interview us together, or separately?"

"Not sure," Aaron replied. "If we have a choice, which would you prefer?" To be interviewed together might be quite embarrassing, but for some reason he felt a need to know the experience from Mary's eyes, however unpleasant. Perhaps he felt the same need for closure that she had mentioned.

"Together, if you can stand it," Mary answered.

*We're on the same track,* Aaron thought. He noticed that Mary was a very natural, pretty woman. Then he looked at her hair. "Your hair looks a lot better than the last time I saw you," he said with a grin.

Mary smiled back. "You are a lousy barber. My hairdresser thought I had put my head in a blender." When he laughed, Mary knew that they were going to get along just fine.

Before entering, Tony knocked on the door. *They are sitting together like two old friends,* he noticed. He wanted a word with Aaron, so smiled at Mary and asked her if she would mind checking in on Scott. "This has been quite a shock for him, Mary. He wasn't told any of this." As she left, Tony received a confident smile from her that did the usual things to his pulse. He watched her walk out the door.

"So the guys tell me that you're quite fond of her," Aaron stated, watching him. He had stood up when Tony approached.

Tony grimaced, but he knew his team did not keep many secrets from each other. They would, however, keep the secrets in the "family". Only the team would know.

"It seems that I've been rather transparent," Tony admitted. Then he noticed that Aaron was standing with his arms crossed and turned slightly away from him. What was this body posture about? "What's up?" he asked.

But Aaron seemed ill at ease, and wouldn't meet his eye. "I'm just sorry you had to hear all that," he said finally.

*Oh hell, he's afraid I'll take this personally. That's what's wrong.* Holding out his hand, Tony kept his voice easy. Any personal feelings he had for Mary had to take a backseat until this assignment was over. "Come on, none of that. You've got enough on your plate without fussing about my feelings." They shook hands, and Tony saw Aaron relax.

*That's vintage Tony,* Aaron thought, shaking his hand. *Hide all those personal wants and desires away. Spend all your energy on ensuring that the men and women under you are safe, happy and productive. Channel all your love and frustration their way and make them your family, but don't ever give yourself a chance at real happiness. As if getting involved with Mary would make you forget to pat us on the back one day. Don't you know that we want you to be happy too? We are more than willing to share you with your friends.*

*Your friends...* Aaron felt a stab of guilt. *I should tell him about Nat. He gives his all for me, and I'm withholding a very big truth from him. Your best friend—I killed your best friend.* For a second, Aaron almost believed he could say it, but their hands had dropped and the moment was gone.

Tony was talking again. "Look, Scott's in a bit of shock," he stated. "That's why I wanted to come in and speak to you. He's been exposed to more than he was ready for since we took him to Cuba, and I think today has been the topper for him. He's developed a fondness for Mary, and I think he has Susan on his mind too."

"Undoubtedly," Aaron muttered.

"So," Tony continued quickly, "I'd like you to come to the house this evening. I've got to 'down-load' Scott and let him get some of this off his chest. Mary and Gavin will be there to help. Can you handle it? You'll probably get the brunt of his questions."

"Of course." It would be a difficult evening, Aaron knew. Scott would want answers that Aaron might not even know. He had to try, though. His chances of marrying Susan seemed very slim now, but if Scott wasn't on his side, they would be nonexistent. Shit, a few days in Cuba had put a lot of strain on his friendships.

Out in the main part of Mr. Walsh's office, Mary had seated herself across from Mr. Walsh, between Sheila and Scott. It was not a place for a private conversation, but since Scott seemed very tense, Mary touched his arm and thanked him quietly for giving her the courage to enter the room and staying with her as he had promised. All he did was hold her hand and sit without speaking.

Tony and Aaron came out of the private room and took the remaining two chairs. Mr. Walsh looked across the table and smiled at Mary. Then he addressed the group in general.

"Paul will be interviewing Mary and Aaron in detail over the next few days. I will be kept apprised as Paul sees fit. That means," he explained to Mary, "that I have to know about anything that affects our chances in court or our public relations. I do not need to know specific details concerning yourself unless they are of particular importance. No one else in this room needs to know exactly what went on, either. I am telling you this because I want you to feel free to talk to Paul without fearing that he is going to be telling tales out of school. Unfortunately, it will probably all come out in the courtroom, and that is why Paul needs to know everything the defence knows." He saw the look of distaste on her face. "I know it will be very unpleasant for you, but remember that Paul will have a much better chance of prosecuting that group of animals if he knows more than the defence knows. That way nothing will be a surprise to him. Do you understand that?"

Mary just nodded.

"I would also," Mr. Walsh continued, "ask that you allow our own doctor to examine you, so ensure us that you are indeed okay, and that you meet with our psychiatrist."

*Oh no,* Mary squirmed. Here she was down here all on her own, surrounded by people she didn't know very well, and he wanted her to meet with a strange doctor and a shrink? Suddenly she felt very much alone, and instinctively looked at Sheila for help.

Sheila seemed to recognise her fear, and smiled reassurance. "Would you like me to come with you, Mary?"

Could she? Mary looked over at Tony to see if that would be allowed. Tony smiled and nodded.

"Yes," Mary answered gratefully. She looked at Mr. Walsh. "Okay."

"Thank you." Mr. Walsh looked around the table. "Okay, you gentlemen can return to your duties. Sheila can take Mary to introduce her to the doctors, then Paul can arrange the interviews with Mary and Aaron."

# XXVII

Hanging up the phone, James Cook stared at it in disgust. Even though he made a very good living saving the careers of foolish rich and powerful people, that didn't mean he liked them all. Richard Harvey was an idiot. An angry idiot right now, of course, because Mr. Pitt had failed again, and this time gotten himself killed in the process with James Thompson's identification on him. Well, he had warned Harvey that it would not be an easy job. Besides, who would have expected the CIA to put one of their top operatives on guard duty? If Richard Harvey had a brain in his head, he would have used his inside connections to find this out. Of course, if he had a brain in his head, he would have checked his contacts to make sure the CIA was not running an operation in Cuba with the very group Harvey had so rashly decided to visit.

Losing Mr. Pitt was a real liability for Cook. He had been a discreet and trustworthy mercenary, and totally reliable. A real shame. He would be hard to replace. In addition, they were now in a worse position because the location of the woman was unknown. Undoubtedly she was under the very close protection of the CIA now. They would take no more chances. Harvey would have to use his contacts to find out where she was being kept. Then the real work would start, and they had so little time. Harvey was pushing Cook to move heaven and earth for a quick trial. The faster this was over and resolved, the better it was for him politically. Before that happened, this witness had to be eliminated. The prosecution would prepare her for trial, and it was now more advantageous to Harvey's case if she never came to court.

Now that they knew the CIA was intending to protect her, any further attempt would have to be an inside job. Someone with access to her had to be reached and convinced to do the job. Or at a minimum, allow Cook's men to do it. Then, of course, the officer who allowed it to happen would have to be eliminated to ensure that it could be made to look like an inside job. It would take a lot of planning, a lot of money and a great deal of luck. All that took time, and they had so little time.

Congressman Harvey wondered how much worse things could get. Cook's men had made a real mess of things. Now he had even more work to do, while going from place to place, using different telephones because he couldn't trust his own to remain untapped. Most of his CIA contacts had been legitimate. They were the people at the top, and these people were not talking to him right now. He was being avoided. He was putting as much political pressure on them as he could, but he knew that he had suddenly lost a great deal of power. The contacts he needed now were fewer in number, and very private. They were people for whom he had done favours, or whom he had assisted in various capacities. A couple actually had their pay cheques enhanced through his accountant. It was payback time.

One of these contacts was currently in the Office of Technical Service, which might come in handy later. The other man was overseas. Contacting him would be expensive and risky. He was on Frank Moseley's team. All Harvey needed from him was information and leads. Who was reachable, and how? Was it possible to turn Gavin Weeks, or were there any hidden secrets they could use for leverage? Who were the other officers involved, and what were their weaknesses? First, though, he had to find this man. He dialled the home number for the contact in Technical Services.

# XXVIII

The evening at 51 Elm went better than Aaron had feared. They were all mentally exhausted from their emotional roller coaster ride that had started in the camp in Cuba. Once they had eaten, and Mary had changed into more casual clothing, Tony told Scott to spit out what was bugging him. At first, Scott would not admit that anything was bothering him, but Tony persisted. Then it was apparent that Scott did not want to talk in front of Mary, but Tony refused to ask her to leave. Frustrated, Scott had finally faced Aaron and blurted out the question that had begun to weigh heavily on his mind.

"How the fuck *could* you?" was all he said.

*How could you?* seemed unanswerable at first. Indeed, Aaron had spent a number of sleepless nights wondering the same thing. With the help of his colleagues and Mary, he managed to explain what reality had meant for him and Mary in Cuba; the fear, the threats, the horror of knowing what Nat was facing, the urgency to remain undetected at all costs, and the need to stay alive so he could save Nat and the women. Mary helped by telling Scott what had happened to her and Juany and Nat, and the confusion she had over "Taz's" dual personality.

By this time Scott was settled on the couch beside Mary. Aaron was on her other side. She sat with her legs curled underneath her, dwarfed by the two men.

"How did you know Aaron's name?" Scott asked unexpectedly.

Fortunately, Mary had been tugging at her pant cuff to straighten it. Her head was down and she took a second to compose her answer. Carefully she put a frown on her face. "I guess Nathanial must have used it while we were talking. I can't remember."

That answer was accepted by Scott, and Aaron appeared to be preoccupied, but Tony was startled. He glanced at Gavin to see if the answer had the same effect on that man. It did. Gavin was frowning. Nathanial Bowman was a veteran officer who had been in a critical, life-threatening situation. To imagine that he would sit there and tell a stranger Aaron's real name when he had just suffered torture to conceal it was not believable. It could not be true. Mary had to be confused.

Or was she? Tony watched them. Her strong defence of Aaron had pleased, yet puzzled him, and they seemed so close. Tony did not pretend to know how their Cuban experience had affected them personally. Sheila had talked about the need for healing, but Tony had the distinct feeling that he was missing something. Nat's death had been nagging at him. The autopsy had found internal bleeding and because the trauma to the body had been so obvious, the cause of death had been accepted. But it had not been conclusive. The doctor had felt it equally possible that Nat could have survived the trauma. In most people's eyes, Nat had just been lucky to die before further torture, so why worry about it, right?

Tony watched Aaron stare off into space. *Or was it luck, Aaron? Would you really have let Nat face more torture? I don't think so. Why do you deny it? You cannot keep secrets like this from me, and I've been trying to give you a chance to tell me. What if Mary saw you? What if someone else guesses? Someone not on our side?*

It seemed to Tony that everything was settling down, when Scott turned suddenly to him.

"There's something else I need to discuss with you."

"Shoot," Tony encouraged.

This time Scott looked pointedly at Gavin and began to talk slowly, as if knowing Tony would interrupt. "It concerns a certain conversation in Cuba."

"Kitchen," Tony barked. Then he abruptly softened his tone. "Might as well turn in, Mary. It's past midnight." To the other two men he said, "Stand by, but ensure privacy, please." That meant *make sure Sheila does not overhear.* He looked for, and received, the nods that told him the men understood. Aaron was turning on a radio as Tony followed Scott into the kitchen and closed the door.

"Okay, son, let it out," he directed.

"Is it a common practise, sir?" Scott began.

He didn't have to identify the topic. Tony knew he was talking about Tony's initial decision to have Mary killed. "Would that be a problem for you?" Tony countered, curious about the response he might receive.

Opening the fridge, Scott took out a can of pop and opened it as if reluctant to give his answer. "A big problem," he admitted finally. He took a sip. "A very big problem. It's not why I joined this company, and I don't want any part of it. I can handle what happened to Aaron, and it would not have bothered me in the slightest if he had killed every one of those bastards. It's murder for the sake of expediency that I want no part of." He had been leaning against the counter, but now straightened to face Tony. "Therefore, sir, if I've been that naïve, and your order reflects the unwritten standard practise of the CIA, then perhaps you would be good enough to tell me now before I waste any more of anyone's time here."

Tony shook his head. "You may be glad to know that what I contemplated in Cuba was absolutely against our mandate, and no, there is no policy, written or otherwise, that allowed me to make that decision." Tony went on to tell him about Mr. Walsh's reaction, and assured Scott that he and Frank Moseley would be most unlikely to make another decision like that in the future. He also told Scott how much he had disliked making that decision in the first place, but the reasons he had felt it necessary. "So," he finished, after considerable discussion, "are you staying with us?"

"Yes."

*One more crisis averted,* Tony thought. This man would have been a big loss.

# XXIX

Several days had been wasted in tracking the man to whom James Cook was speaking on the phone. Cook had insisted that Richard Harvey have the man contact him directly, once located. Harvey could not be trusted not to screw this up. A list of the officers guarding Mary had been provided by Harvey's other contact. That contact was greedy and expendable. He would come in useful. The man on the phone, however, had to be used carefully. He was the kind of man who could provide years of useful service in bits and pieces, and his information was valuable.

"Is Gavin Weeks a possibility?" Cook was looking for someone who would do their dirty work for them, but the list was getting very short, and Cook was getting discouraged. Scott Andrews was an unknown to the caller, as were the daytime Security people. Aaron St. Pierre was too personally involved and rumoured to have a lot of integrity. Sheila Day-Jones was too new for anyone to take orders from. Tony Dune was apt to beat the crap out of anyone who offered him money, and had no known secrets in his closet that could be used against him.

"Gavin would see it as a challenge. He thrives on these kinds of offers," the voice chuckled. "First he'll play with you and suck you in. Then he'll lower the boom, and you'll wish you never set eyes on him. Stay away from Gavin—he's unreachable." Cook swore. That ended the list.

"But," the voice continued, "I do know a little titbit about his boss, Frank Moseley. It wouldn't give you enough pressure in itself, but if you could use it as a grain of truth and build a case around it, you might get lucky. It concerns a married woman..."

# XXX

Gordon Hummel was the psychiatrist hired by the CIA to provide service when their employees needed professional care. It was offered as a free service to all employees because you could not afford to have the staff opening up their deepest fears and secrets to just anyone with a degree. Mr. Walsh had asked Gordon to meet with Aaron and Mary this week, both together and separately, with the idea that Gordon could bring out any hidden feelings of anger or guilt that might otherwise emerge at a very inappropriate time—like in court.

During a Thursday lunch hour, Tony bumped into Gordon at the gym in the basement. Gordon asked him to meet in the cafeteria, after the workout, for a coffee. Tony had the coffee ready and waiting by the time Gordon reached his table. There were few people left in the cafeteria, and Tony had picked a table in the back corner.

"Thanks for meeting like this, Tony," Gordon greeted. "I know your time is valuable, and I've got a two o'clock appointment myself, so this won't take long." He took a sip of coffee. "This stuff doesn't improve much, does it?"

Tony shook his head. "I presume you would like to talk about Aaron or Mary, or both."

"Right." Gordon pushed the coffee aside. "I've read the information you gave me to prepare for their interviews. Of course, I never know if that is all the information, or just all that you can show me, and of course I respect that." Scratching at a tightly trimmed mustache, he continued, "I feel that something is missing."

*Bingo,* thought Tony. "That doesn't surprise me. So do I."

"Is there anything else you can tell me?"

"We've actually given you the whole gist of it—what we know, anyway, and what pertains to your line of work." Tony added another spoonful of sugar to his coffee to try to improve the flavour. It didn't work. "What is the problem?"

"I would bet my life that Aaron's holding something back," Gordon answered. "About what, I can't imagine. Seeing what he has admitted to, I

219

don't know what else could have happened, but he isn't a happy man, Tony. Something is bothering him. It can't have anything to do with Mary, because they seem to have made their peace. In fact," he continued, "that's another puzzle. Those two are like glue. She defends him like a tiger whose cub is threatened. Why? So she knows who he works for. That should hardly have endeared him to her. She should have been even more resentful that he forced himself on her at all. Most people would have looked to him for protection, not abuse."

Tony did not want to ask the question that had been teasing his mind this week, but it was an answer he needed to know. "Any chance those two have fallen in love?"

"No." Gordon had no way of knowing the relief his answer provided. "Their interaction is basically what you would expect from a middle-aged woman and a younger man who are friends. And I can understand Aaron's protectionist feelings, because he feels terrible about what he did to her. She has forgiven him, and now he is trying to make it up to her. He doesn't want to lose her, and he knows people are out to get her. It's Mary I don't understand."

"Do you see the feelings she has for Aaron causing us any problems down the road?" Tony asked.

"No, I don't," Gordon stated. "And I am quite willing to have them explained away by the intimacy they were forced into, and the fact that in the end she believed that he *was* putting on an act, and was really trying to protect her. After all, Tony, how can we look into their experience and complain because the feelings that have resulted are not fitting with our expectations?"

"True enough," Tony agreed, but he couldn't help wondering again what was up with Aaron. Perhaps he should explore an idea with Hummel. "Tell me this, Gordon. Let's speculate that Nathanial Bowman did not die of his injuries."

"Right. I read that autopsy. It's possible." Gordon looked hard at Tony. "Are you suggesting that Aaron may have indulged in a little mercy killing?"

"I'm not suggesting anything," Tony said quickly. "I'm only exploring possible reasons why he is feeling a guilt he will not admit to me."

Gordon was nodding. "This would fit. Your friend was being tortured, and from what I hear Aaron and Nathanial were good friends as well as co-workers. You all were."

"That's true."

"Theoretically speaking, of course, for a man with a personality like Aaron to deliberately take the life of a close friend, even if the friend asked him to, it would be devastating for him. Then to be faced with the necessity of telling your other friends that you did it..." Gordon was looking concerned. "This would not be good news, Tony. *If* this were a true scenario...well, you've got a walking time bomb on your hands. Aaron is what I would call a 'confessor', at least as far as his personal life is concerned. They tell me he is quite different professionally, and I do see that he has a work personality and a private personality. That private side forms strong friendships, and he wears his heart on his sleeve. If he did kill Mr. Bowman and cannot bring himself to tell you, then he must be hurting inside. It's going to come out in one form or another."

"I don't want to force it out of him," Tony muttered.

"I wouldn't try that," Gordon warned. "He is a strong character, and he has to tell you in his own time. Forcing him to take a polygraph right now would damage the relationship between the two of you." Gordon looked across the table at Tony. Years of experience had made him well aware of the type of pressures people like Tony carried around with them. He tried to be an easy man for them to talk to. "Tell me something," he encouraged. "Let's just speculate that your suspicions are true, and say that perhaps Aaron comes to you tomorrow and tells you that he couldn't bear to see his partner in such pain, and he could not rescue him. He admits that he killed your friend." Gordon stared intently into Tony's face. "Tell me how you will react to such an admission."

It was a hard question, but Tony tried to answer honestly. "I'm not sure," he admitted. "It means he took Nat from me, but I need to know anyway. I guess I want to know that Nat did not die alone, afraid, and in pain. If Aaron was with him, then I think it would be easier for me. If Aaron was going to let him endure more torture the next day, then I think I could hate Aaron." Tony looked back at Gordon Hummel levelly. "That's the truth, but I do not believe Aaron would let someone suffer like that. That's my reason for believing that he killed Nat."

"Okay." Gordon nodded. "As long as you realise that your response to him will be crucial to his mental well-being. To admit such a big secret to you will take a lot of courage, and if you react by condemning him, he will carry the scars for life. If he goes to you hoping for support and forgiveness, and finds it, you will have a confidant for life."

"I understand," Tony replied.

"Good. Now, how about you?" Gordon continued, sipping his coffee and turning up his nose at it.

"Me?" Tony found himself squirming under Gordon's penetrating look. "I'm fine."

"Are you? And have you never once thought about what you could have done to prevent this? Perhaps supply better communications, more backup, some hidden weapons? Hmm?" The psychiatrist was smiling kindly. "Not one feeling of regret or guilt?"

"Only every day that goes by," Tony confessed, embarrassed.

"Of course you do. You hide things away, Tony, and pretend they don't exist. Your own health is as much a concern to me as Aaron's. My door is open to you twenty-four hours a day. Use it."

"I'll remember that," Tony promised.

The conversation had reinforced Tony's fears, and it certainly did not make him feel any better. The trial was starting in six days. The days would be full with tying up loose ends, and helping the prosecution with every detail available. The only good thing that was happening was that neither side wanted any publicity. So far, the media had heard nothing. It couldn't last, and both sides knew it, so everyone had exerted the maximum influence to secure the early trial date. It had worked.

*We have to survive this,* Tony knew. Already the Director had fully briefed everyone who needed to know, and Mr. Walsh was feeling the pressure. The panic lay very close to the surface, and public relations was working around the clock to prepare for any conceivable possibility. The little covert operation in Cuba had gotten way, way out of hand, and all because of their poor choice of cover for Aaron. And Aaron was keeping a very big secret to himself. If Tony could figure his secret out so easily, surely the defence would think about it soon enough. A walking time bomb.

# XXXI

Frank Moseley had just returned from a week's trip to the Middle East. They were having some problems there, and Frank had made a personal trip to try to help straighten things out. Not with a great deal of success, but sometimes that was the way it went. He had looked forward to getting back to his small bungalow, having a shower and eating a home cooked meal. There was a woman he knew who might be persuaded to cook the meal for him, and stay for dessert. Instead, he had disembarked the plane and driven home to a nightmare. A few minutes after he got in the door, the phone had begun to ring, and the caller had been an unfamiliar voice.

"Mr. Moseley, I am in possession of some information regarding Tony Dune that might be of interest to you. Of course, I realise that this information should be directed to the Office of Security, but I understand that Mr. Dune is a friend of yours. Perhaps you would rather handle this yourself."

Frank's skin started to crawl. "Who the hell is this?" he demanded.

"Look, if you don't want to get involved, it's no concern of mine. Good day to you."

"Wait." *Damn. I should stay right out of this, but if it's about Tony, for God's sake...what the hell have you done, Tony? Or is this a trick?* "Okay, I'll listen, but that's all. What is it?"

"Not on this phone," the voice said. "How about spending a couple of minutes in conversation with a fellow jogger on your rounds tomorrow morning?"

This definitely sounded fishy, but Frank couldn't ignore a threat to his longtime friend. "You know me, I take it," he answered.

"The west side of the little pond, at your usual time. You always take a break there. Just an innocent little chat."

At 7:30 a.m., Frank reached the west side of the little pond. He did always take a break there to enjoy the morning air. When he was in his twenties, stopping was inconceivable, but he was well past that stage in his life now. This morning, Frank was angry. He hated calls like this, and only hoped it turned out to be some poorly contrived plot that he could expose and be done with. Last night he had thought about it, and decided that Tony just would not do anything that would risk his career. Tony was an uncomplicated, single-minded man who had no life outside his job and the friends he made at work. This meeting was just a waste of time.

A short, slight man in his thirties, with a balding head, jogged towards him without exertion. Some people looked like they were born to run, Frank thought briefly. This man stopped and asked him how his run was progressing. Frank answered, "Fine," and waited.

The man rubbed his face in his towel, and began to talk in a low, casual voice. "Actually, what we wanted to tell you about concerns Mr. Dune's wife," he began.

Carolyn had been dead for three years, but Frank started to feel uneasy. "Who is 'we'?" he demanded.

"You don't need to know that," the man answered, his voice harder now. "I have to admit that I got you here under false pretences. We are not interested in Mr. Dune at all, at least not directly."

Now Frank's mind was on full alert, and his personal alarm bells were ringing loudly. He'd been in this game many times with no difficulty. People thought they could either buy you or blackmail you, but Frank was neither for sale, nor subject to threats. This was going to be another feeble attempt. However, it could be useful to discover who was out looking for information, and then go after the source. "Spit it out," he ordered. "I'm a busy man."

"Then I'll skip the pleasantries, Mr. Moseley. We know that you were having an affair with Caroline Dune for seven years behind your friend's back. You never told him."

Frank actually laughed. "Mrs. Dune has been dead for three years, and their lousy marriage was no secret. Surely you can do better than that."

"We understand that if we revealed the affair to Mr. Dune at this time, it would damage your friendship. After all, even *you* would have to admit that you were not exactly helping their marriage, were you? However," the younger man continued, "we wouldn't bother if that was the end of it."

Frank stared. "What else have you dreamed up? So far, you are batting zero."

"Only the truth, Mr. Moseley." The stranger stared back "We know that you broke up with Mrs. Dune two days before she died. You threatened to tell Mr. Dune about the affair. She died the morning of his return from Peru."

"She committed suicide," Frank stated, puzzled. "Big deal. She was a manic depressive who refused to take medication. Even if what you say is true, Tony was not exactly devastated by her death. In many respects it meant freedom for him. I still don't see where you are going with this."

"Don't you, Mr. Moseley? You should. You see, we know she did not commit suicide."

Something twisted in Frank's gut. Fear. *Don't be ridiculous,* he told himself. *You know that Tony could not have killed her, if that's what they are implying, and they probably are. Unless she was involved with someone else as well. Concentrate on the truth, and ignore their lies.* "She committed suicide," he stated. "Trust me, it was looked at very closely because of Tony's job and the fact that the marriage was poor. Tony was completely exonerated."

"Please! We would never suggest that Mr. Dune killed his wife. Heavens, the poor man apparently was resigned to being miserable forever." The jogger seemed to be enjoying this. "No, Mr. Moseley, it won't do at all. You see, we *know* that you killed her."

"What!" It was the equivalent of a hard punch to the stomach. This was crazy, but why would they even say it? What was going on here?

"Come, come, the evidence was all there. Your people were just too fixated on the wrong man, and you made sure that they were."

"You are fucking insane," Frank protested. "I never touched her." *Damn, be careful. If you sound defensive, they will only try harder.*

"Of course you did, Frank." The jogger had decided he should be on a first-name basis with his potential victim. "You see, it was Mrs. Dune who was going to tell her husband about the affair. You were frantic. He was your friend, and fucking your friend's wife is not exactly a good career move."

Now Frank was angry. "Not a hope, you prick. Get the hell out of here." They couldn't pin a nonexistent murder on him.

"Well, I should let you get back to your run," the jogger announced. "Such a pleasant morning. Just let me leave you with one thought," he added. "It's easy to get that Office of Security all upset. They are so paranoid, and you know how easy it is to make murder look like suicide and vice versa. You've probably done it yourself. Whether you actually killed her becomes immaterial, doesn't it? We just have to present our side, drop a little evidence in their way, and they will believe us, trust me. And so will Mr. Dune. Or at least everyone will have enough doubt to finish you. Such a brilliant career too, at your age. You're smart enough to go right to the top. Be smart now. We would not be asking much—your hands won't even get dirty. Just a little task, and no one has to know. Think about it," he said, as he started to jog in the direction opposite to the way Frank was going. "I'll be in touch very soon. If you see me jogging, stop and have another chat."

As he watched the balding head jog off, Frank felt ill. His own personal nightmare…it could be done. They could make it sound as if he had killed her. He and Gavin had often laughed at blackmailers, and taken them on with enthusiasm, but the secret was to have no dangerous truths involved. It was truth that ruined people and made blackmail hard to fight. No one wanted their dirty deeds revealed. There was enough truth in this threat to make the rest sound believable. The affair and the fact that he had broken it off and threatened to tell Tony. The deceit had bothered him, although he had done his best to get Tony to dump the fool woman. She had used Tony for seventeen years as a meal ticket, and she couldn't face life without him. But she had been good in bed. Not for Tony; he only got the scraps she threw his way. In her mania phases she prowled, and she was a sexual animal. After she died, it had made no sense to hurt Tony with the truth. Now look at the mess his deceit had created. Seventeen years of good conduct and hard, dedicated work ready to go down the toilet, and he didn't even know what they wanted or who they were.

# XXXII

Over the past week, Mary had settled into her new home. What she felt most was the restrictions on her liberty, but other than the fact that she had almost no privacy, the days were actually quite pleasant. The house was kept tidy, and her guardians tried to make her as comfortable and contented as possible. They provided any books, magazines, newspapers, videos or food that she wanted.

Scott had the afternoon and evening shift, and slept in a spare room at night. Gavin took the night shift, but often came early in the evening to visit and work with Scott. Gavin seemed to have taken Scott under his wing, and was constantly teaching him strategies and other things that sounded work related. That is, when they weren't arguing about football teams. Tony stayed over most nights in the second spare room, and usually spent evenings reading with his glasses on the tip of his nose, or talking to the others if he did not have to go to work. If Mary was sitting on the couch, he always sat beside her. Otherwise he had a favourite chair beside a reading lamp on the street side of the house.

Mary was getting awfully used to him being around, and she knew she was going to be hurt when this was all over and he said goodbye and put her on a bus for Canada.

In truth, Mary was getting very fond of all of them. Sheila had the day shift, since her arm was healing so nicely. The sling disappeared after the first day, and only a bandage remained. A routine developed where they all had breakfast together, and then travelled to the office in two vehicles. Tony went directly to his office to work. The other four visited the gym, and then played racquetball. Aaron joined them when he could get away from Tony or Mr. Hedley. Most days they all met for an early lunch, and then Sheila and Mary were dropped back at the house. During the early afternoons, Mary was able to have long talks with Sheila about her experience in Cuba, which helped her immensely.

Scott spent the rest of his free hours doing whatever Scott did in his free time. Sheila was backed up by a random selection of very carefully screened

Security officers familiar with guard duty. Scott did not have to be back until 4:00 p.m., but both he and Gavin had a habit of dropping by for quick visits at irregular times on one pretence or another. Mary had never felt so safe in her life.

One night at 10:30, the phone rang and Scott answered it. A tired-sounding Tony greeted him, asked how things were going, and if Mary had gone to bed. Scott answered positively to both questions. "Are you coming over to keep us company?"

"No. In fact, I'll probably be here for a couple of hours longer. Hedley wants some specifics about how Frank's team planned the operation and I can't give him that. Frank is out of the country this week, so I need Gavin."

"I'll put him on the phone," Scott offered.

"No. I'd rather not have a discussion of that nature over the phone," Tony replied. "Send him to Hedley's office ASAP, will you? Before he leaves, though, I want you to turn Mary's monitor up to maximum. Make sure you stay right on those machines. Do you know how to adjust the monitor?"

"Gavin showed me, but I'll get him to watch while I do it just to make sure I don't mess it up," Scott stated.

"Okay. You're going to be on your own for at least an hour, if not longer," Tony warned, "so stay awake and vigilant. And, Scott—rely on the monitor. You cannot go into Mary's room unless you think she's under attack. Security will be listening, and you don't want them asking any awkward questions tomorrow, right?"

"Please, Tony—a little faith," Scott protested. "I think I can be trusted with guard duty, at least. If she wakes and calls for me, I'll talk from out here, or have her come out."

"Okay, son, see you later."

After hanging up, Scott gave Gavin his message and set the monitor to maximum under his watchful eye. *I hope that light doesn't disturb Mary's sleep,* he thought. *She says she gets nightmares, and last night she was restless. She needs a good sleep.*

No such luck. At 11:35 p.m., Scott heard Mary turning restlessly in her sleep. Ten minutes later he could hear her murmuring, and soon it was apparent that she was in real distress. *She's reliving Cuba, he knew. If I wake her up and talk to her, maybe the nightmare will stay away.* He waited another minute, knowing he had been ordered not to enter her room, but her voice in sleep held panic, and was pleading with someone. *I can't let her endure this,* he decided, *despite what Tony says tomorrow. She'll wake up terrified.* Mary was already starting to scream, so Scott hit the button that automatically overrode her door lock, and flipped the monitor switch down so their conversation would at least have a bit of privacy. He would be in the room, so she'd be safe, and he would just have to explain things to Tony later.

Stepping quickly into her room, Scott called her name softly several times as he approached, to let her awaken without startling her. The nightmare was too intense for her to hear, so he sat on the edge of the bed, speaking her name and touching her arm. It worked. The nightmare ended abruptly. Mary was awake, her face covered in perspiration, staring wide eyed at him.

"It's me, Mar. You had a bad dream. Just a dream—don't be frightened."

"Scott," she breathed, puffing. "It was awful…awful."

She had reached for his hand, and he knew she needed a moment to dispel the nightmare fears.

"Thanks for waking me," she whispered, when she had her breathing under control. Another minute passed, and then she patted his hand and released it.

"Can I make you a hot chocolate?" he asked, then grinned in the dark. "Or perhaps a good stiff drink would help more?"

Mary shook her head and arranged her pillows so she could sit up against the headboard. "Hot chocolate would be nice, and if you are any good at bedtime stories I could probably use one."

"Hah! Not the kind you want to hear, Mar." However, he went into the kitchen, made her chocolate, and then stayed with her and chatted for about fifteen minutes until she was quite relaxed and looked like she could get back to sleep. "No more nightmares," he insisted, leaving her side and taking the empty cup.

"Thanks, dear," she murmured, as she snuggled down into her sheets.

Back at the monitor, Scott reached to turn it up again. Uh-oh, he had turned it off by mistake. *Tony is going to kill me tomorrow,* he thought. *That just shows how lax they are at the office. I should have received a telephone call by now. Some security system this is.*

The next morning found Scott sitting in the chair across the desk from Tony. Scott was fuming. Tony had called him in, announced that he had received a worried call from Security saying that the monitor had been turned off last night, immediately following cries of distress from Mrs. Norland. Security was demanding to know what had happened.

"She was having a nightmare," Scott repeated. "I meant to turn the monitor down to give her some privacy—not off. It was a mistake."

"The mistake was going into her room," Tony lectured. "You were expressly told not to. You've put yourself in a very bad position."

"Why?" Scott did not understand all this fuss. If Security was so damned worried, where were they last night? "I was with her. She was in no danger."

"For Pete's sake, Scott. Read my lips. You were alone in the house with her. You turned off the monitor and entered her bedroom immediately after sounds of distress were heard." Tony was sounding angry and frustrated.

"Whoa, just a minute!" Finally Scott clued in to the problem. "I don't like what you are implying. I woke her up. I made her a hot chocolate, for heaven's sake."

"I'm not implying anything," Tony responded. "I'm stating things as they look to the people reviewing last night's events."

Now Scott was getting angry. "Not good enough. You tell me what you think I did in her room last night."

Tony gave him a level look of authority. "*I* think she had a nightmare. *I* think you woke her up and made a hot chocolate for her. You probably talked for a few minutes. That's all *I* think, but it doesn't matter what I think. I called Security this morning after I talked to you and told them what happened. They are quite upset."

"It doesn't matter to me what anyone else thinks," Scott countered.

"Yes, it does. It matters to you very much," Tony argued back. "They think you were in there for a different purpose."

Scott sputtered. "All they have to do is ask Mary."

"Oh Scott, don't you see?" Tony implored. "They will question Mary, but if you are expected to return to the house, they feel that Mary will be afraid to tell them if anything did happen. She has to know that you will not return to this assignment."

"What!"

Tony ran his hand through his hair. "I have to remove you from this assignment. Take the day off, and I'll call the station chief in Brazil and try to get you a temporary posting there."

"No, that's not fair." Scott had jumped up. "Mary likes me, sir. We're friends—I make her laugh. I didn't do anything wrong," he insisted. "You'll upset her, sir. She's been taken out of her own environment and left here without any friends." Very frustrated, he glared at Tony, but Tony never blinked. Scott knew he had lost, and he'd better back down. Tony would accept quite a bit from him, but if his hands were tied it was foolish to try to back him into a corner. Scott collapsed into the chair again and gave up in misery.

There was nothing wrong with going to Brazil. The station chief had a good reputation, but it wouldn't be the same. Scott knew Tony's team would be reassigned soon anyway, but he wanted to stay and help Aaron and Mary right now. He would miss them terribly, although that was no reason to protest an assignment. Mary would not be happy about this either.

Later that morning, when Scott called Mary to say goodbye, he realised that not only was Mary upset at the news, but the reason he resented Tony's decision so much was because he was feeling so much at home with his team and with Mary. Tony, Aaron, Sheila and Gavin had all become part of his life. Mary needed his support, and Scott knew he had developed a real protectiveness towards her. He understood Aaron's constant concern for her safety. Also, protecting Mary meant protecting Aaron at the same time. The trial would start soon, and they all felt a need to stick together and face this as a team. Now, however, Tony was sending him away. Besides, he admitted, he liked Mary. She made him feel good about himself, but now she was upset.

Mary *was* upset—very upset. They were taking Scott from her for no reason. Stupid, shortsighted people, Mary stewed. First, she told Sheila exactly what she thought about those ridiculous people she worked for. Then Tony arrived to take Mary to the office to talk to some Security people. Mary lit into him and told him exactly what she thought of his Security people and their paranoia. Tony tried to explain, but Mary found the explanation too ridiculous for words.

"I am telling you that all the man did was to give me a cup of hot chocolate! Unless you would like to call me a liar, you should be able to take that as truth." She was standing in front of Tony, staring up at him angrily.

Dr. Hummel had been right, Tony realised. She was like a little tiger, snarling and hissing at him.

"Why are you doing this?" Mary demanded. "Do you really believe Scott would make a sexual advance to me?"

"No, I don't," Tony was finally able to respond. "This isn't about Scott. It's about you feeling secure."

"I feel secure with Scott," Mary countered. "Or perhaps you think I'm such a weak character that if he did make advances towards me I'd be so intimidated that I couldn't say no?"

"Hardly," Tony responded, watching this little fury stand up to him. Out of the corner of his eye, he saw Gavin and Sheila. They looked like they were enjoying the sight of Mary lecturing him.

"Then bring him back," Mary actually ordered. "I refuse to talk to those ridiculous people unless Scott can be with me. You bring me here, lock me up in this house, give me nice people to protect me and who have become my friends, and then you just yank them away because they make a little policy mistake."

"You are *not* locked up," Tony replied, gritting his teeth. "If you want to go somewhere, you just have to tell me, and I'll try to arrange it. But these people are not paid to be your friends. They are doing a job."

"As I am sure you are," Mary spat back, stung by his comment.

This was useless, he decided. The woman refused to understand how things worked here. He was tired of being lectured, and starting to get angry, so he turned to leave.

"Tony." She stopped him with a quieter word. "Please stop treating me like a victim. I don't plan to wear that badge for the rest of my life."

Without another word, Tony left the house, slamming the door behind him. Who the hell did she think she was, telling him what she would and wouldn't do? Now he had to meet with those paranoid Security people and say that she had refused to come. He could just imagine how they would react to that. They could do almost anything, including coming out to search the house for her, or forcing all his team to take lie detector tests to see if anyone had harmed her. Damned woman.

On the way to the office, he tried to settle down. He had a tremendous amount of work to do today, and no time for this nonsense. And it *was* nonsense. If Security had not been sleeping on the job, they could have phoned the house immediately, and Scott would have turned on the monitor. Mary had sounded distressed before Scott had turned it off because she was in the middle of a nightmare. If they had phoned immediately, they could have talked to her and satisfied themselves of her safety. If they had still been concerned, it was a simple thing to send someone over to the house, or even simpler to call Hedley's office and Tony would have called Mary. But no, Security had been asleep on the job, and now they were panicking. So why did he have to take this out on Scott and Mary? Now he would have an upset witness, and was losing Scott.

A sharp right turn took him on a detour to Scott's apartment. Although both Scott and Susan spent a great deal of their free time in the family home, they both kept separate apartments for the sake of independence and privacy. He phoned en route and told Scott to meet him at the front door dressed for the office. In fifteen minutes Scott was in the car beside him; shaved, washed and dressed in a suit that Tony would only dream about affording.

"Okay, young man, you are coming with me," Tony informed. "You are going to see firsthand the trouble you have caused. We are meeting with some people who really need a life. Their job is to be suspicious. This will not be fun for either of us. You will sit there politely, on your best behaviour. And, Scott," he warned, "do not talk to these people the way I let you talk to me. They would not understand. If we succeed this morning," he continued, "you can stay here with me. If we lose, you go. Understood?"

Scott had listened seriously. His tone was respectful. "Perfectly, sir."

It took an hour and a half of arguing, cajoling and promising. Scott's behaviour was perfect....a series of "yes, sir," "an error in judgement, sir," and "I'm very sorry, it will never happen again." In the beginning, one of their interrogators called the house and spoke to Mary himself, promising to keep Scott away from her forevermore if she wished to report any problems. Her response was so strident that Tony could hear her voice from where he was sitting. It was very hard not to look at Scott, but Tony was afraid they would break out laughing at the expression on Security's face. Finally it was over, and for appearances Tony read the riot act to Scott in front of the others. Finished. Over with and done, as Frank Moseley would have said.

As they drove to the house, Tony announced he would drop Scott off and go straight to his office. "I'll be working half the night to make up this time."

Scott looked chagrined. "I'm sorry, sir, I really am. Please come into the house and let me throw a sandwich together for you. It's the least I can do."

At the house, Tony had to watch as Mary threw her arms happily around Scott's neck and receive a hug from the equally happy young man. *I do all the work,* he fumed, *but they get the hugs. All I get is the image of being the heavy.* He waited by the door for Scott to make his sandwich.

"Aren't you coming in?" Mary asked tentatively.

"He can't, Mar," Scott replied as he dashed into the kitchen. "I screwed up his day," he continued in a louder voice, slamming cupboards. "Now he has to make up the time he lost."

Mary approached Tony and touched his arm. "Thank you for bringing him back."

She was so close he had to lock his hands together to prevent himself from reaching for her. "You're welcome. I didn't want to send him away either," he confessed, smiling into her brown eyes. "Oh, and that comment I made about my officers not being here to be your friends, well, that is true. They are paid to do a job, but, Mary, there is no question that they have become your friends."

To his delight, she reached up and kissed him on the cheek.

"I'm sorry I gave you such a bad time," she apologised. "Will you be here for supper? You have to eat somewhere."

The morning spent arguing with Security now seemed entirely worthwhile. He no longer felt tired or overworked. Mary was happy again, and wanted to be with him. With pleasure he agreed.

# XXXIII

"Hey, Gav—how's life on the soft side?"

"Not bad, Finch. Where the hell are you calling from?" Gavin stretched out on the couch and propped his head on a pillow. Scott was sitting at the monitor, reading, and Gavin had been pleasantly reviewing the time he had spent with Sheila earlier in the evening. In his books, she was a good woman who didn't chatter on too much. He was enjoying her company, and it occurred to him that he might like to get to know her a little better.

"Still in the same mess over here," Finch responded. "We could use your help."

"In a couple of weeks, maybe." Gavin was in no hurry to get back for once. "Or whenever Moseley decides I've had too much pampering."

"What are you doing there, anyway? I thought you were supposed to be taking a vacation."

Without hesitation, Gavin told him. Finch was smart enough to check out any telephone he used. Besides, Gavin would not give out the address of the house.

"So you're doing guard duty," Finch concluded. "What a waste. Or are you doing bedroom duty with this broad?"

"Naw," Gavin answered. "Not with her." He left the rest unsaid, and Finch chuckled. "Who do you have for company on your guard duty?"

Gavin told him about Scott and Sheila, and added that Tony spent most of his free time with them. Aaron was an occasional visitor, he added.

Finch seemed to be in a talkative mood, announcing that he was bored with his assignment. He asked a few more questions, then went on to other subjects. After forty minutes, Gavin's ear was sore, so he bid Finch goodnight and hung up. In a couple of more weeks, Gavin knew he would be craving more action. For now, he was enjoying the company he was keeping, and liked taking part in Scott's training. And of course there was Sheila to think about. With a satisfied grin, Gavin slouched down on the couch again.

# XXXIV

Valentine's Day arrived, a clear but cool day, and in the morning everyone followed their usual schedule of getting ready to end or start their shift, and take Mary to the gym. This time, on the way through the office corridors down to the basement where the gym was located, Kevin Whalen hailed Scott in the hallway. Kevin had recently switched from Tony's team to OTS, the Office of Technical Service. He had been one of the people involved in setting up the communications system at 51 Elm.

"How's the new job?" Scott asked, noticing that Kevin was eyeing Gavin with surprise, and Mary with curiosity.

"Great," Kevin answered briefly. He waited patiently until Scott introduced Mary, then said, "So you are Mary."

Scott could tell that Mary did not like that response. She seemed uncomfortable, and shook hands with Kevin politely, but coolly. He gave Gavin a look that said *Someone's been talking*, told Kevin that they were late for a game and hustled Mary away.

*Great,* Mary thought, *I'm getting a reputation. Just what I didn't want.* She fumed all through her workout, but felt better by the time she had managed to win one racquetball game. Of course, she lost four games, but her competition was as fierce as usual.

As they walked back to the change rooms, Sheila fell in step beside her. The men were in front of them, and Sheila grinned at Mary. Both women liked the look of physically fit bodies, and in one of their chitchat sessions yesterday, they had been discussing the men. Why not, they had decided. The men probably discussed them, too. Watching now, Mary suspected that Sheila was attracted to Gavin. *Good taste,* Mary thought, remembering sitting beside him in the car down from Toronto. Although Gavin was not a handsome man, he exuded a sexuality that was hard to ignore. He was a rather mysterious, exciting man, and obviously he no longer gave Sheila the "creeps".

Their normal schedule was to be disrupted in the afternoon. Sheila had plans for Valentine's Day that were to be a surprise for Mary. She had arranged for Scott to take part of the day shift while she went to get a cake and wine for an evening treat. Then she would return to the house and Scott would take a few hours off before supper. The change of plans was mentioned to Mary, but not the cake and wine.

They dropped Mary and Scott at 51 Elm. Sheila had planned to take her own car to the bakery, but Gavin offered to drive her, stating he had no plans for the day anyway. On the way to the bakery Sheila had chosen, they talked about the racquetball games and the gym. Sheila was enjoying this drive. Since she had joined the Company, she had severed a lot of contacts with male friends. She had wanted to get used to the new job and take a look at how her colleagues arranged their sex lives if they weren't already involved with someone. Sheila wasn't looking for a serious relationship yet. Right now her new career was too exciting, and she was being very careful to do nothing that would jeopardise it. Sitting beside Gavin was definitely exciting. Sure, he was quite a bit older than the guys she had invited to her bed in the past, but he attracted her in a way that she couldn't ignore. Oh well, she knew this guy was far beyond her reach, and he hardly seemed to notice that she existed. She would just sit here and enjoy his company while she could.

At the bakeshop, they learned that the cake order had been lost. It would take up to two hours to make and decorate one. Gavin encouraged Sheila to place the order anyway, because the shop had a reputation for making excellent cakes.

Back in the car, Sheila looked at him. "I'm sorry to waste your time like this."

He shrugged and looked at her. "Well, we've got a couple hours to kill. What do you want to do?"

There was only one thing on her mind that Sheila would like to do, but she sure didn't have the guts to suggest it to him. Lost for another answer, she felt a bit of heat in her cheeks. "I don't know," she confessed.

For a moment Gavin stared out the car window, then he turned towards her and met her eyes. She noticed that when his eyes connected with hers, they lost that cool, detached look. A trace of a smile played in the lines around them, and he touched the sleeve of her blouse with his finger. "Well, if you wanted, you could invite me back to your place."

Oh boy, no mistaking that meaning. Now the heat really rushed to Sheila's face, and other places as well. Why not? She didn't report to him, and didn't even work with him directly. And if you couldn't trust a man with a reputation for privacy like Gavin, you might as well join a nunnery. Sheila smiled back. "Yes, I think I'd like to do just that."

Sheila and Gavin returned to the house in the afternoon, relieving Scott, who gave them a strange look and dashed out of the house. People were acting a little peculiar today, Mary decided. On closer observation, she noticed a subtle change in the way Sheila and Gavin were interacting. Definitely less impersonal on Gavin's part, and a little more familiar on Sheila's side. *Well, well, well…what have you two been up to?* Behind Gavin's back she gave Sheila a look, and got a delighted blush in response. *Okay, one minor mystery cleared up.*

By suppertime Scott was still missing, but since he was the main cook they had no option but to wait, unless someone else volunteered to start cooking. Of course no one did, everyone preferring to indulge in pre-dinner drinks. Tony had settled onto the couch beside Mary, with her curled up quite close to him. He had no desire to move. This week had been torture. Having her so close, yet unattainable, was agony. And the worst part was that he was sure that she wanted him, too. He did not dare make a move toward her for two reasons: no privacy was a big one, and also because he was responsible for her, which put him in a total power position over her. It wasn't an even playing field, and he was only too aware of the delicacy of his position with her. While Tony didn't really think Mary would reject his advances, it just wasn't right. There were times, however, that having scruples was exceedingly annoying, and this was one of them. As if reading his mind, Mary sighed. *Damn.* He reached for, and found her hand. Everyone else was forever holding it, he decided. *Why can't I?*

A few minutes after 6:00 p.m., they finally heard Scott coming into the house. A familiar-sounding voice appeared to be lecturing him. "You are the worst driver I have ever seen! Where did you learn to drive—in a maze? We passed that man with the Chou twice going two different directions, and I swear I saw the same brown brick house with green shutters three times." The voice had a playful note to it, and Tony noticed that Mary sat up and stared eagerly at the door.

"Shhh!" That sound came from Scott, as he poked his head around the corner. "Hey, Mar, I've got a surprise for you."

By this time Mary was on her feet, looking as if she couldn't believe her ears. Tony stood up, too. What the hell was Scott up to, and where had he heard that voice before? As soon as she bounced into the room, he knew. Lori. For Christ's sake. He should be angry at Scott, but when he saw Mary run to Lori and throw her arms around the blonde's neck, he knew Scott had just escaped a reprimand. By the look that Scott was giving him, it was clear that

Scott knew he was bending the rules and risking Tony's wrath. Tony just threw up his hands in surrender and saw Scott whisper, "Thank you." Rotten kid.

"Lori, I'm so glad to see you!" Mary did not seem interested in releasing her friend.

Lori laughed in delight. "I can tell. You're squishing me." When Mary let her go, Lori smiled at Scott. "He thought you might want some company."

"Company?" Tony had to ask. Lori certainly could not stay here. Then he saw Mary reach up to put her arms around Scott's neck and kiss him on the cheek. Well, he'd wait until later to clear up this little confusion.

"Thank you," Mary said to Scott, receiving an embarrassed pat on the back in return. Tony watched and fumed. Everyone else could hold and kiss this woman with impunity, but not him. No, he ran close to censorship by just holding her hand.

The only person Lori hadn't met was Aaron. Knowing an introduction was coming, everyone in the room seemed to be holding their breath. They knew Mary had told Lori all about Aaron before leaving Toronto. Tony was wary. *She had better not embarrass Aaron, or this will be a very short visit,* he decided.

Aaron was thinking along similar lines. This was Mary's bosom buddy from Canada, who knew all about Mary's experience in Cuba. It made him uncomfortable, even though he was surrounded by friends. She was hard to read, too. She looked like a bubblehead, but Scott would not bring a woman with no sense here, and Mary wouldn't have one for a best friend. *Wait for the eyes to turn over here,* he decided. *The first few seconds will tell you.*

Mary led Lori over by the arm. Then she dropped Lori's arm and put her right hand into Aaron's left. He gave her hand a light squeeze. "And this is Aaron. Aaron, this is my best friend, Lori Masters." With his free right hand, Aaron offered to shake hands.

Lori was quick on the uptake. Mary was telling her that all was forgiven. It wasn't as much a surprise to Lori as it had been to the others, because Lori was the only one Mary had told about making love with him in Cuba. Then she had been sworn to secrecy. In fact, Lori had known instinctively that Mary's fears about meeting him were caused by embarrassment. Mary had held no hatred in her heart for Aaron. Taking his hand, Lori gave him a genuinely pleased smile. "I'm glad to be able to meet you. I wanted to thank you for taking care of my friend for me."

The people in the room seemed to all breathe out at once. Aaron was actually caught off guard. He hadn't expected approval. It took him a second to remember to respond. "You're very welcome. I'm glad Mary will have a friend to help her pass the time. I think she gets rather bored in this house. Can you stay down here long?"

"I took Monday and Tuesday off work. That gives me almost four full days if I fly back Tuesday night." She smiled at Scott. "I couldn't possibly afford a hotel in this city for that long, but Scott has been good enough to arrange with his parents to let me have a room. As long as I don't drive them crazy, I'm all set."

Gavin had suddenly developed a coughing fit, and it was all Aaron could do to keep from laughing out loud. Scott was giving Gavin an evil look, but really, Scott deserved it. He *never* took his female dates home to daddy. His family home was a private sanctuary, not a place for casual relationships. What this showed was not any great love for Lori, although he must like her a lot, but a real devotion to Mary. Of course, he wouldn't be above taking advantage of his parents being out of the house during his free hours. Aaron managed to just smile and tell Scott that it was very decent of him to make the arrangements.

A little later, Mary and Lori were by themselves for a few minutes mixing drinks in the kitchen by the sink. Lori leaned close to Mary and spoke in a quiet voice. "Mary...that Aaron...wow!" she giggled. "I can at least understand your last night down there."

"Oh, Lori, don't, please." Mary could feel herself blush. "I try not to think about that." She glanced towards the kitchen door to make sure no one came in. "We're friends now, and he's been really good to me. I think he wants to put that in the past as much as I do."

"Sorry, hon," Lori apologised, "but...wow! Is he married?"

"No, but he has a fiancée." Mary added two ice cubes to her drink and closed the fridge again. "I have a feeling he hasn't told her about Cuba yet, though." She frowned. "That would be an awful thing to have to tell the person you hope to marry."

"It would kinda put a damper on her enthusiasm, wouldn't it?" Lori agreed. They rejoined the others. The evening went very well, with the modest party breaking up by midnight.

Aaron decided not to stay at the house. Susan was back in town. Scott had made a point of telling him that this evening. Could it be only weeks ago that he had made those promises and she had agreed to marry him? It seemed a lifetime ago. Having her on tour had been a relief to him, because he had been too ashamed to face her. Scott had told her just a little about Cuba. She knew the promises had been broken. She knew he had raped a woman. Scott had given her no details, but had told her that Aaron was suffering from a deep depression and was being closely monitored. No, he probably couldn't contact her yet.

What would Susan be thinking? Her worst fears had been realised, and so soon. Had she written him off already? No "dear John" letter had arrived—no word one way or another. With surprise, he suddenly realised that he was driving towards the lounge where she would be singing tonight. What he would do when he got there, he didn't know. Would he have the guts to go in? What on earth would he do if she turned away from him? What would he say if she didn't?

It was too late for second thoughts. He was in the parking lot. It only made sense to get out of the car and go to the backdoor—just to see her. Maybe he would simply stand out of sight and listen.

Opening the door and actually going in was extremely difficult. He made it on the third attempt, but his stomach was actually churning. *You are only going to stand in the shadows and listen,* he promised himself. Somehow, he made his feet take him in. He was well known to the lounge staff, who greeted him warmly. Then he was near the stage exit. Sue was singing her heart out to a clearly appreciative audience. It was a popular rock song that had lyrics about a woman who wasn't going to sit around and wait for her lover to return. *Ouch.* It was just a song everyone listened to, but tonight it sounded personal.

That was the moment he saw Stein. Stein was sitting at *their* table. The table that everyone knew belonged to Aaron, Scott and friends. Stein was sitting at Aaron's table, smiling at Aaron's fiancée, and acting like he belonged there. *No, Sue,* Aaron pleaded silently. *You can't let him sit there...not and take my place.* A banker. A banker who didn't hurt people and didn't break promises. A respected friend of the family. At first Aaron saw red, and had an insane desire to clean the floor with that nice banker suit. Of course he couldn't...he wouldn't, but now there was a horrible feeling of loss in his chest. His eyes went to the stage. Susan was still singing, but she had seen him. Her rhythm faltered, but she recovered almost instantly. She was a performer, and would not fail her crowd, but he could see that the smile had frozen a little, and her eyes looked sad. The song was sad anyway, but her voice had a catch to it. *I've lost her,* Aaron knew. *I've lost her to the damn safe banker. Leave her alone and let her sing,* he ordered himself. *Be a man and get the hell out of here.*

Somehow he managed to only walk to the door, but then he ran to the car and drove to the silence of his apartment. In misery, he poured rye into a glass and added an ice cube. It wouldn't help, he knew, but he needed to dull the pain, at least for tonight. The phone sat on the desk beside him. Only because he couldn't bear it himself, he called Scott.

A reluctant voice answered the phone. "Yeh."

"Scott." Suddenly Aaron didn't even know what he wanted to say.

"Aaron? This isn't exactly a good time, my friend."

Oh. Obviously Scott had taken Lori to his apartment before going on to his parents' house. "It's Stein," Aaron blurted. "He's sitting in my chair."

"What are you talking about?" Scott demanded, sounding confused.

"I went to the lounge to see Sue, but she's let that bastard Stein sit at our table, and he's in my chair."

"Good heavens, man. Get a grip." Noises over the receiver indicated that Scott had told Lori to wait a few minutes. "Did you talk to her?"

"No," Aaron admitted. "She was singing, but she saw me. And she didn't look very happy. Stein sure looked happy, though."

Scott sounded exasperated. "And just why would she look happy, Aaron? You haven't tried to reach her in weeks. You've given her no explanation at all. She's had all this time to stew over what I told her. That's supposed to make her look happy?" Then he softened. "Look, Aaron, she hasn't said it's over."

"I haven't given her the opportunity," Aaron muttered.

"Still, if she hasn't given you the word, it's not lost yet. Talk to her, for heaven's sake. Tell her you still love her." His tone became pleading. "Don't give up, Aaron. Fight for her. Don't give up on her, please."

*Don't give up.* "Okay Scott, I'll try. Sorry to disturb you." He hung up. Sue would be at the club for another hour, but she had an answering machine. Carefully, he composed a message in his head and dialled her number. He told her that he loved her; that he was sorry about breaking the promises. With some misgivings, he asked her to attend the trial when he and Mary were in the stand. Then she would hear everything, and after that, if she still wanted the marriage, he would be waiting faithfully. If not, he would trouble her no more. He still loved her very much.

Now he should finish the drink and go to bed, but his fear was too great. He went out again, drove to Sue's apartment building and parked in the shadows of a vacant driveway. The house belonging to the driveway was empty, but no one would notice a car sitting in the driveway away from the streetlamps. He told himself a dozen times to go home and not to do this. *If she takes Stein up and he stays, you'll torture yourself. Go away, leave her alone and respect her privacy.* But he didn't go. He had to know. It was sneaky and she would hate him if she knew, but he couldn't go.

Finally a black BMW arrived and parked in the visitor's parking. Of course it would be a luxury car. Aaron had always known he couldn't compete with her family friends. Aaron drove a leased Chrysler Intrepid, and even that strained the pocket book. Stein had probably bought the BMW outright with his petty cash.

The occupants stayed in the car for a few minutes and tortured Aaron. It made him angry and sick, but he could do nothing. Finally Sue emerged, and so did Stein. They walked to the door. *Don't do it Sue, please.* They walked in, and Aaron's heart sank. *Send him back out. Let him walk you to the apartment, but send him back out. I should drive away; this is insane. I'm the one who broke all the promises. It's my fault, so why should I be surprised? Sue, please...send him away.*

Ten more minutes of torture, then Aaron's heart broke. It must have broken, because it felt torn in two. He started the car and took a final regretful look at the door of the apartment building. Stein! Coming out and going to the BMW. Driving away. *Thank you, Sue. I'll make it up to you, I swear. Now go home, fool, and leave her alone to listen to your message. Let her make her own decision. She has to know everything and still love you, if the marriage is to work.*

# XXXV

Sleep was a luxury enjoyed by people with tranquil minds, not by a man whose life was collapsing around him. Frank Moseley did not even attempt sleep for the next two nights, but sat in his reclining chair, facing a blank television screen. Occasionally his body would doze in an effort to shut down his mind, but unless he found an answer to his dilemma, real sleep would continue to elude him.

He could talk to Tony or to Gavin, or he could go in to see Walsh, a man he scarcely knew, and throw his future away. *Why don't you just kill yourself now,* his mind argued, *because you are ruined anyway.* If only the former DDO, Lester Hardcastle, was still alive, there might have been a chance to work through this. Walsh, however, was a procedure and policy man with political ambitions. You could tell by the way he had managed to land his position. While he had done Frank no harm, he was still an unknown entity.

*I never knew that I was a coward,* Frank reflected. *All these years I didn't feel like a coward, and I don't think I acted like a coward. Yet now it's so clear to me. If I hadn't been a coward, I would have told Tony about Carolyn after the first time. I didn't. I let seven goddamn years pass, and even then I chickened out after her death. Now I can't face the music—the disgrace of being investigated by that bloodthirsty Security section. My enemies are right. This will ruin me even if I am not found guilty of this manufactured crime. I might as well get a job at a donut shop washing floors for all the future I have now.*

*So kill yourself,* his mind suggested. *Have a few stiff drinks and get out of this mess. Be done with it.* The Glock 26 sat beside him on the table. *It wasn't the first time in the last few days that he had thought this way. A couple of times he had actually picked up the gun, but somehow he couldn't get past the finality of it. Another day,* he told himself. *I'll wait one more day and look for a solution.*

In the morning, the unknown jogger met him in the same place. Their demands were simple On February 27, Tony had his regular Thursday

244

evening meeting with his colleagues. Normally, Frank attended. These meetings started at 7:00 p.m. and usually lasted for two to three hours. Gavin started his shift at 7:00 p.m. sharp, although he was known to drop in early. That evening, Scott would be alone from the time Tony left the house after supper, about 6:45 p.m., until Gavin arrived. Frank's job would be to divert Gavin until at least 7:30 p.m. That would give them time to remove the unwanted witness.

"No one will suspect you, Mr. Moseley, and Mr. Weeks will be absolutely in the clear. You've seen the morning papers. The press has heard about the Congressman's arrest, and his accusations against the CIA in regards to Mrs. Norland. I cannot see why you feel that this witness is of any benefit to you now. You people are in a great deal of trouble over her."

Frank had seen the media coverage. It was bad, and had worried him greatly. "Do you expect Scott to sit and watch while this happens?" Frank asked. "The doors are locked and the place is thoroughly monitored."

"Not a problem for us," the man answered. He had told Frank that his name was "Fred". Fred smiled now. "Someone Scott knows will shut down the system, then just knock at the door and Scott will let him in. This man will take care of everything, and we'll have two of our own people outside for backup in case something goes wrong."

One of our own people to kill the witness, Frank heard. Someone Scott knows. "Scott will be killed by a friend?"

"Not necessarily," Fred replied. "We'd prefer a neater operation. Scott's friend will try to convince him to leave and offer to take his place. Something about a girl, probably. We understand that Scott is a real womaniser, and tends to be a little immature, so he'll probably leave. If not," Fred continued, "our man will attempt a substantial bribe. Scott is apparently used to the good life, and that type always wants more. The final option will be to kill him."

From what Frank had heard about Scott, it was quite likely that Scott would risk leaving the house. He'd be in trouble later, but could not be seriously blamed for being tricked.

It would be a hard lesson, but he would survive with a severe reprimand. There would be no blame to the Company—the hit was done by a renegade officer. No one would be able to prove who hired him. Frank didn't need Fred to tell him that the officer who killed Mary would be executed by the two men outside. He would be seen as expendable.

It would be a public relations nightmare, but no worse than things were now. The Congressman would walk, of course, and Frank had no doubts as to who had hired Fred. The Company would lose some credibility, but nothing could be proven, and they would deny and survive. All he had to do was divert Gavin. Gavin was a danger to them, and Fred knew it.

Less than one hour and one dead woman who could be used against them anyway. With a heavy heart, Frank capitulated. It was not the solution he wanted, but he would be cleared of blame and after a respectable period he would resign. Then he would try to start a new life.

That afternoon, James Cook was meeting with Fred. "Are we ready to go next Thursday?" he asked.

"Yes. Our man in OTS will bring the system down at exactly seven p.m. That gives a fifteen-minute leeway in case Tony Dune forgets something and returns to the house. At seven oh-five he will call Scott to tell him the problem is being looked into and he is on his way over. Of course," Fred informed, "our man will not be at OTS. He'll do the disconnecting from the connectors outside the house. At seven fifteen he will knock at the door and say he's there to fix it. Scott won't question him."

"Worst-case scenario?" Cook demanded.

"He gets caught in the house in an attempted assassination attempt. My boys are outside ready for that. Kevin won't live to tell the story. Even if he did, I'm the one who hired him, and they can't trace me. Kevin only knows me as 'Fred'."

"Kevin knows the Congressman."

Fred nodded. "Who did a stupid thing by calling Kevin and asking for information. But Kevin could never prove Harvey was behind this."

"That man's a fool," Cook stated, "but if he stays elected, I'll probably have a lifetime income covering up his mistakes."

"Thursday night will go smoothly," Fred assured. "You can sit back and enjoy the action."

# XXXVI

At the same time Cook was checking Fred's strategy, Sheila was enjoying some strategy being practised on her by Gavin. Oh, this man could make her moan. His mouth was busy between her legs, and it felt so good. They had been at it for two hours now, and it was nearly time for him to get ready for work. This was their seventh afternoon together in a row, and Sheila was glad he showed no signs of boredom yet. The first afternoon he had been quite gentle and polite with her, but once he knew she felt comfortable with him, they had concentrated on the pleasures of lust.

Now his lips moved up her body. This was their third position of the afternoon. The first position had been just so-so, as far as Sheila was concerned, but the second had been fantastic. And she really liked the in-between times, too. This was going to be the conventional way—no, not quite—he had grabbed her wrists and pinioned them with his hands to the bed above her head. Simultaneously he entered her and forced his tongue into her mouth. Normally she would have objected strenuously to someone pinning her down, but the feel of his thrusts inside her and the passion of his kiss aroused her. She knew him well enough now to believe he wouldn't cross any limits she set.

She had discovered that on a personal level, Gavin was all bark and no bite. It was professionally that she would hate to confront him from an opposing camp. He was demanding, though. He demanded that she not be shy, that she use his body in any way she wanted, and that she tell him what she did and did not like. Sheila liked those kinds of demands.

Too soon it was over, and Gavin lay beside her. He was glad Sheila felt no need to talk a lot, and was pleased that he had taken that first step on Valentine's Day. Looking twice at a new recruit was out of character for him. They were apt to ask you a million questions, or worse yet, gossip with their fellow trainees. It had been his policy to stay clear of the new women. Not that he had much interaction with them anyway, but he had picked up the right signals from Sheila.

He ran a hand up and down Sheila's body, and smiled when she stretched like a contented kitten. He was getting to know what she liked. It was easy to relax with her because she made no demands on him. Like him, Sheila was a person who knew what she wanted, and right now she was a woman who wanted to work on her career. He certainly wouldn't be standing in the way.

As if following his thoughts, Sheila looked at him and spoke. "It's been a great week."

"Sure has," he agreed. "I'm getting a real kick out of helping Tony work with Scott, I've been able to visit with Aaron, Frank and Tony, and I get to guard this really nice woman who treats me like I walk on water. Very pleasant for a man's ego. But best of all," he added, teasing her nipple with a finger, "I met this woman who doesn't mind spending her afternoons making mad, passionate love to me."

"Our motto on Tony's team should be 'we aim to please'," Sheila laughed.

"Oh, you do, believe me."

That earned him a smile. "How long until this soft touch of a job is over for you?" Sheila asked.

Gavin thought about it. The trial had started today. "Hard to tell. Apparently the trial moved at the speed of light today, but is expected to slow down when Aaron's turn arrives. Then anything could happen. Even if we get lucky and the defence accepts defeat, it will be at least a couple more weeks."

A couple more weeks. Good. Sheila sat up. They still had lots of time to shower, dress and grab a quick bite to eat. First, though, she was curious. "Is it normal for Tony to fall in love with a woman an hour after he meets her?"

"Hell no," Gavin laughed. Fluffing up a pillow, he propped himself up beside her. "Absolutely unheard of, for him, but he sure is in deep, isn't he?"

Sheila nodded. "It must be frustrating for both of them. They are never alone, and they don't have the freedom to do anything about it, like we do."

"No, they don't." Gavin's thoughts had strayed from Tony and Mary. There was something he wanted to say to Sheila, but he'd have to be careful. "When I'm finished here, I'm apt to be sent almost anywhere. I move around a lot." He sent her a cautious glance.

"A bit of a restless spirit, I'm told," she responded pleasantly. "Matches your job."

"I'm not the settling down type," he stated bluntly.

"No," she agreed neutrally, "you're not."

*So far, so good.* He relaxed. "But I do get a lot of vacation I hardly ever use. If I want to come back I can usually grab a flight without much problem."

Gavin picked up Sheila's right hand and rubbed it. "So this doesn't have to end until you want it to." He looked at her. "I'd call first. No surprise visits."

Sheila was pleased. "I don't know where I'll be." Then she laughed out loud. "Heavens, what a silly thing to say. Finding me would not be a problem for you."

The laugh lines crinkled around Gavin's eyes. "I think as long as Tony believes I'm treating you decently he'll be willing to tell me where you are."

"He *is* a bit of a watchdog," Sheila mused.

"Don't hold it against him," Gavin warned. "You got lucky when he picked you as a draft choice."

Nodding, Sheila played with the hair on his wrist. "I'd like to see you again," she confessed. "I like the way you don't expect anything from me, and I like the way you make me feel."

With his free hand, Gavin turned her face towards him. "Remember the evening of Valentine's Day, when Mary was trying to convince you not to put off having a family for too long in case something happened and it was too late to start over? You're twenty-eight years old. She had a point. If Mr. Right comes along, you'd better not let him slip away."

"Point taken," Sheila replied, "but you've really got to stop hanging around Tony. You are starting to sound like him."

"I'm not Tony," Gavin insisted, and grabbed her to him in the hope of showing her the error of her thinking.

# XXXVII

Tony was tired. It had been the first day of the trial, and already you could see that the defence was saving its energy for a credibility fight. Their lawyer, James Cook, had suggested today that the CIA had originally wanted to back the Sierra Maestra Liberators. The Cuban operation was a bungled attempt by them to save face when they realised that the Sierra Maestra Liberators were not strong enough to be of any threat to Castro. Cook even had the nerve to declare that the drugs and weapons found in the hands of the rebels were actually planted there by, guess who, Officer St. Pierre. Congressman Harvey, Cook said, had indeed gone down to Cuba to meet with the rebels against his country's wishes, but had only done so with the hope of facilitating Castro's release from power.

Tony had expected it all, but it still made him want to throw up. That's how he knew that Cook's plan was to discredit Aaron badly enough to cast doubt in the jury's mind. All that was needed was that doubt. With enough doubt, it did not matter that the defence's story was hard to believe. It was the prosecution who had to fight this war.

During the day, Paul Hedley had been constantly checking his information with Aaron, and Aaron was as tired as Tony. At 10:00 p.m. he gave up his fight against sleep and took one of the bedrooms at the house. Tony had been sitting in his usual place on the couch beside Mary. Gavin was on the computers, and Scott was slouched in the easy chair watching television.

"I'd better go home tonight," Tony announced. "I'll be up early for another long day tomorrow." He turned to Mary. "Are you ready for your hot chocolate?" When she shook her head, he got up. "Come on, I'll make it for you."

They wandered into the kitchen and he made the hot chocolate in the microwave. They didn't say much. She was close, and he found it soothing just to be near her. When they left the kitchen, he stopped at the front door and waved at the men. Then he looked down at Mary. *I'd give anything to take you with me,* he said silently. He hoped his eyes sent her the message. Mary smiled, as if she understood, and reached out to touch his arm. "Sleep tight, and good luck tomorrow," was all she said.

As he walked towards his car, Tony heard steps behind him and a voice say, "Hang on a minute, Tony." It was Gavin, who motioned him into the car and got in beside him. With the door closed, Gavin turned to him. "You love her, don't you?"

No sense denying what was obvious to his friends. "Yes," Tony admitted.

"Look, let me do something for you," Gavin suggested. "It's too risky to let her out of the house, but I want you to trust me on something. That monitor in her room cannot be turned off without questions being asked, but it does have a minimum setting where very little can be picked up. As long as both Scott and I are here, I can turn it down without any questions being asked. I'm the one who does the report in the morning on the night's events. That report doesn't have to say anything about you being in her room."

Tony's conservative nature recoiled. "No way. What the hell are you thinking?"

"She likes you, Tony. She likes you a lot." Gavin looked towards the house, then back at Tony. "It's just Scott and I. You know it won't go any further. I already owe you a bunch of favours, so why don't you let me pay one back?"

"It seems so damned calculated. It isn't the way I want it to be," Tony stated, staring out the car window. It had started to rain, which suited his mood perfectly.

*Poor guy,* Gavin commiserated, understanding how ridiculous the situation was. "Of course it isn't," he agreed. "It's a farce. Look at it. She's a candlelight and roses type of woman. The type you place in a boat and row on a lake in the middle of the afternoon. But this poor woman is kidnapped and presented to one of our officers as bait. She is raped and kept prisoner. After she escapes, we pursue her to her home, where we interrogate her and almost decide to kill her twice. And by the way," he interrupted himself, gritting his teeth, "I take no pride in remembering how close I came to killing that sweet creature."

Beside him, Tony shuddered.

"If that wasn't enough," Gavin continued, "the other side makes two serious attempts on her. So to protect her, we bring her down here, throw her in this pleasant-looking prison, and for entertainment we allow her to visit the gym. When she appears to start feeling the same way towards you as you do for her, she can't do a thing about it because she is *never* alone with you. Even if she had the guts to show you how she feels, the only way you two can express your feelings is in front of us. I feel like a character actor in an absolute farce."

Hearing it spelled out made Tony laugh. The description was perfect, and it was a relief to know that the people he worked with understood and were on his side. A thought occurred to him, and he looked at Gavin and got serious again. "It's not as simple as you suggest. There's one other piece to this, and I need your honest opinion." Propping his elbow on the base of the driver's door window, he rested his head in his hand. "It's about this 'prison'. It *is* a prison for her, even though we have the best of intentions. We cannot afford to let her leave and risk having her killed. I am essentially her jailer, no matter how nice and polite we are to her. That puts me in a position of total power over her, and don't think she hasn't realised that."

"Tony, come on, man," Gavin protested. "I know what you're saying, but for heaven's sake, she's crazy about you. It's obvious to us even if you're afraid to see it."

"I see it," Tony admitted. "At least I've been hoping that's what I'm seeing."

"Then why make her decisions for her?" Gavin asked. "Mary's no extrovert, but she sure doesn't strike me as a woman who would hesitate to say no. She knows her own mind. Remember when you tried to send Scott away? She went up one side of you and down the other. Did you find her unassertive then?"

"Hardly." Chuckling now at the memory of his five-foot-two-inch little tiger, Tony relaxed. "Thanks, Gavin."

"Whenever you want," Gavin said, as he started to open the car door. "Just give me the nod, and don't worry about it. But listen," he insisted, "don't let that woman go back to Canada not knowing how you feel. I would hate to see you let this one slip away from you." He clamped a hand on Tony's shoulder and gave it a shake. "You're a good man, Tony. You should be married. You should have a family."

"Now you've got me married."

"Tell me you haven't married that woman a dozen times in your mind."

Tony did not bother to reply. Then a different thought occurred to him. "You seem pretty free with my personal life, but you haven't told me what is going on between you and my newest recruit."

The car door closed again. "We're having a good time," Gavin answered briefly.

252

"Mm. What's her read on this 'good time'?"

The lines around Gavin's eyes crinkled into their small smile. "Well, she doesn't seem to want me around in the morning, if that's what you mean. Am I intruding on your turf?"

"Of course not. Sheila's well past the age of consent." Tony shrugged. "I was just hoping she was aware of your restless nature, shall we say."

Gavin shook his head. "You've really got to quit worrying about everybody so much," he advised. "Do you really think I'd go anywhere near a clinging type of woman?"

For a few seconds Tony was quiet. "No, of course not. You've always known exactly what you wanted. I'm the only fool who let someone cling to me and waste seventeen years of my life."

The car door was opened again. "Give yourself a break, Tony. It's time to start over," Gavin said as he left the car. He leaned down and spoke through the door before he closed it. "Remember…just give me the nod."

# XXXVIII

That the news would hit the media with a big splash was inevitable. Frank Moseley's reaction to it was no different than the reaction of the people at 51 Elm. It was readily apparent that Congressman Harvey was pulling out all the stops and going on the attack. In Mary's new home, newspapers were received with well-founded apprehension, and the television was no friend. Mary's new friends did a lot of grumbling, and both Tony and Gavin began looking very serious. Aaron would read the papers and then look miserable until the others managed to shake him out of it.

According to the media, Aaron was an out-of-control, sex starved rapist, who had been given free rein by his employers to act exactly as he pleased. When caught in the act, he had concocted a plan to divert attention away from himself, and the CIA was backing him all the way for their own reasons

Mary had written to her parents, in British Columbia, previously to explain where she was and what had happened. She had told them not to worry, regardless of what they heard. Now, however, the whole world seemed to be concerned about her whereabouts and her safety. The rumours were absolutely wild. It was like reading about someone else. Surely all this fuss couldn't be about her! When the press did not find her at home in Toronto, the stories got alarming. Where was she? Was she alive? Had the CIA killed her? Was she being held hostage, locked up someplace by them?

The morning that the CIA was accused of holding her hostage, everyone was looking glum when Mary got to the breakfast table. They had been talking, but ceased at Mary's approach. Tony was missing. Mr. Walsh had called him into the office. The public relations people had wanted to discuss strategy. Mary glanced at the headlines in the local paper and grimaced. The Canadian papers were probably worse.

While she didn't like the tension at the breakfast table, Mary couldn't imagine what to say to make everyone feel better. It seemed a hopeless task. Then Scott came in with a *Toronto Star* in his hand. He looked at the glum group sitting in silence and promptly walked over to Mary, handed her the *Star*, kissed the top of her head and said, "How's my favourite little hostage?"

Relieved, Mary smiled up at him. Sheila laughed and the tension evaporated. Discussion became lively, peppered with earnest grumbling and curses.

Shortly after breakfast, as they were preparing to head to the gym, the phone rang. Aaron answered and listened with a deadpan expression. Upon hanging up, he turned to Mary. "Tony and Mr. Walsh will be here with the car and some people from Security in about fifteen minutes. You are supposed to dress appropriately for a visit to your embassy. They have asked us to produce you. Sheila is to pack your bag in case you end up staying there."

Silence. She was supposed to leave? Mary noticed that no one looked happy. She had a hundred questions, but they would have to wait for Tony. Quickly she changed and helped Sheila with her suitcase.

When Tony arrived, he had a glum reception. Since he didn't feel any better himself, he made no comment. "Your country is worried about you, Mary," he announced. "Your embassy has asked us to produce you. They will probably invite you to stay there, where they can guard you themselves." He forced a smile. "Let's get going. Mr. Walsh is waiting in the car. This will be a high-profile ride for you."

"Wait," Scott said, and ran into the kitchen. He came back out with a can of hot chocolate powder in one hand, and a small bag in the other. "They might not have your kind," he stated, holding up the can.

Mary felt sad. She wanted to hug all of them, but she knew she would only cry if she did. She made herself smile, and turned to follow Tony.

The atmosphere inside the company car was just as glum. Mr. Walsh greeted her politely, but then no one talked much. As they drove through the embassy gates, Mr. Walsh said, "Welcome to a little piece of Canada, Mary."

There were reporters everywhere: outside the gates, inside the gates, everywhere. Horrified, Mary looked at Tony. "Do I have to be here?"

Mr. Walsh chose to answer. "Mary, they are going to ask you if you would like to stay here with your fellow countrymen until you are needed for the trial. You'll be free to go outside and wander the grounds, meet people, and generally have a lot more freedom of movement." He smiled. "It's a nice place, and you'll be well treated."

*But my friends won't be here,* Mary knew, *and neither will Tony,* who was showing little expression on his face. "Do I have to stay?" she asked.

"Mary, you are free to do whatever you chose," Tony responded politely.

Maybe she was too much trouble to look after. Mary wished Tony would give her an indication of his wishes. She changed the question. "Do you want me to stay here?"

Still the polite smile. "I want you to do whatever makes you happy," he responded.

Oh dear, what did that mean? She knew Tony liked her, so maybe he didn't want to influence her, or speak plainly in front of Mr. Walsh. What did he really want? The car had stopped, and all Mary could see were reporters and uniformed guards. She would get squished out there.

Mr. Walsh spoke again. "They can't see into this car, Mary, but once you step out they will start taking your picture. It would be a great help to us if you could try not to look so terrified."

"Smile, Mary," Tony encouraged.

Smile? While in danger of being swarmed? Mary couldn't smile. She wanted to go back to 51 Elm.

"I'll tickle you," Tony threatened. When Mary looked at him in surprise, he jabbed a finger towards her ribs.

"No!" she yelped, laughing and jumping away from him. "Don't do that, I'm ticklish."

"That's better," he announced, trying to ignore Walsh's raised eyebrow. "Now, whenever you don't smile, I will tickle you, got it?"

Surrounded by people in uniform, and with Tony and Mr. Walsh at her side, Mary made it into the embassy with a smile pasted on her face. Once they got to some inner rooms, there were no more reporters. There were lots of official-looking people around, and Tony and Mr. Walsh were greeted politely and led away. Mary was taken into a lavish office and introduced to the Canadian ambassador. It was all a bit overwhelming.

The Ambassador was very nice, and so were the two women and a man who were also in the office. Mary was introduced, and then asked questions about her current involvement with the CIA.

They understood that she was here voluntarily as a witness.

Was this true?

Yes.

Was she being well treated?

Yes.

Had she ever asked to go home?

No.

Did she believe she could go home if she asked?

It wasn't safe, and she did not think they would want her to leave, but she felt that if she insisted, they would let her go.

Was her liberty restricted?

Only in the sense that she was constantly guarded. Mr. Dune had offered to take her any place she wanted to go within reason.

Did she feel like a prisoner?

No, people were too nice to her to feel like a prisoner.

Did she realise that she did not have to stay with the CIA? If she wanted to, she could stay here or return to Canada and protection would be arranged for her. Would she like to go home?

Home. Although she missed Lori and the familiarity of her own country, Mary remembered home as an empty house with depressing memories. With a start, she realised that she had not been depressed since meeting her new friends. "Home" seemed lonely now.

"Am I causing them too much trouble?" Mary asked. "There's a lot of bad publicity, and it's probably awfully expensive to keep me at the house and guarded twenty-four hours a day."

The ambassador actually laughed at that. "Mrs. Norland, please do not concern yourself with their budget. I assure you that you are just a tiny drop in a very large bucket. To answer your other question, the CIA is not unfamiliar with bad publicity, and they have certainly not brought you here because you are too much trouble. They have expressed a great deal of concern for your well-being, and have brought you here in a spirit of reluctant cooperation, shall we say."

"Then I'd like to stay with them at the house, if that's okay," Mary stated.

Once the Ambassador had heard directly from Mary that she was not being held against her will, the interview ended. Mary was given the phone number to call should she change her mind, and asked if she would like to make a statement to the press. At the look on her face, one of the women in the room hurried to say that this could be done on her behalf by a member of their staff. It would assure people that she was alive and well, and here by her own choice. A short statement was drafted in minutes and approved by everyone, and then Mary was led out of the room.

Tony and Mr. Walsh were chatting with some people, but Tony turned at Mary's approach and gave her a look that sent her heart fluttering. Mr. Walsh seemed quite pleased as well, and Mary knew she would have no trouble smiling on the walk back to the car. Tony put an arm loosely around her shoulders, dropping it only when the first reporter came into view. More pictures and questions that received "No comment" answers, then finally they were on their way back to 51 Elm.

By 11:45 a.m., they were already pulling into the driveway of 51 Elm. Tony and two of the Security men took Mary into the house, while the others

257

waited in the car for Tony's return. Only Sheila was inside the house, beaming at Mary while she turned on the computers once again.

Tony checked to see that everything was working properly, and instructed the men from Security to stay with Sheila until Scott arrived in the afternoon. Then he addressed Mary. "I'll carry your bag into your room, and then I've got to run." As he had hoped, Mary followed him into her room. Tony shut the door most of the way, put her suitcase on the bed, then turned and put his hands on her shoulders. "I didn't want you to go," he confessed, "but it had to be your choice. I am so happy that you decided to stay with us."

"I didn't want to leave," Mary assured him. The rest of her thoughts she kept inside her, but knew they were probably showing on her face. Her heart was doing that silly fluttering thing again.

The content, happy look on her face was all the encouragement Tony needed to kiss her. This time it was not impulsive, it was very deliberate. Once again, however, his time was not his own, so he could only hold her warm body in his arms for a minute. Before he reluctantly released her, he whispered against her forehead. "One of these days you and I are going to have that dinner date, and then we are going to go someplace where we can be *alone* together." When her eyes twinkled agreement, he kissed the tip of her nose and started to leave.

"Oh, wait a sec," he remembered. "Come out here." In the living room he dialled Aaron's telephone number. When Aaron answered, Tony told him, "There's someone here you might like to talk to," and handed the phone to Mary. At the front door, he turned back to see Mary listening to Aaron talk, a happy blush on her cheeks. Aaron would not have hesitated to tell Mary exactly how happy he was that Mary had not left. It was good to see her so pleased. He hurried out to the waiting car.

That night, when Mary studied herself critically in the bathroom mirror, she was satisfied with her reflection. *This is as good as it gets for me,* she knew. She had showered and brushed her hair until it shone and hung cooperatively against her head without going off in wild directions. She had also considered trying to liven up her brown eyes with a touch of makeup, but since she rarely wore much makeup, it would feel artificial tonight. But she did put on a light dab of perfume. The nightgown and matching housecoat were a silky, clinging forest-green material that Sheila had helped her select. Mary had never spent that kind of money on lingerie before, but when she tried it on in the store she had fallen in love with it. It was classy and flattering. Carefully she looked it over in the mirror. Yes, it was perfectly decent.

Flattering and possibly suggestive yes, but perfectly decent. Her plan required decency.

*I must be out of my mind,* Mary panicked, almost changing her mind for the fifth time. *Everyone will know what I'm up to. This is insane. Tony won't come in here in front of the guys. I'll embarrass myself totally.* Then she steadied herself. *No, you've thought it all through and mentally practised it a dozen times. All you are going to do is walk out there to take your empty hot chocolate mug back to the kitchen. You will put a smile on your scared face and say goodnight to Scott and Gavin, as if you had no other plans. Then you will walk past Tony, behind the chair, touch his shoulder and ask him what he's reading. It's only to motivate him a little. If he's unreceptive, just say goodnight and keep walking into the kitchen with your mug. Leave it there, go to bed and give up on him.*

If Tony had not spent the evening on the phone working, Mary would have tried this earlier. Now it was almost eleven, which meant the security monitor would soon be on. But perhaps he could order it turned off. *Now go,* she told herself, *before he leaves and it's too late.*

Mary had expected Scott and Gavin to look up, say goodnight, and otherwise ignore her—at least that was what she had hoped. She had not expected Scott to grin and wink, then look over at where Tony had his head buried in a book. Nor did she expect Gavin to do a double take, shift in his chair, and grin down at his computer. That did it! It was all she could do not to turn and run back into her room. She had just gotten the attention of the very two males in the room she was hoping would ignore her. They knew exactly what she was up to.

Blood ran to her face, but it was too late to quit now. Somehow she made it to Tony's chair without him looking up. When he did, she slid around behind him and placed her left hand on his shoulder.

"Ready to turn in, dear?" he asked, covering her hand with his right one.

"Yes." She was close to him, but, conscious of the other men in the room, she did not let her body touch him.

"Sleep tight," was all he said, giving her hand a pat.

Feeling thoroughly humiliated now, Mary wished him good night and went to rinse her mug in the kitchen. *That was awful,* she thought, furious with both herself for trying it, and him for letting her leave. *Give up,* she told herself. *Just give up. I'll never be able to look Scott and Gavin in the face tomorrow, and it was all for nothing.*

At that moment, she heard whispers in the living room, and then Scott strode into the kitchen, pretending to pull his hair out. He opened the fridge and grabbed a pop, then put a hand on Mary's shoulder and leaned down to talk in her ear. "Don't give up on the ole man, Mar. He really is crazy about you, but he's just an old fuddy-duddy."

Mary had to laugh. Scott was not going to allow her to be embarrassed. She shook her head. "I can't do much more, Scott. If he's not interested, he's not."

"Just don't give up," Scott encouraged. "By the way, you look great." He gave the top of her head a light kiss. "Mmm, smell good too." With a parting grin, he left the kitchen.

*There goes my personal cheering section,* Mary mused, following him out. She was now able to smile and say goodnight without embarrassment. In her room, she locked the door and sat down on the bed, dejected.

A knock startled her, and started her pulse quickening. When she opened the door, Tony entered and closed it behind him. He looked a little awkward, but took her by the shoulders and turned her to face the monitor light.

As the light went off, he spoke. "The monitor is turned down to minimum. If we keep quiet, it won't be able to pick anything up. Short of a disaster happening, Gavin will put nothing in his report about me coming into your room." He wrapped his arms around her so that her back was pressed against his chest and his cheek lay against her head. They watched the monitor light flicker on briefly, then off. "If we were to turn it right off, we would have some embarrassing questions to answer," he stated. "Mary," he whispered, "if you want me to leave, just say the word now, please."

"Leave?" She turned in his arms. "Don't you dare leave!" she said in a emphatic whisper.

Tony didn't wait for a second invitation. He wanted her so badly he could feel himself shaking. Her mouth against his was soft, and he could feel her body under his hands as he ran them up and down the silky garments she was wearing. She wanted him; he could tell by the way she pressed against him and stroked his head. What had he been so worried about? Her mouth opened to him, and he felt fire searing through his body. He caught her slight frame up in his arms and carried her to the bed, placing her on it and lying beside her.

Clothes—good grief, he was still wearing a suit, tie and laced-up shoes. The tie was already choking him. In the movies, people seemed to discard clothes either magically or with great abandon, throwing them or ripping them without a second thought. In real life you didn't do that with good clothing, unless you were rich or just plain careless. There was no avoiding it—he had to sit back up and take the time to remove all this. With a groan of disgust, he pushed himself to the side of the bed and fought with his tie.

Normally, ties slide off with ease, but not if your heart is racing and you're in a hurry to get back to the woman lying beside you. It caught, making him frustrated enough to rip it off. Just then he felt Mary move beside him. She straddled him, sitting on his lap and facing him. With nimble little fingers and a determined smile, she unknotted the tie, pulled it off, folded it and placed it in his pockets. All in a matter of seconds. Then she pushed his jacket over his shoulders and he was able to pull it off and hang it over the chair beside the bed.

Next, Mary started to undo buttons on his shirt, but he made her job harder by kissing her. He loved the feel of her lips and tongue, and managed to undo a couple of strategically placed buttons on her housecoat, so he could reach in and feel her breasts beneath it. By the time she had pushed his shirt over his shoulders, he had managed to slide his hand up underneath the silk to her thighs. His hand found the warmth between her legs, and she moved against it, breathing hard into his face. Quickly she reached down to unbuckle his belt and unbutton the dress pants, but then she moved away and back onto the bed. Somehow he finished undressing himself.

Finally he could join her on the bed. She had removed the housecoat, leaving only a scanty nightgown. He lay beside her and took her once again into his arms, feeling her move up against him. His hands ran over her body, pushing the nightgown up to her waist. He felt the firmness of her buttocks, then let his lips travel down her body, feeling her hands running through his hair. The times, many of them, when he had played this scene out in his mind, always revolved around bringing her pleasure. They had all night, and he would be in no hurry. He had dreamt of watching her in orgasmic delight, all too conscious of the fact that her last sexual experiences had been rape. Tonight he had planned to proceed slowly and carefully, to build up her confidence and trust.

What he had not counted on was the desire that was going to betray those plans. To his unexpected dismay, he realised that he was not going to be able to hold off like he had hoped. He had just enough control left to enter her slowly. When he heard her take a breath, he looked at her face. She smiled at him. *I'll make this up to you,* he promised silently. She held him tightly until he finished. He then kissed her and placed his mouth beside her ear.

"Sorry. I honestly wasn't trying to break any speed records," he whispered.

Mary stifled a chuckle. "I know," she responded. "Don't worry about it. I wanted you just as much." It was true. Finally having him inside her and being one with him was just about everything she could want right now. Two people couldn't get any closer, and she had wanted this closeness with him so badly. It would have been nice not having to whisper all the time, but making love silently was a small price to pay.

He lay contented in her arms for a minute, enjoying the release of weeks of pent-up sexual tension he had felt in her presence. "Let me have the rest of the night to make this up to you."

As far as Mary was concerned, it wasn't something he had to make up, but he was more than welcome to have the rest of the night, or the rest of the week if he wanted it. Soon she found out that he was true to his word, as they spent the next few hours exploring each other's bodies. Whenever he was ready, she welcomed him, but in between he seemed determined to spoil her. Mary lost count of her orgasms after the first few, and abandoned herself to the joys of touch and the feeling of being safe in his arms. Safe! Oh no!

Mary froze. How could she forget, after all Lori had talked and joked about it? Not only had Mary not been on any birth control since her marriage fell apart two years ago, but she hadn't even asked Tony any of those other horrid questions. Dating had been easy when she was eighteen, but these days you had to make sure the guy was safe. Blood raced to her face. She couldn't, absolutely couldn't, ask a man things like that. Yet Tony, who had not been in a marital relationship for three years, was probably exactly the sort of man you were supposed to be careful with. *Oh well, too late now anyway,* she realised. *I've just taken up gambling and the cards have been dealt.*

To heighten her embarrassment, Tony had noticed the sudden stiffness in her body, and seen the vivid blush on her face.

"What's the matter?" he whispered.

"Nothing."

"Tell me." He was stroking her neck, which felt so comforting.

"I can't," she admitted.

"Yes, you can," he insisted, still in a whisper. "You can tell me anything."

*Father confessor,* Mary thought wryly, but it did seem easy to talk to him. "I forgot some important things," she admitted into his ear. Thank goodness you couldn't look at someone while you were whispering in their ear. "I forgot all about birth control, and I forgot to ask you any of those…those questions."

Against her neck, Tony buried a chuckle. If this had been able to start as a normal relationship, they would have known they could put worries like this aside, but the thought of an evening discussion in front of Scott and Gavin about birth control, AIDS and other diseases was just too ridiculous for words. To make up for the chuckle because she had been so embarrassed, Tony kissed her and pointed to a tiny scar. "You don't have to worry about birth control," he promised, "and for the other, well, I'll just ask you to trust me on that. You'll have no problem, and I know I won't either."

*Of course you know,* Mary remembered. *I gave you permission to see my medical file when Aaron gave my doctor permission to see his. You probably know a hell of a lot more about me than I'll ever know about you.* It was water under the bridge, though, so Mary decided not to dwell on it. There were more important things to think about right now.

As he reached for Mary again, Tony lost himself to the pleasure he was finding in her. Time flew much too fast, and before he could imagine it, the clock beside the bed said 2:30 a.m. Getting up early in the morning to make an 8:00 a.m. meeting with Mr. Walsh was going to be difficult, because he would have to go home to shower, shave and change first. With great reluctance, he knew he had to get to sleep. For a few minutes he lay against Mary's back She was curled up in his arms, and he suspected that she was close to sleep herself. He was happier than he could ever remember being. Too much of his life had been wasted with a wife who had acquiesced to having sex in order to keep a roof over her head, and to women who gave him pleasure only in return for money. The feeling of loving a woman who came to him eagerly and desired his touch was almost overwhelming. Tonight Mary had given him a sense of self-worth that had been missing for too long in his private life. It made it impossible for him to hold back his feelings for her. Against her ear, he told Mary that he loved her.

Mary rolled in his arms to face him. She put a finger against his lips. "You don't even know me," she murmured. "Not really."

"I know what's important," he insisted.

"You live in a different world from me." As she said it, Mary caressed his temple. It wasn't a rejection, and she didn't want him to think it was, but to admit to love was not a small step. She lived in a different country, with a house and a job. He lived down here, somewhere, and had a job that clearly took a lot of his attention, and was not one that she could ever fully share. On top of that, Mary knew nothing about Tony's hobbies, finances, or how long he was in any particular place at a time. To admit to love tonight meant that all those things could be swept away, but they seemed like very big things to Mary. That she loved him, she had no doubt, but they had a lot of work to do if they were to have a chance together. "We both carry a lot of baggage," she said simply.

Tony knew that she had a point. "We'll sort it out," he promised, "if you decide you want to. Go to sleep now. I'll try not to wake you too early."

The sun wasn't up, and there was only the slightest bit of light to the sky when Mary awakened. Sensing that the bed had an empty feel to it, she opened her eyes in dismay. Gone? Would he have left without a word? A movement caught her eye. There he was, dressing in the dark at the end of the bed. It was early morning, and he would have to go home to get ready for work. That was perfectly understandable, but he seemed to be frowning and gazing off into space. That was not very comforting.

*Just don't ruin it for me Tony,* she pleaded silently. *Spare me the speech about why you should not have made love to me, or how you should stay away from me because you let yourself get too involved, or carried away. Last night was against all the rules and policies, I'm sure. You know it, and so do Scott and Gavin. You, however, are the only one who cares. I'm a mature adult. We come from different lives, and you are probably quite happy with yours. I know my feelings will be hurt in the end, but don't take last night away from me.*

Although Tony's thoughts had been similar, their intent was not what Mary feared. He had woken very happy, but when he looked into himself candidly, he was also feeling a little emotionally fragile. In all his adult life, he couldn't remember feeling like this. This budding relationship could fall apart easily with clumsy handling, and he was so out of practise. Although he really needed to, he could not just wander off with Mary and start the normal courting process. He was involved in a crucial court battle, where he had to balance Aaron's interests with the Company's interests, and at the same time protect Mary. Right now, he had to rush away from the place he most wanted to be, to prepare for a meeting with Carl Walsh prior to the start of court.

Seeing Mary sit up on the edge of the bed, Tony sat beside her and held her close. She smiled up at him, warming his heart. "Happy?" he whispered hopefully. When she nodded and squeezed his waist, he kissed her lips lightly. "So am I," he confessed. Then he told her again that he loved her, which earned him another kiss. No words of encouragement, but no denial. *She's being cautious, or she's not sure yet,* he knew. *Okay, Mary, I'll wait. Somehow I'll make you love me.*

Tony checked the light by the microphone, and spoke between flashes. *Damn that thing,* he thought. "I have to run. I've got a meeting before court. I'll be back this evening to have supper here, but then I've got my weekly Thursday night meeting." He released her, but brushed her hair back with his fingers. "I don't know how often we can be together, but with any luck we'll be out of here soon," he promised. One last kiss. "Don't let Scott tease you too much," he whispered, then left.

In the living room, Scott grinned openly at him when Tony came out of the bedroom, but then disappeared into the kitchen. *Bratty kid,* Tony thought, although in good humour. Gavin gave him a slightly more sedate thumbs up signal. *You are not much better,* decided Tony, although he reached to shake Gavin's hand on the way past. The thank-you was unspoken. They both knew. You did small favours for each other whenever possible. It helped make the job easier. Tony felt lucky in his working relationships. Maybe this time he could be as lucky with his new personal one.

As Tony reached the front door, Scott emerged and handed him coffee in a travelling mug. It occurred to Tony that Scott should still be asleep. The young man had clearly not gone to bed. Then Tony realised that Scott must have decided to stay on guard with Gavin for extra security. Not only had Tony just trusted this twenty-five-year-old to keep a secret about him breaking rules, but this young man had decided on his own to help watch his boss's back to make sure nothing went wrong. Tony thanked him for the coffee and reconsidered his previous evaluation. *Okay, still a brat, but a kind and loyal one, and definitely not a kid.*

Much later, Mary emerged from the bedroom. She received a similar response from Gavin and Scott, but as she walked past them on the way to the kitchen, she grinned back at Scott. "He is *not* an old 'fuddy-duddy'," she announced in a spirit of fun. That got her a loud whoop and a high-five slap from Scott, and a cackle of laughter from Gavin. With a feeling of great contentment, Mary volunteered to make breakfast.

# XXXIX

Waiting aimlessly by his living room window, Frank Moseley watched without pleasure as Gavin drove up his driveway. *The big deceit begins,* he said to himself. *I now have to lie to a man who has been my right hand since he joined my team sixteen years ago straight out of the army. He came to me with a huge sense of patriotism, and has never given me a moment's concern. We've been friends, good friends, for fifteen of those years, and now it will be me who breaks the trust.*

That's what a man like Fred could never understand. *Gavin will never fully believe in this "coincidence". The trust, the faith, will all be gone.* That is why Frank knew he would have to resign. People had faith in Gavin. What Gavin believed, was true. If Gavin had doubts, it was suspect. Today was a very black day for Frank.

Gavin let himself in, and Frank offered him a drink. It surprised Gavin. "I'm on my way to the house, Frank. I take over at 7:00 p.m."

Frank took a breath. This was going to be hard. "Surely Scott can cover a little longer by himself in that place. There's a fortune in security devices built into that house. Your former operation is in a bit of a mess, and I wanted to toss a couple of ideas around with you."

Gavin wasn't pleased, but Frank was his boss, and he was right about the security at 51 Elm. Without showing his reluctance, Gavin let Frank pour a drink for him. By the time it was poured, Gavin knew he'd barely make it by 7:00 p.m. even if he left now. With surprise, he noticed Frank's hand shaking. He frowned at him. "You okay, Frank?"

"Yeh, just a little edgy lately." Frank didn't sit. "I need you overseas, Gavin."

"Whenever you want, of course," Gavin replied. "I'm just grateful to have had the last couple of weeks back here. It's been a nice break."

"A break?" Frank was surprised. "I would have expected you to be bored silly."

"Hell, no," Gavin replied. "Tony has a good group of people, and I've had a chance to teach Scott a few things. He's a quick learner."

Frank stared. "Isn't that the spoiled rich kid who's apt to walk off an assignment whenever a pretty girl walks by?"

Gavin scoffed. "Scott was never *that* bad. Come on, Tony wouldn't have put up with that for a minute. Have you forgotten Scott from Cuba? He's turned into a very reliable, responsible officer. Smart as anything, too. I like the kid."

*Then Scott will die,* Frank realised. How could he have forgotten the eager young man who had trained so hard to be allowed to accompany the rescue mission to Cuba? *That man would not walk away from a job, and he won't accept a bribe, either. If he's responsible, he will die, and now Gavin likes him.* Gavin did not like people who would desert their positions.

It felt as if the ceiling had started to press down on him, and Frank reached for excuses. "Do you still believe that witness is going to do us any good? The press has been horrific."

"Mary? She'll fight to the end for Aaron," Gavin replied, watching Frank's face with concern. *What is bothering this guy?* "It's a bad situation, but Mary is solidly behind us. By the way," Gavin added, trying to cheer Frank up, "you've been away. Did you know that Tony is in love with her?"

"What? Tony...in love with her?" It was getting hard to breathe.

Gavin was getting worried. *God, Frank looks awful.* "Yeh, head over heels. Frank, are you okay?"

Frank had put a hand on the bookcase to steady himself. *I'll kill Scott, then I'll kill the first woman my friend has ever really loved to keep him from believing I killed a woman he didn't love, and then I'll kill myself, because this is too much to bear.* "Did Tony tell you that?"

"Sure did," Gavin replied. "Poor old tormented Tony. You wouldn't believe the change in him." Gavin perched on the edge of the armchair beside the bookcase Frank was gripping. "I guess that's why these last couple of weeks have been such a nice change. Sometimes it's a relief to get out of the hot spots, come home and work with people who have a real loyalty to each other."

The quiet of the house was shattered when Frank screamed and threw his drink against the wall. Gavin jumped up in shock and stared at his boss.

"Get the fuck out of here!" Frank yelled. "Get over to that house, NOW! There's a hit going down on Mary tonight. Someone Scott knows will get into the house. Two men, not ours, will be on the grounds. HURRY!" he pleaded. "You're already late! I'll call Tony and get you some backup." He grabbed the phone.

Years of training meant that Gavin could move even when in shock. "You *bastard*!" he yelled, already running out the door to his car. "You goddamn *bastard*!"

Tony was approaching the gates of Langley when Frank called.

"Tony—get back to the house. There's a hit on Mary tonight. It may be in progress already. Someone inside that Scott knows, and two unknowns outside. I'll call Security."

Tony had screeched the car into a U-turn after the first sentence. "Where are you?" he barked.

"At my home…my hands are dirty on this one, Tony."

"Frank!" But Frank had hung up, leaving Tony in shock. *Mary! Why, Frank? In the name of eighteen years of unblemished service—WHY?* Tony drove as fast as he dared, his mind in two places: 51 Elm, and Frank's home. This kind of betrayal from Frank was unbelievable, and it would totally ruin Frank's career. Or perhaps after a betrayal like this, Frank had other plans.

Tony called Frank back and felt a great relief when he answered. "Go in to see Walsh," Tony ordered. There was silence on the other end. A desperate man with a loaded weapon and a life that was teetering on disaster might be seeking a more permanent solution. "Frank, please. I need you by the phone. I don't know what I'll find there. You've got to help me. Don't you bail out on me. I need you. Go to Walsh and I'll meet you there after. Please."

A sigh. "All right."

It was a defeated response, but it was the right one. Tony hung up and concentrated on his destination.

When the system went down, Scott groaned. *Please, I didn't do it this time.* He wiggled a couple of wires and threw a few switches, but to no avail. Then Kevin called on the direct line from the Security office. That was a relief. Kevin could fix almost anything.

Kevin had wasted no time, Scott thought as he opened the door for him. Aaron was sleeping off a tension headache on the cot in the spare bedroom, and Scott had not wanted to wake him up. Tomorrow Aaron had to be on the stand, and he was trying not to show how scared he was. Scott didn't bother telling Kevin that Aaron was asleep. The bedroom door would deaden their voices. Mary said hello to Kevin, then went into her room. She had taken a dislike to him.

From her bedroom window, Mary saw a dark Cadillac drive down the street, turn off its lights and park in the shadows two houses away. Two men got out and walked down the sidewalk, scaling the fence belonging to 51 Elm and cutting into the backyard. *Strange behaviour, to say the least.* Then another car with no lights drew up quietly. Mary recognised the Mustang as Gavin's. He got out of the car and also scaled the fence. Something was really wrong.

In the living room, Scott shook his head. Kevin had told him that the luscious model Scott had taken home last month was having supper in the Pumpernickel Bar this evening. If Scott hurried, she might still be there. It was tempting, but absolutely out of the question.

"Why not?" Kevin asked. "I'll cover for you until Gavin gets here. I have to be here to fix this system anyway, and Gavin will arrive any minute. Just go," Kevin insisted. "I'll stay with Gavin until midnight. That should give even a Romeo like you enough time."

Scott also knew he could wake Aaron up and ask him to sit with Kevin until Gavin arrived. It was strange for Gavin to be late like this. Then he decided. No. His job was here. To run off would be shirking his duty. Besides, Mary didn't like Kevin. "Thanks anyway, Kev, but I'm working tonight. End of story."

"Too bad," Kevin responded, as if lost in thought. He perched himself on the desk beside the main console and looked down at Scott, who was leaning back in his chair. "Were you aware that some very important people were anxious to have Mary out of the way?"

It had been said quietly, and Scott was sure he could not have heard that intonation correctly. "We've already figured that out up in Canada," he replied steadily, watching Kevin, who was not acting like his usual carefree self. A little alarm bell had started ringing softly in the back of Scott's head, but why? What invisible signal was he picking up? Instinctively, he straightened up in his chair.

"These people would like your help," Kevin said, looking directly at Scott. "After all, you must realise that she's a major liability to the Company. You'd be doing the CIA a favour."

The alarm bell was in full tone now. "I think you'd better speak a little plainer," Scott demanded. "I'm not sure I can believe what you are suggesting."

"Walk out of here now, Scott," Kevin directed, "and it's worth $20,000.00 to you. That's one hell of a lot of money for doing nothing. Pay off some debts or take a broad on a great holiday. All you have to say is that you never imagined it would happen. No one's hurt and you are completely innocent."

No one would be hurt? Mary would be *dead*. It was hard to talk when you were this angry, but Scott knew Tony would need details. "And what will your story be?"

"Don't need one," Kevin laughed. "I have a different career waiting for me—a very lucrative one." He got serious. "Go now, Scott. It will be worth your while."

Scott stood up. "You expect me to stand aside and let you kill Mary? You disgust me!"

While Scott had never deceived himself by believing he knew all there was to know about his job, it still shocked him to have his friend, his ex-friend, pull out a Davis P-380 from his shirt and point it at him. *How can I be so stupid,* he despaired. "What is this?" he demanded.

"It's a gun, Scott," Kevin said quietly. "I thought even you knew that. You can still walk. I don't want to do this—I'll be quite happy if you leave quietly and let me take care of Mary."

"You'll have to go through me to get to her." Scott felt the adrenalin rush. Action time. "Aaron!" he screamed, as he grabbed Kevin's wrist. A shot went off and Scott felt the whiz of the air as it missed him by inches. Scott and Kevin had trained together, so they knew each other's moves. Scott also knew that Kevin was stronger, but he was too angry to think about that now. Somehow, though, Kevin managed to struggle out of Scott's grasp, and suddenly Scott realised that he was staring at the wrong end of the 380.

*My God, this is for real,* was Scott's last thought, as doors burst open around him and he heard several shots. He couldn't move—he was frozen in fear. Then he saw Kevin crumple to the floor. Oh, thank God, it wasn't Kevin's gun that had gone off first. Scott realised that Aaron was at the doorway to the living room with his Colt MKIV in its business position, and Gavin was in the doorway to the house. Both men had fired.

Scott let his breath out in a gasp. "Thank you," he said weakly, his knees feeling like jelly. Then Gavin was beside him, kicking Kevin's gun away.

Kevin was still alive, but immobile. Strangely enough, he looked at Gavin in confusion. "Why are you here?" he managed to murmur. "You're early…" That was as far as he got. Scott had no personal experience with violent death to date, but he knew Kevin had just died.

"You okay?" Gavin asked him. When Scott nodded, Gavin added, "Tony's on his way. We'll get this sorted out. Where's Mary?"

"In her room," Scott answered. "Probably terrified. I'll go to her."

"No, Scott," Aaron interrupted. "Check out the back window for others."

"Right." Of course—eliminate the danger first, then comfort Mary.

Aaron was about to make a very major decision. Gavin had been late tonight, but Kevin's words had shocked him. Kevin had told Gavin he was early! That was wrong…horribly wrong. What it implied couldn't be true. *Please don't let it be true,* Aaron prayed. But it could be true, and if so, they were in the presence of a very dangerous adversary.

Tony had insisted his team learn and use a variety of private codes. Codes that allowed them to work in unison against an enemy without telegraphing their intentions. Aaron knew Scott was about to learn another unpleasant lesson. He needed Scott's help, but his friend was going to be shocked by this. By the time Scott had reached the window, putting a good distance between himself and Gavin, Gavin had holstered his weapon.

Scott heard the command and reacted instantly. It was a crisis code given by Aaron. You had to obey first and then you could question later, but to find yourself pointing your own firearm at Gavin was an unreal nightmare. "Aaron, what are we doing?" Scott questioned desperately. "This is Gavin, for God's sake."

Aaron was at a sixty-degree angle to Scott, if you considered Gavin to be the base point. It had been important to have Scott as far from Gavin as possible for backup. Gavin had years of paramilitary training under his belt, and Aaron knew he couldn't compete with that. To be too close to Gavin could be deadly, so Scott was positioned at a distance, and Aaron had moved back a few steps.

"Kevin said Gavin was *early*, Scott. But Gavin was *late*. Why would he be *early* unless he is part of this attempt? I wasn't supposed to be here, was I?"

"You're wrong, Aaron," Gavin said steadily. "There were two other intruders on the grounds. I've taken care of them."

"Why were you late, Gavin?" Aaron demanded. "And why did Kevin say you were early?"

Gavin didn't answer. He knew how this looked to Aaron. *Oh Frank, look what you've done,* he cursed. *How do I convince Aaron that I had no part in this? Come on, Tony, get here. That is, if Frank called you. Don't do this to me, Frank.* Gavin had no fear of Aaron, who was doing what he believed was necessary. Scott, however, was clearly in shock from his close call with Kevin, and his control was questionable.

Aaron watched Gavin closely. He had been standing still, quietly, but now Aaron saw his eyes go to Scott. That caused Gavin to become agitated. Aaron glanced over quickly. Good heavens, Scott was so nervous that you could see him shaking. Must be shock. No wonder Gavin was agitated. Shaking like that, Scott could fire accidently.

"Scott, I want you to take five deep breaths. Clear your mind and just breathe. Focus on the task—don't think."

Scott tried to do as he was told. *Breathe and focus; breathe and focus.* His muscles settled down. *Breathe and focus.*

Gavin relaxed visibly, but just then Aaron saw Mary open her bedroom door in his peripheral vision. "Go back into your room, Mary," he ordered.

"But, Aaron, you're wrong. Gavin didn't come with those men," Mary said weakly.

"Go back into your room," Aaron repeated. "I may be wrong, Mary, and I hope I am, but go back into your room. Tony will be here soon. Lock your door and don't come out until he calls for you. If I'm wrong, nothing is going to happen here. We'll all stand quietly and wait for Tony. Please, Mary." To Aaron's immense relief, she did as she was asked. He and Scott needed their attention for Gavin. Only a few minutes had passed, but it felt like hours.

Suddenly Aaron noticed that Gavin appeared to be judging distances. Aaron shot Scott a look. Uh-oh, Mary's statement had upset his nerves again. Scott really didn't believe in this, and it was making it hard for him. Aaron thought quickly. *Keep Scott's mind occupied—give him an exercise as if this were a practise drill. Wait for Tony.*

"Scott, what if Tony wasn't called, and he doesn't arrive. What do we do?"

"Check out Gavin's story," Scott responded. "Look for bodies on the grounds."

"Uh-huh, sounds easy. We just tell Gavin to stay put and we walk outside?"

"Nooo," Scott replied. "We have to disarm him and secure him. Then one of us could look outside."

Aaron nodded. "Okay, but you make disarming Gavin sound pretty easy. I need you to break it down—step by step. For starters, what is he packing?"

"Depends on why he is here tonight," Scott stated. "He owns a number of sidearms. He has a Colt, same model as yours, and also a Coonan Compact 357 that he likes. Sometimes he carries his Glock 26, and of course he's got the HK MK23. Oh, and he might have a Smith & Wesson Sigma, the SW380 Auto, tucked out of sight somewhere."

Gavin had relaxed. Scott was under control again, but Aaron was starting to feel ill after listening to that list of weapons. Fortunately, Tony drove in at that moment.

Walking in carefully through the open front door, firearm in the business position, Tony had tried to prepare himself for anything. He felt a combination of hope and dread. What he wasn't expecting to see was Aaron and Scott holding Gavin at gunpoint. A glance showed him Kevin lying lifeless on the floor. "Okay," he ordered, "everyone stay very calm and don't move. Aaron, tell me the reason for this."

"Gavin was late," Aaron stated, "but Kevin said he was early, and wasn't supposed to be here. Gavin won't explain why he was late or why Kevin said he was early."

"Where's Mary?"

"Safe in the bedroom," Aaron replied.

The relief was incredible, but Tony still had a crisis on his hands here. "Aaron, I think you are wrong in this, but I have to be sure. Don't move until I make a phone call." He looked at Scott. The young man's colour was ashen, and Tony realised that he was standing directly in Scott's line of fire, with only Gavin as a partial shield. A hardbacked chair was at his left side. He grabbed it with his left hand, and placed it two steps behind Gavin. "Gavin, interlace your fingers over your head, take two steps back and sit down." Gavin obeyed without comment. "Scott, holster that weapon." Scott obeyed instantly. Tony stepped back so that there was more distance between himself and Gavin, and dialled Frank's cell phone. No answer. Then he dialled Walsh's office and prayed that Frank had gone in.

Aaron watched Gavin. The man looked devastated. Not angry or belligerent; not nervous or guilty. Just quiet, drawn and devastated. Tony had reached someone on the phone.

"I have a critical incident here. I need to know Gavin's involvement." After a moment he hung up and put his firearm away. "Gavin's clear of this, Aaron. He was diverted. I'm to tell you that he always has been and remains a loyal employee of the Company." Those had been Frank's words, spoken in front of Walsh.

Aaron wasted no time putting his Colt away. Cars were arriving in the driveway. "Security," Scott announced.

"Good, we'll clean up here." Noticing that Gavin hadn't moved, Tony pulled his wrists apart and dropped his arms. Then he stood with a hand on Gavin's shoulder.

"Why, Tony?" Gavin asked sorrowfully. "What did they have on him?"

"No idea, my friend," Tony commiserated. "He's gone in to see Walsh."

"He called it off," Gavin stated tonelessly, looking up at Tony.

"I know," Tony sighed, "but I don't know if that will be enough. Look at what has happened and almost happened here tonight. As soon as we are clear here, you and I have to go and see Walsh." Tony looked at the three of them. "I have to know if you men are okay about what happened between you."

At that moment the people from Security came in with all their paraphernalia. Tony directed them to Kevin, then told them to look outside for bodies. He came back to stand with Aaron, Gavin and Scott, ready to help smooth what could be very troubled waters.

Gavin stood up and he and Aaron looked at each other. Aaron made the first move, glad to have been wrong, but a bit worried about Gavin's possible reaction. After all, Gavin was by far the senior officer of the three of them. He had reason to be angry and insulted. Aaron offered his hand. "I was wrong, Gavin. I'm sorry."

But Gavin was not angry. Depressed and a little unnerved, yes, but actually impressed by the way Aaron had handled himself. "You were doing your job," he conceded, shaking Aaron's hand, "and you did it extremely well. You controlled the external interruption and kept Scott under your control." Gavin turned to Tony, "And he even managed not to insult me. Very impressive." Scott had walked over and Gavin shook his hand as well. "A little rough on you, fella, but I appreciated the vote of confidence."

*Thank goodness we made it through that,* Tony thought, trying to act as if they were behaving just as he would expect them to. This could have been very tense. Tony looked at Scott. "Brief me on Kevin's actions quickly, please."

Scott told him about Kevin's attempts to get him to leave, the bribe and the final threat. When it came to the shooting, Scott looked gratefully at the other two. "I was caught off guard like an idiot. I just wasn't expecting him to pull a gun on me. If you two had been a couple of seconds later, I wouldn't be here."

Tony was quiet. So close. Aaron might not have been here, and Gavin might not have made it in time. He would have lost both Scott and Mary. Frank had one hell of a lot of explaining to do. "You all did extremely well considering the circumstances. And, Scott," he added, "I really like it when my faith in someone is proven right."

Scott actually blushed. "That's what you employ me for," he mumbled.

Tony surveyed the scene. Security were removing Kevin. "Okay, I've got to see Mary, and then Gavin and I are out of here. I'll have some of these people stay behind and get this security system up and running. You two need a break, and I need written reports from you.

At Mary's door, he knocked and called her name. The door was unlocked and then he was inside with her. He closed the door. Mary looked shaken, and her bottom lip was trembling. With ease, he swept her off the ground into his arms and sat on the edge of the bed, with her on his lap. "It's over," he whispered, holding her close.

"I was so scared," she cried, her arms gripping his neck. "There was a dead person, and people outside, and then I thought Aaron, Scott and Gavin were going to kill each other. Tony, I don't understand!"

"It's all right now," he assured her. "There was a horrible mistake. Somebody made Gavin late, and Aaron was afraid that Gavin was helping the man who is dead now. Aaron was just making sure. He wouldn't risk anything happening to you."

"How do you ever know who to trust?" Mary's damp eyes stared into Tony's. "I needed you, Tony. I think you're the only person who has never tried to kill me."

He kissed her lightly, praying that she would never know differently. Then he smoothed the damp hair away from her sweaty brow. "Now, Mary, which of my men did you think would hurt you? Huh? Scott?"

"No." Mary shook her head. "I heard him say that he wouldn't let Kevin get me."

"Aaron?"

Mary smiled a tender smile. "No. Never."

"Gavin?"

"No." She rested her head against Tony's shoulder and shook it from side to side. "None of them," she admitted. "I was just so confused."

"I know, dear, but believe me, they were all protecting you. It was confusing for them, too, but you were quite safe once Kevin was taken care of."

Calmer now, Mary wiped her eyes. "Is Gavin angry with them?"

"They are professionals, Mary," Tony stated, "and beyond that they are friends. It was hard on them, but they are almost back to normal already." He kissed her again. "I have to go to the office and find out what caused this. Gavin will come with me, but Aaron and Scott are staying with you, plus some people from Security. Come out now, and you'll see that everything's okay."

She followed Tony out, glancing towards where Kevin had lain. Gavin was standing by the window, and she went up to him first. To Tony's consternation, Gavin put his arms around her and kissed her temple. "Your faith is touching," he was heard to whisper.

*Now even Gavin is holding her, for heaven's sake,* Tony muttered to himself. Then he watched Mary walk to Scott and go straight into his arms.

After holding her for a minute, Scott kissed her cheek, and then they stared into each other's eyes, as if unable to find words to express the fear they had felt for each other.

Aaron was sitting on the sofa. When Mary approached him, Aaron reached for her hand and pulled her down beside him. She curled up against him and he kept an arm loosely around her shoulders. Tony paused on his way out. *She goes to Aaron for protection,* he realised. *Dr. Hummel is right— there's nothing romantic or sexual between them. In fact, Aaron is staring off into space again. What went on in Cuba, Aaron? Why are you two so close, and why can you still not tell me about Nat? Damn.* Aaron would be taking the stand tomorrow in court, with his secrets intact. Not happy, Tony left with Gavin. This next meeting was going to be very unpleasant.

Mary also watched Aaron stare off into space. *I'll bet aiming your gun at Gavin made you think about Nathanial, didn't it, Aaron? Poor Aaron. You should tell Tony. It's not good to keep things like that inside you. Should I tell Tony?* she wondered. *I could, but it's not my secret to tell. Would it be a betrayal?* Safe under Aaron's arm, she decided against telling his secret. Maybe when court was all over she would tell Aaron that she knew his secret. Perhaps then she could help him tell Tony.

At Walsh's office, Gavin was asked to wait in the waiting room. Tony was told to come directly in. Exchanging a grim look with Gavin, Tony reluctantly entered the office. Carl Walsh was at his desk, writing, and Frank sat in a chair across from him. At Tony's entrance, they both looked up.

"Casualties, Tony?" Walsh demanded without preamble.

"Kevin Whalen was killed, sir," Tony reported. "Aaron and Gavin both shot him seconds before Kevin was able to get a shot off at Scott. Kevin had fired once, but missed." He could see both men relax, but he was very angry with Frank. "You almost got Scott killed, Frank."

"I know." Frank looked at him steadily. "I know," he repeated.

"There were two other men killed by Gavin," Tony continued. "Not ours."

"Okay, the FBI is going to give us a hand trying to trace these people, plus this 'Fred' character. We are all expecting the road to lead us back to Congressman Harvey." Walsh pointed at the adjoining room. "Gentlemen, you have things to discuss. That room is private, as you know. Please use it. I'll be here when you are ready."

That confused Tony, but Frank got up and led the way into the room. Tony followed and closed the door behind them. "What is this, Frank?" He chose a seat at the table, and Frank sat across from him. "Why am I in here? This has nothing to do with me."

Frank looked weary, but he seemed determined to face Tony and meet his eyes. "It has everything to do with you."

Tony sat back. It was hard to believe that his old friend had gotten himself into such a mess. "Why, Frank? What could possibly make you put my people at such risk? Why would you kill Mary? What hold could anyone have over you to make you do that? I won't believe you acted alone."

"No, of course not," Frank answered. "It has to do with Carolyn."

"Who?" Tony didn't know anyone called Carolyn, except his deceased wife.

"Carolyn—your wife."

"Huh?" He was totally lost. "What's my damned wife got to do with anything?"

Frank took a breath, then began. "I had an affair with your wife. Someone found out about it."

An affair with Carolyn? Perhaps that explained why she had been such a lousy lover to him. "For how long?"

"Seven years."

"Seven *years!*" Tony sat right up. "Shit, and I never caught on." Could he have really been that blind? "How often?" *Why am I even asking?* he wondered. *What does this have to do with anything?*

"Sporadically. As you know, she was a manic depressive. In her mania cycles she would seek me out if I was in town. It was rather irregular." Frank ran a hand through his hair. "I intended to tell you, but I never did. No excuses. I did try to talk you into leaving her."

Tony shook his head in disbelief. "Did you love her?"

"Hell no," Frank responded. "Sorry, but I didn't even like her. She was using you for a meal ticket. She didn't deserve you. However," he sighed, "when she was in that mania stage she was…insatiable in bed." He dropped his eyes, but then seemed to force them back up again. "Each time I kept telling myself it was the last time."

"I could hardly get her to have sex, for Christ's sake," Tony said, bewildered.

"She threw you the crumbs, Tony. You got the depressive side."

Tony shook himself. This still didn't make sense. "Frank, she has been dead for three years. Are you going to tell me that you almost wiped out people who are very important to me because of an affair with a woman who died three years ago?"

"No," Frank admitted. "There's more." When Tony sat silently, he continued. "I finally found the courage to tell you, but you were out of town at a conference. I told Carolyn that I had to tell you; that I couldn't take being two-faced any longer. She took a fit. I didn't care. I really didn't have any respect for her anyway. But two days later she hung herself, and left you that note of apology. She never mentioned my name. After that it just seemed cruel to tell you."

Tony put his head in his hands. So she killed herself because Frank had ended the relationship. Sad, but... "Frank, you knew we had no kind of marriage. Why, after all this time, would you let someone blackmail you with the threat of telling me this? I mean, it's upsetting, but my God, I lived a miserable existence back then. Her death was a relief to me, Frank." There, he'd said it. He had kept that feeling bottled up for three years; the guilt he felt because her death had freed him.

Frank seemed to struggle to continue. "She hung herself two days after I broke it off. They told me they would make it look like I had killed her. I would have been ruined, Tony. They would not even have to prove it. The story I just told you with a little new evidence thrown in, told to our Security office...you see the picture. Security would have found people who had seen us together."

Yes, Tony saw the picture. A cold, calculated plan by men who would do anything to keep one little witness from reaching the witness box. The story was conceivable. It could have been done, and Frank's career would have ended. "So why did you change your mind at the last minute and send Gavin to the house?"

"I thought Mary was a danger to us, and I thought Scott would jump at the ruse to get him out of the house. When I called Gavin over to my place, he told me that Mary was on our side, that you were in love with her, and that Scott was too responsible to leave his post. I never knew Aaron was there. I believed that Scott would skip out and be unharmed, and that Mary would be the only casualty. But then Gavin made me realise that I would be causing the death of the first woman you've been known to really love, and a young man who didn't deserve to die. Gavin also proceeded to tell me how nice it was to be home and work with people who are loyal to each other. I couldn't do it," he concluded weakly.

For a few minutes there was silence between them. It comforted Tony a little to know that Frank had believed Scott would have survived, however misguided that belief had been. If Frank had not changed his mind, Tony could never have forgiven him. He shivered at the thought of losing Mary. "So what happens now?" he asked.

But Frank did not answer directly. "Tony, do you believe that I didn't kill Carolyn?"

"Ah." Tony understood now. If he believed that Frank did not kill her, then no one could get at Frank that way again. If he didn't, Frank was susceptible, and probably finished at the CIA. He thought about it. What did he believe? This was all new to him. What did it matter? Carolyn was long dead. Losing his longtime friend would leave a much larger void in Tony's emotional life than Carolyn had left. "Frank, I don't know, and it doesn't matter. I've lost Nat. I can't lose you too." He voice had trailed off. His head was hurting again.

"That's not good enough!" Frank suddenly yelled. "I don't want you to save my damned *career*!" He leaned towards Tony and spoke intensely. "I need the truth from you, personally. Do you think I killed your wife?" The lines on Frank's face were accentuated by fatigue and perspiration. The room was cool, but both men were sweating from the high emotional climate.

Jesus. What did he think? It had been thrown at Tony without warning. "Would you have told me about her if she hadn't died?" he countered. "Would you have followed that through?"

Frank sat back and frowned. It struck Tony as ironic that Frank was trying so hard to be honest. They always had been brutally honest with each other. Frank had almost had Mary killed, but he wouldn't even try to save himself now, Tony realised. *He has made a very big mistake, and he knows it, but he won't try to evade the consequences. He'll risk it all to give me the truth, and it would be so easy for him to lie.*

"Yes," Frank said finally. "I was quite ready. I was prepared to carry it out and endure your wrath. There was no doubt in my mind at the time."

*What would have happened?* Tony wondered. They would have argued, maybe even fought. Tony would have left Carolyn and paid huge alimony forever, but he would have been relieved. He would have forgiven Frank eventually, and Frank would have known that would happen. Frank would have stayed close by and waited for Tony's anger to cool, and then would have worked his way back to Tony's side. They had been friends for too long to divide over a woman Tony didn't love. Frank would not have killed her to keep her silent. He would have braved it out, because that was the type of man he was.

Tony looked him in the eyes. "You did not kill Carolyn. I believe that utterly and completely."

Frank almost broke down. "Thank you," he whispered.

Tony allowed him a moment to compose himself. Then he got up and went around to sit on the chair next to Frank, turning it so he was facing the man. Frank's arms were folded, and he was supporting himself by leaning forward with his elbows on the table. Tony waited until Frank turned his head to look at him. "Over with and done?" Tony asked quietly.

"Over with and done," Frank promised. They shook hands.

"Do I go and talk to Carl now?" Tony asked.

Frank nodded. "I still have one more hurdle," he stated, standing up.

"Gavin?" Tony guessed, following Frank towards the door.

Frank nodded again. "He's my most senior officer. The men have almost all worked with him at one time or another. They look to him to know who to trust. They take their orders from me, of course, but Gavin seems to be their mentor. What he believes, they believe. That's why it has always been so crucial for me to make sure Gavin is clear about what we want and why."

"And if he has lost faith now?" Tony asked.

"I'll be removed from Special Operations. The head of this unit cannot lose the trust of its members. Control is critical. If Gavin refused to work with me, I'd lose all credibility with the others. Walsh may still recommend that I continue employment, but I might be counting paperclips."

Back in Walsh's office, they sat in front of the desk. Walsh asked Tony if he wanted Frank to step out of the room. Tony said no. Walsh asked a number of questions and recorded the answers. In the end he seemed content. "Are you ready for Gavin now, Frank?"

"Yes, sir. I should warn you about Gavin, though. If he's given up on me, he'll probably be quiet and withdrawn. He'll show little emotion, and won't want to stay long. However, if I still have a chance with him, he'll be very angry, and he will not take this quietly. The fact that we are in your office will make little impression on him."

Mr. Walsh looked concerned. "He already put a dint in my wall with that pop can the other day. Should I have some Security in here? I don't expect to end up with damaged furniture."

"No, sir." Frank actually smiled slightly. "Any damage will be directed at me. Don't interfere, he won't go too far. It will sound strange to you, but I actually hope he loses his composure. That will mean he cares enough to be angry. For him to be quiet will do me far worse personal damage."

Gavin was asked to enter. Frank stood up on his arrival and walked a little distance from Walsh's desk. Gavin glared at him and stood still, looking towards Mr. Walsh as if for direction. Tony sat back and mentally crossed his fingers.

"Mr. Moseley owes you an explanation, Mr. Weeks," Walsh stated. "He placed you in an untenable situation."

Gavin's attention turned to Frank. "Untenable? You almost killed Scott, you fuck!"

*Angry!* Tony actually rejoiced at the sight of Gavin's aggressive posture and clenched fists.

"I know," Frank admitted, taking a step back.

Gavin followed and pointed a finger at Frank's chest. "You tell me this wasn't about money, because if it was…" He left the sentence unfinished.

"It wasn't money," Frank replied.

Gavin cast a look at Tony and Mr. Walsh. "Do they know?"

"Yes."

"EVERYTHING?" Gavin demanded.

"Yes." Now Frank stood his ground, seeming to mentally brace himself. "It was about Tony's wife."

"What?" Gavin sounded as confused as Tony had been.

"I carried on an affair with Carolyn for seven years." Although it was the third time he had told the story, Frank didn't seem to try to dismiss it. "When I finally decided to tell Tony, I broke off with her and told her of my intentions. She couldn't face a future on her own, I guess, because she hung herself two days later. Tony had been away. He came back and found her. After that I didn't see the point of hurting him further."

For a moment Gavin glanced over at Tony. Tony could tell that it didn't make sense to Gavin yet either. Then Gavin turned back to Frank. His tone was icy. "You caused this to happen over a woman who's been dead for three years? Are you fuckin' *insane*?"

"They threatened to tell Security that I killed her to keep her from revealing the affair to Tony. All they would need was a little fabricated evidence, a couple of so-called witnesses, and the truth about how long the affair had been going on. Somebody knew about that. Security would have bought it, or at least had serious doubts."

It took Gavin a minute to analyze it and review the implications. Unexpectedly, he turned to Tony. "Do you believe him?" He looked back at Frank. "I mean, it's plausible, isn't it? Does he believe you didn't kill her, Frank?"

"He wouldn't have killed her, Gavin," Tony responded. "She wasn't worth the risk to him. I believe he intended to tell me about the affair himself, and that's what set her off."

Gavin squared off with Frank again. He was still visibly agitated, and his voice began to rise. "You caused all this because you couldn't keep your cock in your pants. No—you had to sleep with your best friend's wife." Without warning, Gavin took a half step back, yelled "you stupid *fucking asshole!*" and drove his right fist deep into Frank's gut. The force of the blow could be felt across the room, and Frank almost went down, just managing to stay on his feet, doubled over.

Mr. Walsh started to rise, but Tony shook his head. That blow had to hurt a lot, but Tony would only interfere if it happened again. Frank was gasping for air.

"That," Gavin announced, "was for Scott and Mary. Tony can take care of you himself." He grabbed Frank's jacket lapel and dragged him into an upright position. "Damn you, Frank. I trusted you. I *depend* on you. Why didn't you come to us with this? Tony and I would have helped you."

Frank was not able to speak quite yet, but his breathing was starting to settle down. Gavin stared at him while he recovered. "You tell me," he demanded in a threatening tone, "that there is nothing else. Tell me Walsh knows it all, and there's no other way anyone can reach you again."

Now Frank was able to speak. "There is nothing else…on my word." With Gavin's fist still clenching his lapel, Frank drew himself up straighter. "So don't you *dare* ever hit me like that again."

It was subtle, Tony knew, listening and watching the dynamics. For several minutes Gavin had taken control. Frank had allowed it because Frank was in the wrong and knew it. Had he fought Gavin for control earlier in the confrontation, Gavin would have denied Frank's attempts. It would have been a tactical error on Frank's part. Now Frank had admitted his responsibility and accepted Gavin's anger. It was time to regain control and reassert the chain of command.

Authority is a fragile concept, Tony knew. A man can be put in a position of authority over other people. The man is perceived to have authority by those under him, yet if the people under him decide he does not deserve the authority, then the authority becomes only a word. The respect he is given will be minimal. At the worst, his people will refuse to follow his orders. By his last words, Frank was demanding that Gavin acknowledge his control and authority. It was crucial to Frank's ability to lead. If Frank could not get Gavin to acknowledge that authority, then either Frank or Gavin would have to leave their current positions in Special Operations. Tony knew that Mr. Walsh would remove Frank, because to remove Gavin would create too many questions, and if the reason ever got out, Frank would lose everyone's respect anyway.

As Tony watched, Gavin slowly released his grip and smoothed out Frank's lapel. The seconds ticked by. "Yes, sir," he said finally, and backed a step away. His anger had been dispelled, and Gavin stood quietly while Frank readjusted his suit jacket.

*You've won, Frank,* Tony thought. The tension in the room had decreased dramatically. Frank looked at Mr. Walsh. "Would you like me to leave while you speak to Gavin?" he offered.

Mr. Walsh passed the question on to Gavin. "Mr. Weeks, I have to ask you some questions regarding your working relationship with Frank. Would you prefer to answer these in private?"

"Not necessary, sir," Gavin responded.

The questions, as expected, could have been summarised by simply asking, *"Can you still work with Frank Moseley?"* Gavin answered in the affirmative, and Walsh was satisfied.

"I believe that you gentlemen may have some personal fences to mend, so why don't we end here. Frank, you will stay in your present position, but this was your one and only chance. There will be no more errors on your part. If you encounter something like this again—you tell me first. If we had suffered any casualties other than Kevin Whalen and the two unknowns, my decision would be vastly different. You changed your mind at the last minute, thank goodness, but it was almost too late. Do you understand?"

"Of course, sir."

"Tony, use your judgement, but I would prefer that you give Aaron and Scott a basic sketch only. They'll be waiting for an explanation, of course, but we don't want this spread around, so make sure they understand that. And Mrs. Norland is not to know. It would serve no purpose."

"Yes, sir."

"Good night, gentlemen."

Before they had reached the door to leave the office, Mr. Walsh was on the phone trying to reach someone at the FBI. Gavin opened the door and motioned the others through. Before proceeding, Frank turned to face him. A lot of the communication between the two men was carried on without speech. They had worked closely together for a long time. After a few seconds of not speaking, Gavin offered his hand, and they shook. *Over with and done, Frank,* Tony thought. *You have been very lucky tonight.*

Frank invited them back to his place for a drink. He and Gavin were going to try to figure out who had known about Frank and Carolyn. Tony declined.

It was almost midnight now, and tomorrow Aaron took the stand. Tony needed sleep so he would be sharp tomorrow. Aaron needed his support.

As Tony entered his apartment, he took a couple of aspirin and looked into the bedroom. After last night with Mary, this bed looked empty and cold. She would have caused his headache to go away while she kept him warm. Her softness as she curled in his arms and slept would have comforted him. Soon, perhaps, he would ask to claim her as his own. This case would be over, and she would be safe to leave. Only then would he ask her to stay. Would she give up her life to become part of his? He would be asking her to do something he couldn't do himself. Would she? There was so much they did not know about each other yet. Two middle-aged people carried so many obligations, so much baggage. Did she love him enough to try?

It had been an extremely tiring week, giving evidence at the trial, and tonight had been an emotional roller coaster. He had to get some sleep. With effort, he pushed thoughts of Mary from his mind and tried to count sheep.

# XL

Alfredo listened to his lawyer interpret for Richard Harvey's lawyer. So Cook wanted to go through everything again. Hadn't they covered everything at least three times already? Oh well, it was a break from being in his cell, so Alfredo was content to sit with his lawyer and pass the time. It gave him a chance to talk with Osvaldo and Jose Luis, who were sitting beside him for the same purpose. They had decided to share the same lawyer, as they were being charged jointly. The room was private, although they knew they were being observed closely.

"Let's go over the assaults again," Cook began, counting them off on his fingers. "Thursday afternoon was rape number one. Thursday evening was number two, with the oral sex. Rape number three was Friday morning, against the tree. That afternoon was assault number four, when he urinated on her. Saturday morning was rape number six…" Cook broke off. He didn't mind defending the Congressman, but he was very glad he wasn't the lawyer for these three. Breaking laws and having people killed didn't bother him, but he had seen the pictures of that Cuban girl and the CIA officer. These three men were animals. His only interest in this disgusting mess was to ruin St. Pierre's credibility and damage the CIA sufficiently to allow Harvey to walk away blameless. If it wasn't for that, he wouldn't sit in the same room as this lot.

Osvaldo had not been involved in the assaults on the women, but had undoubtedly been Mr. Bowman's torturer. Cook had not questioned him extensively about the rapes for the simple reason that Osvaldo had not seen them all. This time, he had asked Osvaldo and Jose Luis to join in just to be thorough. In case there was some little detail he had missed.

Holding up his hand, with fingers spread, Cook emphasised what he was saying. "Five times. Five rapes and assaults."

With a frown on his face, Osvaldo turned to his lawyer. There was a barrage of Spanish, with both men counting on their fingers. After a pause, Osvaldo looked at Cook, back to his lawyer, and started talking again. A look

285

of surprise crossed the lawyer's face, and when Osvaldo stopped talking, he asked him a couple of questions, then turned to Cook.

"My client says you have missed one. On the last night, the Saturday night, my client had to go outside. He observed the man they knew as Taz having sex with the woman." He turned back to Osvaldo to double-check the story. "Yes," he continued, "that makes six times if you add it to your five. There were six assaults."

Cook could hardly believe his luck. St. Pierre had admitted to five. Why he had not admitted to the last one was anyone's guess. Perhaps he had forgotten, but it didn't matter. The prosecutor would not be expecting this. It was a piece of information that would be used by Cook to help rattle St. Pierre. One little fact that Cook could use to damage his credibility. It might be important—it might not. But it would help. Everything and anything available would be useful.

They went through the rest of the information. Osvaldo swore that he had not injured Mr. Bowman enough for him to die. Osvaldo had been puzzled by the death, but had concluded that perhaps the CIA man had a bad heart. There had been no marks on the body that explained the death. Osvaldo had checked. The woman tied beside Bowman had raised no alarm. Although puzzled, Osvaldo had accepted the death matter-of-factly.

Cook filed that thought away for future consideration, and turned to another topic. "When their rescue arrived, you said everything was confusing and people were yelling. Where was Taz during this?"

When translated, this made Osvaldo laugh. "He came after me with a knife while two other men were walking me towards the trees where they were tying up their prisoners. I am alive because one of his own people tackled him."

*A pity,* thought Cook privately, *but that's none of my business.* "Would you say St. Pierre was out of control, then?" Cook prompted.

"Completely," Alfredo chimed in. "When they walked me past the cabin door, he was yelling at his own people who were standing around."

"Could you understand any of it?" Cook asked. "Your lawyer tells me that you speak some English."

"Yes, some," admitted Alfredo proudly. Then he concentrated. "He seemed to be pleading with them, and he was very upset. I heard him say, 'No, not Gavin. Don't send Gavin, she doesn't deserve that.'"

"She?" Cook was puzzled. "Who was he referring to? Gavin is a strange name for a woman."

"Oh." Alfredo looked confused. "I didn't understand then, but now that we know he didn't kill the woman tourist like he said he did, I thought that he might be talking about her. But I don't know who Gavin is."

On his drive home after the interviews, Cook thought about the death of Bowman. The autopsy had shown no obvious sign of death, although the body had clearly suffered trauma. Bowman had not had a bad heart, and in fact he was found to be generally in good condition. It had been accepted that a combination of shock and trauma had been too much for the man. Now Cook wondered. Would St. Pierre have allowed his buddy to be interrogated another day? St. Pierre's cover, and therefore his life, were at risk. Surely St. Pierre had been trained on the body's pressure points and would know how to kill without leaving a sign. Could he kill his fellow officer if his own life was threatened? Possibly. Very possibly.

There was one other titbit of information Cook possessed. Before the botched attack on the safe house, Kevin Whalen had pumped Scott Andrews for information. It had not been rewarding, but one peculiar fact had emerged. Mary had seemed to know St. Pierre's first name before being told. It was odd, since St. Pierre was trying to protect his cover. Why would he suddenly tell her his name? She had not known anything else about him. Cook sighed. Was it too farfetched to think she might have witnessed Bowman's murder? Would Bowman and St. Pierre have talked first?

Speeding up, Cook headed for his office. He needed to talk to Finch again. Finch would understand what it was like to be without supervision in a hostile environment in a critical situation. Cook could guess at St. Pierre's actions, but he couldn't imagine himself at the scene. Finch could help him. Then Cook would know if he was on the right track.

# XLI

From the witness box the next morning, Aaron surveyed the courtroom. Tony had told him where Susan was sitting to prevent him from wasting valuable energy looking for her and wondering if she had come. She had taken a seat at the back, near the aisle, as if she wanted an escape route. At least she was here. He hadn't seen her since that night at the lounge, and his heart took a leap at the sight of her now. It wasn't over yet, then. There was still a chance, even if slight.

There was no time now to think about his personal life. Mr. Hedley rose and started the questioning. It was Friday morning, and Aaron had no idea how long his turn on the stand would last.

The questions began with what Aaron's role had been in Cuba, identifying the accused, explaining his drawings and the financial transactions that he and Nat had completed. Mr. Hedley's questioning was extensive, interrupted occasionally by the defence, and it took the entire day to set the scene, explain the Liberators' involvement in importing drugs and weapons to the United States, and explain the blackmail schemes.

Events of the previous night had tired Aaron, and by 4:00 p.m. he was exhausted. From the time court had started that morning, he had been in the witness box. Only at lunch did he get a chance to relax. The CIA had three rows of representatives at the front of the courtroom, but Aaron scarcely noticed them. Mr. Hedley had led him step by step through the day, and Tony had been at his side during lunch and court breaks. From the relieved looks on the faces of the CIA personnel, Aaron knew he had performed well. Most of his evidence today, however, had been impersonal. Hedley had only touched on Nat's death. Monday would be the day that Nat's torture and the rapes would be discussed. The stage had been set, and the defence had made surprisingly few objections. Monday would be the nightmare.

Before leaving the witness box when court was adjourned for the day, he looked towards Susan. She was watching him. He tried to smile, but felt self-conscious in front of the large audience. It earned him an equally strained smile back. *Let her be, and don't push her,* he told himself. *Let her sit through Monday. She needs to hear the worst and decide if she can live with what you've done. You told her that you love her. Now it's her turn to decide if she still loves you.* With effort, he turned away and left with Tony.

# XLII

When Cook finally received a call from Finch, he could tell that Finch was not in a good mood.

"This is twice in as many weeks. Do you think I'm staying at a Holiday Inn with a private telephone?" Finch demanded.

"You'll be compensated appropriately," Cook promised. It had cost a lot in terms of paying contacts just to find Finch again this fast, but Cook was ready to grasp at any available straw. St. Pierre had been good on the stand yesterday. Could they have missed something that was useable?

In detail, Cook reviewed the testimony to date with Finch as it related to St. Pierre. They needed more leverage, he told Finch. St. Pierre had sounded too credible, and if the witness backed him up, the jury seemed ready to give him a standing ovation.

The needed break came when Cook mentioned Bowman dying.

"Whoa...hold on there," Finch interrupted. "Bowman and St. Pierre had worked closely together for a couple of years, I believe."

"Yes."

"And your client's friend worked Bowman over so he couldn't walk under his own power?"

"Well...yes. But my client knew nothing about that."

"So St. Pierre couldn't escape with Bowman, and Bowman was facing more torture the next day."

"Correct," Cook agreed.

"Was the cause of death proven?" Finch asked.

"Not conclusively. The other lawyer is hoping to use that to get his man off," Cook responded. "There was internal bleeding, but he could easily have lived. It sounds like the doctors were a little surprised that he died. The individual who, um, did the damage, is very surprised."

A pause. "I think you just found your solution, Mr. Cook. Did you know that St. Pierre's nickname is 'puppy dog'? He's a softy. He could never have let Bowman suffer once he found out he couldn't rescue him. Think about it.

I'll bet you anything that Bowman died by St. Pierre's hand. If so," Finch continued, "you've got a guilt-ridden young man in your grasp. And he probably didn't dare tell his boss, because Bowman and Dune were best friends."

*Jesus. I was right,* Cook realised. This was getting very exciting. "That means that the prosecution has no prepared story that St. Pierre can fall back on," Cook stated. "He's up in that stand all alone, and once his counsel hears the big secret, they'll drop him like a hot potato. Mr. Finch," he concluded, "you have been a great help."

"Wait," Finch ordered. "One more thing. Has it never occurred to you guys that this female witness you can't seem to kill is a real liability to the CIA? Why don't you use her?"

Cook sighed. "We'll try, that's for sure. Our problem is that she seems to be on their side. Our source at their headquarters had told us that it's all 'buddy-buddy' between Mrs. Norland and the CIA. Somehow they've won her over."

"Well, that may be true now," Finch snorted, "but I bet that wasn't what was going through Frank Moseley's mind in Cuba. Once St. Pierre told Moseley and Dune what he had done to her, I'll bet their first thought was to make her disappear permanently."

Alfredo's phrase jumped back into Cook's memory. "Is that something that Moseley or Dune would do themselves?"

"Hell no," Finch replied. "Not if they could help it. They would send the best man they could find. They wouldn't dare leave a trace. She was a political disaster for them." Suddenly Finch laughed. "Christ, Cook, they had their best man right there with them."

Crossing his fingers and hoping the answer matched his thoughts, Cook asked almost fearfully, "And who would that be, Mr. Finch?"

A slight pause ensued. "Why, Gavin Weeks, of course. He was with Moseley in Cuba, leading the rescue."

*Bingo. "No, not Gavin. Don't send Gavin. She doesn't deserve that,"* had been the cry of St. Pierre to his superiors. Finch was right. The CIA had planned to kill the witness to protect themselves. St. Pierre, whom Finch had called "puppy dog", had been begging them not to do it. This was it. This was the piece that could be used to rattle the witness and destroy any intention she had to help the CIA. She had no clue that they had planned to kill her. Perhaps only the intervention of Mr. Pitt had saved her. Once she had been seen in their presence, the CIA could hardly risk having her disappear mysteriously. The case was won before it had barely started.

"Mr. Finch, you can name your price," Cook informed. "I think Congressman Harvey is going to be grateful. Very grateful."

When Finch hung up the phone, he heard a noise behind him. With a sinking feeling, he turned to see that Hammond had been standing in the room. The other team members were now in the doorway. Hammond did not look amused as he kept his weapon aimed at Finch.

"Finch, my man," Hammond said in a tense, hostile voice. "We thought you were on our side. Moseley tells me that you got him and Gavin into a lot of hot water, and it sounds like you're causing trouble again. I don't know how long this has been going on, but it's about time that you went home to face the music."

# XLIII

On Sunday after lunch, 51 Elm had an unexpected visitor. Gavin arrived with Frank Moseley in tow. Mary had been sitting on the arm of Tony's favourite stuffed armchair, leaning against his shoulder as they worked on a crossword puzzle. Hearing Scott announce a visitor whom she didn't recognise, Mary tried to slip off the chair before he entered the door and saw her sitting so close to Tony. Tony's hand on her arm told Mary she could stay put.

"Hello, Frank," Tony greeted his friend, surprised to see him here. "Drop by for a visit?" For Frank to come visiting was highly unlikely. He had no reason to do so, and he risked confronting Scott for the first time since Thursday night in front of other people. Scott and Aaron had figured out on their own who was responsible for making Gavin late last week, and although he had said little about it to Tony, Scott surely would have no fond feelings for Frank Moseley.

Frank surveyed the room. He saw Mary and Tony cosily sharing the same chair, and Sheila on the sofa reading a book. Aaron was also on the sofa, with his feet on the coffee table, watching him. Scott was seated in front of the computers, eating an apple, with his feet up on the desk. In all, the scene looked like an advertisement for family living.

"This is work?" Frank asked Gavin.

"It's pretty quiet here most of the time," Scott stated pointedly, "with only the occasional adrenaline rush."

Tony noticed that Frank flinched slightly. *Well, Frank,* Tony thought, *what did you expect?* Tony considered how to handle this. Scott was well within his rights to be angry, but on the other hand, Frank had been allowed to continue in his position. That meant that Scott still had to acknowledge Frank's authority, regardless of whether he had any respect for Frank. Tony hoped the two men could repair the damage eventually, but that was not something that would happen quickly. He decided that he would step in only if Scott got noticeably out of line. *Let's see how Frank handles this,* he thought, *and how Scott responds.*

Before anything further could be said, Mary seemed to jump, and suddenly spoke up. "This is Frank?" she asked, puzzling Tony. "The Frank that Nathanial knew?"

*For heaven's sake.* "Yes," Tony answered. "Another message?" he asked. When she nodded, Tony looked at Frank, who had turned all his attention to Mary. "Prepare yourself, Frank." He patted Mary's arm. "Why don't you take Frank into the kitchen and tell him?"

She did so, and they stayed in the kitchen for almost half an hour. Scott seemed edgy, and kept looking at Aaron, who shook his head and finally told him to relax. When Frank emerged with Mary, looking like he had endured a shock, he caught Tony's eye, and Tony could see the emotions behind his friend's carefully controlled face. *If she had died, you never would have heard that,* Tony said silently, *and you know it. You probably feel like crap right now.* Tony got up and walked to him. "You don't have to do this, Frank," he said quietly so no one but Gavin could hear him.

Frank shrugged and nodded his head at Gavin. "He thinks it's time I got to know these people." Frank glanced towards Scott. "And I owe someone an apology."

"No guarantees on the reception," Tony warned his friend.

"I know."

As Frank walked over towards Scott, Aaron tapped Sheila's shoulder and indicated that she should follow him. On the way past the armchair, Aaron reached for Mary's hand. Mary was puzzled, but followed without comment. *Aaron the leader,* thought Tony. *They do what he says, and save their questions for later.* The dynamics of the entire team had been changing as Aaron gained experience. He was a natural leader, and before the team was separated, even the more experienced men had already started treating him as an equal. In a very few years, Aaron would be close to Tony's heels on the promotional ladder, and Tony expected Aaron to pass him at some point. If he could only help Aaron survive this crisis, that is.

Scott had removed his feet from the desk and was watching Frank without expression. In truth, he didn't know what to make of this approach. This man had almost gotten him killed, but he was a close friend of Tony and Gavin, two men for whom Scott was developing a deep respect. Moseley was also equivalent in position to Tony, with a lot more experience in the position, which meant that Scott didn't dare start a fight with him, although he sure felt like it. All he could do was wait and hear what this Moseley fellow was going to say. He could always refuse to talk to Moseley or have anything to do with him that wasn't directly work related.

Frank stopped beside Scott's desk and accepted the younger man's challenging stare. "I put you in a position of unacceptable risk the other day," Frank began. "That happened because I seriously underestimated your commitment. While I did not know who was to be sent here after Mary, I was assured that you would jump at an offer to be relieved of your shift. I thought that you were unprofessional enough to leave an assigned job. I was wrong."

He took a breath. Scott was still watching him warily, saying nothing. "Gavin couldn't believe that I had forgotten you from Cuba. I can hardly believe it myself." That was true, and Frank felt like a fool having to admit it. "The only explanation I have for that is that I just wasn't thinking clearly. I was in shock to find myself in such a vulnerable situation, and I couldn't seem to think past my own personal crisis. If I had gone to Gavin or Tony, they could have snapped me out of it, but I didn't."

The challenge had gone out of Scott's eyes, and Frank saw those eyes flicker towards Tony. *He doesn't quite know what to do about this,* Frank realised. *After I leave, he will talk to Tony, so it's best that I apologise and get out.*

"I'm sorry," Frank offered. "That sounds terribly insignificant for almost killing you, but I really am sorry that I ever put you in that position. And I'm sorry that I didn't appreciate your dedication to your job."

Scott shrugged, and finally spoke. "Well, I guess I'm the only one responsible for that reputation," he admitted. He didn't feel like fighting this Moseley guy any more. The man had screwed up in a big way, and he was admitting it. It took balls to come here and do that. Scott made a decision. He didn't have to like this man, but if the other guys felt highly enough about Moseley to give him a second chance, then the least Scott could do was to accept an apology. The same apology should be made to Mary, but Tony had told him that Walsh specifically ordered them never to let Mary find out about what had gone on. It would do no good, and could do a lot of harm. Giving in, Scott stood up and offered his hand. "Okay," was all he said.

*"Okay" is a good start,* Frank decided in relief as he shook the younger man's hand. Gaining everyone's respect back was not going to happen overnight, even among his friends. Perhaps *especially* among his friends. Leaving Scott in Tony's capable hands, Frank left with Gavin.

For the rest of the afternoon, after Frank had left, Scott kept his distance from Tony. Tony, he decided, was pleased with him. He had that look on his face. Scott was in danger of being hugged, and he *hated* being hugged. It was too embarrassing for words.

# XLIV

Paul Hedley had been busy all weekend, and it seemed that there weren't many people he had not talked to. Carl Walsh was under a great deal of pressure from the Deputy Director of Central Intelligence, who was as nervous about this case as his boss, the Director. Walsh and Hedley had talked and met frequently over the past two days. Public affairs had been hovering nearby, and had checked in too often. They probably anticipated another disaster. Three attempted murders, one of them being by their own staff member, was a little too much for their collective ulcers. Walsh's colleagues, who headed the other Directorates of the agency, would also pop in occasionally to see how things were going.

Actually, the weekend had flown by, as Paul had practised his approach, reviewed his notes, tried to anticipate the defence, and prepare for the unexpected. This morning he was primed for the fight, but he had to admit to a certain nervousness. Today was important. It was credibility day. There was no question that the defence would attack, so Paul had to try to take the wind out of their sails first. All the sordid details had to be exposed, but they would be supported by explanations and defences of their own. He had to guide Aaron along the delicate path of maintaining public support in the face of actions that the public abhorred.

The courtroom was packed and the press smelled blood. Aaron was sitting in the witness box looking like the ideal public servant. Hopefully he would still look like that when this case was over.

"Now, Mr. St. Pierre," Hedley began. "On Friday you identified the accused and gave a full account of their actions as they related to many of the charges brought before the court. I now want to explore your own actions and the actions of others as they relate to the death of Nathanial Bowman, Juany Martínez and the kidnapping and rape of Mary Norland." Hedley paused. "For review, Mr. St. Pierre, who did the accused believe you to be?"

"I was known to them as a drug trafficker named Taz," Aaron responded.

"And did they believe you to be anything else besides a drug trafficker?"

Aaron nodded. "Yes. I had a record for rape and murder."

Paul Hedley glanced at his notes. "And did they know that in advance?"

"Yes." Aaron sat straight, with his hands resting on the front of the witness stand. Tony was sitting in the front row again, directly in front of him. If Aaron got nervous or confused, he was to look at Tony for moral support. It should not be necessary while Hedley was questioning, but could be needed later.

"Did you do or say anything to reinforce that image?"

"Yes. That was my cover, and therefore my protection."

"Who did you discuss this with and why?" Hedley asked.

"The defendant, Mr. Pérez," Aaron responded. "He initiated the conversations on the first few days."

Hedley looked up. "Why do you think he would do that?"

"I believed at the time that he was testing me, to find out if I was really Taz."

"And did he seem satisfied?"

"Yes," Aaron replied. "He did."

Hedley checked his notes again, and then moved away from the desk. "Tell the court about the conversation you had with Mr. Pérez on Wednesday night."

"Mr. Pérez invited me to go into a village with him the next day," Aaron stated. " He and Mr. Rodríguez were taking the group leader, Mr. Sánchez, in to conduct some business. Mr. Pérez told me that he knew of a house where some girls would 'make us happy', as he put it."

"And you interpreted that to mean what, Mr. St. Pierre?"

"That he wanted to visit a prostitute," Aaron responded.

"What was your response?" Hedley asked.

"I told him that I did not want to go," Aaron answered, knowing that Hedley would take this further. "I made up a story to get out of it."

"Why?"

"Because he expected me to want to go," Aaron stated. "To simply say no would have put me under suspicion, because it would have been out of character for Taz. Taz did not have high moral standards."

Hedley looked directly at him. "Did you at any time suggest in any way that they should bring a woman back to the camp for you?"

"Absolutely not," Aaron replied. "I told Mr. Pérez that I would not visit the women with him because I only used prostitutes when I was desperate, and that I was not desperate."

"Tell the court about the story you made up for Mr. Pérez," Hedley ordered.

This was where it started to get embarrassing. Aaron looked at Tony, mainly to prevent himself from accidently looking at Susan and getting flustered. "I told Mr. Pérez that I preferred to stalk middle-aged housewives and keep them captive. I said that I liked to keep the women to myself, and terrorise and rape them. That is what the real Taz was known to do. He was also known to kill women at the end of their captivity, so I told Mr. Pérez that I liked to do that, as well."

"Mr. St. Pierre," Paul Hedley said slowly, "did it ever occur to you that Mr. Pérez and Mr. Rodríguez would kidnap a middle-aged woman as a result of this story?"

"No," Aaron insisted. "I did not expect to see them back until Sunday. Mr. Pérez never suggested or intimated that he was going to kidnap anyone."

*So far, so good,* thought Hedley, *but this is only the beginning. Now we get into what actually happened.* "Did anything unexpected happen during the following day?"

"Yes. Mr. Pérez and Mr. Rodríguez returned with two women bound and gagged: Miss Martínez and Mrs. Norland."

"Did they tell you of their intentions towards these women?" Hedley inquired.

Aaron swallowed. His hands were getting clammy, so he crossed them in front of his body. "Yes. Mrs. Norland was a present for me to enjoy on my vacation. Miss Martínez was for everyone else who wanted her."

Hedley stood still and looked at the crowd in the courtroom. "What did they mean by that, Mr. St. Pierre?"

"They expected me, as Taz, to want to rape Mrs. Norland. She appeared to fit the description of a middle-aged housewife." Aaron kept his eyes on Tony.

Hedley turned to face him. "Did you say no?"

"No," Aaron responded. "I couldn't."

"Why not?"

Aaron felt a catch in his throat. He coughed, then continued. "Because Mr. Rodríguez had recognised Mr. Bowman. They had met on a previous assignment, but neither of them could place the other at first. Mr. Rodríguez drew a gun on Mr. Bowman and identified him as an officer with the CIA. I realised then that the reason I was being presented with Mrs. Norland was because Mr. Rodríguez did not trust me. He had suspicions about my role. I had to keep him believing that I was Taz, so I could rescue Mr. Bowman and hopefully we could escape and free the women at the same time."

"Were you armed?" Mr. St. Pierre.

"No," Aaron answered. "I only carried a knife because that is all the real Taz carried. All the Cubans had guns of various types, so I couldn't free Mr. Bowman with them all standing around."

"Tell the court what you did next, Mr. St. Pierre." Hedley looked at Aaron, who stared back at him.

"I raped Mrs. Norland," Aaron stated quietly. He could hear the courtroom gasp.

"You admit that?" Hedley asked.

"Yes."

"Couldn't you have simply walked away?" Hedley asked.

"No," Aaron replied. "I would have been taken prisoner with Mr. Bowman. We would both have died, and Mrs. Norland would have suffered the same fate that Miss Martínez did."

"What happened to Miss Martínez?" Hedley had moved a step or two towards the centre of the courtroom.

Aaron drew a breath. "She was raped by ten of the Cubans, including Mr. Pérez, repeatedly, kicked, knifed and beaten until she was almost dead from her injuries. Mr. Pérez killed her in front of myself and Mrs. Norland with a knife on Saturday."

Hedley was quiet for a minute. "Now tell the court where Mrs. Norland is."

"She's in the courthouse, sir," replied Aaron.

"And what is she doing here?" Hedley asked.

"She is a witness for the CIA," Aaron answered.

"For the CIA," Hedley echoed. "She is speaking on your behalf, even though you raped her."

"Yes, sir."

"What condition was she in when she left Cuba, Mr. St. Pierre?"

Aaron stared at Tony again. "She had cuts, bruises, and she was very traumatised, sir."

"Did you at any time cut her with a knife?"

"No, sir."

"Beat her?"

"I slapped her, sir."

"Kick her?"

"No, sir."

"Mr. St. Pierre, how many times did you rape Mrs. Norland?"

Aaron swallowed again. "I raped her three times and assaulted her twice." He had been told to anticipate some disorder in the courtroom, and he wasn't disappointed. It was humiliating, but he knew he had to accept it. The judge brought the court to order.

Hedley started up again. "Now, Mr. St. Pierre, we are going to go through this step by step, but first could you explain why you had to keep assaulting Mrs. Norland?"

"I was expected to put on a show for the defendants," Aaron stated. "If I had appeared to grow bored with Mrs. Norland, not only might they get suspicious, but they would have taken her for themselves. I was doing everything I could to make the attacks look violent, yet cause Mrs. Norland as little pain as possible. I didn't want her to suffer the same fate as Miss Martínez."

"Did all the accused rape Miss Martínez?" Hedley asked.

"No." Aaron had been prepared for this question. Hedley, with Walsh's approval, had arranged a plea bargain with Lino. In return for identifying Osvaldo as Nat's torturer, and implicating the three Cubans in the blackmail scheme, Lino would receive a minimal sentence. Lino had not helped anyone escape, but he had not hurt anyone, either. Walsh had even suggested that if Lino would agree to act as an agent for them, he would be able to return to Cuba. That, however, would be discussed later. "Lino Viltrez took no part in the rapes, nor did Mr. Rodríguez or Mr. Sánchez. Mr. Rodríguez, however, was the one who tortured Mr. Bowman."

"What time did you first assault Mrs. Norland?" Hedley asked.

"Shortly after three p.m. on the Thursday," Aaron replied.

Mr. Hedley shuffled some papers. "And when was the second assault?"

"Around six p.m. that same evening," Aaron responded. "The sun was just beginning to set." He had tried his best to avoid the second assault, but Alfredo wouldn't shut up about wanting to see how Taz "trained a bitch," and some of the others were impatient for another show. Alfredo had been watching Taz carefully that first evening.

"What happened?"

"Mr. Pérez wanted to see Taz in action again," Aaron stated between clenched teeth. "I didn't want to hurt Mary…Mrs. Norland…again, but I had to do something that was convincing." Aaron noticed that his jaw was getting sore, so he tried to relax his muscles. He had a long way to go yet. "Mr.

Rodríguez refused to feed the women because he planned to kill them Sunday morning, and he didn't want to waste the food. They had nothing to eat or drink all day." Now Aaron hesitated. This would sound disgusting and cruel.

"Just tell the court as briefly as possible what you did, Mr. St. Pierre," Mr. Hedley urged.

"I had granola bars with me. I cut two of them up and made Mrs. Norland do tricks like a dog for the first one." Aaron took a breath. The quiet of the courtroom was already being interrupted by gasps from the audience. He struggled on. "For the second one, I forced her to perform oral sex on me." Now the courtroom was buzzing audibly.

Mr. Hedley persevered. "Did anything else happen that day?"

"In the evening I went outside to try to help Mrs. Norland," Aaron stated. At least this part was less painful to recount. "I gave her some water to drink and some antibiotic cream for cuts. She was cold, so I gave her my jacket to wear, and left another granola bar in the pocket for her."

"And did you go back into the cabin after that?" Mr. Hedley asked.

"No," Aaron answered. "I spent the nights outside. I slept about ten feet away from Mrs. Norland, to make sure she was left alone."

Mr. Hedley pressed on. "What happened the next morning?"

*Oh boy, this is going to be awful,* Aaron knew. "In the morning, Mr. Pérez cut Miss Martínez' face with a knife. I heard Mrs. Norland scream, and ran out in time to stop Mr. Pérez from cutting her face as well. He was angry at her, so I told him I would take care of her."

"Tell the court what you did," Mr. Hedley directed tonelessly.

"I had been eating breakfast, and still had a heavily buttered piece of bread in my hand. The Cubans had come out and were watching again, so I taunted Mrs. Norland, and managed to smear butter on both of us to make the sex easier for her." Talking about this was as bad as Aaron had feared, even though he and Mr. Hedley had practised it. "Then I held her up against a tree and had intercourse with her."

"Did Mrs. Norland sustain further injury?" Mr. Hedley asked.

"Scrapes to her back from rubbing against the tree, sir," Aaron responded shortly.

Mr. Hedley paused. "Was there any further assault against Mrs. Norland that day?"

"Yes, sir."

"Explain, Mr. St. Pierre."

*Here we go,* Aaron thought. "Two of the Cubans, not the defendants, attempted to rape Mrs. Norland. She called me for help."

Mr. Hedley held up a hand. "For help, Mr. St. Pierre? Were you not her attacker?"

"I had told her to tell me if anyone else tried to touch her. She knew she wasn't supposed to let them do that."

"And how did you handle this, Mr. St. Pierre? You have said that you could not appear to be nice to her, yet here you were coming to her aid."

Aaron took a breath. "Yes. I had to continue with my act and not appear to be sympathetic to the victim, yet I didn't want anyone else hurting her. So I told her that I would ensure that no one else was interested in her." He paused, but saw Mr. Hedley waiting expectantly. "So I made her take off her clothes and...and...urinated on her."

It took the judge several minutes to settle the court down this time. Aaron didn't dare look at Tony. Only Hedley and Mary had known the details that were now being discussed. Aaron forced himself to keep his eyes on Hedley and try not to think of what Susan and Tony must be feeling right now.

At the first opportunity, Mr. Hedley continued. "And did you leave her like that Mr. St. Pierre?"

"For about an hour," Aaron answered. "Then I got some soap and a towel, and took her over to the waterfall. I told Mr. Pérez that I was bored and I didn't like the way she smelled. I let her swim around for a while, then I gave her a bath."

"How did Mrs. Norland react to this treatment?" Mr. Hedley asked.

"At first she was terribly humiliated, but after the bath she seemed quite relaxed and calm," Aaron replied. "Her hair was all matted, so I used my knife to cut it. I stayed with her for quite a while. I felt awful for what I had done to her."

Mr. Hedley once again referred to his notes. "Mr. St. Pierre, between these attacks, were you doing anything else?"

Aaron nodded. "I was searching for Mr. Bowman, but I couldn't go far, because I couldn't be seen looking for him or doing anything that looked suspicious. At other times I was arranging with Mr. Pérez to purchase drugs and weapons for people who were supposed to have sent me to Cuba for that purpose."

"When did you next see Mr. Bowman?" This time Mr. Hedley's voice sounded almost gentle. He knew how badly Aaron felt about his co-worker.

"Friday afternoon," Aaron began in a dull voice. "Mr. Rodríguez showed up on horseback with Mr. Bowman."

"What condition was Mr. Bowman in?"

302

At this point, Aaron looked back at Tony. "He had been tortured. His hands and feet were swollen, and he couldn't walk." Trying to blot out the image, Aaron closed his eyes, but it didn't help.

"Did you have a chance to talk to him?"

"Yes. I convinced Mr. Rodríguez to tie him beside Mrs. Norland," Aaron advised. "Later, I saw Mrs. Norland holding his hand, so I used it as an excuse to come over and taunt her. I retied her ropes so she could sit closer to him."

Paul Hedley looked out at the audience. "Did Mr. Bowman identify his assailants to you?"

"Yes," Aaron stated through clenched teeth. "He told me that Mr. Rodríguez had interrogated him and been the cause of his injuries." Aaron swallowed. "Mr. Bowman had somehow managed not to reveal my identity."

The courtroom was very quiet, and Mr. Hedley waited for a few minutes before continuing. The sympathies of the people in this room were bound to swing back and forth during this testimony. Right now that sympathy was shifting to Mr. Bowman and Aaron. It made sense to pause and allow them to picture the dilemma that Aaron had faced.

"When did Mr. Bowman die?"

"Sometime during the night," Aaron answered, not quite able to look at Tony. "He was dead when I woke up in the morning." He hoped Mr. Hedley would move on from this topic.

Paul Hedley did deliberately move on. "On the next day, Saturday, were there any further assaults on Mrs. Norland?"

"Well, yes," Aaron responded, "but it wasn't much of an assault."

"Explain that please, Mr. St. Pierre," Mr. Hedley ordered.

Aaron was getting tired, and he had to force his mind off Nat and concentrate on what had happened next. Oh, right. How could he forget? "Mr. Pérez decided it would be fun to have anal sex. I didn't know at the time that Mrs. Norland spoke Spanish, but she had understood him. I missed that, but all I knew was that I couldn't hurt her any more. I was mentally sick by that time, between the violence and the loss of Mr. Bowman." Aaron looked at Tony. "She was begging me not to do it. I couldn't...but I had to at least pretend. There were some small bushes that partially shielded us. I wasn't capable of any more forced sex, so I just pretended. I faked it."

Mr. Hedley paused. "Mr. St. Pierre, wouldn't Mr. Pérez be suspicious if Mrs. Norland had exhibited no distress?"

"Well, she was scared and crying, but I did have to make it seem real, so I grabbed her breast and she cried out. When I went to do it a second time, she cried out before I touched it, so I didn't have to. That happened a third time, as well." Aaron looked over to where Mr. Hedley was standing. "That's probably when she started realising that I wasn't this Taz person. She knew I was faking the sex act, and as long as she played along I wouldn't hurt her. When it was over, I stayed with her." Now he glared over at Alfredo. "I pretended that I wanted to terrorise her with the knife. Mr. Pérez didn't suspect a thing. Mary…Mrs. Norland…clung to me and I was able to stay with her for several minutes."

"Was that the last assault, Mr. St. Pierre?"

"Yes," breathed Aaron, relieved.

"Did anything else happen that day?" Mr. Hedley inquired.

"Some tourists rode past," Aaron stated. "They weren't supposed to be there, and we never figured out where they came from. By some miracle they didn't stop, because Mr. Rodríguez ordered the group to kill them if we were spotted. Mr. Pérez and I ran out to keep the women quiet." Aaron looked over at Alfredo again. "Miss Martínez was badly injured by that time. Mr. Pérez finished her off with his knife." He looked back at Tony. "I held Mrs. Norland and told her to keep quiet or the tourists would be killed." He noticed that his fists had clenched on the witness box, so dropped them to his lap. "Before Mr. Pérez went back into the cabin, he told me that Mrs. Norland was to be killed the next morning, but first the Liberators wanted her for themselves."

Alfredo's lawyer was trying to object, and for a few minutes Hedley was engaged in a spirited argument. Aaron took advantage of the short break to try to relax.

Finally Mr. Hedley continued. "How did Mrs. Norland react to being told she would be made available to the others, and then murdered?"

"She was terrified."

"What did you say to her?" Mr. Hedley asked.

Aaron looked at Mr. Hedley intently. This was the part that their public relations team had really debated over. It had finally been decided that Aaron should stick with the truth, since Aaron had in fact *not* killed Mary, but this was extremely risky. "I told her that I would not hurt her any more, and that if she wanted me to, I would kill her myself that night."

A collective gasp came from the courtroom, and once again the judge had to intervene. Mr. Hedley waited. "How did Mrs. Norland react to that, Mr. St. Pierre?"

"She wanted me to," Aaron replied. "She couldn't bear the thought of what would happen otherwise. I went to her later that night," he continued, "but she was scared. I couldn't bear to see her scared now that she knew I wasn't Taz. So I held her and told her that I would do it when she was sleeping, but I fell asleep without tying her up. She escaped."

Mr. Hedley was pacing. "How did she know you weren't Taz?"

"I don't know," Aaron responded. He had been amazed at that himself. "She just seemed to figure it out. I must have let my guard down around her."

"Why didn't you just let her go, Mr. St. Pierre? Mr. Bowman was already dead."

It was another crucial question for the public relations team. Aaron took his time answering. "If I let her escape, I expected her to go directly to the authorities, if she wasn't caught by the defendants, first. Our people were coming in the next afternoon to rescue us and were expecting to remove the leaders of the Liberators to the United States. I had hoped to keep Mrs. Norland unharmed until then, but it wasn't going to be allowed." He took a breath. "The defendants had tortured and killed Mr. Bowman and Miss Martínez. They had forced me to rape a Canadian tourist, and they were blackmailing American businessmen. I wanted them captured. I couldn't stand to think that they might escape us if the Cuban authorities arrived. It would also put our own people at incredible risk."

"Mr. St. Pierre, do you think you could have killed Mrs. Norland?" Again, the million-dollar question.

"I don't know," Aaron responded truthfully. "When she escaped, I didn't have the heart to pursue her."

Mr. Hedley nodded. "And did Mrs. Norland go to the Cuban authorities?"

"No," Aaron answered. "She went straight home to Canada without telling anyone what had happened."

"Mr. St. Pierre, have you met with Mrs. Norland since your return from Cuba?"

"Yes, frequently."

Mr. Hedley smiled. "And how would you describe the relationship between yourself and Mrs. Norland now?"

"We've become good friends, sir."

"Doesn't Mrs. Norland blame you for your assaults on her?"

"No, sir. She understands that I was trying to keep her from being harmed, and she's forgiven me for terrorising her."

More questions followed, but for Aaron the worst was over for now. It was noon, and Mr. Hedley's questioning had taken a day and a half. Now Tony would take him to lunch, then the defence would attack. At least everything had been admitted regarding Mary, and the defence couldn't possibly know about Nat. They would attack Aaron's credibility, and it would be hellish, but Mr. Hedley would protect him and the CIA's interests as far as he could. With relief, Aaron left the stand.

# XLV

Lunch was a rather crowded affair because of the number of Security people present. The proprietor of the restaurant was used to serving this clientele under various conditions, and had a private room waiting for them. Aaron knew that a simple lunch would be served quickly in respect for their timetable. Now that Mr. Hedley was finished with his questions, Aaron knew he had to prepare himself for some real unpleasantness.

Beside him, Tony was quiet. Aaron was glad of the people around him, because he didn't want to discuss the morning's revelations with Tony. They would have to talk privately about it at some time to diffuse any tensions this morning might have created between them. Of course, Tony might simply be quiet because he was worried. Aaron knew Tony had to be feeling the pressure from his superiors. So far Tony had shielded him from that pressure, but it had to be intense.

Although it was probably good, the sandwich tasted like paper in Aaron's mouth. He gave up trying to eat it, and sipped on ice water. The afternoon's questioning would run from 2:00 p.m. to 4:00 p.m. For two hours he had to stay alert and not let the defence trick him. Two hours of a fencing match with potentially disastrous consequences for his personal life. He saw Tony eying the uneaten sandwich. It was not unlike Tony to try to order you to eat if he felt you needed the energy. Today, however, Tony just gave him an encouraging smile and said nothing. Good, he wasn't too upset.

*"Trust Tony completely,"* Nat had said. Now that Aaron's stomach was in knots, he wished that he had told Tony everything. Perhaps he could have made Tony understand about Nat. If he had told Tony, much of the fear inside him would have been relieved. Tony could have told Aaron what to do if the defence started asking about Nat. Or maybe not. Maybe Tony would have withdrawn his support completely. Aaron wished he knew how Tony would react. Not that it mattered now. It was too late and there were too many people around. Aaron knew he was on his own with this one, and it scared him.

Back in the stand, Aaron waited expectantly. Being a witness in a court case was no new experience for him, but this time he had been warned that he would feel as if he was the one on trial. In a sense, he was on trial; he and a very large organisation called the CIA. It was an ominous feeling to know that you were representing their credibility right now. Thousands of men and women made up the CIA, but how he, Aaron St. Pierre, conducted himself on the stand today was going to have a disproportionately large impact on their reputation. That was why there were three rows of the Company's employees: public relations people; lawyers; the Deputy Director, Peter Geraldton; Mr. Walsh; Tony; Moseley; Sheila; and a heavy Security detail all over the building.

Gavin and Scott were in another room on standby as witnesses, also guarded by Security. Mary was with them, because she was the next scheduled witness. Mary's job was to convince the world that Aaron had not wanted to hurt her, and the CIA had not been responsible for this happening to her. Indirectly they *were* responsible, of course, but they couldn't let the blame shift from Alfredo to them. Aaron's cover had been a poor choice, but Alfredo and Osvaldo had planned the rapes and cornered Aaron. Somehow, Aaron and his defenceless victim had to convince the world of that. *Not too much to ask,* mused Aaron.

Mr. Cook stood up and strolled over towards the witness box. Today he had to play his cards carefully, because his research told him that Mr. St. Pierre was no fool, and was not a renegade. He was a committed employee with a bright future, and it was Mr. Cook's responsibility to destroy that future. In Mr. Cook's favour was the fact that Mr. St. Pierre had been under considerable stress during and since the affair in Cuba. He was under a doctor's care, and his employers were watching him very closely. Mr. St. Pierre had to be rattled sufficiently so that he would let the blame of this affair fall on himself and the CIA. Not only that, but Mr. Cook had a further objective, and that was to prevent Mrs. Norland from testifying.

Over the weekend, Mr. Cook had gathered his material and practised his approach. First he would portray Mr. St. Pierre as a man out of control who raped a Canadian citizen of his own free will. Then Mr. Cook would reveal the Saturday night attack, which should suffice to knock the support of the CIA staff from under Mr. St. Pierre's feet. Then Mr. St. Pierre would truly be on his own, and he would feel betrayed. At that point, Mr. Cook would change tactics and sympathise with Mr. St. Pierre for being made into the fall guy in this affair. He would trick Mr. St. Pierre into blaming the CIA for the events in Cuba. That would be sufficient to ruin the credibility of the evidence, but Mr. Cook wanted guarantees. Therefore, he would finish by informing Mr. St. Pierre that it was clear that he had killed the other CIA officer, and that Mrs. Norland was the only living witness. With a bit of luck, that would push Mr. St. Pierre over the edge enough for him to kill Mrs. Norland to protect himself. Mr. St. Pierre could not afford to have his employers know that he had murdered one of their own.

Mr. Cook stopped and looked up at the witness. "Mr. St. Pierre, you have stated that prior to Mrs. Norland arriving at the camp in Cuba, you had some conversations with Mr. Pérez about your activities with women."

"Yes."

"How many conversations did you have?"

"I cannot recall," Aaron admitted. "Mr. Pérez was quite vocal on the subject, so I would estimate that we had at least one of these conversations every day."

"Now, you said that it surprised you when Mr. Pérez brought women back to the camp, didn't you?" Cook asked.

"Yes." Aaron was on his guard. Mr. Cook's back was to him, hiding the receding hairline, as well as any expression on Cook's face.

"Yet you admit that you had numerous conversations with him about exactly that subject, did you not?" Mr. Cook was still staring at the courtroom audience.

"Yes, but I at no time—" Aaron didn't get to finish.

Mr. Cook spun around. "Then Mr. Pérez could be in no doubt of your desires," he accused.

Aaron remained quiet. That had not been a question.

Mr. Cook approached him. "Mr. St. Pierre, you have said that you were protecting your cover. You had numerous conversations with Mr. Pérez in which you expressed your sexual desires in great detail, to such an extent that your fellow officer had to walk away from the conversations because he couldn't stomach them. Is that not true?"

"That is true." The courtroom was getting very warm suddenly.

"Then could Mr. Pérez have been in any doubt of your habits of forcibly confining and raping women?"

"They were not *my* habits," Aaron retorted.

"But you were this Taz person. They were his habits, were they not?" Cook asked.

"Yes."

Mr. Cook kept staring at him. "Then Mr. Pérez had no reason to doubt that they were your habits, did he?"

"No."

"How," Mr. Cook asked, turning away again, "can you possibly blame Mr. Pérez for thinking to bring those women to the camp when you asked him to?"

"I did not ask him to," Aaron insisted. "I never suggested—"

"You never dissuaded him," Mr. Cook interrupted. "You talked about it, encouraged him…in fact, Mr. St. Pierre, where do you think he got the idea from?"

The room was definitely getting warm. "He was testing me."

"I submit, Mr. St. Pierre, that he was giving you exactly what you asked for."

"I did not ask for—"

"She was your *present*, Mr. St. Pierre. He got her for you as a favour because you told him that's what you wanted!"

"No!"

Mr. Cook stood with his hands in his pockets, watching the rows of CIA employees. "You never raised a hand to help her, Mr. St. Pierre. You could have released her at any time, couldn't you?"

"No." While *no* wasn't quite right, *yes* was the wrong response, Aaron decided. Physically, yes, he could have released her, but it would have been a disaster for himself, Nat and the operation.

"No?" Mr. Cook looked surprised. "Are you telling me that you could not have left her untied any night so she could escape?"

"I could have left her untied," Aaron answered, "but the ramifications of doing so were not worth the risk."

"Ahhh. It was inconvenient," Mr. Cook concluded.

By having Mr. Hedley jump up and protest, Aaron was spared the necessity of trying to explain further. He had to remind himself that Cook was trying to rattle him, and getting rattled had to be avoided at all costs. Looking at Tony earned him a small reassuring smile. *This is no fun, Tony,* Aaron thought.

It was time to move on. Mr. Cook summarised the assaults again, leaving out the details, thank goodness, then asked Aaron an unexpected question.

"Mr. St. Pierre, how often do you normally have sex in a week?"

This time Aaron felt his jaw fall open. What kind of question was that? Mr. Hedley protested vigorously, but this time Mr. Cook was able to convince the judge that Aaron's sexual habits were somehow relevant. Aaron was caught off guard. How many times did he have sex? When he was home with Susan, before Cuba, as often as he could. Away from Susan, not at all. Grab an average figure, he told himself, refraining from looking anywhere near Susan's direction. "I've never tried to average it before," he answered, "but maybe twice?"

"Mmm."

For a minute Aaron hoped that Mr. Cook had changed his mind about pursuing that, but then he found out the intent.

"About twice," Mr. Cook repeated. "But with Mrs. Norland as a captive, you could have sex as often as you wished. Isn't that right, Mr. St. Pierre?"

*Oh God,* thought Aaron. *This is getting worse and worse. Think before answering.* "Mrs. Norland had no say in the matter, if that's what you mean."

"No," Cook agreed, nodding. "No say at all." Suddenly he raised his voice. "Mr. St. Pierre, you were having the time of your life, weren't you?" He never gave Aaron a chance to answer. "No supervision, no one to account to, all the sex and domination you wanted, and *there would be no witness,*" Cook dropped his voice, "because she would be dead, wouldn't she, Mr. St. Pierre?"

Aaron felt himself shaking, but he refused to answer until he knew which question he was answering.

Strangely, Cook didn't pursue the questions. He walked to his table and consulted his notes. "Now, Mr. St. Pierre, you have told us about five assaults, is that correct?"

"Yes," Aaron answered, guardedly.

"You admit to those five of your own free will?"

"Yes."

Cook looked up at him. "What about the sixth?"

"What?" It shocked Aaron. What sixth? What was he talking about? Looking at Hedley told him that the prosecutor was confused and worried.

Cook looked innocently at Aaron. "The sixth assault."

"There was no other assault," Aaron insisted, chills running down his backbone. What was Cook up to?

"Mr. St. Pierre, may I remind you that you are under oath?"

Perplexed, Aaron looked at Tony, who seemed very confused. Their staff were starting to squirm nervously in their seats. "I don't know what you are referring to," Aaron finally replied.

Approaching him, Cook stopped about three feet away. "Perhaps you'd better think again, Mr. St. Pierre. We have witnesses to the rape. Don't perjure yourself."

This was irritating, but also frightening. "I know I'm under oath," Aaron stated. "There was no other assault."

Cook actually smiled. "No? Then what do you call what Mr. Rodríguez saw you doing Saturday night?"

*Oh no!* Shock hit Aaron in the stomach like a blow. He had been sure no one had seen them. Everyone had been asleep. But Cook couldn't have made up this coincidence, and if Osvaldo had seen Aaron and Mary making love, then it would be suicide to pretend nothing had happened. He had to try to explain this, and hope Mary would survive the cross-examination.

"That wasn't rape," Aaron stated, feeling his way.

"You are going to stand there and say it didn't happen?" Cook asked incredulously.

"I'm saying that it wasn't rape," Aaron repeated. "It was consensual."

Actual groans could be heard in the courtroom, and Aaron had a horrible feeling they had come from his own people. He looked at Hedley, who had dropped his pencil and was staring at him in dismay. Then Aaron looked at Tony, and wished that he hadn't. Tony had his head in his hands, and his shoulders had sagged. *Don't give up on me Tony,* Aaron begged in a silent panic.

Even Cook seemed sincerely amazed, and if Aaron had known, Cook was actually ecstatic. This couldn't have been more perfect. Tie a woman to a tree, rape her for three days, and then try to tell people that she had consented to have sex with you. It took a real effort on Cook's part to keep his composure. He had found the key to his defence. He had won.

After a minute, Cook could again trust himself to speak in a manner befitting a courtroom. "Mrs. Norland consented," he stated.

"Yes, sir." By now Aaron's palms were sweaty, and perspiration had started to run down under his shirt.

Cook paused again. "Mr. St. Pierre, Mrs. Norland had been held captive for three days, am I correct?"

"Yes."

"She had been tied to a tree throughout her captivity?"

"Yes."

"Uh-huh." Mr. Cook nodded. "And you testified that you had 'trained' her to do everything you wished, is that not so?"

There was no other answer. "Yes," Aaron replied regretfully.

"You even taught her to sit on command and bark like a dog for food, is that true?"

*He's winning,* Aaron knew. *I have to stop this, but I don't know how. Why isn't Hedley helping me?* A glance at Hedley told the story. The lawyer was sitting passively, watching the interchange between Aaron and Cook as if he were watching a video he did not understand. *I was supposed to tell him everything,* Aaron knew, *so he would be prepared. That was the deal. He's given up on me.* Aaron looked at Tony, who was also watching with a dejected expression. *You too, Tony? I should have told you I made love to your girlfriend, but I thought no one saw.*

"Isn't that true?" Cook repeated.

"Yes," Aaron admitted.

"So," Cook continued, "this woman had been tied to a tree, taught to be totally obedient to you to avoid further pain, had been raped for three days, and all of a sudden she decides she wants to make love to you?" Cook's voice was booming. "Mr. St. Pierre, can you *possibly* be that naïve? Do you really think this woman had any choice at all?"

It sounded fantastic, Aaron knew. No one would believe it. Mary's desire for a human touch on the eve of her expected death was something most people would not understand. No one else had seen the change in their relationship since Nat's death. No one who had not faced death could imagine what she was going through. Only a person who had lived through their awful experience in Cuba could understand that.

By the time Cook finished questioning Aaron about Mary, Aaron's shirt was soaked with sweat. Hedley had objected halfheartedly to a few questions, but Aaron had the distinct feeling that he had been abandoned. Even worse, Tony seemed to be avoiding his eyes. It was a terrifying feeling, and Aaron now realised how much he had depended upon Tony's support. The CIA was a good employer, but the administration had to protect the organization first. Without Tony to run interference for him, Aaron was sunk. Aaron had made a deal to keep Mary alive. He had promised to accept the consequences. Now Aaron was watching the case crumble over the little word *consent,* and the likelihood that charges would be laid against him to protect the agency suddenly seemed frighteningly possible.

He could go to prison for this. For something he had wanted no part of, his life could be ruined and his liberty stolen. It made him angry. A promise made in desperation in Cuba was coming back to haunt him, and it wasn't fair. *Damn you, Tony. Help me.*

Was it over? Cook seemed to be consulting his notes, deep in thought. What other little tricks had the defence prepared? Hammond had called Frank to warn him that Finch had been caught on the phone with someone, but there had been no time to interrogate Finch properly. How much of what Finch had suggested could possibly be put forward in a court of law? It was all guesswork.

"Mr. St. Pierre," Cook began loudly, startling Aaron, whose nerves were now on edge. "Who is Gavin Weeks?"

Instinctively, Aaron looked at Hedley for guidance. Why was Cook asking about Gavin? At Hedley's cautious nod, Aaron told the court that Gavin Weeks was a CIA employee.

"And what is Mr. Weeks' function in the agency?" As Hedley rose to protest, Cook held up his hand. "I'll reword that question, Your Honour," he interrupted quickly. "To what section of the CIA does Mr. Weeks belong?"

Another cautious nod from Hedley. "Operations," Aaron responded briefly.

Mr. Cook was not satisfied. "Is it true that Mr. Weeks is attached to the Special Operations unit?"

Aaron carefully did not look at Hedley, but paused to allow him a chance to protest. When Hedley did not protest, Aaron replied in the affirmative.

Cook looked towards the rows of CIA employees, as if deep in thought. Aaron could feel the tension emulating from his colleagues. What was Cook up to this time?

"Now, this Special Operations unit consists of some very highly trained individuals, does it not?"

Again a pause, and again Aaron answered in the affirmative. Hedley had to feel coiled like a spring inside, wondering at what point to interject. It was imperative at this point that Aaron respond slowly and carefully, at least until he knew where Cook was heading.

"These individuals are extensively trained in the use of a variety of firearms, plus the ability to go places undetected and perform very delicate and sensitive operations about which the public knows nothing..."

Hedley was up and protesting. What purpose was there to these questions; and besides, it was touching on protected information not for public distribution.

Cook accepted the protests too meekly. Whatever this was about, it wasn't over, Aaron knew. Once Hedley had wound down, Cook smiled his acceptance.

"I'm sorry, Your Honour," Cook said almost gratefully. "I never meant to pry into any CIA *secret operations*." Then he turned suddenly to Aaron and his smile disappeared. "Mr. St. Pierre, when Gavin Weeks led a group of men into Cuba to rescue you, why were you overheard begging Tony Dune not to send Mr. Weeks after Mrs. Norland?"

*I'm going to faint,* Aaron thought, but he didn't. Shock left him speechless, though.

"Come on, Mr. St. Pierre," Cook chided. "Your exact words were 'No, not Gavin. Don't send Gavin. She doesn't deserve this.'" Cook walked up close to Aaron, but kept his voice loud. "What didn't she deserve, Mr. St. Pierre? What was Mr. Weeks ordered to do to her?"

Aaron hadn't recovered from the questions about Mary. He wasn't prepared for this attack either. This one was not his fault. Tony had been the one foolish enough to give the order to kill Mary, but if the public *ever* found out about that order, the CIA would come down on Aaron like a ton of bricks. They would deny everything of course, but they would need to deflect the public's attention, and Aaron was the available scapegoat.

Now Tony was looking at Aaron intensely. *Sure, Tony,* thought Aaron angrily, *now you need me. Where were you fifteen minutes ago, you prick?*

Hedley protested, but lost. The question stood. Aaron still hadn't answered. His mind was racing for an appropriate response. "I was on the verge of a nervous breakdown," he stated. "I have no idea what I said. Mrs. Norland had taken my jacket with her, and it had some drawings in it. We had to get it back. Mr. Dune was going to send Mr. Weeks to get it."

"Come on, Mr. St. Pierre," Cook almost yelled. "Mr. Dune was going to send a trained killer into Canada for a jacket?"

Hedley almost came over his table. There was no question of his objection being allowed, and yes, it would be struck from the records, and yes, Mr. Cook was reprimanded. All of that didn't matter a hoot, because the public now had formed their own very good idea of what Mr. Weeks did for a living. It took the judge quite a while to quiet the courtroom this time.

*Doomed,* thought Aaron dejectedly. *We've lost and I'm doomed.*

Mr. Cook resumed. "You were begging for Mrs. Norland's life, weren't you, Mr. St. Pierre?"

"Mrs. Norland was not in any danger," Aaron replied automatically. "The CIA has never, and would never intentionally cause the death of a Canadian tourist." The order had been rescinded, so that was true enough.

"Only because you begged for her life," Cook stated.

Hedley protested again. Aaron said nothing. No question had been asked.

Cook came back with a different approach. "You know, Mr. St. Pierre, I've changed my mind."

Aaron looked at him warily. *What now?*

"Yes," Cook emphasised. "I've looked into your history, and I believe I have done you a disservice today. You have an upstanding reputation."

There was no movement among the CIA ranks. Something else was coming, there was no doubt.

"In fact," Cook continued, "you are known to be a decent, compassionate man. So," Cook admitted, "I believe you. I believe that you never wanted to hurt Mrs. Norland. I believe you were given a cover story that got you into great trouble when you had to defend yourself and your colleague. In fact," Cook added, "I believe that you truly thought that Mrs. Norland had consented to the final sex act."

When he paused, Aaron glanced at Tony. Tony and the others sat as if frozen, waiting for the pounce.

Cook pressed on. "What I don't understand is why you are taking the blame for all this. You are, aren't you, Mr. St. Pierre?"

"No," Aaron croaked. That was a lie. He certainly was taking the blame.

"Sure you are, Mr. St. Pierre," Cook insisted. "You are the fall guy, aren't you?" He pointed at Hedley. "Who hires your counsel?"

"The CIA," Aaron replied.

"So your counsel is here to protect the CIA, correct?"

"Yes."

"And if your interests conflict with the CIA's interests, who does your counsel represent?"

"Mr. Hedley is retained by the CIA," Aaron repeated, without enthusiasm.

Mr. Cook nodded. "Your counsel is hired to protect the CIA, Mr. St. Pierre, not you. Does your counsel know that you had to *beg* your boss not to kill an innocent woman you spent three days trying to protect?"

Aaron was losing control—he could feel it. Hedley was up and protesting. Cook ended up being warned again, but Aaron knew it wouldn't do much good. Cook smelled blood, and Aaron felt himself getting confused.

"Mr. St. Pierre," Cook recommenced quietly. "Prior to being on this assignment, did you ever rape a woman?"

"Of course not," Aaron replied quickly.

"No. In fact, you have had an unblemished career, have you not?"

"Yes," Aaron admitted. An unblemished career that was turning to shit before his very eyes.

"And for three days in Cuba, you were forced to assault a woman to protect your identity. You hated that, didn't you, Mr. St. Pierre?" Mr. Cook's tone was sympathetic; soothing.

"Yes." It was almost a whisper. Three days of hurting and terrorising Mary. All because they told him to be Taz.

Cook shook his head. "And at the end of these three days, when your rescue arrived, Mr. Dune ordered Gavin Weeks to go up to Canada and find Mrs. Norland, didn't he?"

Aaron barely managed not to answer. The answer was *yes*, but *yes* was dangerous. He looked at Tony, who was staring intently into his eyes.

"Mr. St. Pierre," Cook repeated. "Mrs. Norland's existence as a witness was a threat to the CIA, wasn't it?"

Aaron couldn't seem to get his thoughts together fast enough. Why was all this his responsibility?

"You aren't answering, Mr. St. Pierre," Cook insisted. "Why do you insist on taking the blame for their decision? You spent three days keeping Mrs. Norland alive because you are a decent man, and then you were heard begging Mr. Dune not to send Gavin Weeks after her. You knew what it meant to send Gavin Weeks after Mrs. Norland, didn't you?"

Too many questions and innuendos. Too much pressure. Aaron felt his heart racing. *I can get out of this,* he knew. *Damn you, Tony, you were supposed to protect me, but now this is falling apart and I'm the one who will suffer. My life will be ruined unless I save it now.*

He looked at Tony, feeling his breathing quicken. Tony still stared at him, his eyes begging Aaron to stay in control. *Why, Tony? Why should I take the fall? You gave the damn order, not me. I could get out of this right now. Mary and a good lawyer would keep me out of jail. All I have to do is tell the court you gave the order. No one would care about me any more. You guys would be the ones fighting for your careers. I could crucify you.*

Cook was still talking. "Mr. St. Pierre, please tell the court what it meant to you when Mr. Dune ordered Mr. Weeks to go after Mrs. Norland. Why were you begging him not to?"

*I'll do it,* Aaron decided. *To hell with them. I don't deserve to take the fall. The public has a right to know whose fault this is.* He met Tony's eyes again. *Damn you, Tony, it wasn't my fault. I don't deserve this. I'll tell them—*

"Mr. St. Pierre, please answer my questions."

Aaron was literally shaking. Tony's gaze remained steady, asking Aaron to hold together. *Trust Tony,* Nat had said. *Tony will stand behind you. Tell him everything. Aaron had not told Tony everything, and things were falling apart.* Aaron couldn't think any more, couldn't fight this any more. He gripped the front of the stand. He would end this now…but Tony's eyes never wavered. Tony, who had been a friend to him for almost five years; encouraging him, yelling at him, sleeping on his couch. Tony would be ruined by this, absolutely ruined. With a gasp, Aaron knew he couldn't do that. He couldn't sell Tony out.

Aaron took a breath and kept looking at Tony. "I don't know what I was saying in Cuba. I was distraught. The CIA would never consider sending anyone into Canada to kill an innocent civilian."

There was complete silence in the courtroom. Almost there, Cook decided, hiding his disappointment. Damn, this man was loyal. It had been so close—the man had almost cracked. You could tell by the way his hands had gripped the witness box, and the wild look in his eyes. So close, but just not quite. Cook shuffled some papers to give himself a minute to regroup. This next attack should do the trick. St. Pierre was on the edge, and needed just another little push. It had to work, because Cook knew the judge was losing patience. It was time for a direct attack on St. Pierre to get him to confess to the murder of Bowman, or at least rattle him so much that he would forget to defend his employers. Cook was fairly confident that St. Pierre had killed Bowman, and was absolutely certain that he had not admitted this to Dune. You just didn't admit to murdering a well-respected fellow officer, especially when the victim was known to be your boss's best friend.

Of course, the ultimate goal was to shock St. Pierre into realising that Mrs. Norland was the only eyewitness to Bowman's murder. If enough pressure was applied, it was conceivable that St. Pierre might lose his head and make Mrs. Norland disappear. That would close down the case, and they would have no worries about Mrs. Norland's testimony. Mr. St. Pierre would have crucified himself and brought his employers into disrepute.

*Okay,* Cook decided. *It's showtime. St. Pierre had his chance, and he blew it.* "Mr. St. Pierre, your nickname is 'puppy dog', is that correct?"

*Oh, for God's sake,* Aaron groaned inwardly. *Get off of my personal life. What are you up to now, Cook?* "Some people call me that," he admitted reluctantly.

"Why?" Cook asked simply.

"Why?" *Give me a break. People call me that to piss me off.* "To annoy me, I guess."

But Cook didn't buy that. "Come now, Mr. St. Pierre. Isn't it because you are known to be the kind of man who hates to hurt anyone or see anything suffering or in pain?"

*Shit.* Alarm bells were ringing violently in Aaron's head. *Please don't let this be about what I think it is.* "Maybe," he answered vaguely.

"How long had you known Nathanial Bowman?"

Fear made Aaron suddenly feel cold. "Almost five years," he responded.

"He helped with your training, did he not?" Cook inquired.

"Yes."

"And you were both on the same team—you worked closely together throughout those five years, did you not?"

"Yes."

Cook nodded. "I believe it would be fair to say that you and Mr. Bowman were close friends, is that true?"

"Yes." *Very close. Close enough to make this hurt for the rest of my life. Especially if Tony guesses now.*

Cook changed course a bit. "How tall are you, Mr. St. Pierre?"

*Tall?* "Six feet, two inches," answered Aaron, puzzled.

"And how tall was Mr. Bowman?"

"Six feet."

"How far were you from the American base in Cuba?"

*Oh, I get it.* "About 250 kilometres, if you travelled the roadway."

"So although you are apparently a tall, strong man, there is no way you could have carried Mr. Bowman to safety when you found out that he couldn't walk."

"That is correct." Aaron had never committed outright perjury before, but he suspected that the first time would be arriving shortly. Oh well, he was ruined now, anyway.

"And Mr. Bowman could not walk," Cook reflected, "so if you had tried to hide him, the two of you would be sitting ducks if the Liberators organised a search."

"Yes," Aaron replied.

"Did you have any way of calling for assistance?" Cook asked.

"A signalling device," Aaron responded.

Cook walked over to glance at his notes, then looked across at Aaron. "A signalling device with a global positioning system built in, I believe. Did you use this?"

Aaron nodded. "Yes. Mr. Bowman had sent a signal for a rescue on the Sunday."

"Could you not send another signal after Mr. Bowman was taken captive? After all," Cook stated, "the base was only 250 kilometres away. Help would have arrived swiftly."

"It was broken." Aaron felt a tightness in his throat. "The device malfunctioned and we were stuck with the Sunday rescue."

"Let me see if I understand this, Mr. St. Pierre," Cook mused. "You had no chance of being rescued until Sunday. Mr. Bowman had been tortured and could not walk. You had no identity papers to use with Cuban officials to protect you. It would have been an impossible feat for you to carry Mr. Bowman to the American base. Hiding with him would have been a game of Russian roulette." Cook stopped and gazed out at the courtroom. "And to make matters even worse, you *knew* that Mr. Bowman was facing more interrogation the next day. Is that correct?"

*Oh hell, I'm finished if I confess to Nat's death,* Aaron knew. *Somehow I have to keep from admitting this.* "That is correct," Aaron responded nervously.

Cook still faced the audience. "You would have had to stand by and allow your friend to endure more torture trying to protect you and your operation. Isn't that true, Mr. St. Pierre? You would have had to watch your friend being carried away to be subjected to who knows what pain."

"That didn't happen," Aaron stated quickly. He couldn't have people thinking he would be that callous.

"No, it didn't," Cook said slowly, turning to walk towards the defence's table. "Mr. St. Pierre, how did Mrs. Norland know your name?"

"What?" *Knew my name? When?* Aaron was confused.

"When your colleagues met Mrs. Norland in Toronto, she knew your real first name. How did she know that?" Cook stood motionless.

*You're bluffing,* Aaron knew. Still, it threw him. Scott had mentioned something about that, but Aaron hadn't paid attention. Scott must have told Kevin. "I don't know," Aaron responded honestly. "I never told her. Mr. Bowman must have." It made no sense at all for Nat to tell her, but how else could she have known?"

"Don't you, Mr. St. Pierre?" Cook turned towards him and started to speak in an accusing tone. "Mr. St. Pierre, you were Mr. Bowman's *friend*. You couldn't bear to see him suffer, could you?"

Aaron didn't answer, but felt his nerves start to twitch.

Cook wasn't about to give up. "I submit, Mr. St. Pierre, that you went to Mr. Bowman that night. He was weak, he was in pain, and he had to be terrified at the thought of facing another day of torture. You talked to him, didn't you?"

"I talked to him that afternoon," Aaron insisted, his jaw tense.

"You talked to him that night, Mr. St. Pierre, didn't you?" Cook continued. "He called you 'Aaron', and Mrs. Norland heard him. Mr. St.

Pierre, you killed Mr. Bowman because you couldn't bear to see him suffer any more, and Mrs. Norland *saw you do it*!"

"No!"

"*That's* how she knew your name. *That's* why she knew you weren't Taz. *That's* why she trusted you to kill her without pain."

"No!" Aaron had broken into a sweat, terrified that he would start to stutter. It had never occurred to him that Mary had been awake. She had said nothing, but everything Cook said made sense. Nat *had* called Aaron by name. The next day Mary *had* lost her fear of him. She *had* asked him to kill her. Then a forgotten phrase jumped into his head. *"Don't let me die by their hand, Aaron."* My God, he had missed it. It was true, she had seen it all.

"She knew your *name*, Mr. St. Pierre," Cook insisted.

"Nat…must ha…have told her." No, no, don't stutter. Don't give it away.

Cook actually snorted. "Mr. Bowman had just finished enduring a day of torture protecting your cover, Mr. St. Pierre. Do you expect anyone to believe that he would then turn to a complete stranger and say, 'By the way, that man isn't Taz, his name is Aaron'?"

No, of course he wouldn't, Aaron knew. Everyone else would know too. Now Tony would know, and so would Walsh. It was over for him.

"You killed Nathanial Bowman, Mr. St. Pierre, and Mrs. Norland is the only living witness to it."

Mary. Mary saw him. Mary, who couldn't lie to save her life; who would *never* pass a lie detector test. Aaron couldn't look at Tony now. He was shaking, and Tony would see through him.

Cook was smiling inside. St. Pierre was a wreck. He had him in the palm of his hand. "The CIA sent you to Cuba as a rapist. Your friend was captured. You were forced to wait while he was being tortured." Cook raised his voice. "The only witness to all of this was Mrs. Norland. For three days you were forced to rape that poor woman. That is why you had to beg for her life, Mr. St. Pierre. That is why you were heard begging Mr. Dune not to issue the execution order—"

Hedley was up, yelling.

"—the execution order that would have protected—"

Pandemonium was occurring in the courtroom, despite the judge's gavel.

"—was the *only* way the CIA could protect itself." Somehow Cook had gotten it out.

Aaron stood motionless while the judge tried to install order. Cook would be in trouble. Hedley was panicking. Aaron hardly noticed. He was cold inside. They were ruined and he would pay the price. Finally order was restored. Cook was looking at him. Had there been a question? Aaron couldn't remember. He muttered an automatic response. "The CIA would never deliberately cause the death of a Canadian citizen."

Cook gave up. This man was unshakeable. It would be pure luck if St. Pierre killed Mary. Cook had given his last shot. If Mary were still alive tomorrow she would be a lot easier to rattle.

"No further questions, Your Honour," he stated.

Done, finally. Thank God. Now Hedley would try to repair the damage. Aaron waited. And waited. Hedley was looking at Walsh and his advisors. Walsh finally made a slight negative motion with his head. Hedley faced the judge. "We have no further questions, Your Honour."

*What? No! Damn you, Walsh!* Aaron's heart started racing. After that…after all that…they had just betrayed him. Tony's face was grim, but he didn't look away. *Damn you again, Tony. I protected you. You were supposed to protect me.* Aaron felt a terrible fear and loneliness as he left the stand. He would go to prison for something that wasn't his fault. They would make him take the fall for something they had caused. All because he hadn't wanted Mary to die. Anger swelled in him. From the corridor he ran into their private room where Mary sat with Gavin and Scott.

"Mary, come with me," Aaron ordered. As she got up and followed, he took her hand and hurried her towards the door to the parking lot.

"Aaron, where are you going?" Tony had followed him out, with Walsh and the others right behind.

"Mary and I are going for a ride," Aaron retorted, half dragging Mary along towards his car.

"Like hell you are. Get back here."

*Fuck you, Tony.* Aaron kept walking, with Mary at his side.

"Mr. St. Pierre, you get back here."

Aaron knew an order when he heard it, but was too angry to care.

"Mary." Tony's voice had changed, appealing to Mary, hoping she would stop going with Aaron.

Aaron spun around, wanting to hurt the man who had abandoned him. "What's the matter, Tony? Don't you trust me with her?" He held the car door open for Mary and she got in meekly. "Why don't you send your dogs after me then?" Jumping into the driver's seat, Aaron started the car and spun out of the parking lot.

"Why are you standing there?" Walsh demanded of Tony. "St. Pierre just ignored your orders and drove off with our witness. Where the hell is our security?"

As Walsh looked for staff, Tony touched his arm. "No, Carl. He's testing me."

Walsh looked astonished. "Testing you? Didn't you hear what went on in there? We know he probably killed Bowman, and Mary's the only witness to that. St. Pierre could kill her. He knows what we did in there, and he's panicked."

Tony was shaken more than he would ever let Carl Walsh see, but he held on to one belief. "He won't hurt Mary." *Please, Aaron, let that be true,* Tony prayed. *You hate us right now, but don't take it out on her.*

Carl Walsh wasn't satisfied. "You're taking a huge chance with that woman's life, Tony. St. Pierre didn't trust you enough to tell you about Bowman. Why do you think you can trust him now?"

*He won't hurt her,* Tony kept repeating to himself. In desperation, he looked over at where Scott and Gavin were standing. Scott looked astounded, but must have seen the appeal in Tony's eyes.

"Aaron would never hurt Mary," Scott stated simply to Walsh. "He just wouldn't."

"He did before," Walsh retorted.

Scott met Walsh's look without flinching. "He didn't have a choice, sir."

For a moment there was dead silence, then Walsh addressed Tony. "It's your call, but St. Pierre comes in by nine p.m. or we send people after him. And, Tony," he continued, "he admits *everything* to you or we let him sift for himself, understand? If he comes clean, we'll take care of him, but men who keep secrets like that are no good to us." Walsh sighed, "And if he kills Mary, he hangs and carries the blame for all of this. His guilt clears us." Walsh touched Tony's shoulder. "Nine o'clock, total confession, and we're still behind him, okay?"

Tony nodded. He couldn't expect more. *For God's sake, Aaron,* he pleaded silently, *come back. You're angry and scared, but don't lose your head. I didn't desert you. Our back was to the wall, but I didn't desert you.*

# XLVI

Mary could tell that Aaron was very upset, but at least his driving had improved after the first couple of blocks. Tony had not wanted her to go with Aaron, but Aaron had clearly needed her. If Aaron needed her, she would be at his side. They drove to a spot by a creek; a bit of a park with trees and picnic tables. Aaron drove around a bit more, seeming to choose a position for the car. Once he was satisfied with his spot and had parked, he leaned back, breathing heavily.

Keeping a careful watch around him, Aaron reached over and opened the glove compartment. Mary saw him take out a gun, check it, and leave it lying on the open glove compartment door. "Don't touch," he said to her. Mary moved as far back in her seat as she could. *Not on your life would I touch that, Aaron.*

"What happened in the court?" she finally asked when he remained silent. "Was it bad?"

"Yes." Aaron stared out the windshield, trying to collect his thoughts. In his head was a vision of Nat in the darkness, and Mary supposedly sleeping at the base of the royal palm. Of course Mary had never said anything about witnessing Nat's death. She had to have known that she witnessed a murder. "You saw me kill Nat, didn't you?" he asked her.

*Oh dear. How did they find out about that?* Mary wondered. "Yes." She wasn't going to try to lie, but she hoped Aaron wasn't angry because she hadn't told him that.

Aaron turned and looked at her, and Mary was reminded slightly of Taz II. His eyes were a little less personal than normal. "Why didn't you tell me?" he asked.

Mary shrugged. "That was your secret to tell, Aaron. It wasn't for me to tell."

"They've guessed," Aaron stated, "but I denied it." He tried to remember what had been said, but it was all confusion. He turned to face her. "Didn't it occur to you that they might guess? You are the only one who knows for sure about Nat." He reached over to touch her shoulder. "How did I do it?"

324

Mary touched her neck around the throat, trying to visualise that horrible action. "You put your hand on his neck while you were telling him not to be afraid. Then he shook a bit and he was dead."

Aaron sat in silence. There was no doubt Mary had witnessed it. If she was asked this tomorrow, or if they ever gave her a lie detector test, the truth would be out. Slowly, he let his breath out. "I'll show you."

As he leaned over, Mary sat quietly. When he put his hand on her neck, she stretched her head back so his hand had room. It was scary. It did occur to her that she was in a very defenceless position, and he was very upset. Her heart fluttered a bit as his fingers found their mark. Mary looked bravely into his eyes. *I know you won't hurt me, Aaron. You're upset and things didn't go well today, but I know you won't hurt me, because you're my friend now, and you want me to be alive too badly.*

"It's right there," Aaron murmured. "See, you were off almost two inches." Then he moved his hand back and touched her cheek, smiling into her trusting face. "You're not the slightest bit afraid of me, are you?"

"Why would I be afraid of you, Aaron?" Mary asked, trembling just a little in spite of her words. "You never wanted to hurt me."

He sat back, slipped an arm around her shoulders, and pulled her to lie against his side. "If that's so easy for you to understand, why am I having so much difficulty convincing everyone else?"

"They weren't there," Mary told him plainly, relaxing against his side. Since she had come to know Aaron as a friend, her nightmares of Taz had disappeared. Those days in Cuba seemed to be a long time ago. She patted Aaron's hand. "Why didn't you tell Tony about Nathanial?"

"I didn't think I could," Aaron replied. "They had been friends for a long time. I thought Tony would hate me, and I needed him."

Mary shook her head. "Don't you think he probably knew anyway? If other people have guessed, surely Tony, who knows you best, had figured it out. He's probably spent nights wondering what he would have done if he had been there." When Aaron looked at her with haunted eyes, Mary could see how hard it had been for him to carry this burden alone. "I suspect that if you tell him, Tony won't even be surprised," she guessed.

"Well, at least not now," Aaron admitted gravely. "But keeping it from him sure was a mistake today." A big mistake. "I'll tell him tonight," Aaron promised. "It's too late, but at least I'll have cleared my conscience, and maybe he can help prepare you for tomorrow. We can't let them know I killed Nat."

"Tomorrow's my turn," Mary stated fearfully. Clearly it must be an awful experience to have upset Aaron so much.

"Oh." Right…he had to tell her what else had been 'discovered'. She would be embarrassed, but he had to warn her. "Mary, remember that Saturday night?" He saw the concern on her face. "Osvaldo saw us. That's what else went wrong today. I was accused of raping you again, and *nobody* believes you could have consented. By the time they got done with me, even I could hardly believe it. That's what ruined it today. My reputation is now shit, and the case is falling apart." His hands had gripped the steering wheel. "Tony is going to have to lay the charges tonight, and my life as I know it is over."

"It's so unfair," Mary stated. "You knew you should have killed me in Cuba, and now look what's happened."

Aaron stared at her, incredulously. "No. Mary, can't you see that the only reason I've been able to bear this is because of you? You sit beside me, you defend me, and for a reason I'll never comprehend, you forgave me. If it weren't for you, I'd have ended my own life, Mary."

For a moment, Mary stared out at the creek. "Aaron, I never did thank you for that last night. You made me want to stay alive." When she looked at him, she knew she was blushing. The five o'clock shadow, the dark hair and eyebrows, and the soft, caring eyes belonged to the same Aaron she had met in Cuba. Only his clothes and neat appearance differed.

"You don't have to thank me for that, Mary," Aaron whispered intently, smiling at her embarrassed gaze. "I needed to be kind to you as much as you needed it from me. I'm just sorry that you are going to have to talk about it tomorrow."

*He's probably one of the nicest men I've ever met,* Mary thought, *and he's in trouble for doing something he couldn't avoid.* "I'm going to tell Tony that if he charges you, I will tell everyone that you are being unfairly blamed."

"No, no, no, Mary." Startled, Aaron turned and held her shoulders. "Don't you do that." He softened his voice. "You'd be playing games with some very powerful people, Mary, and they are very good at games. If you try that, it will only hurt me more." She looked disappointed, and he had to laugh. "Mary, you are such a darling. Do you want to help me?"

"Yes, of course."

"Then, when you take that stand tomorrow, remember that you have to convince the world that what happened to you in Cuba was not the fault of the CIA." He grinned at her. "Just a small task, right? Don't lie, and don't let the defence trick you. If you don't like the answer he has led you to, think about how you would like to answer the question. Try not to get trapped. Remember that to the public I represent the CIA. If you can get me off the hook, without implicating them, then I'm free and clear."

"I'll get you off," Mary promised. Somehow she would do it.

The gun was restored to the glove compartment, and Aaron drove to a fast food drive-through. They ate in the car and were still back at 51 Elm by 7:00 p.m. As Aaron walked into the house with Mary, Tony was hanging up the phone. Scott and Gavin were standing by the computers, and the tension in the room was unmistakeable. To Aaron's surprise, Frank Moseley was also there.

Tony greeted Mary pleasantly, then looked at Aaron. "Kitchen," was all he said.

Meekly, Aaron followed Tony into the kitchen and closed the door. This would not be a good scene. Tony faced him, his high colour showing Tony's visible effort to maintain control.

"Did you enjoy putting me through that tonight?"

Aaron leaned against the kitchen counter and crossed his arms. "You dumped me today," he accused. "You gave up on me. First you put me through all that, then you just gave up without a fight."

"You're wrong," Tony responded. "I never gave up on you." In anger, he paced the length of the kitchen and back, stopping in front of Aaron. "Christ, Aaron, I love that woman. What do you think I'm made of? Have you forgotten that I had to sit there and listen? And just when I thought I had finally heard the end, you admit that after all you did to her, you then made love to her." He held up his hands in a plea. "If you say she consented, then I want to believe you—but, Aaron, she was *tied to a tree!* How can I believe that she had a choice?"

Tony wanted to believe him. That's all Aaron needed to know. He forced himself to look Tony in the eye. "She was scared. She had asked me to kill her, but she was crying. All I did was hold her and kiss her once. Mary didn't expect to be alive the next day. She was lonely and she thought her life was over. She reached out for me because she knew I wasn't who I was pretending to be. It had nothing to do with assault, Tony. It was completely different, and she definitely consented." Aaron unfolded his arms as he saw the anger leave Tony's features. His boss had experienced enough to know what loneliness and fear were all about.

"I'm sorry that you had to hear all that today," Aaron offered, "but I won't apologise for making love to Mary. I won't," he repeated. "I needed her as much as she needed me. It was the only decent thing that happened in that hell hole."

"Okay," Tony whispered, raising a hand to end the topic. "It's okay. I understand now." Then he waited. "Anything else?" he prompted, bracing himself.

*Oh god, here we go,* Aaron realised, his body tensing once again. "Nat," he began, looking at Tony fearfully and feeling himself swallow. "They were right. I did kill Nat."

Tony experienced a strangely incredible sense of relief. "Of course you did," he managed to choke out.

*Of course I did?* Aaron suddenly felt an enormous weight roll off his shoulders. *Of course I did?* Tony had known all along and stood behind him anyway? There had been no accusations and no polygraph tests. Tony had guessed, but had not dragged him in to Security to find out the truth? "You knew all the time," Aaron breathed in astonishment.

Tony stepped forward and gripped Aaron's forearms. "Do you think I could have stood to ever look at you again if I thought for a minute that you let Nat lie there alone and in pain, knowing he was going to be tortured again the next day? Aaron, don't you think I know you a little better than that?" He dropped his hands. "You could never have let Nat suffer like that."

Aaron ran his fingers through his hair in amazement. "Man, I wanted to tell you so badly. I didn't think I could tell you," he confessed. "He was your best friend. How could I tell you?"

"I know, son," Tony responded. "I knew you were afraid to."

"Can you imagine what it's like," Aaron asked, "to have to hold someone you love in your arms and end their life?" He fought the constriction starting in his throat. "One minute he's your friend, and he's alive. Then he's dead, and you did it, and you can't…can't undo it." It was getting hard to speak. "I wanted any other way, Tony, but…but I couldn't think of one."

Tony was staring hard at the kitchen wall. Neither man spoke for a minute, then Tony broke the silence. "Mary saw you," he stated.

"Yes," Aaron admitted. "I thought she was asleep. She saw the whole thing."

"Does she know how you killed him?"

Aaron nodded. "Oh yeh. Well…she didn't know exactly how it was done. I had her demonstrate, but she only knew that I had touched his neck. She was off on the location."

Tony nodded. "Aaron, I need to confirm all this with Mary. When I come back, would you do me a favour?"

"Sure." *Anything,* Aaron thought, *just don't turn your back on me now.*

"Frank, Gavin and I have this empty spot inside us," Tony began. "Nat was our friend, and we didn't get to say goodbye. It feels unfinished for us." Tony looked hesitantly at Aaron. "You were with him at the end. It would help…it would make us feel better if we knew what was said and how, well, how it ended. I think we could deal with this emptiness better. Could you tell us? Would you be able to do that?"

*Good heavens,* thought Aaron, *I wasn't expecting that.* He looked at Tony and nodded. "Yeh, okay. I think so. I'll try—it's the least I can do."

"Thank you," Tony sighed. He pulled out his cellular phone and dialled Walsh. Carl had decided that he did not want to be told officially about Nat's death. He only wanted to be reassured that Aaron was not keeping secrets. When Walsh answered, Tony said only, "We have an understanding." Walsh would know what he meant. Carl was still feeling his way around the agency, but Tony was becoming more impressed with the man each day.

"Aaron, do you understand that things are going very badly, and I have to charge you with the offences against Mary in Cuba?" Tony asked as he put his phone away.

"Yes."

"I will not leave you alone in this," Tony promised. "I'll be working to get you out of this mess until it is finished. And just so you'll know, Mr. Walsh is backing us, Aaron. He's turning out to be a pretty good head, and he carries a lot of power, don't forget. He's sending over a personal friend now, who is highly placed at the FBI. His name is Al Norton. Norton is coming here for two reasons. He will lay the charges against you, so that everything is nice and official. We can't be accused of sweeping this under the rug. But if we survive Mary's testimony tomorrow, which is critical to us, the charges are withdrawn and Norton never took part in it. It just goes away. Only Walsh, Norton, and the people in this house will know you are charged, Aaron. Walsh is prepared to leave Security in ignorance unless we have to go public."

Tony checked his watch. It would be a long night for him, but even longer for Aaron. Aaron had a resigned look on his face. *Hell, does he know how much I hate doing this?* Tony wondered. *I can't even promise him it will all turn out okay, because it might not. All I can do is give it everything I've got.* "Aaron, you have to trust me. It's not over yet, and I don't know where we're going, but you have to trust me to do whatever it takes to get you out of this. I've been working with Walsh, and he's on board. Once we know what's going to happen, we have a lot of weight to throw behind you. Don't give up on us."

Aaron felt sick. "God, Tony, today I almost—"

"—but you didn't," Tony interrupted intensely. "You didn't sell us out. 'Almost' means shit. You didn't." He slapped Aaron on the shoulder. "I have to talk to Mary, then I'll be back with Frank and Gavin. By that time Norton should be here."

Tony found Mary in her bedroom, sitting on the edge of the bed, looking very serious. He closed the bedroom door behind him, and sat down beside her. They exchanged a look, but neither smiled. Mary waited for him to begin.

"Aaron has told me about what happened between you on your last night in Cuba," Tony began quietly, pretending that it didn't hurt. "He had to admit to it today in court. He has also talked to me about Nat."

Mary nodded. She didn't know what to say. Tonight, Tony seemed to be a combination of the working Tony and the personal Tony. His voice was gentle, but she could tell that he needed information from her. He looked away, then looked back at her.

"Mary," he continued with effort, "Aaron has told me that you consented to the sex that night. Is that true?"

"Yes." She made herself look at him. "I did."

"You were tied to a tree, Mary," he stated bluntly. "You had been his hostage for three days. You had no freedom of choice."

"Yes, I did," Mary answered. "Aaron didn't force me. I wanted him." This was really hard. Mary felt her eyes leave Tony's face, but forced them back again. "I thought I was going to die, Tony. No one had cared about me or treated me nicely for three days. I was all alone. Then I realised that Aaron was not really Taz. He was being kind to me. I needed...someone to hold me. I didn't want to die alone." There were signs of emotion on Tony's face, but Mary couldn't read them this time. "I'm sorry if this hurts you, Tony, but I can't take it back, and I wouldn't. That night I needed someone. I can't apologise for that."

"I'm not asking you to apologise," Tony whispered. He reached over and patted her knee. His voice was not to be trusted right now, so he stared out the window for a minute. Then he changed the subject. "They may ask you about Nat."

"What should I say?"

Good question. What should she say? She believed that she witnessed Nat's death, which she undoubtedly did. On the other hand..."Aaron says you were off on your guess about where you would need to apply pressure to kill someone."

Mary nodded. "Almost two inches, he said."

Tony looked over at her. "Then you don't know exactly how he was killed."

"Well, not exactly," Mary admitted, "but it's kind of obvious, isn't it?"

"But you don't *know*," he insisted. "You are assuming that to be the cause of death. Nat could just have been unconscious, right?"

"I suppose so," Mary answered doubtfully.

"When you are asked questions tomorrow," Tony said, "you can only state as true the things that you know are true. Paul Hedley will not let you sit there and make presumptions. Remember that the autopsy concluded that Nat died as a result of the trauma he suffered at the hands of Osvaldo. This is not a murder case against Aaron, Mary, although the defence will try their best to turn it into one. They are only guessing. For all you know, Nat could have died on his own later in the night, or someone else could have killed him during the night. Even if Aaron was charged with murder, you would have a hard time proving it, and believe me, we have no wish to charge Aaron with Nat's death."

"I'm afraid about tomorrow," Mary admitted. "I'm afraid I won't be smart enough, and they'll trick me."

"I know, dear, but this case is probably doomed anyway. All you can do is your best." Depressed, Tony rested his elbows on his knees. "I have to go now and ruin the career of someone who didn't deserve any of this. I have to charge Aaron with raping you and prepare him for the role of sacrificial lamb. In the end we will try to clear him, or at least get a minimal penalty, but he'll be ruined in the process. He's young enough to start over, and we'll help him as much as we can, but it's all such a damn shame, and a real waste."

Since this was about the worst day of his life anyway, Tony decided he might as well risk it all. He reached for Mary's hand and looked into her sad face. "Do you love me?"

"Yes."

The answer had been given without hesitation, and Tony managed a slight smile. Any other day he would have been dancing on the clouds after hearing that answer. "Try to remember that tomorrow, will you? The defence is going to use any trick at their disposal to turn you against us. They may say anything. Some of the things are just guesses. Some may be true." He shuddered inside. How would she react if she was told about the order in

Cuba? He had planned to tell her, but he chickened out. She loved him now, and he couldn't bear the thought of losing that love. Surely she wouldn't believe anything Cook tried to tell her.

"Remember that to protect Aaron, you must fight for us, Mary. If, by some miracle, you can make us look like the good guys again, then Aaron goes free. By protecting us, you protect Aaron. Look at me whenever you get in trouble. Paul will do his best to guide you." He leaned over and kissed her lips lightly. "Remember that no matter what happens, I have loved you since the day we met, and I would never, ever have done anything to hurt you. Can you remember that?"

"Of course." Tomorrow was going to be awful. She could tell by the way he was talking. It was up to her to save Aaron, and she was pitted against a defence lawyer who had been playing these legal games for years. Mary had no illusions about her abilities. She lived in a simple world and tried to tell the truth. Tomorrow the truth could be dangerous.

"Don't perjure yourself tomorrow," Tony warned, "but don't say anything you don't know to be true. And never offer them any extra information."

"Okay."

A final small kiss, then Tony got up. Now he had to face Aaron and do what was required of him to protect the agency. Today he hated his job.

Aaron had been sitting by himself in the kitchen, wondering how all this had happened to him. Part of him wanted to jump into his car and simply run, leaving it all behind, but the other part knew that he could never live as a fugitive. He had a much better chance if he stayed and let Tony try to help him through this.

When Tony brought Frank Moseley and Gavin into the kitchen, Aaron looked up from his chair with a feeling of dread. They were standing around him as if encircling him. He felt very much trapped, with them on the periphery.

At Tony's encouragement, Aaron managed to start talking. They listened quietly as he described Nat's last day. When they asked questions, Aaron answered, and eventually they knew everything, right down to what was said and what was felt. It was draining, but it was also a relief.

In the end, the men stood without speaking. No one had moved, but somehow everything was different. Aaron no longer felt alone in the centre, with them on the outside. He now felt as if he was cushioned behind a protective barrier. They were not outside...he was inside. He felt an incredible strength surrounding him. When he looked up into their serious faces, he realised that he no longer feared what was ahead. They were now on his side, and they would do their best for him. That best would be formidable indeed. Aaron sat back and felt the world roll off his shoulders. His job was done, he could do no more. He had placed his future in their hands, and they would take care of him.

The silence was interrupted by Scott's knock on the kitchen door. "Mr. Norton is here," he called.

As Tony guided Aaron out of the kitchen, Moseley and Gavin both told him not to worry. It was a strange way to end a career, Aaron decided. He was introduced to Mr. Norton, who shook his hand and then proceeded to state the charges in an even, detached voice, as if he wished he were doing almost anything else. Definitely a strange way to end your career, having your boss standing beside you with his hand on your shoulder, looking like he wanted to cry; with Moseley staring out a window; with Scott, well, Scott looked as if he had just lost his best friend; and Gavin was pacing agitatedly by the computers, as if he would like to pick one up and smash it.

When Mr. Norton finished, Tony turned to Gavin and Scott. "Will you two come to the court early tomorrow morning? I need someone to watch Aaron."

"I will *not* be his jailer," Gavin spat. "This isn't right, Tony, and you know it. Do your own dirty work."

Tony's face flushed with anger. "Read between the lines, Gavin," he said in an icy tone. "As it stands now, no one outside this house knows what is going on except Mr. Walsh. That's the way we want it. I have to be in the courtroom tomorrow. If you won't agree to take control of Aaron, I'll have to turn him over to Security. Is that what you want?"

"All right," Gavin growled, still furious. "All right, I'll do it." He glanced at Scott for consent, got it, and looked back at Tony. "We'll be there."

Aaron was taken away, leaving Gavin and Scott in the house. Extra Security would be arriving shortly. Tony had timed their arrival so they would not see Aaron being charged. Mary had not come out of her bedroom. Scott picked up the telephone and looked for a number in his personal address book.

"Who are you calling?" Gavin asked out of curiosity.

"My financial advisor," Scott responded, starting to dial. "I have to liquidate some assets."

Gavin wanted to throttle him. "Your what!?! Your best friend just gets arrested, and you're worried about liquidating your fuckin' assets?"

That earned him a stony look from Scott. "Aaron will need a lawyer...a good one. The last time I looked, Aaron couldn't afford the kind of lawyer I have in mind. I can." He finished dialling, then noticed that Gavin was still staring at him, but this time with a look of respect. Scott felt a little embarrassed. "Well, hell," he grumbled, "what's the good of having money if you can't help your friends when they need you?"

Gavin found that he could smile again. "Kiss your financial advisor for me, will you?"

# XLVII

Today was Mary's turn in court. At her insistence, Tony took her into their waiting room to see Aaron. As they entered the room, Aaron stood up, his wrists cuffed together in front of him. Gavin and Scott were close by, but Tony knew it was more for support than for guarding purposes. Mary crossed the room and took Aaron's hands. He managed a smile for her and told her not to worry, that everything would be okay. For a moment she gazed up at him, then returned the smile.

There was a knock on the door. Tony moved in front of Aaron to block anyone's view of the handcuffs, but it was Walsh who entered. Carl was accompanied by an unexpected visitor, who followed him into the room.

Aaron was puzzled. He recognised the visitor, but what was she doing here? Mr. Walsh was talking to him, so he left that question for later.

"Aaron, I want you to understand exactly what our plans are," Mr. Walsh began. "As Tony has told you, if at the end of the day our public relations people feel we survived without major damage, we will drop all charges against you. If anyone else were to try to bring the charges forward again, they would meet with some very stiff resistance from us. If, however," he continued, "this turns into disaster for us, we will make a public display of charging you. Then we will wait for as long as it takes for the furor to die down. Once we are out of the limelight, we will proceed as quietly as possible, and work to your benefit as much as possible. In the meantime you will continue on our payroll."

Suddenly Mr. Walsh seemed to remember the visitor, who had remained near the door. He waved her over. "Oh, and this is your lawyer, Cynthia Woodsend." He smiled slightly. "Normally we are not exactly thrilled to find ourselves opposite her in court, but in this case I believe she will find us quite easy to get along with."

His lawyer? Aaron greeted her politely, but felt the heat of embarrassment in his face. "There must be some mistake, Ms. Woodsend. I'd love to hire you, but I couldn't possibly afford—"

"I have been retained by the Andrews family to represent you," she cut in quickly, "should that become necessary." Ms. Woodsend then nodded in Mr. Walsh's direction. "Your employer had no objection to my dropping in to make your acquaintance and give you my card, since I was in the building today anyway."

Scott. Aaron looked at his "wannabe" brother-in-law. Although Scott had a bit of colour in his cheeks, he met Aaron's look defiantly. Scott had to know that it would take years for Aaron to repay this debt, if ever. Yet to refuse this gift would be an insult to the generous nature of his friend. The feeling of gratitude was almost overwhelming. Aaron accepted Ms. Woodsend's card with thanks, and watched her leave. He felt better. Now he had the support of his friends *and* one hell of a good lawyer.

They were calling Mary's name over the speaker system. It was showtime for her. Aaron wished her luck, and Mary walked to Tony's side, glancing back at Aaron as she left the room. Before they entered the courtroom, Tony saw her stop and look up at him. He knew she was afraid.

"Fight for him, Mary," he whispered. She lifted her chin in determination and entered the courtroom.

The courtroom was very quiet when Mary took the stand. Scott had told her where his sister was sitting, and what she was wearing, so Mary looked quickly at that spot. Then Mary couldn't help but smile. The young woman was just what she had expected. Of course Aaron would be engaged to someone as pretty as that, with a kind-looking face. When Susan hesitantly returned Mary's smile, Mary was pleased. *She seems nice, Aaron,* Mary thought. With luck and a lot of embarrassing work on her part today, perhaps Aaron and Susan could get on with their future. Determined, Mary faced Mr. Hedley and waited for the questions.

Mr. Hedley began with questions that were easy for Mary to answer: her name, where she lived, and family status. Then he asked how she had come to be in Cuba. The questions were not a surprise to Mary. Mr. Hedley had met with her a couple of days ago to practise them. The next ones centred on the kidnapping, which Hedley had her describe in detail, including the horseback ride into the mountains and the fact that the women were given no food or water. Particular attention was paid to Alfredo's comments when he had put Mary in the van, about how she was to be a "surprise" for Taz on his vacation.

"From what Mr. Pérez said to you, did you think that this 'Taz' knew about the kidnapping?" Hedley asked.

"No."

On to the arrival in camp. The courtroom audience was silent when Mary described how she and Juany discovered that they were to be used by the men in the camp for sexual purposes. Numerous questions were asked about how Taz reacted, and what he said to Mary, Alfredo, Osvaldo and Nat. Mary had not heard Osvaldo call Nat a CIA officer because Osvaldo had been facing Nat, and was about fifty feet away from her. Taz had been easy to hear because he had been speaking loudly, in a wild type of manner.

"Did 'Taz', and let's refer to him as Mr. St. Pierre, appear surprised to have you given to him as a present?"

Mary nodded as she replied. "Yes, he was definitely not expecting it."

Hedley asked if Mr. St. Pierre had seemed pleased. Mary answered in the negative. "Taz" had been agitated and excited, but had not indicated through his actions that he was particularly pleased. He had not rushed over to claim her.

Once Mr. Hedley had established that Mary believed Mr. St. Pierre had not known about the kidnapping and had appeared to be caught off guard with his "present", he moved on to the questions Mary dreaded. She had to describe the assaults, briefly, thank goodness, to all the people in the courtroom. The things Aaron had done to try to alleviate or prevent pain were embarrassing to describe, as was the oral sex. Mr. Hedley was patient, even though he had to ask her to speak up several times so she could be heard. Mary told about Taz I and Taz II, and her confusion about their personalities. Fortunately, no one in the courtroom seemed to find it at all amusing. Although they had heard most of this from Aaron, they sat in silence, as if in shock. At one point Mary found the courage to look at Susan. The young woman was white.

Mary was also asked to describe Juany's treatment, which she did to the best of her memory. Under Mr. Hedley's guidance, Mary described her fear of being hurt, and of the knife. No, Mr. St. Pierre had never cut her with the knife. She had been slapped a couple of times, and terrified, but he had not beaten her. Mr. St. Pierre had kept the others away from her, and she had emerged relatively unharmed. Nat's situation was discussed, and Mary could sense the anger from the CIA benches.

There was a pause. Mr. Hedley was pleased. This was going well. He continued by questioning Mary about what she had overheard regarding the Congressman and the activities of the Liberators. The threat to the tourists who rode through was also mentioned. That left one hard topic: the "consensual" sex act. Tony said that Mary had consented, so Hedley would do the best he could with that. The courtroom audience was very definitely on Mary's side, and would believe anything this quiet, sincere victim said. After that topic, he would wrap up with her escape wearing Aaron's jacket.

"Now, Mrs. Norland, we have arrived at Saturday night in the camp," he began. "You have told us why you did not want to be given to the Cuban men the next day. Mr. St. Pierre had offered to kill you, and you were resigned to the fact that you would die that night. Did Mr. St. Pierre come over to you that night?"

"Yes," Mary answered. "It was late. The stars had been out for a while, and I had been watching them. I thought it would be my last time."

Hedley took a second to observe Mary. She had just unknowingly created a setting for the audience. A setting of a clear night during which a scared woman waited for death. Amazing. The impact that this small person had on this case was frightening. He ploughed on.

"What happened when Mr. St. Pierre came over to kill you?"

"I started to cry," Mary admitted. "I seemed to do a lot of crying down there, because I was so afraid all the time. I had asked Mr. St. Pierre to kill me, and he had promised not to hurt me, but I was still afraid, and I didn't really want to die."

"What did Mr. St. Pierre do?" Mr. Hedley prompted.

*Here we go,* thought Mary. *Now I have to bare my soul to all these strangers to help Aaron.* "He held me and tried to reassure me. He…he kissed me."

Hedley took a few steps and stood on an angle to the witness box. "Mr. St. Pierre says that he had sexual intercourse with you at this point. Is that true?"

"Yes."

"He also states that you consented to this intercourse."

"No."

Hedley froze. It had been a very quiet *no*, but it had been a definite *no*. What the hell was going on? He glanced at Tony while he tried to collect himself. Tony was staring at Mary in shock. Hedley knew trouble when he saw it. Why had Mary changed her mind? He had to feel his way through this. The courtroom was buzzing.

Slowly, Hedley faced Mary. "No, you did not consent?"

"Correct."

She was sitting there looking very nervous, but determined. Why? "Then he did rape you." It was the obvious conclusion, but he asked anyway, thinking frantically.

"No."

*What the hell....?* This was not making sense. Judging by the movement in the courtroom, you could tell that he was not the only person confused. "Mrs. Norland, I don't understand. You had sex with Mr. St. Pierre. Either you consented, or you didn't."

Mary unconsciously ran a hand through her hair. *I hope I'm doing the right thing,* she prayed. Taking a deep breath to calm her nerves, she began to explain. "I was going to die. For three days I had been tied up, assaulted, starved, and I was alone. No one had been kind to me except Mr. Bowman. When I realised that Taz was Aaron, and Aaron was kind, I asked him to kill me. There wasn't supposed to be any tomorrow. Aaron...Mr. St. Pierre...was holding me, and he kissed me." She faltered, then forced herself on. "I needed to feel that someone cared for me. I needed someone to love me before I died."

Mary could feel herself blushing furiously, and the tears were starting in the back of her throat. She sniffed and kept going. "After...after he kissed me, I kissed him back and started to...well, touch him. I wanted him to touch me...to make love to me." The courtroom was once again totally silent. "He didn't understand at first, but then he did. He never intended to make love to me. He asked me if that was really what I wanted. In fact," she insisted, "after a while he hadn't even taken any of his clothes off." Mary looked in appeal at Mr. Hedley. They had not practised this, and Mary knew that she was floundering.

Cautiously, as if testing thin ice, Paul Hedley responded to the eyes that were asking for his help. "He was making love to you, fully dressed."

"Yes."

"When," he asked, "did that change?"

"Fifteen, maybe twenty minutes later," Mary guessed, wanting the floor to open up so she could disappear from sight. "Then I undid his belt. He said I didn't have to do that—he thought I wouldn't want to. I told him I wanted to." She couldn't, just couldn't, look away from Mr. Hedley in case she saw Susan or Tony watching. The tears had escaped and were running down her face. "So you see, I didn't have to consent," Mary concluded, "because Aaron never asked me to do anything. I asked him. It was Aaron who had to consent."

*Amazing...again.* Paul Hedley waited while Mary composed herself. The courtroom waited in silence, except for sniffing that could be heard from a number of people. *There is not a dry eye in this room,* Hedley was sure. *The audience is seeing a lonely woman in Cuba, waiting to die and needing to be loved. We've won. Barring unforseen disaster from the defence counsel, we have won.* When Mary could speak again, he led her gently through the escape. One more gem came out of that.

"You were able to escape because Mr. St. Pierre forgot to tie you up," Hedley summarised at one point.

"Aaron wasn't Taz any more," Mary answered. "Taz would have tied me up. Aaron St. Pierre would never tie a woman to a tree."

Court recessed for lunch, and Tony watched Carl Walsh walk beside Mary back to their private room. Carl was looking cautiously optimistic for the first time in weeks. He was clearly pleased with Mary's testimony, and seemed genuinely impressed with her personally. Mary had gained another admirer.

Lunch had been ordered in, mainly because Aaron was to be kept included. While things were looking good, they still had to live through the cross-examination before they could breathe easy and give Aaron back his freedom. Tony stayed by Aaron's side. He felt hopeful, very hopeful, and he noticed that Aaron's spirits were picking up because of that confidence.

Back in the witness box after lunch, Mary was ready for Mr. Cook. Mr. Walsh and the Deputy Director, Peter Geraldton, had been very flattering this morning. They said she had done an excellent job. That made her happy, because it meant that Aaron would not be in trouble any more if she could keep it up. Only a little longer, then it would all be over. Tony had not let her be embarrassed by her confession, either. He said she had been very brave to do that. Paul Hedley had laughed and expressed a desire for a stiff drink. Soon, her turn would be over.

James Cook knew he had a hard job ahead of him. He had to rattle this woman and shake her faith in the people she currently viewed as her protectors. It had to be done very carefully, too, because everyone in the courtroom was on her side. There was no doubt in anyone's mind that she was the victim, and he could not be seen to prey upon her. This would be very tricky. He could not afford to alienate the jury.

"Mrs. Norland," he began, "you have been staying someplace as a guest of the CIA, is that true?"

"Yes sir." Mary was well prepared. She was to answer questions politely and not to get defensive. If she did not know the answer, she was to say so. It was dangerous to guess. If she felt that she was being tricked, she was to think about what she really wanted to say. Mr. Cook would try to trap her into saying yes or no, when the real answer was entirely different. She was never to offer additional information. Mr. Hedley would try to help whenever it was necessary. Above all, she was not to lie. Everyone believed her now, and that must not change.

"Were the doors locked?"

"Yes, sir."

"Were there alarms on the outside doors?"

"Yes, sir."

Mr. Cook smiled at her. "Did you have a key?"

"No, sir."

"So, Mrs. Norland," Cook concluded, "you could not walk out of that place unless someone let you out, is that true?"

"Yes, sir."

"Were you allowed out?"

Mr. Cook wasn't looking at her. He was staring at the jury. "Oh yes," Mary answered. "They took me to the gym every morning."

"They took you?"

"Yes, sir."

"Mm." Cook paced a bit. "What would have happened if you had said you wanted to go for a walk by yourself? Could you have just walked out the door?"

"Oh no," Mary answered. "Not until they turned the alarm off."

Cook looked at her. "Would you have been allowed to go out by yourself?"

"Nooo," Mary answered cautiously.

"Why not?"

"It wasn't safe for me to do that," she explained. "I would have needed people to protect me."

Cook turned to face the audience. "What you are saying, then, is that you were unable to leave the custody of the CIA."

Hedley protested. Mrs. Norland had never been in custody.

Cook continued. "I will change my terminology. Mrs. Norland, could you simply have said goodbye to the CIA, told them you no longer wanted to cooperate, and walked away?"

"But it wasn't safe," Mary protested.

"Please answer yes or no, Mrs. Norland."

Stuck on the first subject, Mary realised. This was not good. If she said, *"No,"* that would sound bad. Then she remembered something. "Yes."

"Yes?" Mr. Cook sounded incredulous. His tone turned to one of pity. "Mrs. Norland, do you really believe that?"

"Yes," Mary answered confidently. "They took me to the embassy one day, and my ambassador said I could go home right then if I wanted, or I could stay at the embassy. All I had to do was call them and ask Mr. Dune to take me there."

Cook swore to himself. Why the hell hadn't his contacts told him about that? He had just lost some leverage with this witness.

Tony and Carl Walsh looked at each other. Walsh had been absolutely right in his decision to produce Mary at the embassy's request.

Mr. Cook changed subjects quickly, as if that one had not been important. Today was not going well for him. After Mary's performance over the "consensual" sex this morning, he had decided it would be suicide to pursue that topic. That left him only two other avenues of attack. He proceeded to one of them now.

"Are you familiar with a man called Gavin Weeks?" Cook inquired casually.

Mary nodded. "Yes."

"In what capacity? How do you know him?"

"He guards me at night," Mary responded.

"He guards you," Cook repeated, as if in deep thought. "Do you believe that to be his normal job, guarding people?"

"He probably has other jobs, too," Mary replied carefully, "but I don't know what he does." She didn't, either. All she had heard about him were generalities and rumours.

"No, you probably don't," Cook agreed, cutting off Mr. Hedley's protest before it was uttered. Hedley had sat down again, warily. "In your mind, Mrs. Norland, do you suspect that he has functions that are quite different from what he is doing now?"

*"Think about what you want to say,"* Mary remembered being told. "I do not think Mr. Weeks is a regular security guard," she stated.

"No," Cook agreed, "he is not. Have you ever had an occasion to be afraid of him?"

"No," Mary replied. Not really. He had never done anything to frighten her. That incident in her car had been a fluke, and he had tried to keep her from being scared.

"Mrs. Norland, do you watch television or go to movies?"

*Television? Movies?* Mary was confused. "Yes."

Cook nodded and faced her suddenly, knowing he was about to cause some trouble. "Mrs. Norland, do you know what a 'hit man' is?"

Hedley was on his feet, but Mary didn't hesitate. She was angry. Gavin was her friend, and Mr. Cook was insinuating that he was no more than a hit man. Gavin, who had promised to protect her personally, when she *knew* that was most unlikely to be part of his job description. Gavin, who had saved her life twice.

"Gavin's not a hit man!" she responded indignantly. Then she caught herself. Offering information or saying extra things was dangerous, she had been told. Besides, for all she knew, being a hit man could indeed be part of his job description. It was best to keep quiet.

Hedley stated his objection in no uncertain terms, and won, but that wasn't what pleased him the most. When he sat down, he had to smile at the angry-looking Mary. That little outburst from the innocent witness had been lovely. People now knew that she was not only unafraid of Mr. Weeks, but that she was absolutely convinced that he was not a paid killer. *One more point for our side,* he counted mentally.

*Boy, this woman is naïve,* Cook decided. It was time to teach her the facts of life. "Mrs. Norland, you are the only non-Cuban witness to the events that happened in that camp in Cuba aside from Mr. St. Pierre, is that correct?"

"Yes."

"Now, Mr. St. Pierre is employed by the CIA. That makes you the only independent witness to those events, is that correct?"

"Yes, I guess it does," Mary conceded.

"In fact, Mr. St. Pierre had planned to kill you because he realised what a danger you were to the operation, is that true?"

"I never understood that part," Mary admitted. Mr. Hedley was up complaining again, which gave Mary a chance to wonder where this questioning was going.

"Mrs. Norland," Cook began again. "You have stated that it is your belief that Mr. Weeks has a job other than guarding people. He is, in fact, assigned to Special Operations. Why do you think," Cook asked slowly, "that on the Sunday afternoon in Cuba, Mr. St. Pierre was overheard begging Mr. Dune not to send Mr. Weeks after you? He said, 'She doesn't deserve that.'"

Mr. Hedley was on his feet trying to stop Mr. Cook from talking.

"Why would Mr. Dune send Mr. Weeks after you, Mrs. Norland?" Cook demanded, yelling over Mr. Hedley.

"No," Mary protested weakly, but she felt ill as the truth suddenly dawned on her. The judge was trying to get order, and the courtroom was buzzing.

Mary sat in shock. Tony was going to send Gavin after her? Aaron had begged him not to? Aaron, who had made an agreement to take the blame…an agreement that had never made sense to Mary?

Several inexplicable puzzle pieces suddenly fell into place. Aaron had agreed to take the blame in return for her "protection". Shouldn't her protection have been automatic? Tony had asked her all those questions…the ones almost the same as Gavin's…and Gavin had been contemplating killing her. Tony had told her how dangerous it was to their case that Aaron had assaulted her—a fact borne up by his statement that Mr. Pitt had first wanted her as a witness. Tony had come to Toronto to see if it was worth the risk of protecting her. He had originally planned to send Gavin to kill her, but Aaron had begged him not to.

Why hadn't she figured this out before? Because she had fallen in love with Tony. Tears started to run down her face as the lawyers argued. She looked at Tony, who had paled and was staring at her as if he too was in shock. Last night he had warned her that the defence would say anything, and some of the things would be true. He had wanted her to still love him.

Now she was being asked something by Mr. Cook, but she didn't care. She wouldn't help any more. Last night, against her better judgement, she had admitted to Tony that she loved him. A man she didn't really know, who had a whole secret life about which she knew nothing. She had finally decided to take the huge risk and tell him she was in love with him. And he had tried to kill her. What a loser she was. What a naïve fool!

It was as if all her pent-up fear and emotion wanted to come out at once. All she could do was cry. Tony looked miserable, and Hedley was obviously agitated, but Mary didn't care. *To hell with all of them.*

Cook was actually dismayed. The witness was crying. That was not what he had been aiming for. She should have been shocked, angry, puzzled or outraged. Why was she crying as if she had just lost her best friend? This was backfiring on him. The judge had allowed him to browbeat St. Pierre to a certain extent, but that was because St. Pierre was trained, coached and supported by a large organisation. Mrs. Norland was a victim who had come voluntarily across the border to give evidence to the court. The judge was letting Cook know in no uncertain terms that he would not be allowed to harass this witness. Cook also knew the jury would have little patience with him.

What had gone wrong? Cook looked to where Mrs. Norland was staring— right at Anthony Dune. Good heavens. Dune looked almost as upset as the witness did. Cook cursed himself and his sources. Why hadn't they known? Mr. CIA himself, the ever so ethical workaholic Dune, must have found his way to this woman's heart.

Now what? Cook was momentarily lost. Could he use this to his advantage, or was it time to admit defeat?

Without warning, Mary took things into her own hands. She decided not to play this game any more. Before anyone could stop her, she ran from the stand and straight out the closest door. People were yelling at her and running after her, but she didn't care. Once in the hall, she realised she had no plan, and no place to go. The women's washroom was to her right, across the hall, so she ran in there, finding it thankfully empty. There, she gave up trying to control her sobbing, leaning against the wall by the paper towel dispenser. Behind her, she heard Sheila dash in.

"Mary." Sheila came over and peered into her face. "He wouldn't do that, Mary. They're just trying to upset you. Tony would never do something like that."

"Yes, he would," Mary insisted, feeling the tears running down her cheeks. "It's true, he did. That's why he asked me the same questions that Gavin did. It's all true."

At that moment, Mary heard Tony's voice as the door opened. Someone was protesting, but Tony was saying he knew damn well that it was a woman's washroom. He came in anyway, and stood in front of her.

When he looked at the woman who had won his heart, Tony felt a wave of despair go through him. Mary was huddled in the corner, hating him. She knew he had given that order, and now he would lose her. In spite of that, he had to somehow keep her fighting for Aaron. She was looking at him with tears in her eyes and a sob in her voice.

"It is true," she accused him. "That's why Aaron had to plead for me. That's why he had to make the deal with you. Not to have you protect me…to keep you from killing me." It ended in sobs.

She was so hurt, he knew. She felt betrayed by him, and he could not undo what he had done. How could he possibly make her understand those minutes in Cuba? He turned to Sheila. "Please leave us alone for a few minutes." Sheila looked at him, shocked, but obeyed.

He touched Mary's shoulder. "Mary, I walked into a disaster in Cuba. My best friend had been tortured and the only independent witness we had to what happened down there had been raped by one of my officers. To protect us, I made a decision I had no authority to make." She was wiping her eyes, so he fished in his pocket for a tissue and handed it to her. "I never tried to have you killed, not *you*," he continued. "I hadn't met you—you weren't real to me. You were real to Aaron, though. That's why he had to change my mind. You're right," Tony confessed. "Aaron bargained for your life, and because he did that, he saved you for me. That's why I'm begging you to go back in there and fight for him. He deserves that."

Taking a breath, Tony tried to smile into the wet brown eyes, but failed dismally. There was a huge lump in his throat. "You may hate us now, Mary. You hate me. But please don't take it out on Aaron. He's fought for you every step of the way. All he's ever tried to do is protect you. Please go back in there and fight for him. They can't hurt you any more. You know the worst now."

The tears had stopped, and Mary wiped her eyes. It seemed to Tony that she had accepted the truth. When she nodded, he felt a great relief. She would still help Aaron. It was all he could hope for. When she moved, she paused in front of him and looked into his face.

"Mary," he whispered, but caught himself. He struggled to control his own personal pain. There was no time left. Personal agonies had to be put aside. Whatever small chance he had of crossing the divide he had placed between them had to be put on hold. They were two small pegs in a very big wheel, and Tony's private life had to take a backseat once again.

Mary looked into his face searchingly. What was she looking for? *Can you see the pain?* he wondered. *Can you see what is happening in my heart when three conflicting forces are tearing it apart?* His love for her, his loyalty to his employer, and the deep responsibility he felt for Aaron were all in opposition to each other. Somehow he had ended up on a tightrope high above the earth, and he could see no net below.

Looking away, Mary felt dull inside. She realised that they were standing together talking in a washroom. "You know," she said, "I had really hoped that someday we could have been together someplace normal."

It hurt a lot, and Tony knew he had winced. "We have to get back into court," was all he said. Obediently, and without apparent interest, she let him guide her out.

# XLVIII

Lino Viltrez sat in his cell beneath the courts, deep in thought. So far he had been treated well, and his worries about his personal safety had diminished. His captors had no idea who he was, so it had been easy for him to agree to their deal without threatening his country's security. In return for confirming that the Liberators were blackmailing American businessmen, and that Osvaldo had tortured Mr. Bowman, Lino was offered a reduced sentence and told that he would be deported back to Cuba at its completion. Little did the Americans know how much Lino looked forward to being deported.

Mr. Simmons, his court-appointed lawyer, appeared to be negotiating on his behalf in good faith, but Lino did not trust the CIA. For all he knew, Mr. Simmons could be on their payroll. Lino had asked for, and received, daily copies of a Canadian newspaper. Once the case had hit the media, his country had discovered what had happened to the Canadian tourist. His government was doing its best to reassure the Canadians that the Liberators remaining in Cuba would be severely punished. Canadian tourism was vital to the Cuban economy, and Canadians like to feel safe. His government was being profuse with apologies and assurances that nothing like this would ever happen again. Security would be increased. Tourists would be protected.

What was not reported in the paper were the secret negotiations going on between certain officials in the Cuban and Canadian governments, which were undoubtedly occurring. Lino's government would want him back. Lino was a high-ranking Cuban Intelligence officer, who knew a great deal too much to be sitting in an American jail cell. He had volunteered to infiltrate the Liberators himself because of his knowledge of the United States. They had known the CIA had contacted the Liberators when James Thompson had been seen in their country. They had started watching his activities.

Lino had been livid the day Alfredo and Osvaldo had brought the women into camp. It had been difficult for him to look unconcerned. His plan had been to let the women escape, but "Taz" had rarely left them alone. Mr. Simmons had told him that St. Pierre had been protecting Mrs. Norland and the two had become friends. When he thought back to Taz's behaviour, that didn't actually surprise Lino. He had heard the knife story from Alfredo, and had also heard two of the Liberators grumbling about Taz not letting them have Mrs. Norland.

It also explained Taz's reaction when the women were brought into camp. Taz had seemed to be taunting Bowman, almost putting on a show. Looking back now, Lino could see that St. Pierre had been caught off guard and was looking for a way out. It explained the initial look of shock on his face that no one else seemed to notice, and that disguised appeal to Bowman. Mrs. Norland had been fortunate to suffer no major damage. Lino planned to round up and personally kill every Liberator he could find when he returned to Cuba in repayment for what they had done to the village girl, Juany.

What Lino wanted most of all was to get back home and take Jose Luis with him, as a "present" to his government. It would be difficult, he knew, for his officials to negotiate through Canadian officials without letting the Americans know who he was. They would be instantly suspicious. Once they knew, it was unlikely the CIA would let him leave. No, if he hoped to get home, Lino would have to do his own bargaining.

The CIA was in big trouble, because the world was waiting to see how they had treated the tourist. Lino wished he could watch the trial. The Liberators could walk free if St. Pierre lost his credibility. That thought did not please Lino at all. He wondered how far the CIA would bargain in exchange for having a Cuban Intelligence officer back St. Pierre and clear him of all blame. Realistically, the CIA would recover from its disgrace even if St. Pierre did badly. Heads would roll, surely, and positions would be shuffled, but they were too strong to be down for long. His country would have enjoyed watching them squirm, but Lino had a feeling that it was more important to his government that he be returned to them with his secrets intact. It was also important that Jose Luis be presented to the Cuban people as the worst of all evils: a traitor and a man who had tried to put a stain on their entire tourist industry.

One big problem remained. What assurance did he have that he would be returned safely to Cuba? He was in a foreign country with no protection, surrounded by people he could not trust. He was surrounded by CIA officers and one small famous tourist. An idea was forming. Mrs. Norland was a small Canadian tourist.

# XLIX

As Mary walked into the witness box, Paul Hedley observed her closely. He spoke briefly to Tony, who told him that Mary would continue for Aaron's sake, but for no other reason. Hedley understood. They were once again on the edge of a crisis. If Mary could survive the remainder of Cook's cross-examination, then he had one last brief chance to repair any damage. Fortunately, although the jury had seen Mary upset, Cook had been unable to prove his point. He had been trying to rattle her and had succeeded, but she had not agreed with him. Her distress could be seen as a witness's reaction to being continually bombarded by questions. If only Mary could remain strong enough to endure the remainder of his attacks, they still had a chance.

On the stand again, Mary felt her resolve harden. She was tired of this game, and very tired of Mr. Cook. He was trying to trick her into saying things that would hurt Aaron. This time she was ready for him. Aaron deserved to be protected, and protect him she would.

Cook knew he would only have a few more chances with this judge. Since he had lost his momentum on the last subject, he would move on to the final issues.

"Mrs. Norland, when you were contacted by the CIA in Toronto, you already knew Mr. St. Pierre's first name, didn't you?"

"Yes."

"When did you learn his name?"

Mary tried not to avoid Cook's eyes. "Mr. Bowman must have told me."

"He turned to you and said that 'Taz' was not really Taz, but a CIA officer named Aaron?"

"No, he didn't say that," Mary admitted. "He must have just let it slip out." That was true enough. Nathanial would not have intended Mary to overhear him.

"You don't remember him telling you?"

"No." He hadn't told Mary. She had just overheard.

"Then you don't remember *when* you heard it."

Mary sidestepped the question. "I was only talking to him in the afternoon and evening."

"Did you not question him about this new name?"

"I don't remember exactly when he said it," Mary insisted, with a feeling that she should be crossing her fingers. This was awfully close to lying. "I remembered it later."

"Did anyone approach Mr. Bowman during the night?"

"I don't think so," Mary replied honestly. "Aaron, Juany and I were the only people near him."

"Did you see Mr. Bowman die?" Cook asked.

*See him die? Not exactly.* "No, but he must have died after I lay down to sleep, because he was dead in the morning."

Cook looked sternly at her. "You saw Mr. St. Pierre kill Mr. Bowman, didn't you?"

Hedley jumped up. There was no evidence that Mr. Bowman had died of anything other than the physical trauma of being tortured. The witness had already stated that she did not see Mr. Bowman die. Mr. Cook was insinuating once again that Mr. St. Pierre had murdered Mr. Bowman, but there was *no* evidence of this. Mr. Bowman had died as a result of torture, and the coroner had already testified to this.

Mr. Cook lost the argument, but threw in one last question. "Can you swear, Mrs. Norland, that Mr. St. Pierre did not kill Mr. Bowman?"

*A trick. What do I want to say?* "I cannot swear to that. Mr. Bowman was alive when I went to sleep, and dead when I woke up." She did not bother to tell Mr. Cook that she had gone to sleep but woken up again when Aaron came over to talk to Nathanial.

*Damn woman,* Cook swore to himself. Okay, final subject and their last chance.

"Mr. St. Pierre was sent to Cuba by the CIA disguised as a known rapist. Is it fair to say that if Mr. St. Pierre was not in Cuba, you would not have been raped?"

That was rather obvious. "That would be fair," Mary agreed.

"So it was Mr. St. Pierre's fault that you were assaulted," Cook concluded.

"No." It was not Aaron's fault, in Mary's mind.

"No?" Cook had wandered away, but now approached her again. "You just said it happened because he was in Cuba."

Mary dug her heels in. "No, I said it could not have happened if he had *not* been in Cuba."

"Therefore, his being in Cuba caused you to be raped," Cook insisted.

*Wrong,* Mary knew. "No. I was raped because the defendants kidnapped me and gave me to Mr. St. Pierre as a test."

It was turning into a fencing match. "The defendants did not rape you," Cook insisted.

"Only because Aaron protected me," Mary countered.

Cook would not give up. "Mr. St. Pierre raped you."

"Yes," Mary admitted.

"He is therefore the cause of you being raped," Cook concluded.

Wrong again. There was a difference, Mary knew. "No. Aaron doesn't rape. 'Taz' was being tested by the defendants."

Cook held up his hands. "'Taz' *is* Aaron."

Mary could be very stubborn when she knew she was right. She set her jaw. "Mr. St. Pierre would not have raped me if he had any choice."

"He *had* a choice," Cook insisted.

"The *choice* was torture and death. That was not a choice. Besides, I would have had the same fate as Juany." That was the absolute truth, Mary knew.

Cook had a sinking feeling in his gut. He couldn't shake her. It was incredibly frustrating. The judge soon tired of his efforts and asked him to move on. He had lost. There was nothing to move on to. At least he could protect the Congressman as far as possible.

"Mrs. Norland, did you meet Mr. Harvey in Cuba?"

"No, I left before he arrived." Mary welcomed the change in subject.

"So Mr. Harvey never harmed you, Mr. Bowman or Miss Martínez."

"No." Mary noticed that Mr. Cook had dropped his confrontational tones.

"As far as you could tell," Cook continued, "was there any indication that Mr. Harvey knew of the presence of yourself, Mr. Bowman or Mr. St. Pierre in Cuba?"

"Not as far as I know."

"Thank you. I have no further questions, you honour." Mr. Cook sat down.

Were they finished? Mary could barely stand the relief. She looked at Mr. Hedley, who stood up and smiled at her. He had been whispering with Tony and Mr. Walsh.

"Just to clarify, Mrs. Norland, you told the defence that Gavin Weeks was not a hit man. Why did you say that?"

Mary answered carefully, because Mr. Hedley had sounded very cautious. "Gavin saved my life twice. And I wouldn't be here at all if he was a hit man and someone told him to kill me, would I?"

Paul tried not to smile. The next question was crucial from a public relations perspective. Mary had already answered it, but it needed to be said clearly and without hesitation.

"Mary, who do you blame for raping you?"

Mary had no doubt about that. "The defendants. They kidnapped me and *gave* me to someone they believed to be a rapist, for a *present*! They treated me as if I wasn't even a human being!"

"Thank you, Mrs. Norland. No further questions, Your Honour."

Court adjourned for a break, and Mary found herself surrounded on the walk back to their private room by a group of very happy CIA employees.

Everyone entered the private room, and at the sound of the chatter, Aaron and Gavin stood up. *Here we go,* thought Aaron. His knees felt weak, and he looked at Gavin gratefully when he put a hand through Aaron's arm.

"I'm right here, man," Gavin whispered.

Mr. Walsh walked directly over, followed by Tony. "Get those cuffs off him," Walsh ordered. "You missed quite a show, Aaron," he continued, grinning and pointing at Mary. "She did one hell of a job." Then he got serious. "We owe you one, Mr. St. Pierre. You will stay off work on sick leave until Dr. Hummel says you are ready to return, and then we are going to talk about where you want to go in this company."

Aaron managed to croak out a "Thanks." He was astounded, and leaned in relief against Gavin.

Before Mr. Walsh had taken two steps away, Gavin had his key out and was removing the handcuffs. As he took each one off, Tony took Aaron's freed wrist and rubbed it. Aaron smiled. The handcuffs had not been tight. In fact, the whole process had been conducted in the most polite and delicate manner possible. Poor Tony had hated it, though. The look on his face told Aaron how sorry he was, and how much he wanted it put behind them. He did not need to massage Aaron's wrists, but as Sheila would have said, it was a healing thing.

"It's okay, Dad," Aaron whispered. Tony blinked, smiled slightly and dropped Aaron's wrist. *Over with and done,* as Moseley was apt to say.

Mary was standing a few feet away, with her eyes shining, a smile on her face and her hands clenched in front of her. She was so excited that she could hardly stand still. Her Aaron was free.

Aaron looked at her, grinned at her happy face, walked towards her and placed his hands around the petite waist. With little effort, he picked her up, shoulder height. "You are incredible," he said honestly, ignoring her gleeful screech at being lifted so high. The door opened behind him, but Aaron didn't pay any attention.

"Aaron," Tony said in a warning voice.

*Oh Tony, you're such a stick in the mud,* Aaron thought, as he pulled Mary to his chest and wrapped his arms around her. Mary didn't mind, he knew. She had her arms wrapped around his neck for support, and was laughing happily in his ear. "How did you do that?" he asked her. "How on earth did you do that?"

"Aaron," Tony said again.

At the same time that a voice spoke behind him, Mary stopped laughing and was tapping frantically at his shoulder to be put down.

"She has incredible inner strength," the voice said.

*Susan!* Carefully, Aaron put Mary down and turned to find Susan on Scott's arm. Scott was beaming.

"I'm sorry," Mary said to Susan, as Tony placed his hands lightly on Mary's shoulders to draw her back a bit from Aaron.

"Good heavens, don't apologise," Susan replied, looking a little nervous. "After what you two have been through, you deserve a chance to celebrate."

Aaron seemed to have lost his ability to speak, so Tony spoke for him. "It's good to see you again, Susan."

Susan looked apprehensively around the room. "I hope it was okay for me to come in here," she said to Tony. Then she looked into Aaron's face. "I just wanted to make sure you were all right."

"Of course it's okay," Tony assured her, wondering if he would have to kick Aaron to snap him out of his shock. "You're one of the family."

"I'm sorry you had to sit through all that," Mary said. "I felt so badly for you."

That surprised Susan, who looked at Mary firmly. "Don't you apologise," she ordered. "You don't have to apologise for *anything*," she emphasised. "Either of you," she added, looking at Aaron.

That finally snapped Aaron out of it, and he reached for Susan's hands. "Sue, I'm so glad you are here," he managed, in a husky voice.

Scott strolled away to talk to Gavin, and Tony found that Mary was willing to be led away a few more feet, although she virtually ignored him. She stood with her hands clasped loosely, beaming at Aaron and Susan.

*Yes, my dear,* Tony thought, *they are very happy. We would be feeling that way now too, if I hadn't blown my second chance at happiness.* It hurt inside. His professional side wanted to celebrate, but personally he was in agony.

Mary had not pulled free from the hands he had rested on her shoulders, but there seemed to be a great distance between them. He wanted to try to pull her closer, but was afraid his little tiger would turn and snarl at him. It was safer to stand here like this; apart, but at least close. He couldn't bear the rejection today. They needed a chance to talk, so he could try to explain why she should forgive him for that order in Cuba.

Hedley popped his head through the door and gestured to Tony, Walsh and Peter Geraldton. "Court's ready to reconvene."

*Time to go.* Tony sighed and dropped his hands from Mary's shoulders.

# L

The courtroom was invited to sit after the judge had seated herself, and Tony tried to make himself comfortable. It was Lino's turn on the stand, and Tony hoped Lino would testify well. If he did, it should wrap up this case. Surely the defence would decide to plead. The FBI had done its domestic research thoroughly, and the defence did not have a leg to stand on. Lino was simply the icing on the cake, and important personally to the CIA because he would confirm Osvaldo as Nat's torturer. If Lino did his job well, he would receive a light sentence for his involvement with the Liberators. Lino seemed eager to return to Cuba, and this was possible following his time in jail. His interpreter stood in readiness.

As Lino approached the witness stand, he hesitated. His guard was trying unobtrusively to move him forward. Tony frowned. What was the matter with this guy? He had made an agreement that was in his own best interest. There would be no forgiveness if he backed out now.

Lino took the stand with obvious reluctance. Paul Hedley eyed him apprehensively. There had been more than enough surprises in this case already. Couldn't anything go smoothly? He asked Lino to state his name, and was relieved that after a slight pause Lino was at least able to do that.

"Mr. Viltrez, you have been a member of the Sierra Maestra Liberators, is that correct?" Hedley reached down to shift a page of notes that had slid out of order.

"Not exactly," was the response.

Hedley froze. Not exactly? What the hell was this? He stared at Lino. This was not in the script. Couldn't anyone follow the script in this case? *Okay, time to think fast. What does "not exactly" mean?*

"Mr. Viltrez, please explain what you mean by 'not exactly'." *And it had better be good,* Hedley thought, *or your goose is cooked.*

Tony's mind was racing. "Not exactly" could be an attempt to distance himself from the Liberators, or it could be something much more important. He really wanted to hear what "not exactly" meant.

Lino was looking directly at where Tony and Frank sat side by side. He was not looking much like a guitar player now. They could see him swallow. His response silenced the courtroom.

In perfect English, Lino answered. "I joined the Liberators following the murder of James Thompson." Then he stopped.

Mr. Walsh turned to stare at Tony. On Tony's other side, Frank whispered, "Get that man the hell off the stand."

Hedley was no fool. He turned to check for direction. Tony gave him a sign to "cut". Who the hell was Lino? This could get very exciting if the suspicion forming in Tony's mind was true.

Hedley faced Lino. "Mr. Viltrez, I plan to ask you once again to identify yourself to the court. Before I do so, do you wish to consult with your counsel?"

"Yes."

Hedley asked for, and received, a recess. Cook didn't even object. He looked like a man who knew he had lost, and he was already whispering to the Congressman. Tony, Walsh and Moseley led Lino away in the company of Hedley and Lino's lawyer. Tony took a quick detour to let the others know about the change in events.

Tony dashed into their private room where everyone was waiting anxiously. He noted that Susan and Mary were talking at one side of the room, so he waved the others into a group. "Lino is not who we think he is," Tony blurted quietly. "He's talking to his lawyer now. It is possible, just faintly possible, that you may have scooped a Cuban Intelligence officer, Aaron. We'll know shortly, I hope."

The group was speechless until Scott dared to look like a fool. "Is that good news for us, or worse?" he ventured.

"It should be good news, shouldn't it?" Aaron guessed. "He'll have no use for Jose Luis, and he'll probably agree to almost anything in exchange for being allowed to go home."

Tony nodded. "That's my guess. If he is Intelligence, he's a real find for us, but we'll be handling this very carefully. We've got a lot at stake here."

Speaking of a lot being at stake, he looked over at Mary. She met his gaze, but her eyes were expressionless. Her work was done here, but she couldn't leave until the trial was over, just in case she was needed again. There would be no further danger for her now, though. Everything she knew was known to all. Mary could leave the safe house and stay elsewhere, although the CIA was still responsible for her while she was needed by them.

"Mary," he beckoned, hating the coldness in her eyes, "it's not necessary for you to be kept at 51 Elm any longer. You're quite safe now. I'll arrange another location for you. Perhaps you could stay with Sheila."

At that remark, Gavin gave Tony a look that said a sarcastic, *Thanks a lot.* Scott saw the look and knew the reason for it. Tony wasn't thinking, but after the pressures of the last two days, that wasn't surprising.

"I'd love to have Mary stay at my parents, Tony," he offered. "I'll stay there to keep an eye on her, and we have staff who will be glad to take care of her." That earned him a grateful, if sad, look from Mary.

Tony bit his lip and nodded, cursing the fact that he had to run off again. He desperately needed to talk to Mary. Now he only had time to thank Scott, smile at Mary and dash out.

Mary watched him go, then felt a touch on her shoulder. Gavin nodded in the direction of the door, so Mary followed him out to the smoking area. It was deserted at this time of the day. To her surprise, she saw Gavin remove a single cigarette and a pack of matches from his pocket.

"I didn't know you smoked," she commented.

Gavin smiled. "It's rare. I have to keep in top shape, and it's getting harder every year." Lighting the cigarette, he leaned back against the outside wall of the building. "Actually, I bummed this from one of the Security guys." He looked at the cigarette and laughed. "That's pretty ironic when you consider that I only smoke when I'm going to talk about things I'm not supposed to talk about."

"Don't bother," Mary protested, holding up her hand to stop him. "I don't need one of those 'lectures from a friend' discussions. I knew better than to fall in love with Tony right from the start." She smiled up at Gavin. "You guys live in a life that I have no understanding of. My better judgement told me, 'Hands off,' but I didn't listen." She sighed. "I suppose he pretended to fall in love with me to make sure I would help you guys out."

A frown had crossed Gavin's brow. "No. Absolutely not. Mary, we also have personal lives, although I know you haven't had a chance to see that. Tony loves you very much. I mean, here is a man who normally plays by the book, but since he's met you he's been breaking one rule after another."

"Yeh, he loves me so much he was going to have me killed," Mary replied dully.

Gavin shook his head as he turned to his side so he could face her, still leaning against the building. "Mary, he didn't go to Toronto to kill you."

That didn't convince her. "Yes, he did. In Toronto he asked me the same questions you asked me in the car. He was going to kill me all along, and he sent for you."

"Not true." This was wrong, and Gavin had to correct it. "Yes, he probably questioned you, but he sent for me because he needed backup. We didn't expect the attacks on you."

"You asked me the same questions," Mary insisted. It seemed bizarre to be having a relaxed conversation with a man about whether or not he had intended to kill you, but Mary was getting used to bizarre experiences.

"Yes," admitted Gavin, who was finding the conversation equally bizarre, and way, way off limits. "I had to ensure that you weren't intending to cause us irreparable damage. Tony and I never had a chance to talk about you." Gavin butted the cigarette. "You were no threat, Mary, and Tony knew that as soon as he met you. When he found out about our little 'conversation' in the car, he looked like he'd seen a ghost."

For a couple of minutes, Mary was quiet. She wanted to ask a question that Gavin might not answer; an answer she was sure of, but was afraid to hear. Needing to know, she pushed herself. "What happened in Cuba? Did Tony order you to kill me then?"

At first she thought Gavin wasn't going to answer, but then he did. "Yes, but I want you to listen to me," he continued as she started to speak. "You know what was going on down there. We didn't. When we got there, Tony found that his best friend had been tortured and was dead. Aaron was hysterical. That Cuban girl had died a horrible death. Tony and Frank would have liked to shoot the lot of those rebels, but the damned Congressman was there." Standing in front of her, Gavin put a hand on Mary's shoulder. "And they knew—they knew—that if you went to the media or the police like they expected you to, those rebels would walk away laughing, and we would endure the wrath of the public. We've had black eyes before, Mary," Gavin told her, "and we continue to prosper. But we have never had a black eye for a reason like this. Political stuff upsets people, but raping innocent tourists from friendly countries is not something we ever wanted to learn how to deal with."

Mary sighed. "I hope you're not expecting me to agree with that decision."

That made Gavin let out a laugh. "Good heavens, no. I'm only trying to give the reasons, not make it right. Tony had no right to give that order. None. But it wasn't a normal world down there, was it, Mary?"

"No, it wasn't," she admitted. The rules were different and the way people treated each other was different. The Cuban camp had held little resemblance to the real world. "If Aaron hadn't convinced Tony to change his mind, would you have killed me?"

Gavin decided to answer with a question. "I heard that you told the world that I wasn't a hit man. You are right," he informed her, "although a lot of people would say that was just a matter of semantics. I hear that Cook called me a trained killer. That was really flattering." He looked at Mary questioningly. "Why do you believe I'm not a 'hit man'?"

Mary frowned and thought about it. "I just know you're not. Not exactly, anyway. If you were, you would not have cared whether I was a problem for the CIA. You would not have asked me any questions, and I'd be dead now. They would have said, 'Shoot,' and you would have done it."

"Right," he agreed. "First of all, Mary, Tony did not want to give that order. That's why Aaron was able to talk him out of it. And he wanted to send *me* after you. If I had been sent to Canada, I would have checked out the damage: newspapers, radio, police broadcasts. There was no story anywhere. That would have surprised me. So then I would have called Frank and Tony to tell them. They would have told me to use my judgement. That means that I would have found you and questioned you as I did in the car. The result would have been the same. No," he said finally, "you had not told anyone what happened. When you found out who Aaron was, you made no threats, no lawsuits, nothing. You are not vindictive, you liked Nat, and you wanted to protect Aaron." He smiled at Mary. "I would never have killed you. Tony did not contemplate sending a 'hit man' after you, Mary. He did consider sending me, but that's because he knows he can trust me."

"Well, that's reassuring, at least," Mary responded.

"You're still hurt that Tony gave that order even though he had no idea who you were, and there was no time to figure things out down there." It was a statement.

Looking up, Mary saw Gavin's eyes on her. They never looked cold to her any more. When he was comfortable with you, they could actually look warm, like they did now. "It doesn't seem a good way to start a relationship," she stated.

"You two have had a terrible time starting a relationship," Gavin agreed. "Nothing's been normal for you, but I still think you are perfect for each other."

The door opened at that moment, and it was Tony who poked his head out. "Mary, would you come with me? Lino wants to talk to you."

"Lino? Why?"

Tony looked at Gavin. "He wants to talk to us, but he doesn't seem to trust us. It's possible that he was infiltrating that group for the Cuban government, but before he talks to us he wants to see Mary." Tony smiled at Mary. "We don't know why he wants to see you, but we'll be in the room with you. If you would talk to him, we would really appreciate it." Mentally, he crossed his fingers, hoping that she wouldn't refuse.

Mary did not hesitate. She had no objection to talking with Lino, and besides, she was rather curious. She walked down the hall at Tony's side, and did not pull away from the hand on her arm. His touch was comforting, and already she was resigned to the fact that she still loved this man in spite of everything that had happened. But she was also still angry.

As they walked, Tony heard her mutter, "You tried to kill me."

There was no one in the hall, so Tony stopped, spun Mary around and looked down at her face. "No. I never tried to kill you. I didn't know you."

"That almost makes it worse," she retorted. "You weren't even going to give me a chance."

This road was getting them nowhere. This road would only lead to heartache. Tony decided that he had to change directions. "I'm sorry," he spoke softly. "If I could take that order back, I would, but I can't. Maybe I should have told you, but for heaven's sake, Mary, it's not something you tell a person you love. It was a bad decision, I didn't know you, it didn't happen, and I can't take it back. I don't know what else to say," he confessed.

The brown eyes searched his face. "Do you really love me?"

"You know I do," he professed with emotion. It was the right answer, and he gasped with relief when she stepped forward and wrapped her arms around his waist. "Thank you," he whispered, as he rubbed the back of her neck and kissed her temple. A third chance at happiness—nobody got three chances. This time he would not make a mistake. "You and I are going to have a nice, long talk tonight," he promised, "with no one else around. Right now, though, we have to see what Lino is up to."

Tony led Mary into a room, which was occupied by Mr. Walsh, Lino, Lino's lawyer and Frank Moseley. A couple of the Security men were standing outside the door. As Mary came in, Lino rose slowly to his feet and smiled at her. The other men were already standing, perched in various places around the small room. Aside from the chair in which Lino had been sitting, there was only one other chair, and that was across the table from him. Tony guided Mary toward that chair.

"Hola!" Mary greeted. The room seemed to hold an atmosphere of anticipation.

"Hola! Thank you for meeting with me, Mrs. Norland," Lino replied in perfect English, sitting down again.

The change in Lino from a suspected Intelligence officer preparing to negotiate with the employees of the CIA, and the Lino who was addressing Mary, was quite remarkable. Tony now saw the soft-spoken, friendly guitar player greeting a tourist for whom he had played folk songs during her time of trouble. This was the man who had peeled and given Mary an orange. To give someone an orange seemed like a very insignificant thing in this world, but to Mary, who had been left to starve without an ounce of human compassion, the gesture had made a great impression.

"I have told these people that I wish to return to my country," Lino began. "We have much talking to do. First though, I want to apologise for the treatment you received while in my country. This is not treatment which is tolerated by the people of Cuba. I can assure you that we are most distressed by what happened to you."

Mary said nothing, but smiled at him.

Lino returned the smile. "I wish also to ask a small favour of you." He ignored the shifting of positions among the men in the room. They were wary of him. "If our talks go well," Lino continued, "I hope to go home. If I give you my name and a telephone number, would you promise to call me after I get home?" He glanced at Walsh, then back to Mary. "We would talk about the songs I sang to you in Cuba, so you would know it is me you are talking to. If no one can find me, or you think it is not me you are talking to, would you tell this man?" Lino gestured towards the man Mary did not know. "He is my lawyer. I would also ask you to tell your own government and contact our consulate in Toronto."

Mary did not know what was going on here, but clearly Lino was looking for a way to ensure that he would be sent back to Cuba. It was not a big request, so she promised to call him.

"Do you think you will be permitted to do this?" Lino asked, indicating the other occupants of the room.

That caused Mary to send a challenging look at Tony and Mr. Walsh. Carl raised his hands as if in surrender, and nodded. If all the king's horses and all the king's men could not prevent Mary from doing something she felt was her right and duty, what chance did a mere intelligence community have? He could not prevent her from making a telephone call.

"No one will prevent me," she answered Lino.

"Mrs. Norland," Lino said, as he scribbled on a card, "my government is in debt to you. You had a terrible time on your vacation. If you would come back as our guest, I can personally guarantee your protection." He handed her a card.

It seemed to Mary, as she took the card, that the others in the room would have liked to snatch it away, they seemed so eager. Mary read Lino's writing. His last name was different, and so was something else. "Oh, Lino, are you in the army?" she asked, surprised at what she read.

"Something like that," he smiled. Then he rose. "Thank you, Mrs. Norland. I look forward to your phone call."

This time, Tony let one of the Security men take Mary back. They had some fast negotiating to do with Lino.

# LI

Waiting for Hedley to come in with the results of the trial made the afternoon drag for the people waiting in the private room. Gavin was glad that Sheila had been allowed to observe the trial for the sake of experience. Having her, Mary and Scott in the room helped him pass the time. Aaron probably didn't notice the time dragging. He was obviously ecstatic to have Susan at his side again, and the handcuffs off. You couldn't blame the guy for that.

Mary was quiet, but had a happy, serene look on her face. She smiled frequently when she looked at Aaron and Susan. *Tony had better not let this woman get away,* Gavin thought. *She's exactly what he needs—a perfect antidote for that temper.* Actually, in temperament she was a female version of Frank; calm and steady, with a big stubborn streak.

Speaking of Frank, Gavin wondered where Frank would send him next. Surprisingly, the thought depressed him a little. He would miss them all, and he would miss the evenings he had spent with them at the house. It was a strange sensation for him. Usually he couldn't wait to get back to the field. It was the life he had chosen to live until…until what? He was forty-three years of age. In a very few years his body was going to start objecting to the extreme physical demands he sometimes had to make of it. With a start, Gavin realised that he had never thought past the next few years. How did he ever become forty-three? The years had crept up on him. *Great,* he thought. *Today everyone should be happy, and I'm starting a mid-life crisis.*

Well, what was the answer? If he asked Frank to assign him to something else, Frank would try to accommodate the request. Hammond was ready to take Gavin's place. The only problem was that Gavin couldn't imagine what else he wanted to do. Administrative work was out, and the politics of the office scene would drive him crazy.

Then a thought occurred to him. If Tony accepted his new position permanently, someone had to lead his team. Central America was being underserviced in Tony's absence. A position as a station chief with Tony's team under him might just be the answer. Gavin was sure the team would like working for him, because his other teams had never objected.

Tony had a few more months to try out the position, and by that time Sheila's placement would be over. She would have to be assigned to a different team for a while, of course. He couldn't possibly supervise her while they were… Good heavens. What was he thinking? Mentally, he had just included Sheila in his future plans. His mind had started exploring the possibility of settling down. Looking at her now, he told himself to slow down. *No reason to panic—she will want a couple of years to get going on her career.* After that, who knew if they would even still be in touch?

Actually, he hoped she would still be around. He like being with her, and was finding being intimate with her far more fulfilling than the encounters that had become the habit in his transient lifestyle. Approaching her had been a risk that was paying off in dividends. She had placed no demands on him, which left him free to control the extent of his involvement. What would she say if she knew where his thoughts were heading now? *No rush,* he told himself. *I'll take it as it comes, but I just might have a word with Frank about the possibility of applying for Tony's position.*

It was Walsh who announced the good news, accompanied by Tony, Frank Moseley and Hedley. "They are going to plead," he stated with glee when he entered the room. "And following sentencing, the FBI has a little surprise for Harvey and Cook. The Bureau has traced out the line to Mr. Pitt." He turned to Mary. "Once the others have been sentenced and we have checked out a few things Lino has told us, we'll be shipping him home with Jose Luis in tow. Jose Luis is not exactly pleased about going back with Lino, but he's arrogant enough to think his connections down there will keep him out of serious trouble. I suspect he is in for a real surprise."

"By the way," Walsh added, "we are all invited to dinner tonight with Mr. Geraldton."

As Walsh left, Gavin looked at Tony. "Do we have to go?" Gavin hated formal dinners.

"Of course," Tony answered. "Don't you recognise a command performance when you hear it?"

Making a face, Gavin waved Scott over. "You sit beside me," Gavin insisted. "You've got that social chitchat stuff down pat."

Scott agreed happily. As far as he was concerned, the day was turning out just great. He looked over at Aaron and Susan and decided to help plan a wedding.

The pleas were finally finished, and they were free to leave. Sentencing was set for next week. Dinner reservations had been made for 7:00 p.m. at

Solomon's, the same restaurant that had served them lunch the day before. It was only 5:00 p.m. now, for which Aaron was thankful. He and Sue had a chance to be alone together before the dinner, and he had asked her to come home with him.

At his apartment, he stood with her in the foyer. He felt as if he had been through a war, which, in a sense, he had. During the last few weeks he had been subjected to incredible pressure, and the tension had taken its toll. Mentally, he was exhausted. Right now, he wanted more than anything to make love to Susan, yet at the same time he was afraid she would be thinking about what he had done to Mary in Cuba. Whatever the reason, he was feeling extremely tense, and the sense of arousal he had hoped for was missing.

*Great,* he cursed silently, *just great. Sue still loves me enough to try again, and now I'm going to let her down.* It was incredibly frustrating, which only made him more tense.

"You okay?" Sue asked, when he didn't move.

"I'm afraid all this has taken its toll," he admitted.

She kissed him lightly on the lips. "Then you'd better give yourself a chance to relax. I imagine that you've been under an awful lot of stress since the last time I saw you. Why don't we sit down and have a drink? Nothing has to happen tonight. We've got all the time in the world."

"But I *want* something to happen," he protested.

Sue put her hands on his shoulders and kissed him with a little more meaning. Aaron could smell traces of her perfume. He had to ask about their future. "Are you still going to marry me?"

Her look was kind and loving. "Oh, Aaron, of course I am. I never stopped loving you." With a smile, she started loosening his tie. "Do you remember our first date?"

"How could I forget?" Aaron answered her. "It was the happiest day of my life."

"Mine, too." She had the tie undone, and stuffed it into his pocket. "I was so nervous," she confessed. "I thought you would compare me with all the other women you knew. I was so far in love with you, but I was afraid I'd be a disappointment."

"That was crazy," Aaron told her. "I had loved you since Scott introduced us. No one could hold a candle to you."

"Flatterer," she accused. Now she started to unbutton his shirt, stopping to stroke his face and kiss him again. "You were wonderful. You kept telling me how beautiful I was—"

"You *are* beautiful," he interrupted.

"Finally you suggested that we get out of the foyer, so you led me into the bedroom."

Aaron looked around himself and laughed. They were still in the foyer, and it hadn't even dawned on him. When Susan took his hand and led him to the bedroom, he followed willingly.

Once in the bedroom, Susan turned and slid her arms around his neck. He met her kiss, and wrapped his arms around her, pulling her close. Her fingers were in his hair, and her body pressed against him. Ah yes, he remembered this. It felt good, very good.

After a minute, Susan spoke again. "I was hooked, you know, after our first night together. I thought I was just one of many, so I wanted to stay away from you, but I couldn't bear not being with you. I was totally, absolutely addicted to you. I still am." Her kiss this time was passionate.

What on earth had he been worried about? He wanted her so badly now that it seemed to take forever to get their clothes off and scramble onto the bed. Once in her arms, it felt as though he had never left. She loved him, she would be his wife.... He was home. His life hadn't ended. It had just started again.

Like Aaron, Tony took Mary back to his apartment, but with the opposite intention. He wanted to talk to Mary. The next time he made love to her, he wanted it to be in his bed, *alone*, with no microphones and without rushing. Tonight, after supper, they would have the whole night to make love, and Tony even planned to be late for work tomorrow morning. That would really shock his co-workers.

Inside the door to his apartment, Tony picked Mary up and kissed her. Then he surprised her by carrying her into the living room, placing her on the sofa and sitting down beside her. Her happy brown eyes were looking at him with a question in them. He answered by spending the next few minutes kissing her, then settled down with his arm along the back of the sofa, behind her shoulders.

She might say no, he knew. Mary had a home and a job waiting for her, and a life in another country that she might not wish to give up. He would be asking her to make a change he would not have been willing to make himself. He took a deep breath and gambled.

"I know that by asking you to marry me, I am asking you to give up a lot," he began. "I am asking you to give up your job and your home, because I want you to be here, with me." He paused. "If you wanted to work, I could help you with that, or you could look on your own. I would only ask that you tell me where you were looking."

"What restrictions would I have?" she asked him.

She was considering it! His heart jumped, but he kept his face perfectly serious. "Absolutely no table dancing. I won't tolerate that."

For a second Mary looked at him in astonishment, then she broke out in laughter and punched him in the ribs. It was good to hear her laugh, and even better to realise that she had not said no to him.

"I have a temper," he warned, wanting to be honest, "but you've already seen that."

Mary frowned. "Do you hit?"

"No," he said quickly. "Absolutely not. You've seen the worst of it. I say nasty things, then I feel lousy about it."

Mary nodded and continued to look at him.

*She still hasn't said no,* he realised. *She's cautious, but she is considering it.* He had a suggestion to make that he hoped she would like to hear.

"And, Mary, if you want to start a family, tell me right away, so I can try to get this little operation reversed—" He didn't get any further. He had struck gold. Finally he had said the absolutely right thing. He knew it by the way she had scrambled onto his lap with a cry, and was now choking him with the arms she had wound so tightly around his neck.

"Mary," he protested gently. "There won't be any children if you don't let me breathe."

*Oops.* Mary loosened her grip, but proceeded to kiss him all over his face. This wonderful man wanted to be her husband, and now he wanted to give her children. Mary had not been this happy in a long, long time. Tony was laughing at her now, but that was okay. She settled down against his chest and sighed contentedly. Then she thought of something else.

"Do I have to give up my citizenship?" she asked.

He chuckled at this. "Heavens no. If you did, you wouldn't be able to hold it over my head every time I tried to boss you around, would you?"

They sat in peace for a while, then he asked, "Do you hear that?"

"What?"

"The sound of solitude," Tony answered her. "No people, no monitors, and hopefully no bugs."

"Bugs?" Mary looked quickly around for signs of crawling insects. When Tony started laughing hysterically, she realised her mistake and blushed. "Oh, wrong bugs."

It felt great to laugh. This woman was going to be his lover and companion for the rest of his life. They would have a family and a home…maybe even a house with a lawn. Contentment, that's what he was feeling right now. Tony thought about houses and things like lawn mowers. Then he chuckled again. He had never thought about a lawn mower in his life before today.

"Why are you laughing this time?" Mary demanded.

"I just caught myself thinking about lawn mowers," he answered.

"You're planning to cut some grass?"

"At our house," he answered. "How do they work? Do you still pull a cord to start them?"

Mary shook her head in amazement. "I don't think I'll be looking for a job. Between raising children and doing home maintenance, since you obviously can't, I think I'll be too busy."

Happy together, they continued to listen to the sound of silence until it was time to meet the others for dinner.

# LII

By the time Tony and Mary arrived at the restaurant, Aaron and Susan were just ordering their first drink. Tony noticed that Aaron looked weary, but relaxed and happy at the same time. *Thank goodness that relationship survived,* Tony thought. With Susan at his side, Aaron was likely to bounce back quickly.

Dr. Hummel would insist on Aaron staying off work until he had made a full recovery, but it probably wouldn't be long. Carrying the secret of Nat had been Aaron's heaviest and last burden, and now that it was disclosed, it would weigh him down no longer. Frank and Gavin would make themselves available, as would Tony, if Aaron felt the need to discuss it in the future. Dr. Hummel would be privately informed so he could help Aaron with feelings of grief, guilt and loss.

Frank, Gavin and Scott had been sitting and conversing for a while, and looked up to welcome the new arrivals. They noticed that Tony and Mary were still standing.

"Well?" Tony demanded with a grin. "Aren't you going to congratulate us? We're getting married."

That earned Mary kisses, and Tony handshakes, until it was Scott's turn. Aaron had just sat down again when Scott finished giving Mary a kiss and telling her how happy he was. Then he turned to Tony. To Aaron's astonishment, Scott actually hugged Tony, surprising the "ole man". Aaron couldn't help bursting into laughter, but tried his best to cover it up. There was no question about Scott being happy that Mary and Tony were marrying. The dirty look Scott sent Aaron for laughing wasn't even a serious one.

Once everyone settled down again, they ordered a bottle of champagne. Frank Moseley was sitting between Gavin and Tony. He whispered something to Gavin, then got Tony's attention.

"Have you made a decision about your new job yet?"

Tony shrugged. "Not completely, but I'm leaning in the direction of accepting it. I like the wider view it gives me, and there is never a dull moment. I'll probably end up taking it if Walsh is in agreement."

"Got anyone picked to fill your old one yet?" Frank asked.

Tony felt a pang of loss. "I did," he responded quietly. "I was working on Nat to take it." He tried to shake off the depression. "So I'm back to the drawing board," he admitted. If Aaron had a few more years of experience, Tony would not have hesitated giving him the position, but it was still a bit early. "Why, is someone interested?"

Both Aaron and Scott were obviously listening in on the conversation, but Frank decided that it didn't matter. He jerked a thumb in Gavin's direction. "Our friend here has become rather attached to these two eavesdroppers. Gavin would like to reassemble your team and take it back down to help work Central America.

"Excellent," Aaron offered, without caring if his input was wanted. Working for Gavin would help him not miss Tony as much.

Scott pretended to be horrified. "But, Aaron, Gavin will make us jump out of fuckin' airplanes! His idea of a good time is to practise swimming in an alligator-infested swamp. I hate alligators."

Gavin gave Scott a stern look, but the crinkles around his eyes softened it. Tony thought about the personalities and the interaction between Gavin and his team. It would be a good fit, and he wanted to leave his team with someone with whom they would work well. "Will it be enough excitement for you?" he asked Gavin.

"I think they'll keep me busy," Gavin replied. He was pleased to realise that Scott and Aaron were receptive to the idea.

"Sheila will have to be told," Tony said simply, watching Gavin.

Gavin returned the look with complete understanding. "Yes." A movement at the door caught his eye. "Here she is now."

The restaurant had a cloakroom a few feet down the hall. Gavin met Sheila by the door and guided her into it. With the sun shining outside, no one was checking overcoats today, and the cloakroom was deserted. There was no door, however, so privacy was minimal, and they were in full view of passing patrons.

Gavin needed Sheila to know of his plan to formally request Tony's old job before she reached the table and was caught off guard. Sheila was a good trainee, and as such was viewed as a valuable commodity by the Company. The need for her to switch teams would be handled with sensitivity, and every effort would be made to avoid causing her any personal embarrassment over her relationship with him. That would be Tony's job, and he would do it well. It was Gavin's responsibility to be courteous enough to forewarn her.

In the cloakroom, Gavin broke the news to her. Sheila was surprised, and he could see her analyzing the implications.

"You'll want to switch teams, of course," he said in an attempt to help. "You would have been reassigned then anyway." The team would probably have been dissolved with Tony absent, and a general reshuffling of people would have occurred.

Sheila was a little confused. It sounded as if Gavin wanted her to switch teams now, instead of finishing her placement. Oh, now she understood. He wanted to end the relationship. Perhaps he hoped to fill Tony's position now, or perhaps he was simply getting bored of her and didn't want the embarrassment of seeing her around. Well, she had walked into this with her eyes wide open, and if he wanted to end it, it was certainly his right to do so. No commitments had been made.

Privately, Sheila was disappointed and a bit annoyed. At the least, he could have had the decency to tell her this in private, instead of in a public place, in a cloakroom, a few minutes before she had to make polite conversation with the Deputy Director and the Deputy Director of Operations. *Thanks a lot, Gavin,* she fumed. *I wouldn't have done this to you.*

In truth, she would not have ended the affair at all. Sheila was only intimate with one man at a time. Gavin's offer last week had been perfect. She could have worked on her career and enjoyed his company whenever he was around. Besides, she had come to like him. He made no demands on her, and he expected her to put her career first. On top of that, she had discovered that under that gruff, unemotional exterior, Gavin hid a nice personality. You could see it in the kind way he treated Mary. Sheila had also been discovering it herself over their few weeks of intimacy. *Oh well, things change.* It was expected. She bit back her annoyance. It would do neither of them any good to end on bad terms.

"Okay, Gavin," she said, "if you want to end it, it's over. I'll talk to Tony and get reassigned."

That startled Gavin, and made him realise that he had handled this badly. "No," he protested. "I don't want it to end."

This made Sheila more confused, and she was starting to get embarrassed. "Then I don't understand what this is about, Gav. I don't know what you want. You're confusing me. Just tell me what it is that you want."

To Sheila's shock, what the normally private, undemonstrative Gavin wanted was to put a hand behind her neck, pull her roughly towards him, and kiss her soundly on the mouth. When he was done, he kept his hand on the back of her neck while she recovered from her surprise.

"I want you around," he was saying, looking terribly awkward. "I like you being within reach. It isn't something I usually want from anyone, and I don't know where this is taking me." A look of confusion had settled on his features, and he seemed almost embarrassed. "I like being with you," he told her. "I don't want to end this."

"Okay, Gav," Sheila spoke to end his discomfort. His hand was still on the back of her neck, and she rubbed his forearm. "That's fine. We've got lots of time to figure things out. I'll be around if you want me to be," she reassured him. "I've got a career to work on for a while before I try to get the rest of my life settled."

"Are you okay with things left that way?"

Now he seemed more relaxed, but also concerned for her. Sheila smiled. The man really did have a heart, he just didn't know what to do with it. "It's perfect," she reassured him. "Hell, I've got a great day job, and you on the side for my leisure time. What more could a working girl want?"

Gavin laughed. Things had worked out well in spite of his fumbling. Sheila was an unusual woman, which was exactly why she appealed to him. Impulsively, he dropped his arm and took her hand, leading her back to the table. This would raise a few eyebrows, but so what?

Frank Moseley was the first person to observe their approach. His eyebrows did indeed rise. "Tony," he said quietly. "Gavin is coming back. He's holding Sheila's hand."

Tony tried to hide a grin. "Is this a problem for you, Frank?"

"No, seriously," Frank insisted. "Gavin is holding her hand...in public!"

"Quit staring, Frank. You'll embarrass them," Tony chided.

Under Tony's stern look, Frank managed to behave himself and hide his astonishment, but just barely. Tony then turned to watch Gavin seat Sheila. "Have you updated Sheila?" he asked. When Gavin nodded, Tony smiled at her. "It won't be for a few months yet, dear. We've got lots of time to find something that would be of interest to you. There are a number of places we could use you."

It was hard to sit still, Scott decided, when you were so happy that you wanted to jump and shout. If Walsh and Geraldton weren't expected, he would have immediately invited everyone back to his family's home for a party. Perhaps he and Sue would plan one for the weekend, instead.

Everything was working out perfectly, as far as he was concerned. Instead of losing Mary back to that frigid country up north, she was staying here and marrying Tony. They would probably get married quite quickly. Scott was very impressed with the way Tony had stood at Aaron's side since the Cuba affair. As far as Scott was concerned, Tony deserved his promotion, and he deserved Mary, too.

Even better, Sue still loved Aaron, and now Aaron was going to be his brother-in-law. That marriage wouldn't happen for at least a year, though. Being the only daughter, their father would want to throw a large wedding for Susan. Scott would help Sue try to convince him not to go too crazy with the planning. Aaron didn't want to wait any longer than he had to. Soon, Scott hoped, Aaron and Sue would get busy and produce little nephews and nieces for him. It would be a riot to take a little Aaron to a baseball game.

Despite the crack he had made about Gavin and alligators, Scott was delighted to learn that Gavin wanted to be his boss. Actually, Gavin was a better personality fit for Scott than Tony had been. To have Gavin as a station chief, and Tony supervising the Covert unit, was a great piece of luck. A job couldn't help but go well with two people like that over you.

Moseley was turning out to be okay, too. Gavin was backing him, and had told Scott the background to the blackmail. It was hard to feel a lot of sympathy when you were one of the targets, but Scott did believe that Moseley had not expected him to be killed. So if Gavin believed in Moseley, Scott would accept that the man had made a rather large but isolated mistake, and would not do so again.

Walsh and Geraldton were late, which suited everyone just fine, although no one would ever say that. It was more enjoyable to chat in a relaxed atmosphere before the two senior men arrived.

Two empty chairs at the table awaited them, but to Tony the empty chairs reminded him of Nat. It still hurt, like a punch in the chest, and could make his throat constrict, as his emotions threatened to betray him. He breathed in heavily and out slowly. This had to be controlled. Tomorrow he would talk to Dr. Hummel himself, because something told him that this kind of pain would not be controlled by his usual method of hiding it away. This was a pain that would sneak up on you when you least expected it, and lay you defenceless. Tony was starting a very important job, and he had a marriage with a wonderful woman ahead of him. He could not afford to take the chance of either part of his life being harmed by this unpredictable pain. Hummel would help him control it. If Aaron had no problems talking to Hummel, then Tony knew he should take advantage of it too.

Aaron was watching him now. *You know, don't you,* Tony thought, meeting Aaron's look. *You're starting to read my mind, just like Nat did, and*

*the way Frank and Gavin can. We'll miss each other, you and I. You were the
only one who could have stood in Nat's place.*

A thought jumped into Tony's mind. Without warning, and without
thinking, Tony had voiced it. "Do you play golf?"

Although the women kept talking to each other, the men all heard the
question and went silent. Aaron knew instinctively that this was not an idle
question, because Tony already knew that he golfed occasionally. This
question was much more important than it sounded. In case Aaron had any
doubts, Scott kicked him lightly under the table.

"Well, yes...badly, but yes," Aaron stumbled.

Tony paused. He had asked this without consulting with his other two
surviving partners, one of which would probably be directly supervising
Aaron in the near future. Looks were exchanged.

Aaron and Scott sat silently while the nonverbal communication flew
around the table. First, Tony and Frank exchanged a look. Frank smiled very
slightly and looked at Gavin. Gavin read Frank's assent and looked briefly at
Tony. Then Gavin addressed Aaron directly.

"Do you throw your clubs?"

That caught Aaron by surprise. "Uh, no. Why would I want to throw a
perfectly good club?"

At that, Gavin looked at Frank, nodded slightly and then turned to Tony
and made a slight hand motion that might have meant *It's okay with me.*

When all that was done, Tony let out a breath and addressed Aaron. "I
need someone...we need someone, to take Nat's place...as a fourth." He had
to clear his throat.

Aaron looked at each of them in turn. "Oh, I could never take Nat's place,"
he said quietly, "but I'd love to make up a fourth."

*Perfect answer, Aaron,* Scott thought, looking at the pleased looks on the
faces of the other men.

"Good, it's settled," Tony announced. He smiled at Aaron, then reached
for Mary's hand. The near disaster that had started in a camp in Cuba was
"over with and done". Life had a lot to offer, and right now it was looking
pretty good.

\*

Printed in the United States
65941LVS00003B/7-54

9 781424 135936